Air

Bargain with the Wind

SHARON SHINN

Elemental Magic

Sharon Shinn
Rebecca York
Carol Berg
Jean Johnson

BERKLEY BOOKS, NEW YORK

THE BERKLEY PUBLISHING GROUP
Published by the Penguin Group
Penguin Group (USA) Inc.
375 Hudson Street, New York, New York 10014, USA
Penguin Group (Canada), 90 Eglinton Avenue East, Suite 700, Toronto, Ontario M4P 2Y3, Canada
(a division of Pearson Penguin Canada Inc.)
Penguin Books Ltd., 80 Strand, London WC2R 0RL, England
Penguin Group Ireland, 25 St. Stephen's Green, Dublin 2, Ireland (a division of Penguin Books Ltd.)
Penguin Group (Australia), 250 Camberwell Road, Camberwell, Victoria 3124, Australia
(a division of Pearson Australia Group Pty. Ltd.)
Penguin Books India Pvt. Ltd., 11 Community Centre, Panchsheel Park, New Delhi—110 017, India
Penguin Group (NZ), 67 Apollo Drive, Rosedale, North Shore 0632, New Zealand
(a division of Pearson New Zealand Ltd.)
Penguin Books (South Africa) (Pty.) Ltd., 24 Sturdee Avenue, Rosebank, Johannesburg 2196,
South Africa

Penguin Books Ltd., Registered Offices: 80 Strand, London WC2R 0RL, England

This book is an original publication of The Berkley Publishing Group.

PRINTING HISTORY
Berkley trade paperback edition / November 2007

Library of Congress Cataloging-in-Publication Data

Elemental magic / Sharon Shinn . . . [et al.].
    p. cm.
    ISBN 978-0-425-21786-3
1. Fantasy fiction, American. 2. Magic—Fiction. 3. Four elements (Philosophy)—Fiction. I. Shinn, Sharon.

PS648.F3E44 2007
813'.0876608—dc22

2007023095

PRINTED IN THE UNITED STATES OF AMERICA

10 9 8 7 6 5 4 3 2 1

CONTENTS

One

I was there the first time the master caught sight of the woman who would destroy him.

I had just left the kitchens, where I had paused to reassure myself that Ermintrude had preparations for the meal well under control. I was heading for the front hall to check on the footman, for Martin was quite young and had never had to greet so many people in one evening before. I didn't need to pick my way through the muddy yard to inquire on the situation at the stables, for Dawson was wholly reliable; he would be able to handle the onslaught of coaches and teams. On my way to the foyer, I could not resist pausing at the discreet servants' entrance to the ballroom and taking a moment to observe the celebration under way.

It was a marvelous sight, all whirling color and dancing candlelight, and for a moment my heart swelled with pride. At last, Grey Moraine was resuming its place as the finest manor home within fifty miles, the social center of County Banlow. Oh, the balls we had had when the old master was young and healthy!

The summer hunts, the winter holidays! The house would be full to bursting with elegant ladies and witty men. Nothing in these parts had been prized more than an invitation to spend a week at Grey Moraine.

Nothing had made me happier than the announcement that the new master was planning his first grand entertainment.

He had arrived at Grey Moraine six or seven months previously and instantly won the hearts of all the servants who had served his uncle so faithfully for many years. A few of the elderly grooms and cooks were pensioned off, and quite generously too, but everyone else was kept on. He had almost no staff of his own to bring along, for he had been a soldier before Grey Moraine unexpectedly fell into his hands. Therefore, the only servants to accompany him were a well-mannered valet and an elderly groom who cared about nothing except earning a place near horses. Both were properly deferential to those of us who had served at the mansion for so long. One could hardly have expected a transition to go more smoothly.

And then the news that the master wanted to have a ball! Throw open those wide, carved doors, fill the great expanse of the ballroom with flowers, trail rose petals and candelabra down the sweeping stairway that led out to the side gardens. The cook and the butler and I were in transports. Ermintrude had menus made up before the end of the day, and Harlan had immediately toured the wine cellar to see what else we might need to stock. Such a bustle of cleaning and cooking and festooning as you have never seen while we prepared the house for its first major event in more than fifteen years.

And then *she* walked in the door, and with a single smile laid out the brief and disastrous course that the master's life would take.

⚬↷

Martin announced her as Lady Charis. I had a moment to get a good look at her face—she had small, sculpted features, absolutely pure white skin, and enormous dark blue eyes—before she sank into a graceful curtsey. Her dress was the same shade as her eyes and it seemed to spread around her as she dipped low and straightened, so that she almost appeared to be a water nymph rising from the sea. The guests standing near enough to see her began murmuring to each other, their faces alive with interest and admiration. I could easily guess what they were saying. *But she's so beautiful! Who is she, do you know? Look at that girl's face! I haven't seen her in County Banlow before. Who is this lovely creature?*

The master, who had been standing a good twenty yards away, abruptly broke off his conversation with Debrett Horton and made his way through the crowd to greet the new arrival. "I am Duncan Baler, owner of Grey Moraine," he introduced himself, taking her small hand and bowing over it very low. She might have been the queen herself, to judge by his obeisance. "Welcome to my house! I am very glad to have you here."

A faint color washed over her white cheeks. You would have thought she was both embarrassed and exhilarated at the attention of a rich and attractive lord. And yet Duncan Baler, despite his many fine attributes, was actually not a handsome man. His face was a bit sallow, though good-natured and honest; the skin was weathered from his years of soldiering. He bore more traces of his military past in his upright bearing and air of physicality, and his broad shoulders were not easily confined to the polite dimensions of a dress jacket. He wore his brown hair shorter than the current fashion and did not bother with some of the sartorial excesses practiced by other young men of the time.

But he was master of Grey Moraine and had inherited, besides the property, quite a sizable fortune. Any young lady with the slightest interest in making her way in society would have acquainted herself with both those facts.

"Lord Duncan," she said, and her voice was rich and deep. "I hope you forgive my forwardness in arriving at your home without an invitation."

I practically gasped at her words, for that was bold indeed. Lady Charis was beautiful, and every line of her face and body bespoke generations of exquisite breeding. But such an action shouted, *Adventuress!*

The master smiled down at her. I could not be sure, but it appeared as if he squeezed her hands, which he still held. They were so small they were lost between his big ones. "I can only be grateful that you were brave enough to do so!" he replied. "How did you hear of such an insignificant event as my ball?"

The people nearest him laughed a little at that, and Lady Charis smiled back. "I have been traveling from Lefton to Manningham," she said, naming two cities separated by at least three hundred miles. Any journey between the two of them would take a traveler through County Banlow. They were each decently sized towns—not that I would know from firsthand observation, since I had never left County Banlow—and both were respectable destinations. Yet neither was a seat of high fashion, and it was unlikely that many of our other guests had spent much time in either.

In fact, no one in this gathering could be expected to know her.

"I stopped at the Red Owl Inn last night to break my journey," she continued. "There, the talk was of nothing but your grand ball! The first one to be held at Grey Moraine in more than a decade! I admit to an ungovernable curiosity. Even in Lefton, we have heard of Grey Moraine. I simply had to come and see it for myself." She made a quarter turn to bestow her smile on all the nobles gathered near enough to overhear. "I hoped that the presence of an army of witnesses would dissuade you from throwing me back out in the night. I will be very quiet. You will hardly notice I'm here. I would just like to peek in a few corners and gaze at a few marble statues. Then I will be on my way."

"You will do no such thing!" the master declared, tucking her little hand in his arm and drawing her deeper into the room. As if connected to him by ropes and tethers, the small crowd of revelers stepped right after him. "You will dance with me. And perhaps you will dance with a few other fellows. And then you will dance with me some more. Dinner will be provided at midnight, and I will be delighted if you sit beside me to eat. Then more dancing—until dawn. Perhaps past dawn, if the musicians can still feel their fingers to keep playing. Won't you stay for it all?"

"If you're sure," she said.

"I'm certain," he replied.

Just then, the musicians, who had seized this opportunity to refresh themselves with wine, took their chairs again and offered up a waltz. Smiling even more broadly, the master drew Lady Charis into the figures with him, and soon the whole ballroom was once again a spinning mosaic of color and beauty. I ducked back through the doorway and hurried down the hall toward the front door to check on Martin as I had originally intended.

All the while, the sounds of violins and flutes and cymbals accompanied me, rhythmic and lighthearted. I imagined their bright music could be heard from the highest room of the mansion or the farthest dark corner of the garden. But over their crescendo and beat I heard another sound, one that chilled my skin and squeezed my heart: the whispering, ghostly laughter of the wind.

∽

The guardians of the earth will nurture your crops and sustain your fortifications, if you respect the land and show them honor. The nymphs of the water will soothe your hot blood if you burn with fever; every healer keeps a shrine to the living rivers somewhere in her house. But the sprites of the air are capricious and willful and full of jealousy. Invite them into your life at your peril. They will exact a penance you may not be prepared to pay.

Someone, I thought, had invoked the demons of the air tonight, for there had never been such a lovely autumn evening. The dancing had paused long enough to allow guests to crowd around the buffet and pile their plates with delicacies. Some people sat at the informal tables; others wandered through the ballroom and the nearby salons, admiring the portraits on the walls and the tastefully arranged furniture. Young couples stood so close they might still be in the embrace of the waltz. Matrons gathered in far corners of the room and whispered about their friends, while their husbands retreated to the master's library and engaged in friendly gambling. I wished the musicians would not linger so long over their meals, though I understood that they needed to recruit their strength for the second half of the night. But I preferred it when all of the guests of the house were gathered more or less in one space. I felt uneasy when anyone could be anywhere engaged in unobserved activity.

The master himself was nowhere to be found.

Neither was Lady Charis.

I stood again at the servants' entrance to the ballroom and sent my glance to every corner. Not there. I had just been at the front door, checking with Harlan, and I was reasonably sure he would have mentioned it if the master had gone outside that way, perhaps to smoke a pipe and enjoy the warm night. A quick visit to the library confirmed that he was not among the men laying absurd bets and laughing very loudly.

He must be in the garden.

Perhaps it was not my place to follow him. Perhaps that seems too presumptuous for a housekeeper, a mere servant, even one who has served Grey Moraine for as long as I have. But I tell you this: Grey Moraine belongs to me every bit as much as it belongs to the Balers, who have held it for a hundred years, or the Fittledons, who owned the property for three centuries. I have poured my life into its wood and stone. I know every passageway; I can recite for you the contents of every room. Without glancing at the engraved register hanging at the front door, I could name for you every individual who spent even a day as master of the house. I love Grey Moraine more than anything I have truly owned. My worst fear would be to have something or someone harm it.

And so I went sneaking into the garden, gliding along on cloth-soled shoes and sticking closely to the shadows. It did not take me long to find my quarry. They were pacing very slowly along the circular path that led all the way around the formal gardens. A few widely spaced torches showed them the way but left many convenient passages of darkness to traverse. I could catch a glimpse of other couples similarly engaged in making the circuit in as laggardly a fashion as possible. The night could not have been more suited to romance. The air was almost as warm as summer, and the late roses in the garden sent up a voluptuous scent. Overhead, a full moon made a yellow and languid shape against the spattered stars.

The wind was so still that every word carried.

"Your house is beautiful, milord," Lady Charis was saying in her husky voice. "Despite its exceptional elegance, it has an air of warmth and welcome."

"I am glad to learn that it seems inviting to *you*," the master replied gallantly. "But alas, I cannot take credit for any of its amenities."

"Why is that?"

"I inherited it less than a year ago, and I have made very few changes. Much of what you see stands as it did during my uncle's day."

"Your uncle had no sons? That must have been a disappointment to him."

"In fact, he had *two* sons. My cousin Ronald died when we were boys, but my cousin Ralph seemed reasonably healthy, and he was engaged to marry a girl from Kingston. I had no expectation at all of inheriting. To tell you the truth, I've only been here a few times in my life. My father and his brother had not been on the best of terms, so we visited here rarely. And once I joined the army—" The master shrugged, or I imagined he did. It was difficult to see clearly, and I had to carefully mind my steps as I pushed through the scrubby undergrowth that lay outside the hedges that lined the walkway. But I was determined to hear as much of the conversation as I could, so I persevered. "I was out of the country for much of the last five years. And not much interested in visiting elderly uncles when I was back."

Lady Charis laughed softly. "So you were a soldier. Live hard, fight hard, love hard."

There was a smile in his voice. "Something like that."

"I take it an unfortunate accident befell your cousin—Ralph, was it?"

"Yes. My uncle had been ill for quite some time. His death was expected. Ralph was spending more and more time here, consulting with his father and taking over some of the management of the land. The very day my uncle died, Ralph was thrown from his horse as he came back from a morning ride. Broke his neck." The master shook his head. "Terrible thing."

It *had* been a terrible day. Dawson had urged Lord Ralph to take a gentler horse on his morning ride, for the rawboned young stallion was still not easy with a bridle and Dawson himself had trouble getting the horse to behave. Lord Ralph, let me just say, had always been hotheaded and a touch too sure of himself, and it had taken someone with consummate skill to direct him. Dawson, though a most excellent man with horses, was sometimes impatient with men, and he had not quite possessed the knack of handling the young master. Lord Ralph had ridden out on the stallion, and the stallion had returned alone two hours later.

Of course, searchers went out immediately. It never occurred to any of us that anything worse could have happened than a bad fall and a broken leg, or perhaps a concussion. I was just as glad I had not been among the party that found Lord Ralph's broken body lying beside a hazard that had apparently been too high to jump.

What chaos! What consternation! The old master dead just three hours when the new one followed him out of the world! Fortunately, the estate agent was already present, for he had been going over the will with Lord Ralph. He knew who the next heir was and how to get in touch with him immediately.

I later had the melancholy thought that this agent would also know whom to notify if Lord Duncan were to suddenly fall ill.

To my dying day, I will be just a little ashamed of myself that my first emotion, upon hearing the news of Lord Ralph's death, was not grief. In truth, I was a little relieved. Although I had loved the old master deeply, I had never cared much for either of his sons. All my hopes had been pinned on Lord Ralph's betrothed, the calm and clear-sighted woman who was destined to be the new mistress of Grey Moraine—and mother to the next heir. The property could survive one or two indifferent owners, I had always thought. It was the next generation that truly mattered.

"Where were you when the news reached you about your change of estate?" Lady Charis inquired.

I could hear the grin in my master's voice. "In a gambling club in Kingston. I had just lost my last gold coin and risen from the table, thinking, 'Well, what shall I pawn tomorrow?' That's when this very sober young man came up to me and said, 'If you're Duncan Baler, you must come with me right now to the law offices of Keller and Kait.' I thought maybe an old arrest warrant had caught up with me—"

"You did not!" Lady Charis said with a laugh. "You don't strike me as the type who's ever been in trouble with the law."

"True enough," he admitted. "Except for the occasional run of bad luck gambling, I've been a steady sort my whole life. What I really thought was that there had been some trouble with my commission check. I'd sold out of the army just the week before, and it had taken a while for the money to arrive."

"You'd left the army just the week before?" she repeated. "It was as if you'd known, somehow, that your life was about to change."

He laughed. "I *wanted* it to change, that's for certain. The army was good to me, but I found myself losing the restlessness that had pushed me so much when I was younger. I'm almost forty. Time to settle down. I didn't have any specific plans, but I thought I might buy a small property. I might invest my funds. I wanted to look around, pick a spot, and settle in." He stepped into a circle of light thrown by one of the torches and made a broad gesture with both hands. "I certainly didn't expect that *this* would be where I would come to rest."

She stepped beside him into the light, and once again I had a chance to compare them. You could have hardly found two people more dissimilar. Lady Charis was so small, so delicate, that the master—never too concerned about elegance of dress—looked as rough as a laborer beside her. She had to be nearly twenty years his junior, with skin so flawless that his own seemed pockmarked and coarse by comparison. And there was a glow to her, a radiance that was almost visible, fueled by something more than youth, I thought. Excitement, perhaps. Intensity. Desire.

What did the Lady Charis want so much that yearning toward it lit her from within like a candle behind a leaded glass window?

Against that glow, Duncan Baler looked stolid, ordinary, exceptionally plain. But Lady Charis smiled at him as if he were the most beautiful man she'd ever laid eyes on.

"I think it's marvelous that Grey Moraine has come into your possession," she said, her voice very low. "Everyone speaks of you so highly. You will be a wonderful master." She turned away from him and began slowly pacing forward on the path again, casting him a provocative look over one shoulder. "Though one wonders if Grey Moraine might become even more magnificent once you've installed a mistress."

He caught up with her in two strides. "I have given no thought at all to taking a wife!" he exclaimed.

Her laugh pealed out. "Well, you are the only one! All the talk tonight has been of you and whom you might choose to be your bride." She gestured toward the house. "You must know that all the unmarried girls of County Banlow dressed in their finest clothes and offered you their most practiced smiles tonight! Everyone hopes to catch your attention and be considered for the highest honor in the region—that of mistress of Grey Moraine."

"Dreadful news! This is positively the last ball I shall ever plan! I will not be able to enjoy a single dance, knowing how I'm being sized up as a matrimonial prospect."

"All you need do is choose a wife," Lady Charis replied, amused. "Then all the speculation will end, and you can hold as many dances and dinners as you wish."

"There's an idea," he said, his voice thoughtful. "Perhaps I should place an ad in the county newspaper. 'Wanted: Sensible woman who knows how to run a household. Must be able to communicate with servants and understand a budget. Also desirable are skills related to planning grand entertainments for large country mansion.' That might net me some reasonable candidates, don't you think?"

"Quite a few!" she answered with a laugh. "But perhaps you have left out a number of important qualifications."

"I can't think what."

As they passed through another circle of torchlight, she gave him a second glittering sideways smile. "Don't you care if she is beautiful? If she is accomplished? If she inspires in you feelings of great passion?"

Though his answering smile was so much less incandescent

than hers, I much preferred it for its sincerity and genuine warmth. "Ah, I am hardly the sort of man to inspire feelings of great passion in women," he said. "I don't expect to be lucky enough to find a woman who both wakens my heart and burns to marry me."

She came to a dead halt. "Why, Duncan Baler!" she said. "What a very sad thing to say! And completely untrue. There might be a hundred women who would love you with their whole hearts."

"I only need one," he replied.

"Then you should most definitely look for her," Lady Charis declared. "No pretending you aren't good enough to find someone who will marry you for love."

"And how long will you be staying at the Red Owl Inn?" he wanted to know. "So that I can tell you of my progress in my various courtships, of course."

She laughed again, but there was an undercurrent of sadness in the sound. "Oh, I must be on my way in the morning."

"No!" the master exclaimed, and he sounded truly perturbed. "I had thought you would remain in the area a week at least."

"Did you? And why?"

"Well—because—because I wanted you to, I suppose."

"I am expected in Manningham," she said. "I must not be tardy."

"Expected by whom?" he asked.

The question seemed to catch her off guard, and for a moment she fumbled in her response. "Well, my—my—I have an aunt there, and several cousins. They are all most eager to see me."

Even I caught the echo of wistfulness in her voice, and the master fairly pounced on it. "It is obvious that you are speaking an untruth," he said, but his voice was very gentle. "May I be permitted to ask why you are really traveling to Manningham, and why you do not wish to go?"

She tried to keep a brave little smile on her face, but it was clear the effort was beyond her. "My aunt has only my best interests at heart," she said at last.

"That is hardly an answer at all," he protested. "Who is this aunt, and what does she want you to do that seems so oppressive to you? And why were you required to leave Lefton, if you didn't want to go?"

She resumed her pacing, even more slowly, and her story came out while she was in one of the dark spaces between torches. I had to creep along very quietly so as not to be overheard while she spoke in such a low voice.

"My parents died last year, leaving behind more debts than money to cover them," she said at last. "I have scraped by for a while, but it is clear to me I must change my situation. My aunt— my father's sister—has friends who are in need of a governess. I am in need of funds. The arrangement suits us all."

"It suits nobody!" the master exclaimed. "For someone as beautiful and vital as you to be hidden away in someone's attic, teaching vile and thoughtless children—"

That made her laugh. "You have no reason to suppose they are vile and thoughtless."

"All children are. It goes without saying. It would be madness to condemn someone like you to such a life."

She hesitated and said, in an even softer voice, "The other options seem even more insupportable."

"What options?" he demanded. "Surely you don't think— you wouldn't—I know there are men out there who might make clandestine offers—"

"No, no, I would die before I sank to such a level!" she returned with heat. "But my aunt—my *other* aunt, my mother's sister—she believes I would do better to marry my way into a comfortable existence. Oh, and she has picked out just the groom for me! Never mind that he's seventy, and hideous, and that at least one of his *three* wives died under circumstances that had all of Lefton talking! He is quite wealthy, you see. That is all that merits her attention." Lady Charis's voice grew hard. "I would rather earn my way in the world, no matter how hard the work, than sell myself in such a way."

The master was silent for so long that Lady Charis was moved to speak again. "I've disgusted you," she said, and she sounded close to tears. "I'm sorry, I didn't think—let me go back to the house. I'll call for my coach."

I saw her lift her skirts with both hands, but the master stopped her by touching her wrist. "No. Disgusted me? Impossible. You have made me think about how different life is for a man without prospects and a woman without prospects. A matter of months ago, I was not so differently situated than you, but I knew there were several possibilities open to me. Even if I had left the army without a coin to my name, I'd have been able to find work of some kind, and I wouldn't have railed too much against my lot. I wouldn't have been forced to decide between choices that were degrading or merely disagreeable. I would have been able to make my way through the world with some degree of happiness."

"You seem to be singularly blessed with a happy spirit," she murmured. "I imagine you would have been happy no matter what your circumstances."

"But I cannot bear to see you go off so soon to such a dreary existence," he answered. "How quickly are they expecting you in Manningham? And answer truthfully."

She shook her head. "There was no set date. I am obliged to present myself before the month is out, but I had hoped to enter into an employment contract as soon as possible. My funds are nearly gone, and I have wasted enough time as it is."

"But stay just another few days," the master said in a wheedling tone. "Your life will be filled so soon with such drudgery! Give yourself a week of pure, uncontested indulgence. I will arrange for bountiful dinners and pleasant carriage rides and perhaps an expedition to a ruined abbey not far from here. Your aunt need not know," he said, speaking over her when she attempted to protest. "We will send her a message saying that your coach lost a wheel and the yokels in this backward county could not make you a new one with any dispatch. She might be aggrieved, but *you* won't care. You will be very penitent when you arrive, and she will be forced to forgive you."

Lady Charis laughed, but she instantly sobered. "You paint the most tempting picture," she said, laying a hand upon his arm. "It is a very sweet offer, and I have not had many of those in recent days. But I cannot accept. I will be on my way to Manningham in the morning."

"And I say you will not," he said, smiling down at her. "And I think I am more stubborn than you are."

"You would be surprised at how determined I can be."

"Ah, my lady, I am a soldier. I am used to winning, no matter how steep the odds against me. I say you shall stay three more days before you head on to Manningham, and that the memory of those days will sustain you all your life."

✑

Who can really blame her, then, for remaining at the Red Owl Inn for another day, and another day after that, and still another day? The master was ingenious in the stratagems he used to keep her from leaving. I believe he himself went to the inn that first morning and ordered the removal of the wheel from her battered travel coach. Another day he paid the head groom of the inn to say that there were no horses available for hire; she could not depart. The third day—oh, I forget. Perhaps the cook was bribed to burn the breakfast or the housekeeper was induced to mislay some clothes. In any case, some small trouble arose that forced the guest to cancel her plans for leaving.

Certainly someone who had desperately wanted to travel on would have found ways to overcome these setbacks, but it was very clear that Lady Charis infinitely preferred to stay. Her laughter could be heard from every corner of the house in the days that followed—from the dining hall, where the master gathered the younger nobles of the neighborhood for teas and breakfasts; from the gardens, where the master escorted her on long, aimless walks; from the stables, where he led her as they set out on yet another ride around the countryside.

Naturally, he made sure she got her fill of the most spectacular feature offered by Grey Moraine. The house was built on a rugged terrace that overlooked a jagged, tumbling chasm of stone, but most views of the house did not show you that prospect. Indeed, the front and the sides of the mansion overlooked sloping lawns and manicured gardens. But Grey Moraine itself, when seen from the road as you first approached, was a turreted three-story structure silhouetted against empty sky. Behind it was nothing but air and canyon.

I myself showed Lady Charis to the observatory that forms the upper level of the house. From the front windows, of course, you can see the gardens, the trees, the drive, and the lawns. From the back windows, you see a panorama that makes you gasp—a two-thousand-foot plunge into a steep and virtually inaccessible gorge. The whole back wall of this room is nothing but windows, so that the view seems to go on and on. At sunset, the smoky rock is washed with pink and gold, but at any other time of day, Grey Moraine is a slash of icy menace, beautiful and stark.

Some people refuse to stand too near those windows, as if afraid some hungry spirit of the mountain will suck them to the edge and over the sills. Or perhaps the more weak-minded ones fear that they will be somehow induced to fling themselves through the glass to go tumbling to their deaths. The old master used to joke that he would never invite anyone into the observatory unless he was absolutely convinced the other fellow meant him no harm. Myself, I am neither dizzied by great heights nor worried about the spite of the earth gods, but I find the observatory an unsettling place to be. The sky seems too close there, the air too thin. I am much happier when I can lay my palm flat against the ground.

Lady Charis was not at all unnerved by the signature view of Grey Moraine. She did take a sharp breath the moment she stepped into the room, but she instantly crossed all the way to the window and pressed her nose, and then her hands, flat against the pane. For a moment, I saw her breath spread fog across the glass.

"*Duncan,*" she said in a voice of deep awe. I instantly noticed that she was addressing him by his name without his title. "It's utterly magnificent."

"My favorite room in the house," he said.

She didn't even turn to look back at him, just kept staring out at the harsh and fantastical landscape. "Has anyone ever climbed down this mountainside?"

"Not successfully," he said. "One or two have tried. And there's a story about a worker who fell to his death when the house was being built. Another tale about a woman who jumped through the window at night, killing herself, of course. But any old house will have tales like that, if it's been around as long as Grey Moraine."

She finally turned to face him, leaning her spine against the window. Her ease with the chasm behind her made me shiver a little. I tried not to turn my back on that view for any length of time. "Are there ghosts?" she asked with a smile. "The spirits of unhappy people who have died at Grey Moraine?"

"I don't know. Nettie, are there ghosts?" the master said, turning to me.

I had my hand on the door and was just about to leave (though perhaps you will say I should have exited before this; I confess I had tarried a moment to witness Lady Charis's reaction to the observatory). I glanced at him as I made my answer. "There have not been ghosts at Grey Moraine for many years now," I said. "Legend has it that the wife of Lord Walter—the third of the Fittledons, that would be—roamed the hallways for a hundred years, crying for her baby who was lost in a fire. And the daughter of the fifth Fittledon was said to have died of a broken heart when her lover spurned her to marry another. She was often to be seen drifting around the gardens, tearing the petals off of roses. Even now when it's a bad season for roses, the gardeners will say that Lady Lacey has been at the bushes again. But it has been years now since either of them was seen here."

"I am disappointed!" Lady Charis cried gaily. "Grey Moraine seems exactly the sort of house that would harbor all manner of wraiths and phantoms. Perhaps you merely have not lived here long enough to grow acquainted with them."

The master smiled at me. "She has been here as long as *I* can remember," he said fondly. "Nettie, when did you first go into service at Grey Moraine?"

"So long ago even *I* sometimes forget," I said with a light laugh. "I even remember your uncle's father, that's how long it's been."

He spread his hands and gave Lady Charis a rueful look. "So you see? If Nettie cannot remember ghosts, then surely none of them walk these halls."

He nodded to dismiss me, and I quickly stepped back out into the hall, thinking, *I didn't say I couldn't remember any ghosts. I said there had not been any seen here for quite some time.*

⤿⤺

I have no idea what conversation passed between Lady Charis and the master while they stood together in the observatory, gazing out on that dramatic view. I can only guess what they talked of on that slow, pretty ride to the broken abbey five miles north of the house. They had no private conversation over dinner that night, for the master had once again invited a handful of local scions in to provide ready laughter and lighthearted banter. Everyone stayed late, and it was the master who drove the visitor back to the Red Owl Inn.

He was up quite early the following day to fetch her one more time. I had overheard her protesting mightily the night before as he wrapped her in her cloak and escorted her to the door. "Positively not!" she was saying in answer to some question that I had missed. "Not one more day! I will stay through tomorrow, for I would dearly love to see the church at Clermist, but the morning after that I will be on my way, and nothing you can say will dissuade me."

"I'll think of something," he had promised as he shepherded her out into the night. "Have a little faith in me."

"And *you* have a little faith in me! I stand by my word."

"As do I, milady," he replied. "As do I."

For myself, I was hoping that this really would be the last day we would see Lady Charis, with her blue eyes, her pale skin, and her hint of melancholy. The master was altogether too taken with her—a penniless girl setting out to make her way in the world! Not at all the sort of woman he should be wooing, no matter how carelessly—and I wanted her gone. I wanted him to settle in at Grey Moraine, realize what a grave and momentous responsibility he had inherited, find himself a well-bred woman of gentle disposition, and quickly begin to produce happy and attractive children. Who wouldn't enjoy a life like that? Why couldn't he pursue it immediately? I didn't want him wasting any more time with shallow and unsuitable women who might turn his mind from its proper direction.

You can imagine my dismay, then, when the master came back from Clermist that evening with the news that he had married Lady Charis in the ancient little church that was the small town's only claim to distinction.

TWO

I sometimes think it would have been easier on me if I had ever been able to hate Lady Charis. Ermintrude did, as did Harlan; with them she was capricious and difficult, impossible to please one moment, singing their praises the next. Young Martin, on the other hand, adored her, and if she smiled at him or thanked him or actually called him by name, he was in blushing transports for the whole of the day. The rest of the staff was evenly split between absolute worship and fierce dislike, which made for some spirited arguments in the servants' quarters during the first few months of the master's married life.

As for myself, I was mostly puzzled and wary. Despite her inconsistent behavior with every other member of the household, she never treated me with anything less than careful courtesy, which occasionally modulated into teasing warmth. I can't say I was convinced she actually *liked* me, but I think she respected me—for my age, perhaps, or my long years of service, or the accumulated wisdom these two factors had combined to give me.

And I, though I did not respect her, found myself occasionally liking the new mistress. Or—no—that's not the right word. I found myself protective of her. I found myself feeling compassion. Why would a lovely young woman who had just married the richest and kindest man in three counties require a moment's compassion, you might ask? I'm not sure I could explain it myself. I think it was because, from time to time, despite the quite spectacular change in her fortune, I still caught that hint of wistfulness on Lady Charis's face.

It was easy to miss, of course, between her fits of temper and her childish petulance and her erratic and unreasonable demands. It was possible to dismiss because of its sheer ludicrousness. But Lady Charis, Duncan Baler's storybook bride, carried a core of sadness around with her, and no excess of lavish dinners, aristocratic company, or spousal affection could dispel it.

The first month that they were married, the house was never still.

I had wished Grey Moraine would entertain again. Well, my wish was answered a hundredfold! Every noble who lived within a hundred-mile radius of Grey Moraine must needs be invited to a five-day hunting party or a weekend masquerade. Lady Charis and the other young ladies of the district wrote and performed an amateur theatrical, while the young men made up the audience and applauded loudly. There were four grand balls within as many weeks, and a day didn't go by without half a dozen ladies from the neighborhood dropping by to leave their calling cards in the morning or take tea in the afternoon.

One of these tea parties sticks in my mind as being peculiarly representative of this particular period.

Our visitors this afternoon were a Mrs. Horton and her

daughters, Emmeline and Corabelle, who lived about ten miles away on a tidy property that was almost as prominent as Grey Moraine. Although Mr. Horton had no title, he was a wealthy and well-respected man who was considered a model landlord, if a little on the tight-fisted side. His son, a sober and rather dull young man, had married the year before in an event that had been the most talked-of wedding in the neighborhood until Lord Duncan eloped with Lady Charis.

Accompanying Mrs. Horton and her daughters were the vicar's wife, Mrs. Dolnat, and two elderly maiden sisters who were of the highest respectability, Leonie and Therese Jacard. While the company was certainly not as exciting as some of the groups that had gathered at Grey Moraine in recent days, you would have thought Lady Charis's very favorite friends had come to call. She practically sparkled with delight when the carriages arrived at the door and Martin showed the six visitors to the parlor.

"Nettie, please bring us refreshments," she said as she welcomed the women into the room. "Come in, come in, sit down! I have been so impatient to have all of you over to see me! You were here for the ball, of course, but no one can ever talk properly over the music."

I spent much of the next two hours carrying trays of tea and plates of sweets between the kitchen and the parlor. Normally, of course, one of the serving girls would handle such a task, but one was down with a cold and another had twisted her ankle. And I was curious. I was always willing to wait on the young mistress if it meant I might overhear some of her conversation. In fact, I might confess here that I hovered just outside the doorway for much of the afternoon—to be near at hand if Lady Charis had need of me, but also to listen to anything she might have to say.

Most of the conversation was quite ordinary, consisting of gossip about the unfortunate neighbors who weren't present this afternoon, commentary on fashions that had been on display the week before, supposition about who might be about to marry whom, and news about friends and family members who were absent.

The Misses Jacard were pleased to announce that their brother, his wife, and his children would be coming to visit over the winter holidays. "We shall entertain, of course," Therese said. "Just a small dinner or two. Of course, all of *you* will be invited, but we don't have the space to invite *everybody*."

This was said in a regretful tone, as if implying that Therese Jacard truly wished to open her home to the whole neighborhood, but in fact everyone accepted it in the spirit in which it was truly intended—that is, that only a small fraction of the people living in County Banlow were good enough to be invited into the Jacard household, and most of them were already sitting in the room.

"Oh, we will be entertaining as well over the holidays!" Mrs. Horton said. "David will be bringing the family, and Stephen will be home on leave."

"Stephen," Corabelle said with a little sigh, and then laughed. Everyone else laughed with her. Stephen was her cousin, though removed by a marriage or two; he had been raised by the Hortons when his own parents died young. He was a soldier by profession, a good-looking young man with a somewhat roguish disposition. It was no secret that Corabelle had nursed an affection for him most of her life.

"I quite look forward to seeing Stephen again," said Leonie Jacard. "He vanished so abruptly last spring when he was home on leave. I didn't get a chance to say good-bye."

Mrs. Horton wore a pained look. "Truth to tell, I was just as glad to see him go back to the regiment! The last time he was home—well. Let us say I was not always pleased by his behavior. He's very high-spirited."

"Oh, Mother, every girl in three counties flirts with him!" Emmeline exclaimed. "You can hardly expect him to refrain from flirting back! Even Father would misbehave given some of Stephen's incentives."

Mrs. Horton gave her daughter an icy stare. "I hardly think so."

"But surely—he's such a delightful young man—surely he did nothing too awfully terrible," the vicar's wife said. Her tone of voice implied that she was so good-hearted she could hardly bear to believe anyone capable of sin, but I knew better. She was an inveterate gossip and really wanted to hear of grave transgressions.

Emmeline leaned back in her chair. "Well, I myself caught him kissing one of the cook's assistants in the kitchen, but I think there was something worse," she said in a spiteful voice. Emmeline was not nearly as pretty as her younger sister, and my guess was that Stephen did not pay her as much attention, hence her eagerness to tell stories that reflected badly on him. "Because he was supposed to stay another whole week, and then one night there was this dreadful row with Father, and the next day he was gone."

"Kissing servant girls was quite enough incentive for your father to send him away," Mrs. Horton said firmly. "But I'm sure another six months in the army have curbed his wildness somewhat."

"I *hope* not," Corabelle said. "At any rate, I cannot wait to see him again."

"Well! All of you with such exciting visitors scheduled to arrive!" Lady Charis said. "We shall have to plan something very special."

"Perhaps you can have a winter ball at Grey Moraine," Corabelle suggested. "Everyone dressed in white, like snowflakes."

"How very boring," her sister drawled.

"Emmeline. That's unkind," her mother reproved.

Lady Charis laughed. "I shall think of something," she promised. "We would want it to be very grand."

Talk turned next to food and fashion. Lady Charis was organizing a dinner to be held in a couple of weeks, a much smaller affair than some of her recent diversions, but quite elegant; she planned to order desserts from a famous bakery in Kingston. I noticed—I am not sure why—how often Lady Charis specifically asked Mrs. Horton's opinion about details of this event and other matters. Mrs. Horton is not my favorite of the neighborhood ladies, but she has superb taste and impeccable manners, and I found myself heartened that Lady Charis would turn to someone so obviously equipped to guide her through some of the tangles of society. *The new mistress is young, but she is willing to learn,* I told myself. *That must be a good sign.*

A few days later, Lady Charis sent out invitations for the small dinner party. No one from the Horton family was included on her list.

⁊

I first became aware of the omission when the vicar's wife dropped by Grey Moraine two days after the invitations were sent. Lady Charis and the master had left an hour previously to spend the afternoon in the nearby town that held the Red Owl, a few taverns, some shops, and very little else. The day was sunny and breezy, not too chilly, and both of them had looked forward to the excursion. Harlan sent for me when Mrs. Dolnat made it clear she wanted to leave a message.

"So awkward—but so important," the vicar's wife said when I met her in the parlor. "It seems that Lady Charis's invitation to the Horton household has somehow gone astray. Mrs. Horton is too proud to speak up herself, but I knew Lady Charis would want to rectify the situation immediately. I can't bear to think of those sweet girls being left out of such an exciting event."

In fact, it was clear she was thinking of such a thing with relish. Her dark eyes snapped with hope and venom, as if she expected me to share a particularly tasty piece of news. But all I said was, "Thank you so much, Mrs. Dolnat. I will certainly make sure Lady Charis is informed."

The master and his bride returned from their expedition laughing and happy, and they headed straight for the observatory, where they liked to spend some time together every day. "Nettie—be a dear and bring us something to drink," the mistress called out to me as they swept up the stairs arm in arm. "Preferably something sweet. I'm parched."

"Something alcoholic!" the master added over his shoulder. "And something to eat as well."

So I made up a tray of lemonade and champagne, added a few pastries, and carried it upstairs. They had flung themselves onto a low settee that sat against one wall and were sprawled on it with all the appearance of people who had exhausted themselves in pursuit of pleasure. Late-afternoon sun sent gold washing through the great windows and across the wood floor and lent the room a burnished glow.

"What in the world did you do today to tire yourselves so completely?" I asked in amusement.

"We walked the length and breadth of that silly little street you people call a town," Lady Charis said. "And then Duncan thought it might be a good idea to stroll down some path that he said led to a very pleasing prospect—those were his exact words! A very pleasing prospect! But he didn't mention how you had to clamber down boulders and across fallen trees and get your skirt all muddy before you came upon this little hillock where you could stand and gaze at a few knobby mountains that he considered a spectacular view!"

He was laughing. "I don't recall that I had a lady companion the last time I made that exploration," he admitted. "And it's probably been five years since I attempted it myself. But I still think it's quite a lovely scene. And you would agree with me if the effort of getting there hadn't upset your delicate disposition."

"I shall borrow Martin's boots next time you offer to take me on any expedition," she replied. "Nettie, you angel, you've brought me lemonade! Do pour me a glass."

It was as I was handing the master his champagne that he asked if anyone had come to the house while they were gone. "Yes, milord, the vicar's wife dropped by with a message for Lady Charis."

She had the glass pressed against her mouth, but I swear I saw her lips curve into a smile against the rim. "Indeed?" she asked. "And she wanted to tell me what?"

"It appears that you inadvertently neglected to send an invitation to the Hortons for the dinner next week."

"Oh, there's a disaster in the making! Overlooking Sarah Horton!" the master exclaimed. "Even I know how highly she is regarded in this county, and I have resided here scarcely longer than you have."

Lady Charis rested her glass on a nearby side table. "It was not inadvertent," she said.

The master and I were both surprised, but only he said so. He sat up more straightly on the settee. "What? You mean to leave her out deliberately?"

"I do."

He looked bewildered but not particularly upset. Myself, I was closer to dumbfounded. If there was an arbiter of taste in County Banlow, it was Sarah Horton. She was strict, proper, at times harsh, and always on the arrogant side of civil. But no one wielded more social power than she did. "But why?" he asked.

Lady Charis considered. "I do not like her."

He gave a short laugh. "There are plenty of people I dislike in the world, and a good number of them live in County Banlow, but I treat them decently when I have to deal with them at all," he said. "It might not be worth the shock and outcry that will ensue if you shun her."

Lady Charis tilted her head and regarded him with those wide blue eyes. "Are you telling me I must invite her?"

He shrugged. "It is your party. It is your house as much as it is mine, and you should not have to entertain anyone you dislike. But if I were you, I would consider carefully before opening up such a breach."

She hesitated a moment and then said, "I will think about it."

That seemed to satisfy him, but it left me feeling even more uneasy. I could almost read her mind. He believed that her soft answer meant she was truly chastened, and that she would behave properly; he would not ask her again to amend her decision. And absent a direct instruction from him, she would not amend it.

"Lady Charis is mad," I said to Ermintrude as soon as I was downstairs. It is a measure of how disturbed I was that I chose

Ermintrude as my confidant, for in general I find the cook over-emotional and a little silly. "Or perhaps she's only cruel."

"She is probably both," was Ermintrude's instant response. She kissed her fingertips and laid them briefly against her heart. It was the gesture we country folk used to turn aside the mischief of the air demons, though it could also be employed to ward off the onset of general disasters.

"But I didn't think she was stupid," I added and I told her the story, which left her baffled as it left me.

"What possible reason could she have for making an enemy of someone so powerful?" Ermintrude demanded. "This will cause turmoil for months to come, mark my words."

"Or even longer," I agreed.

For those who enjoyed that sort of thing, the news that Lady Charis had excluded Sarah Horton from the party at Grey Moraine was a delicious scandal. The house buzzed with the news, as even the footmen and the housemaids understood what the insult implied, and any time I went to town during the next week, I heard it discussed. Whenever I happened to encounter servants from the Horton household, they turned their heads away and refused to acknowledge me, leaving me no choice but to ignore them in turn. What a ridiculous situation! How petty! How strange!

Why were we in it?

I worked closely with Lady Charis to plan the party, helping her decide how to arrange sprays of dried flowers around the dining room and the order in which to serve some of the more elaborate dishes. We were sitting together in her little study the morning before the dinner when she abruptly said to me, "You think I made a mistake, don't you?"

I pretended not to know what she was talking about. "With the marzipan? No, indeed, I think it is just what is needed to finish the meal."

She waved a hand impatiently. "In excluding Sarah Horton from my little event."

I gave her a direct look. A servant should not be too honest with her employer, or so they say, but I have found that there are times it pays to be forthright. As long as one is tactful, of course. "I think you have humiliated her. And that you set out to do so on purpose."

Her smile was very faint. "Why would I want to do that, I wonder?"

"I suppose you have a reason that seems very good to you."

"I do," she said. "Though I do not propose to share it."

"If it is not too presumptuous, I would ask if you intend to go on ostracizing her, or if you will be content to humiliate her just this once."

Lady Charis pulled on one of her dark curls, winding it around her finger as she appeared to consider the matter. "I am nobody," she said at last. "A parvenu bride with no social connections. Surely no one will care too much that I choose to exclude one person from one dinner at my house."

"You are married to the richest man in the county," I said, though surely she needed no reminding. "You have set yourself up to be a leader of local fashion. Already some of the other girls are copying your mannerisms and your styles of dress. Where you lead, others could surely follow. Do I think that your mistreatment of Sarah Horton will lead to her exclusion from the other houses in the district? I do not. Do I think it will cause ongoing speculation spiced with enough ill will to hurt her standing in the community? I do."

"And her daughters?" Lady Charis asked. "Will they suffer as well?"

"Inevitably. Again, I believe the Hortons' social credit is so great that they will easily survive, but they will be looked at askance. They will be whispered about."

Lady Charis was silent a moment. I sat forward. "It is not too late," I said. "You cannot expect them to accept an invitation *now* to tomorrow's affair. But this can be remedied. Just single them out in some highly public fashion. Invite the Hortons, and the Hortons only, on some enjoyable outing. Show them extreme attention. This can all be smoothed over."

She gave me that deep and mischievous smile that I had already learned to distrust. "Oh, no, Nettie. You misunderstand. I *want* them to suffer. All of them. And their brothers and cousins and fathers and uncles as well, if that is possible. A little thing like being left out of a meal can hardly be enough to truly harm them, but it is the only thing I can think of to do at the moment."

I gave her a grave stare. She had taken the end of her lock of hair and was idly brushing it across her face as if applying rouge to her cheekbones. She looked as pretty and dainty as a particularly angelic child. "Might I ask why?" I said.

She debated. "They are cruel," she said at last.

"Not that I ever heard," I felt obliged to answer.

"Perhaps I know something about them that you don't."

I phrased my next words very carefully. "I was unaware that you had been in the district long enough to have formed any impression at all of the Hortons."

She smiled. "Even in Lefton, we have heard of the Hortons," she said.

I was even more careful with my next sentence. "She is

unlikely to meekly accept being disgraced in such a way, particularly by someone so young and so new to County Banlow."

The smile remained on her face. "I know. But it really scarcely matters what she does to me later, as long as she is unhappy now."

What could I possibly say in reply to that? I merely nodded. "After the marzipan," I said, "should we consider more wine?"

⁓

The dinner, not surprisingly, was a resounding success, the more so because all the people who *were* invited to sit down at the table spent much of their energy mocking those who were *not*. Not the master, of course—he and one or two of his cronies (thoughtfully included on Lady Charis's guest list) withdrew almost immediately to the library to smoke.

And not Lady Charis, I noticed. She said very little about anyone else, whether absent or present, though she listened intently to the gossip everyone else had to offer and laughed whenever something particularly cutting was said. She didn't even have any observations to make about Mrs. Horton or her daughters, though she almost purred any time someone else made a derogatory remark.

"But what of their sire?" she asked late in the evening, after two inebriated young men had spent twenty minutes mocking Emmeline's plump figure and Corabelle's nasal voice. "No one speaks of him."

One of her companions shrugged; the other shook his head. "He's a dull dog," the first one said. "Can name his ancestors back to the time of the first king, but he doesn't have much conversation."

"So the delightful Sarah married him for his lineage, not his charm," Lady Charis surmised.

The second young man snorted. "Only man in five counties whose blood was as pure as hers," he said. "And you can bet those two daughters won't be allowed to wed anyone who's not of the highest caliber." He sketched a bow and indicated his friend. "Certainly not mongrels such as the two of us are."

"But I quite like mongrels," she replied. "I much *prefer* them to truebloods."

And so the conversation went for much of the night—at least, the portions I was privileged to overhear when my duties took me near enough to listen.

The party itself did not send any new ripples through County Banlow society. Indeed, there was more discussion about the Hortons before the event than afterward, which I suspected was a disappointment to Lady Charis. Still, she seemed quite happy in the days immediately following the event, though whether buoyed up by malice or the afterglow of a good party I could not say. At any rate, we had a week or two that I would describe as absolutely serene, focusing on trivial domestic issues and the mere ordinary business of existing.

Of those days, only one really stands out in my memory. The master had gone to town in the afternoon to run some errand that escapes me now. He had planned to be home early enough to join Lady Charis for the rare quiet dinner that would feature no guests at the table. The weather had been cold enough that frost had greeted us several mornings in a row. This particular day had been frigid and dreary from the very moment of dawn, overcast, gray, and intermittently filled with rain. Lady Charis had spent the entire day inside the house, and most of that time in the observatory.

I went up just about sunset to see if there was anything special she wanted for the dinner table. She was sitting quietly on one of the sofas, a book open on her lap, though she did not appear to be reading. A smile lit her face as I opened the door, but it faded somewhat as she realized it was only I.

"Oh! I thought you might be Duncan," she said. "Surely he's home by now?"

"I don't think so, milady," I replied. "I was merely coming to inquire if you had any instructions about dinner."

She waved an impatient hand. "No—anything Ermintrude wishes to prepare is fine with me. But you say Duncan has not returned yet? What could be keeping him?"

"He might have met a friend in town and stopped at one of the taverns for an hour," I said.

"I suppose," she said and glanced toward the window. The last of the sunlight illuminated the sleety, pelting rain that was even now hitting the glass. She shivered. "Dreadful weather to be traveling in."

"The master was a soldier for a long time," I said. "He's traveled in worse."

"Still, I don't like it that he is yet on the road. I expected him back an hour ago."

For a moment, I was reminded of the day Lord Ralph had died. He, too, had headed out on a routine ride in which nothing should have gone amiss, and he, too, had failed to return when he was expected. I felt a stir of uneasiness, which I tried to quell. "I'm sure he'll be at the door soon with some excellent reason for his tardiness," I said. "Shall I bring you some wine while you wait for him?"

"No," she said, and she laid aside her book and stood up. "I'll come downstairs where I will hear him when he arrives."

Her perturbation quickly communicated itself to the staff. Both Harlan and Martin hovered in the front hallway for the next hour, opening the front door every few minutes to peer through the curtain of rain. Ermintrude set dinner back and whispered devotions under her breath. I didn't know if she was praying to the spirits of the air to leave off their usual malevolence and allow the master to pass unharmed, or if she was invoking the guardians of the earth to shield him with their own bodies as he wended his way from town. I didn't ask; I prefer not to engage in conversations about religion with anyone, Ermintrude in particular.

Lady Charis paced up and down the length of the parlor, the room nearest to the foyer, and every ten minutes or so stepped through the door to inquire if anyone had spotted Lord Duncan. I pretended to be about my ordinary work, but in truth I found many excuses to pass through the hallway, hoping to be within call as soon as there was news.

Finally, nearly two hours past sunset, Martin opened the door and let out a great shout of relief. "There he is! I see him! The master's home!"

I happened to be in the parlor, urging the mistress to take a glass of wine. She sagged briefly against the wall and then instantly straightened, her face tinted with anger. "Well! At last he deigns to come home! I must ask him what he was about to make all of us worry so."

She strode into the hall and I could not help but follow, but both of us were thunderstruck to see the master when he stepped through the door. He was absolutely drenched, and his feet and lower legs were coated in mud. He had no coat, his hat was missing, and his hands and face were red from the assault of the weather.

"Duncan! What has happened to you? Come immediately to the fire!" Lady Charis exclaimed, instantly seeming to forget her ire in a surge of concern. "My dear, you look like you walked all the way back from town."

With Martin's help, he was peeling off his boots in an effort to avoid tracking mud throughout the house. The efficient Harlan had already hurried off to find a dry coat to wrap him in. I had to think the man might have caught his death of a chill.

But he laughed in complete unconcern. "I did!" he said. "How could I have forgotten that the way was mostly uphill? Took me almost three hours, though I thought I could make it in two."

"But—but why?" Lady Charis demanded, bewildered. "Didn't you ride a horse to town? Did he throw a shoe?"

Harlan was back with a towel and a smoking jacket, and the master accepted both gratefully. "No, the horse is fine as far as I know," he said, wiping his face and then shrugging into the coat. "I gave him away. There's a fire in the parlor, you say? Let's warm up a bit and then ask for dinner."

He put out his arm to escort his wife into the next room, quite a parade of us behind him. No power in this world could have prevented me from following him to hear the rest of the story, and Harlan and Martin were right behind me. It didn't seem to occur to any of us that we had no right to listen.

The master pulled up a footstool right before the flames, extended his stockinged feet, and sighed in contentment. Lady Charis settled on the edge of a nearby wingback chair and prompted, "Your horse? You gave him away?"

The master nodded. "I was just mounting so I could ride on home when I encountered a man in front of the pub. His own horse was lame, covered with lather—all done in. The man was sort of talking to her the way you talk to your horse—'Come on, girl, you can go on a little more, I know you can.' I paused to tell him he could probably rent a mount from Sawyer, the tavern-keeper, you know, but he turned to me and said, 'I can't pay a cent for a new beast. I can't even afford to buy a night's lodging and hope she's recovered enough to go on in the morning. I *must* be on my way tonight. I'll walk if I have to.' So naturally I asked where he was off to in such a hurry, and he told me his daughter had fallen ill. She was not expected to make it through the night. She and her mother live in a little cottage up near Crossholt—what do you think, Harlan, thirty-five miles from here?"

"More like forty, milord," said the butler.

"So I said, 'Well, you can take my horse, then,'" the master resumed, but before he could say another word, Lady Charis interrupted.

"You *believed* him? This—this desperate stranger? He could have been a criminal! A thief! Riding away from pursuers! He could have been a swindler just trying to find a credulous fool!"

The master shrugged. "Both thoughts crossed my mind," he admitted. "But, yes, I chose to believe him. I handed him the reins of my horse and took charge of his own, which I engaged to board in Sawyer's barn until this man was able to return my own animal to me. I gave him my coat, too, since he had so far to go," he added as an afterthought. "He thanked me at least fifty times and then took off." The master wriggled his toes and smiled. Clearly his feet were warming up. "I left his horse with Sawyer's hostler and set off for home. I must say, by the time the first hour passed, I was cold enough and wet enough and tired enough that I was beginning to rue my impulsive actions, but now that I'm in front of the fire in my own house, I'm rather pleased I helped the man out."

"Duncan," Lady Charis said, her voice very calm. "You realize you'll never see your horse again."

He shrugged. "And if I don't, I don't. Never gamble what you can't afford to lose. I have five more horses in the stable—yes, and the funds to buy a dozen more if I want them. My bet was that this stranger was an honest man, and if he's not, then no real harm done to me. I'd rather think I helped a liar than that I hurried past a man in need."

I glanced at Lady Charis, to see what retort she might have to make now, and found a most peculiar expression on her face. She had put a hand to her throat, as if to shield it from a draft; her lips were parted as if she were having trouble drawing in enough air. She no longer looked angry—indeed, I thought she appeared confused more than anything. As if she had stepped into a familiar room in her house and found it crammed with furniture she'd never seen before. As if she had found herself married to a man who turned out to be completely different from the person she had believed he was.

"That was—I suppose your behavior was exceedingly kind," she said in a halting voice. "Not one person in a hundred would have been so generous. Not one person in a thousand."

"And that's the saddest part of the tale, if true!" he replied. "I like to think any man will be kind if given the chance. Any woman, too."

"One would *like* to think it, perhaps," Lady Charis said, seeming to recover some of her usual asperity, "but one would probably be wrong."

The master hauled himself to his feet and gave himself a

little shake as if to resettle all his clothes. He grinned at the servants still clustered by the door. "Martin, perhaps you would be so good as to find me a dry pair of shoes. Nettie, could you let Ermintrude know that we're ready for our dinner now? And Harlan—the best bottle of port in the cellar. I think I need a little extra help tonight to warm my bones."

Three

Winter had barely settled in when some of our neighbors began entertaining for the holidays. Mrs. Horton announced she was holding a small dinner party, to which the Balers were pointedly not invited. The vicar's wife was quite gleeful when she brought the news to Grey Moraine, though she pretended to be shocked that such a long-standing member of the community could behave in such a petty fashion. Lady Charis received the information with weary boredom, but the instant Mrs. Dolnat was out the door, she jumped to her feet and laughed in delight.

"What fun!" she exclaimed to me as I gathered up the tea things I had brought in for her and her guest.

I gave her a baffled look. "To be excluded from a social engagement?"

"To create such consternation! You watch, there will be a procession of visitors up the drive over the next few days, as every other young lady invited to the Hortons' dinner drops by to debate with me whether she should attend. They won't come right out and *ask,* of course, but what they'll want to know is if, by accepting Sarah's invitation, they will be forfeiting any chance to be invited to Grey Moraine again."

Not for the first time in my life, I found myself glad that I had not been born noble and ambitious. Such machinations gave me a headache. "What will you tell them?"

"Oh, I shall be very warm and affectionate. 'My *dears,* don't fret at all! I couldn't *possibly* expect you to pass up such an opportunity. You will *always* be welcome at Grey Moraine. Don't worry about it another moment!' The delicious thing is," she said, spreading her arms and twirling around like a schoolgirl, "they won't know if I mean it or not! They'll be in agony, trying to decide whom to offend—Sarah Horton, who has dominated County Banlow society for thirty years, or the fashionable and wealthy Charis Baler, who is so interesting—but so capricious."

I couldn't help but smile at that. "So you call yourself capricious."

She laughed lightly. "I imagine everyone does, yourself included."

I bowed my head a little and assumed a meek expression. "I would not presume to comment so about my employers."

"Dear Nettie," she cooed. "So loyal—and so discreet."

It might have been a barb; it might have been sincere. I merely bowed my head again as I turned toward the door with the tea tray in my hand. "Always loyal to the masters of Grey Moraine," I said. "Till my dying day."

✐

She was right, as it turned out. A dozen of the younger folk of the county made their way to the mansion in the next few days, trying to get a feel for how she would react if they attended Sarah Horton's dinner. I later heard that three of the people who had received what would ordinarily be extremely prized invitations had found excuses for turning them down, which caused *another* ripple of scandal throughout the neighborhood. And Lady Charis didn't immediately make it clear how she intended to react, for—after more than two months of almost constant entertainment—she passed a good two weeks without scheduling, or attending, any major events.

In truth, she might not have planned it that way. She had taken a cold or some ailment that left her tired and listless, and she spent those two weeks sleeping late and huddling in the observatory, sipping hot drinks. She was fretful but somewhat pathetic, and even Ermintrude softened toward her, trying to tempt her flagging appetite with savory broths and crusty breads. The master coddled her, of course, reading aloud to her in the evenings and bringing back treats for her if he had been out during the day—ribbons and buttons from the shops in town, perhaps, or an armload of holly he had found on a bush alongside the road. But unfortunately, business called him away for three days during this period, and then she really moped.

Oddly enough, the one thing that seemed to cheer her the most was hearing stories about past owners of Grey Moraine. I brought her the three hand-bound volumes of personal family history that had been compiled by the old master's grandfather, and she spent a great deal of time leafing through their pages, utterly absorbed. They included sketches of the house at various points during its construction and renovation, copies of wills and tax statements, letters between owners and their heirs, copies of marriage certificates, and a number of pen-and-ink drawings of past masters and mistresses of the estate.

"Now, who is this?" she would ask me, pointing to some cameo portrait, and I would tell her all the additional tales that had been handed down about each owner through the generations. She was surprisingly good at keeping track of which Fittledon was which, and she had no trouble at all with the Balers.

"We'll have to have someone in to sketch your picture soon," I remarked one rainy afternoon as we sat together in the observatory. "Yes, and the master's as well. And of course we'll need to commission both portraits to be done in oil."

She rather self-consciously brushed back a lock of her black hair. "I've never sat for a picture before," she said.

"I'm sure any artist would be glad to have you as his subject."

She laughed a little. "What will future generations think of me, I wonder?" she said. "When they look at my picture. Will they say, 'Isn't she lovely? But such a cold expression!' Or will they say something kinder?"

As was so often the case, I had to work hard to phrase my answer politely. "Perhaps what they say about you will be influenced by what they know of your behavior during the time you serve as mistress of Grey Moraine."

"You mean, if I am a good woman, they will find me more attractive?" she replied dryly. "That might be how it works as you are viewed through the lens of history, but while you are actually *existing*, people seem to only notice you for your looks."

"Your ladyship has nothing to worry about on that score, then," I said.

"Yes," she said a bit moodily, "I cannot help but know that I am considered very beautiful."

The instant she said the words, there was a flare of lightning, followed seconds later by a growl of thunder. The lightning made me jump; the openness of the observatory always made it seem as though the room itself were at the epicenter of any storm. My nervousness made Lady Charis laugh.

"Nettie! Why, you're as edgy as a colt! It's just a little rain."

"I don't like rough weather," I admitted. I kissed the middle three fingers on my right hand, then pressed them to the center of my chest.

"What's that?" she demanded. "I've seen you do that before—yes, and Ermintrude, as well. What's that for?"

It had been a habitual and unthinking gesture. I was a little embarrassed that she had caught me out. "Folk superstition," I said. "A ward against wicked spirits."

She sat up straighter on the sofa, more animated than I had seen her in the past two days. "What wicked spirits?" she said. "Tell me about them."

I did not like to talk about the elementals, for they were drawn to the sounds of their own names and seemed to cluster closer whenever you spoke about them. Particularly the sprites of the air. And yet her face was so bright with curiosity that I knew it would do no good to try to fob her off with vague explanations.

"Fancy folk tend to have fancy gods," I said, "but country people believe in more intimate deities. Farmers who have worked the land all their lives will tell you that guardians of the earth reside in the soil. Those guardians have their hands outstretched to catch every seed as it's planted, and they tend every blade of grass, every stalk of corn, with the care humans might give each living infant. Soldiers and townsfolk also pray to the guardians of the earth, for these spirits can watch over *places*— keep walls strong, prevent foundations from crumbling. Some believe that certain sites have acquired their own guardians who take human shape and watch over their particular spots for centuries."

"And these guardians are always benign?"

"Usually," I said. "But if they are angered by thoughtless abuse of the land, they can rise up to destroy roads and fields and whole mountain ranges, if they choose."

"Very impressive," Lady Charis said.

"The water nymphs are more mercurial, for they have the changeability of a wild brook," I continued. "They can shower you with gifts or they can leave you desolate and abandoned. Young girls pray to the water spirits, because they are believed to have power over emotions. They may persuade a man to fall in love with you, but they may easily turn his love into another channel. They are thought to have some affinity with the blood that moves through your body, and if they are moved to do so, they can cure you of fever or any other illness. So it is believed."

"But this is so appealing!" Lady Charis said. "Although just a little quaint."

"It is the spirits of the air who are the most powerful and the most dangerous," I went on. As I spoke, I glanced at the windows, which overlooked a hard, steady rain. An ordinary storm, or the air demons expressing their rage over something? Hard to know. "Even the other elementals fear them, just a little. Like the wind, they can go anywhere. They can be soft as a whisper of breath, or as noisy as a thundering gale. Unlike the other elementals, they have no fondness for men. They envy us our position—lords of the living world—and they constantly scheme to bring about our downfall. They harm us in small ways, if they can, which is one reason I am so afraid of storms! I know the air demons would like to rattle the glass right out of these casements and come rushing straight into this room to torment us. But the air demons are also responsible for most of the great miseries that have been inflicted on men."

"What miseries? How inflicted?" she demanded.

"They make bargains with men," I said flatly. "They offer great power to individuals who will effect great destruction. If an obscure king suddenly commands the resources to invade his neighbors, it is because he has sold his service to the spirits of the air. They bestow upon him the money and skill and charisma to become a leader—and in return they specify a sacrifice that he must give them when they so demand."

She appeared fascinated, though still slightly skeptical. "What kind of sacrifice?"

I shrugged. "They might require him to slaughter an entire town and torch its buildings, for they love nothing so much as pure annihilation. They might push him to such excesses that he bankrupts his own country and every territory he has annexed, leaving whole lands and untold generations wretched, disorganized, and poor." I shrugged again. "But more often they work in smaller ways, through ordinary people, causing mischief instead of true sorrow."

"Give me some examples."

"They always make some kind of offer to a dissatisfied mortal," I said, adding hastily, "at least according to the stories. Say a man is poor and wants wealth. They will promise him gold, and they will deliver it. But once he is a rich man, they will require him to destroy the good men around him. Perhaps he uses his money to outbid an honest merchant and drive him out of business and send all his dependents begging in the streets. Perhaps his new funds will go to support a political uprising that will bring down a steady government. The spirits of the air flourish in chaos, no matter how it is brought about."

"They do sound most unlovable," she said. Her voice was steady, but I thought she was probably mocking me. It is hard for most sophisticated people to believe tales of the elementals. They are *so* convinced that they make every decision of their own volition, uninfluenced by forces not immediately visible to their eyes.

I leaned forward, determined to finish my tale now that I had started. The rain had slackened a little, but the windows were still wet, and the sky visible from every prospect was a louring gray. "The demons of the air particularly love to make pacts with young women, and they can take a variety of pleasing shapes," I said. "There's many a girl who thought she was invoking the water spirits as she prayed to have a young man fall in love with her, only to learn later, to her rue, that she had made a deal with a wind demon instead. She got her wish—she got her husband—but the cost was much steeper than she was prepared to pay."

"Oh, now, you must tell me what kind of price was exacted."

"Most often," I said, "the demons steal the soul of her first child."

Lady Charis merely stared at me out of her enormous blue eyes.

"While it is still in her womb," I continued slowly, "they suck out its human essence. In its place they leave the spirit of one of their own—a soul of greed and vapor. It comes into this world as any human child, and is raised as human, and goes through life like any mortal man or woman, with all the advantages its inheritance can give it. And yet all this time it is an air elemental, bent on havoc and destruction, and everywhere it goes it brings grief to men."

Lady Charis seemed to recover from a moment of stupefaction. "Why is it I have never met any of these changeling children walking about in the world? There must be hundreds of them, judging by the number of girls I know who would be willing to make any covenant to get the men they want!"

"There are," I said grimly. "And you no doubt have encountered a dozen of their offspring in your lifetime. Think of the men you know who behave cruelly or irrationally, who mistreat their wives and subordinates. They are the children of the wind, masquerading as humans. Think of the most spiteful woman you have ever encountered, who terrorizes her servants and loves to spread hurtful gossip."

"The vicar's wife," she said with a smile.

That actually surprised a smile out of me in return. "I wouldn't doubt it," I agreed. "She, too, could be an air demon, walking among us as a child of man."

"Well, it is a most interesting philosophy!" Lady Charis said with a little laugh. "But I think your elementals might find themselves balked in many instances. What if the newly rich man refuses to sow dissent among his fellow merchants? What if the new bride never conceives a child that the demons can alter to their own specifications? What if the humans accept the largesse bestowed upon them but refuse to uphold their part of the bargain? The pretty girl is still married to the man she loves. The king has still conquered half the world. What can your demons do then?"

I shuddered a little. How many foolish mortals had thought they could outsmart the elementals? Had any of them ever succeeded? Not in any of the tales I had heard. "The humans who fail to honor their pacts die most dramatic deaths," I said. "That is another thing that the countrymen believe. A man who flings himself from a bridge into a river was pushed into the water by the wind. A woman who stumbles down the stairs and breaks her neck was tripped by a sprite of the air. There are tales of men who begin gasping for breath—choking, as if unseen hands are strangling them—when no one is near enough to touch them. You do not make a bargain with the wind and fail to honor it. Which is why it is best not to make such a bargain at all."

"No! I quite see that!" Lady Charis said, drawing a deep breath. She let it out on a laugh that, to my ears, sounded a little shaky. "Nettie, I must commend you. What a storyteller! You have shocked me from my megrims, I think—though you have left me in a state of terror, which may not be much better!"

I bowed my head in a subservient manner. "I only told the tales because you asked, milady."

"Yes, and I am most intrigued by all you have related. I presume Ermintrude feels as you do—and Harlan, and Martin, and all the servants?"

"Ermintrude certainly," I said. "Though she believes the spirits of the air can be moved to kindness now and then, if you supplicate hard enough and resist their blandishments. She will petition them to protect travelers on the road, or at least refrain from offering them harm. I confess, I have never seen any signs of their benevolence myself, but perhaps I have not lived long enough. Someday I may be surprised."

"Live long enough, and all of us are surprised," she said, rising to her feet. "Well. Let me go downstairs and see what Ermintrude has found to tempt me for dinner."

⁓

Shortly after that conversation, Lady Charis seemed to shake off her unaccustomed malaise. Perhaps the sickness passed—or perhaps she was energized by the social events that clustered thick and fast during these weeks of the winter holidays.

First the Misses Jacard held a set of dinners to celebrate the visit of their brother and his family. *Two* dinners, they said, because they had so many friends the house wouldn't hold them all for a single event; but everyone knew this was their way of appeasing both Sarah Horton and Charis Baler, while keeping them separate by inviting them to different meals.

"A masterstroke," Lady Charis said to me when she heard the news. "I own, I did not expect those two old dowds to come up with such a clever scheme! I must reward them in some fashion."

Then the vicar's wife had an intimate breakfast in the morning and a small dinner in the evening; again, the guest lists bore no crossover. A few bolder matrons of the district simply invited both the feuding factions to the same functions, and the stories I heard about those events told of the complicated choreography the other guests performed to keep Lady Charis segregated from Mrs. Horton even when they were in the same room.

It was not to be expected that Mrs. Horton would invite the Balers to her house for any of the entertainments she devised when her son and her nephew were in town, nor that Lady Charis would include any of the Hortons at the sumptuous banquets she planned during that same period of time.

What was even less expected was that Stephen Horton would come to Grey Moraine to pay a visit to his aunt's social enemy. And yet he did.

He arrived on a day that was exceptionally sunny, though very cold. Snow that had fallen three days previously still lingered in the shadows and outlined the black tree branches, though the walks were mostly cleared and travel was relatively easy. I had been upstairs when the sound of horses' hooves caught my attention, and I peered from one of the second-story windows to see who had arrived. All I could tell was that the visitor was a dark-haired man wearing a scarlet uniform and riding a spirited black horse. Just the set of his shoulders was enough to tell me he was a personable rogue; I didn't even have to catch sight of his face.

I instantly thought of business I had in the foyer and hurried downstairs just as Martin was showing the guest to the parlor. He might have been young, but Martin was a quick study, and he instantly knew that anyone with the surname Horton might cause consternation at Grey Moraine these days. He looked relieved to see me, since Harlan was nowhere in sight.

"Nettie," he whispered. "Here's Captain Horton come to call, but milord is out to the Chesney place. I told the captain the master won't be back for another couple of hours. He said, 'Then is Lady Charis home to visitors?' What should I do? Should I tell milady? Or simply show him the door?"

"I'll tell her for you," I said. "In the meantime, do offer our visitor some refreshment, whether or not she chooses to see him."

He nodded gratefully and hurried away, while I went back upstairs to find the mistress in the observatory. I was curious to see what reaction she might have to Stephen Horton's arrival. Would she be angry that he dared to visit Grey Moraine despite the fact that she had made it clear she despised his relatives? Would she be offended at his presumption? Impressed by his determination? Won over by his recklessness?

I shall never forget her expression when I gave her the news. She was standing by the bank of windows, and her porcelain face was limned with afternoon gold. She should have looked goddesslike, the clean lines of her face and body sculpted as if in marble, but instead she looked soft, wondering, astonished, and hopeful as a child offered a treat she had never dared to hope for.

"Captain Horton has come to see *me*?" she said, and her sweet voice matched her sweet expression. "Really he has? Oh, show him up, Nettie, do!" She patted her ringlets. "Is my hair mussed? Do I have any smudges on my face?"

She was vain of her appearance, as any young lady might be, but her eagerness to appear to her best advantage was extraordinary for the circumstances. I said, in a somewhat repressive voice, "Indeed, you look perfectly presentable for entertaining visitors. I will bring the captain up."

You will think badly of me, perhaps, when I say that I planted myself firmly on the other side of the door once I had shown Captain Horton to the observatory and procured refreshments. That Lady Charis had a fondness for Captain Horton had been impossible to overlook, and I thought it was my duty as a loyal servant of the house to discover just how far that affection extended and whether the young man returned it. I have some practice in listening at keyholes, and the observatory is particularly resonant. I am fairly sure I heard every word.

To my relief, none of those words was incriminating. In fact, had I not witnessed Lady Charis's smile and blush a few moments ago, I would have said the two had no history together at all.

"Captain Horton!" she greeted him, her voice friendly enough but not particularly warm. "I am so sorry my husband is not here to meet with you. It is very good of you to come calling."

"I heard from many sources the romantic tale of Duncan Baler and his fetching young wife," the captain replied. His voice was playful, but I imagined that was its natural tone; during my surreptitious study of him as we climbed up the stairs, I had come to the conclusion that this was a man constitutionally incapable of refraining from flirtation. "I determined to come see you for myself at the earliest opportunity."

"And here you see me!" she replied. "I hope the gossip presented me with tolerable accuracy. Please, sit."

"Oh, you just want me to say how woefully inadequate the descriptions of you were!" he said with a laugh. "But I won't say it. I don't know you well enough to begin showering you with fulsome compliments."

She laughed. "I don't know you at all, but somehow I get the sense that you have made a career out of showering young women with outrageous compliments and that you will find it hard to desist just because I am a stranger! Before too many minutes have gone by, you will be admiring the color of my eyes or the grace of my carriage. I think I know your type, Captain."

He sounded both rueful and amused. "What a low opinion you have of me! And so soon! What can I do to make you believe I am a sincere and worthy man?"

"You may first tell me what prompted you to come calling at Grey Moraine," she said. "You must be aware that a certain coldness exists between your aunt and me. Surely she would not be happy to learn you were idling away your afternoon with *me*."

"I am my own man, not bound to abide by my aunt's likes and dislikes," he replied. "I did not get a chance to meet the new master of Grey Moraine last time I was home, and you know we army men like to gather together and exchange tales of the soldiering life." His tone changed; he was clearly grinning. "And then, you know, I was consumed by curiosity to meet *you*! The very fact of my aunt's displeasure made it imperative I introduce myself as soon as possible. Everyone in the household expects me to behave in a contrary fashion. I swear they'd be disappointed if I *didn't* come see you."

"Hmmm—a thin enough explanation, but I suppose I will accept it, since I was very bored until you knocked on my door," she said. "But if you're to stay longer than ten minutes you must earn the privilege by being entertaining! Tell me what you have discovered about our friends and neighbors during your sojourn home. I like a juicy tidbit as much as the next woman."

"Well, the Jacards are incredibly smug and pretentious—but you know that already if you've spent five minutes in their company," he said. "Their brother is a good fifteen years older than I am, so I have never encountered him much, but I was forced to endure a whole evening with him two days ago, politely discussing foreign policy, of which I know nothing, and banking exchange rates, about which I do not care at all. His oldest daughter is as uninteresting as her aunts, but the young one hinted at a certain wildness of spirit. If he doesn't pay attention, she will commit an indiscretion. She has that air."

"Oh, I cannot imagine a Jacard doing anything that puts her beyond the pale! The stuffiest people imaginable."

He laughed. "You would be surprised at the secrets hidden behind some of the most respectable doorways in County Banlow," he said. "People you would never suspect of a moment's wrongdoing! Completely guilty."

"Let me think. Whom do I consider absolutely blameless? The vicar, surely."

Captain Horton made a rude noise. "Addicted to the bottle. I was told once that he never gives a sermon completely sober."

"Mrs. Milsap?"

"Eloped with a fortune hunter when she was a very young girl. Her father and her uncle caught them at the border. Two days later she was married off to old Milsap—which turned out to be an excellent arrangement for both of them, as far as I can tell."

"Mrs. *Milsap*? I don't believe you."

"True, on my honor."

"What about—I know. Your uncle. Debrett Horton."

"Ahhhh," the captain said. I imagined him leaning back in his chair and stretching his legs out in front of him. "Had a liaison with a village girl that resulted in the birth of a bastard daughter twenty-some years ago."

"No! That is an out-and-out fabrication."

"I swear! Truth! No one knows it, and if you ever tell anyone I said so, I'll deny it with my last breath."

"But—what happened to the girl? Was she sent away?"

"Not at first. She was raised not far from here by some severe but respectable matron who was paid a pretty sum to care for her. She was sent away last year, I believe, though I couldn't tell you where. I suppose she's a young woman now."

"This is such a remarkable story! Does she know her parentage? Does she have any claim upon the Hortons at all?"

Captain Horton made that noise again. "You've met my Aunt Sarah—and, if the rumors are true, you despise her—so you can guess the answer to that question. The girl knows who her father is, and I think Uncle Debrett would have acknowledged her in some fashion except that Aunt Sarah absolutely forbade it. As far as I know, Emmeline and Corabelle aren't even aware of the young woman's existence. Wouldn't want to sully their ears with such scandalous talk, you know. Wouldn't want to tarnish their image of their father."

"How did you come to hear of her, then, if her existence is such a secret?"

"David told me—Debrett's son, you know. He's not quite as much a prig as his father, but *he* was only told because he's the heir, of course, and apparently there is some small sum of money that goes to the girl every year. Enough to keep her from starving, at any rate. And if something were to happen to Debrett, well, David would be expected to continue the payments. He was practically dumbstruck the night he repeated the story to me. Debrett Horton, of all people! It's still hard to credit."

"And did David ever introduce himself to his—well, I suppose she would be his half-sister, wouldn't she?"

"No, but I did," Captain Horton said.

"*Really*? Why?"

I pictured a careless shrug of those scarlet-clad shoulders. "Because I was curious. And because I like women. And because I myself have suffered just a little at the hands of Debrett Horton and his haughty wife."

"What was she like?"

"Oh, an odd little creature! She had something of the look of Emmeline about her face—not especially pretty—but much livelier than either of her sisters. Very nervous—hardly would sit still for a moment—and rather intense. Asked me all sorts of questions about the household. About my uncle. About her sisters. And then asked me what she should do with her life. Go to Kingston and try to make her way? Take a position as a lady's companion? Confront her father in some public fashion and force him to make better provision for her? She had a lot of ideas, and a great deal of energy, but she lacked purpose and a plan. I couldn't tell if she was angry or hopeful or wretched or determined to make her life better. All of those things at once, I suppose."

"So what advice did you give her? Though may I say right now that you do not strike me as the sort of man who could offer wise counsel to *anyone*."

He laughed again. "A most incisive insight! I forget what I told her, but I don't know that she would have taken my advice in any case. I did visit her a number of times last spring, and then one day she was gone. My uncle claimed not to be responsible for her removal from the county, but I have to wonder if he or my aunt decided they did not like her living so close after all. I have no idea where she's gone off to. I wish I could discover if she's well, at least. Maybe David can tell me where the money is being sent these days."

"That's very commendable of you," Lady Charis said. "To care so much for a penniless bastard girl."

The smile was back in his voice. "As I said. I like women."

"Captain Horton!" she exclaimed, mock reproof in her tone. "Am I to understand that you *flirted* with this girl? Unsuitable by every measure—class, situation, and ties of blood!"

"Ah, well, I might have offered her a compliment or two— of the type I've been most conscientiously *not* offering to you, since you warned me against excessive flattery," he added. "I hope you've noticed how good I've been."

She seemed to instantly accept the change in topic. Indeed, I thought perhaps she was tired of hearing Stephen Horton talk about another woman, however pitiful and nameless that girl might be. "I never said I didn't like excessive flattery, only that I didn't like *insincere* flattery," she replied. "I quite like being given a compliment as long as the other person means it."

"Well, I'm entirely truthful when I tell you this has been the most enjoyable half hour I've spent since I returned to County Banlow," he answered.

"So I am more amusing than Therese Jacard and Vicar Dol-nat," she said gravely. "Yes, I think even someone as suspicious as I am can believe praise as tepid as that."

"In fact, I have enjoyed our conversation so much that I hope you will be willing to repeat it during the all-too-brief remaining duration of my stay," he said. "Would you go riding with me some day? I hope your husband can accompany us, of course."

"You must come in the morning if you want to include Duncan on any outings," she said. "He spends the last half of most days attending to estate matters and visiting with tenants."

"But I am a soldier on leave!" he exclaimed. "I never rise before noon! I am making up for all the sleep I have missed during my recent months in the barracks. Will you come riding with me even if your husband is not present to chaperone?"

There was a short silence. I held my breath. The correct response, of course, would be *No*. Or even, *Bring one of your cousins along and we shall all ride together*. Certainly both Lady Charis and Captain Horton knew that they should not court gossip—or even worse trouble—by planning unsupervised excursions throughout the countryside. "I would be happy to," she said at last. "When would you like to go?"

"Tomorrow," was the prompt reply. "I shall be by shortly after lunch."

I could hear the smile in her husky voice. "I shall be dressed for riding."

∽

For the next week, Captain Horton and Lady Charis were constantly in each other's company. Two of those days, they were out late enough that the master had returned to the house before they did, and each time, the captain was invited to join them for dinner. If the master disliked the easy intimacy that had sprung up so quickly between his bride and the dashing young soldier, he showed no evidence of it. Judging by what portions of the conversation I was able to overhear as I helped the kitchen girls serve the meals, Lord Duncan was genial to the new guest, happy to swap stories of officers and enlisted men they both knew, and completely innocent of suspicion.

I cannot admit to any such sanguine attitude myself. I eavesdropped shamelessly whenever they were together in the house, and I watched from the windows the whole time they were gone, ceaselessly imagining conversations and indiscretions. They returned one day, laughing and windblown. Had her hair been disordered by the breeze or by his careless hand? Had her lips been reddened by the cold air or by a passionate kiss? I could not ask, and I could not know, but uncertainty and anxiety drove me to several sleepless nights.

I most certainly was not the only person to notice their sudden friendship. Through roundabout channels of servants' gossip, I learned that Sarah Horton had pitched a rare fit one afternoon, demanding that Stephen Horton never cross the threshold at Grey Moraine again, and the vicar's wife made a point of dropping by one morning to gently warn Lady Charis against being "too particular" in her attentions to the handsome soldier. "For you know how people like to talk, my dear," she said in her honeyed voice. "Surely you do not want to cause any additional ill will between you and Sarah Horton? Or any uncertainty about your own sterling character? And you so newly a bride!"

But the friendship, or whatever it was, was of very brief duration, for suddenly, the captain was gone. His leave over, he had headed back to his regiment. I had no way of knowing if he and Lady Charis had exchanged soulful good-byes that final day while they were outside the house and off the property, but I could not help thinking that they had. For a day or two after he left, she was mopey again, but simultaneously restless. She moved through the house like an unsettled spirit. You never knew where you might find her, listlessly staring out the windows and seeming to watch for shadow men to come riding up on shadow horses.

Her mood changed quickly enough when the master told her he wanted to invite company to visit.

"I believe I should have young Callum and his wife to stay with us a week or two," he announced over breakfast shortly after the holidays. The world was in the grip of grimmest winter, the darkest time of year, and the weather had been particularly cold the past few days. The master didn't seem to notice such things, but Lady Charis was constantly draping herself in shawls and robes, and she looked a little woebegone. Or perhaps she was still missing the captain.

"Who's Callum?" she asked without much interest.

"The son of my second cousin. I checked with the estate agent and I was right—he's my closest male relative." As Lady Charis still looked blank, he added, "My heir."

That did make her sit up straight in her chair and assume an expression of alarm. I noticed, because I happened to be in the dining room at that moment, ladling out soup. "Your heir! But, Duncan—our children will be your heirs."

"And I hope we have a dozen," he said warmly. "But Ralph's unexpected demise makes me realize how quickly the world can change, and a man must look the future squarely in the face. Who knows? I could be thrown from my horse tomorrow, just like Ralph, or go down with a fever, and then Callum would have to step up in a hurry, just as I did. I'm not sure he's ever *seen* Grey Moraine. I'd like him to have some kind of idea what he might be in for, if the circumstance ever arises."

"And once he *does* see Grey Moraine, he'll be tempted to ensure you *do* meet an untimely death!" she exclaimed. "Who wouldn't want this place the instant he laid eyes on it? He'll push you down the steps for certain!"

At that, the master laughed. "I sincerely doubt it. But in case he turns out to be the covetous type, I'll be constantly on my guard."

"Duncan, I wish you would think about this for a few days."

"I *have* thought about it," he said, his voice very gentle but quite unyielding. "I believe I will invite them to come at their earliest convenience."

⟡

In fact, Callum and Letitia Donaldson found it convenient to arrive ten short days later. I confess, I was prepared to dislike them as much as Lady Charis was, for the Donaldson line was so remote from the Baler heritage that I could not consider them truly worthy of the property. I was sure they must be ill-bred upstarts, encroaching and crass. But in fact, I lost my heart to both of them at first sight.

He was perhaps thirty, fresh-faced and smiling, a rather slight man with medium-brown hair and a boyish expression. She was as fair as Lady Charis was dark, a blond fairy princess of a girl, delicate and sweet-faced and shy. They might not have come from the highest echelons of society, but their manners were flawless.

They were also expecting their first child. Letitia was one of those women who looked even more radiant when they were pregnant, and it was clear she was unbearably excited about the child who would be born in about two months.

"Just wait till you're expecting a child of your own," she said to Lady Charis over tea one afternoon. The master was taking Callum around to meet the tenants and ride the entire perimeter of the property, so the women were left to entertain each other. "The whole world looks different! Everything seems like a miracle. I saw a baby turtle the other day, so awkward and so marvelous, and it made me cry. A turtle! And yet it seemed like a divine creature."

It was hard for me to tell exactly how Lady Charis viewed these potential usurpers of her place. She had greeted them with perfectly pitched civility and performed excellently as a hostess, though she had never exhibited the playful side that showed her to her best advantage; she seemed always on her guard around them. But this comment caught her by surprise, I could tell. I dawdled a while over the tea things to hear her response.

"Indeed, I hope to have children, and quite soon," she said slowly. She brushed her hand very lightly over her stomach, an almost unconscious gesture that I had sometimes seen women make in the early stages of their pregnancies. I narrowed my eyes? Could she be with child? If so, she had not mentioned it to anyone, and not even the sharp-eyed Ermintrude had suspected. "That will cut Callum out of the succession, of course."

Letitia laughed merrily. "I cannot even picture it—Callum as master of Grey Moraine!" she replied. "We have the most adorable little place near the property where Callum grew up. It looks like a cottage, only a very large one, and I love it so much that I almost can't stand the thought of moving to the main estate once Callum's mother has passed on."

Lady Charis thought that over. "So his father is dead, and

Callum owns the family property, but he has elected not to move you into it?"

Letitia gave her a smile brimful with mischief. "We could hardly displace his mother, you see—well, she simply wouldn't move! She's told him so already—and Callum absolutely *refuses* to live under the same roof with her. She is—I do try to love her, but she is very *commanding*. And very loud. It is much more peaceful in the cottage. Callum administers the estate, of course, but everyone is much happier with the current arrangement."

Clearly the heir and his bride were not the type of people who would scheme to do away with the current master of Grey Moraine so that they could take up residence in his place. I saw the same thought pass through Lady Charis's mind, and then she offered Letitia her first true smile since the couple's arrival.

"More tea?" she asked, lifting the teapot. "Nettie, could you see if Ermintrude has made any of those cherry pastries that I love so much? I'm sure Letitia would enjoy them as well."

So, after all, the visit with the presumptive heir went extremely well, and the two couples parted with many expressions of affection and promises to visit again in the future. "You let us know when that baby is born," the master said, handing Letitia up into her carriage. "Boy or girl, you send us word."

Lady Charis had kissed Letitia on the cheek, and she did the same to Callum. "Travel safely," she said. "Let us hear from you soon."

The two of them stood in the drive, waving good-bye until the carriage was out of sight, and then arm in arm they promenaded back into the house. It wasn't until that night, as master and mistress shared a quiet dinner, that I realized Lady Charis was still troubled by the very existence of the Donaldson family.

"We'll have to go visit them next," the master was saying as I brought in a pie and prepared to serve it. "After the baby is born, perhaps. Once spring has come. We'll take a few days and make a long, slow journey to their property. That part of the country is very pretty, I understand."

With one hand, Lady Charis toyed with her fork. With her other, under the table, she stroked her belly again. I felt myself grow tense—with anticipation or a kind of dread, even I couldn't have said—and I thought, *She's going to tell him she's pregnant.* But all she said was, "Yes, I would be delighted to see them again. I quite liked them."

He laughed. "You say that in such a mournful way! Do you mean it? Or do you just think that is what I want to hear?"

I put a piece of pie in front of her, and she hesitated before answering. Obviously she did not want to have this conversation while I was in the room. I hastily served the master as well and exited through the door to the kitchen. And then I stood very quietly on the other side of the door and listened.

"No, I truly did like them, which is saying a great deal, as I expected to despise them," she said at last. "But I can't help wondering why you wanted—why you think—what your reason was for having them here. That's all."

"I thought I told you my reason. It seemed bad policy for me to inherit Grey Moraine without having the slightest idea of how much responsibility that entailed. I wouldn't want the next heir to face the same situation."

"Would you have any reason—any particular reason—for thinking you could not have an heir of your own body?"

"No, none at all," he said, sounding surprised. "You, at least, are quite youthful, and I'm pretty sturdy despite my relatively advanced age." He laughed.

"I just thought—if you were intending—I mean, if you didn't view me as the kind of woman who would be a good mother—"

Now he finally seemed to understand that she was truly agitated. "Why, Charis! Whatever can you be thinking? Of course I expect you to be a splendid mother! And I hope you will have the opportunity to be one very soon. Why would you say such a thing? Why would it cross your mind?"

She seemed to answer with some difficulty. "I know that while—while Captain Horton was in town, there was some gossip—unfounded accusations!—because of the amount of time I spent with him. People can say such cruel and terrible things. And I thought—I wondered—he was barely back with his regiment before you invited Callum to the house, and I thought— was there a reason—did you think—"

I heard the rustle of clothing; surely he had jumped up and circled the table so he could draw her into his arms. "Charis," he said, his voice even more gentle. "My dear. I was glad you enjoyed the captain's visit. It didn't occur to me to think there was anything untoward in your behavior. I have not been thinking of how I could rid myself of my wife and perhaps find someone more pleasing to put in her place."

There was a strange gulping sort of sob, and I realized that Lady Charis must be weeping unrestrainedly. "No—but then I—and you said—if you were to *die*! Callum would be master here and I would be all alone! You gone, and me full of despair, and where would I *go*? I liked them so much—Duncan, I *did*!— but what would become of me then? I never thought—I never thought about it—and then—and then, there they were, and you were showing him the house, and I—I—I could not bear it if something were to happen to you!"

The next few moments were empty of conversation, though

he made soft, soothing noises and she continued to cry. I wondered if he had swept her into his arms and then dropped into her chair, holding her on his lap, or if they stood beside the table, tightly embraced, she with her face buried in his jacket. It took a little while for her to grow calmer, but eventually her sobs quieted and he spoke in a crooning voice.

"There, are you better? Nothing so terrible has happened. Nothing terrible is *going* to happen. Charis, my darling, don't you know how much I love you? I have already made provision for you. I do not expect to die soon—no, no! let's see no more tears!—but if I *do,* you will be taken care of. Callum will assume the management of Grey Moraine, it is true, but there has been money set aside for you. You shall never go hungry. You shall never be forced to seek a post as a governess, or marry some horrid old man, merely to put food on your table. You will be able to live quite comfortably—though not if you spend every cent on new clothing the very first year I am gone—"

The words made her laugh, as they were clearly meant to, though even her laugh was bordered with tears. "Well, I would have to buy *some* new clothing, since I don't have a single black dress, and of course I would be in deep mourning," she answered in a somewhat ragged voice. "I hope you have made allowance for *that* in your will."

"I shall write my lawyer tomorrow and insist on a codicil," he promised. "Are you feeling sufficiently reassured to sit down and eat your pie now? It looks particularly good this evening."

"Yes, I believe I can finish the meal with no more histrionics," she said, and I heard the sound of chairs moving back and forth across the flooring. There was a period of silence, as I imagined they tasted and appreciated their dessert, and I turned to head back to the kitchen. The sound of her voice stopped me before I had taken a step.

"Duncan," she said, very low and very serious.

"Yes, my dear?"

"You are so good to me."

"It is easy to be good to you. I love you very much."

"You have made me much happier than I ever expected to be," she said.

"That is exactly how I feel about you," he replied.

She didn't answer, but I had the strangest impression that she wanted to—that she was having to struggle mightily not to make some kind of reply that she knew he would dislike. I couldn't guess what it might be, and, in any case, she didn't utter it. I loitered a while longer, but they exchanged no more words, and I eventually quit the area and went back to the kitchen to sample my own piece of Ermintrude's excellent pie.

Four

There followed a period that I can only describe as idyllic. During this time, Lady Charis showed no disposition to entertain. She did not plan extravagant dinner parties or crowded dances; she often pretended not to be home when company came to call; and she turned down virtually every invitation that came her way. When Sarah Horton planned a very fancy dress ball and pointedly did not invite the Balers, Lady Charis didn't even seem to notice. The vicar's wife came to commiserate with her over the indignity of being excluded, and Lady Charis said, "Oh! She's having a party? I do hope it's fun." Mrs. Dolnat left extremely disappointed.

She spent every possible moment with the master during those two months it took for winter to unfold into spring. She rode with him when he went to see his tenants; she sat in on meetings he had with his agent. When he traveled to Kingston on business, she accompanied him. In short, she gave every appearance of being a woman who had fallen madly in love with her husband—and I truly believe that, during this period, she had.

Spring brought Captain Horton home on another visit, but this time he found his reception at Grey Moraine much cooler. No more long, flirtatious conversations upstairs in the observatory with Lady Charis; no more unsupervised rides through the gentle countryside. The captain seemed at first a little regretful, and then philosophical. He did return twice for dinner, but didn't sit too long at the table. No one encouraged him to do so.

Spring also brought the news that Letitia Donaldson had borne a baby boy, and the master and mistress drove off for a visit that lasted nearly two weeks. When they returned, he seemed quite jolly, extolling the joys of parenthood, but she seemed very pensive. At first I thought the travel itself had worn her out, but in the days immediately following their return, she grew even quieter, almost melancholy. She looked pale, I thought, so I wondered if she might have picked up some kind of ailment on the road. But, no, her appetite was still good, and she looked quite healthy, and so—

And then I knew. She *was* pregnant, after all. The full skirts hid the changes in her figure, but the contours of her face had altered; the sheen of her hair was more lustrous. She must be three or four months along, I thought, far enough to be sure. Far enough to be ready to tell her husband the joyous news.

But she did not tell him and she did not tell him. Duncan Baler was not a man who tried hard to keep his emotions to himself. If he had known his wife was pregnant, every person within fifty miles would have been privy to his excitement.

Which meant that *she* did not think the pregnancy a cause for joy. But why? Why? The only possibilities that presented themselves to me were too awful to contemplate, and of those, infidelity was the least abhorrent. I found myself obsessed with watching her, trying to gauge her mood, trying to guess what she might do next. I eavesdropped on conversations she had with anyone, from Ermintrude to Mrs. Dolnat, so it should not be surprising that, one spring evening, I overheard the entirety of her discussion with the master that took place outside in the garden.

Lady Charis was sitting on a small stone bench that was situated beneath a spreading oak and faced the gardens just now shyly coming into green. Despite the season, it was cool outside, particularly with night drawing on. I had followed her into the garden, but did not plan to spy on her for any length of time until I heard the master's footsteps coming down the walk. Then I hid myself behind the convenient tree and listened to what they had to say, peering out from time to time to get a glimpse of how they stood or sat.

The master greeted her with some surprise. "What in the world are you doing sitting outside on a day as cold as this?" he exclaimed, leaning over her. "You'll freeze!"

She shook her head. "I wanted to be in the last of the sunshine."

He took hold of her hands. "Your fingers are ice! Come inside this very instant." He tried to tug her to her feet, but she resisted.

"Another minute or two," she said. "I find it easier to think when I'm not in the house."

He dropped down beside her, wrapping one arm around her shoulders and covering her folded hands with his free one. "And what do you need to think about that requires open vistas and chilly sunlight? Which, I might point out, you could see just as well from the observatory."

"I'm just—sometimes I think—do you ever wonder why life has turned out the way it has?"

"Do you mean something in particular?"

"Well—you, for instance. Inheriting this house, when you had no such expectation. If your uncle had died a year or two later, Ralph would have been married, might even have had a son, and *that* boy would have inherited instead of you. What combination of events and circumstances conspired to make *you* the master of Grey Moraine?"

"It's unfathomable. And completely outside my power to control," he said in a comfortable voice. "So I don't waste my time worrying over such things."

"But I *do*," she said in an intense voice. "If you were not master at Grey Moraine, I never would have met you that night when I was passing through the town. I might have met Ralph instead, perhaps, and he might have politely showed me the house, and I would have been on my way the next morning. And I would be a governess and you would be dicing in some establishment, and we never would have known each other! Never would have married! Is that the way our lives were supposed to turn out—would have, except for an accident of fate? Is it right that *we* have had so much happiness because of the misfortune that befell your cousin? Should we not have to pay for that happiness with some misfortune of our own?"

"Why, Charis," he said in the soft, gentle voice that he had used the night she wept over Callum's visit. "What dark thoughts are in your head! It is true that a random confluence of unforeseen events has brought us to the place we are now, but that is true for everyone who draws breath! Who can predict where their lives will take them? If my mother had not chuckled at a terrible joke someone else told her, my father might not have turned his head to see who was laughing, and *they* would not have met, and *I* would never have been born. How far back do you want to trace the impossibilities of coincidence? Things happen, good and bad, and some we can influence and some we cannot. But we do not have to *pay* for good fortune. Suffering is not the automatic cost for joy. Who ever told you that?"

"No one told me. It is just something I have always believed. There must be a balance in the scales, and mine are tipped so far over to one side that I feel—I think—sometimes I can't sleep at night, dreading what might come next."

"Charis," he said again, hugging her more tightly to his body. "And all this fear and anticipatory dread because you have married *me*? I cannot think such a commodity can carry a very steep tax. It is not such a marvelous reward."

She had turned her face into his shoulder and now she giggled against his jacket, but even so I could tell that she was on the verge of tears. "Well, it seems like a marvelous reward to *me*," she said, her voice muffled against his sleeve. "It came so close to not happening! I almost did not have the courage to come to your house that night, uninvited. And think if I had not! Our paths never would have crossed."

"Don't be so sure of that," he said. "You fret about the randomness of fate. Well, I subscribe more to the theory that there is a destiny that guides our decisions. If you had not come to my house that night, I am very sure I would have ridden into town that morning, and caught sight of you at the Red Owl. Perhaps your carriage really *would* have lost a wheel, and you would have been standing hopelessly in the courtyard at the inn. And I would have swung down from the saddle and said, 'Madam, you look most distressed. What might I do to aid you?'"

"You would not have," she said. "You would have ridden on by."

"And if, by fell mischance, I failed to see you that morning, I most assuredly would have encountered you in Manningham," he went on. "I have a friend in that city. I visit him all the time! I would have spied you on the street some day and instantly demanded to be introduced."

She lifted her head and regarded him suspiciously. "You have no friends in Manningham," she accused.

"I do, I assure you! Dozens."

"You have never once been to visit them in all the time I've known you."

"They're very dull."

"Then you would *not* have gone to see them, and you would *not* have noticed me walking down the streets!"

He lifted one of her cold little hands to his mouth and kissed it. "I would have," he said firmly. "They are dull, but life without you at Grey Moraine would have been duller still, and I would have been seeking entertainment and social interaction in every city where I have the slightest acquaintance. I would have been *looking* for you, don't you see? Not even knowing I was on a search. I would have found you, no matter where you lived or what you might have been doing."

Her face was very forlorn as she stared straight at him out of those drowned blue eyes. "But what if I didn't look the way I do now?" she said. "What if I had been homely, and drab, and poor? You never would have noticed me then."

"I would have," he averred. "You think I love you for your looks?"

"I think my face is what everybody notices first," she said. "And sometimes they don't see beyond it. What if I looked like

Emmeline Horton? You would not have given me a second glance."

"Emmeline is a very attractive girl," he said, but it was clear he was struggling to bring Emmeline's face into focus.

"She's not," Lady Charis said dryly. "If one of the footmen didn't announce her every time she set foot in your house, I don't believe you'd remember who she was from one visit to the next."

The master laughed. "It is true, I must confess, that I much prefer your face to hers," he said. "But your face isn't what I fell in love with. Your face isn't what I married. It is your heart that moved me so much. I think, even if it had come in a much plainer package, your heart is what I would have noticed first."

Now she turned her head away, as if she couldn't bear to look at him any more, but she covered up the action by resting her cheek against his shoulder. "My heart is much less beautiful than my face," she said in a soft voice. "It is spiteful and ambitious and full of jealousy. And very small, I think. Not nearly as generous as yours."

He lifted a hand to stroke her silky black hair. "Your heart? Oh, it is a timid little mouse of a heart," he said. "It wants to come prancing out and take part in the banquet, but it's been scared back into its little cubbyhole too many times by fearsome mean cats and great stomping rat-catchers. Your heart was designed for joy, but your life was not, and so your heart learned to cower, and scheme, and make do." He kissed the side of her head. "My job is to coax that scared little heart out of hiding."

Now she lifted her head again and drew back so she could stare at him. Astonishment had dried her eyes, and they were huge pools of wonder in her face. "How long have you believed that?"

He kissed the tip of her nose. "Since the day I met you."

"And you married me anyway?"

"That's *why* I married you."

"I don't know what to call you that would be more insulting, or more truthful," she said. "A romantic or a fool."

He laughed a little. "A man in love," he said. "So I'm a little of both."

She shook her head ever so slightly. "You leave me speech-less."

He kissed her nose again. "Good. So does this put your fears at rest? Make you stop worrying about what price the universe will exact for your happiness?"

Her headshake grew more emphatic. "It makes me even more afraid," she said. "The costs are even higher than I thought."

"What costs?" he said. "What levy will be assessed?"

She freed her hands from his grasp so she could lay them on his shoulders, and she leaned so close her nose almost touched his. "I think you will break my heart," she said, very low. "And I know I will break yours. I am so afraid, Duncan, that you will be sorry you loved me."

"No," he said, so instantly that his word slurred over hers. "Not if Grey Moraine comes crashing in on my head, brick by brick. Not if every man I meet shuns me, every woman despises me, and the world itself comes to an end."

She loosed a long sad sigh and settled back into his arms. I had the sense that she was draping herself across him, not so much to absorb his strength and heat, but to shield him with her own body from any assault that might come at him from unexpected sources. "Oh, my dear," she said in a voice that shook, "if only it were no worse than that."

∽

Three days later, the master woke me sometime after midnight with a furious pounding on my door. "Nettie! Nettie! Help me, please!"

I slipped on a robe, picked up a candle, and flung open the door. He was fully dressed, but in clothes he might have picked up from the floor where he had discarded them upon retiring for the night, and he too held a candle. "Milord! What's wrong?"

"Do you know where Lady Charis is? She's not in her room and I cannot find her anywhere in the house."

"Did you check the observatory? She spends much of her time there."

"I glanced in, but the room was dark. And she's not in the parlor, or the library, or the kitchen—or anywhere. The doors are locked from the inside or I would be afraid she had gone outside." He actually shivered. "And on such a night."

For a spring storm was lashing the house, pellets of rain skittering against the glass and gusts of wind howling around the corners. "Let's check the observatory again," I said, picking up the skirts of my nightdress. "And work our way down."

But once we attained the top floor of the mansion, we learned we did not need to search any farther. Both of us stepped deep enough into the wide room to send our candlelight to the far wall—and both of us could see Lady Charis curled up on the sofa that faced the largest bank of windows. She made a small, dense shape against the fabric, and she did not move or speak when we entered, but the feeble light showed us her eyes wide open and fixed on the view before her. It was spectacular. Lightning writhed across the limitless sky, throwing the rocky chasm into stark relief, and then everything fell to darkness. Another shock of lightning, another sudden ghostly glimpse into the void. Then darkness again.

The master rushed to her side, hastily set down his candle, and put his arms around her. "Charis! My dear! I woke up and couldn't find you, and I grew so worried! What are you doing up here? Are you ill?"

She looked up at him a moment in silence. His face was so close to hers that she did not have to stretch very far to kiss him briefly on the mouth. She unclasped one of her hands, tightly wrapped around her ankles, to lay a palm across his cheek. "Duncan," she said.

He dropped down beside her on the sofa. "What's wrong? Only tell me, and I'll take care of it."

Her laugh was soft as a breath. "You can't take care of it," she said.

"Tell me," he pleaded.

I was standing close to the door, hoping they would forget my presence, but she looked straight over at me. "Nettie knows," she said.

I almost dropped my candle. "What do I know?" I asked fearfully. Oh, I did, I did, but surely I was wrong—

Lady Charis came to her feet with a single graceful movement. The master made as if to rise as well, but she extended a hand, palm outward, as if to hold him in place. He settled back. "Let me speak," she said. "Do not interrupt me." She glanced at me again. "You may stay and listen if you like. Perhaps you will be able to explain to him later the things that I find difficult to say now."

"What things?" he asked in a choked voice. "Why difficult?"

The lightning cracked again, illuminating the saddest of smiles on her lovely face. "I made a bad bargain," she said. "I asked the elementals for a favor, which they granted, and now it is time for me to pay. And I find, suddenly and to my horror, that the price is too steep. So I am going to refuse. And I believe that means I am going to die."

The master did jump to his feet at that. "No! Who would harm you? You are safe as long as I am by your side."

She reached out a hand again and gently pushed him back to his seat. "You cannot fight the wind," she said. "You cannot outwit the storm. I made a bargain with the gods of the air, and there is no reasoning with them."

"What bargain?" he whispered.

She looked at me and I answered for her. "She asked them to make her beautiful—so beautiful you could not help but fall in love with her."

"See?" she responded. "I told you Nettie knows."

"But—but you *are* beautiful. I *do* love you."

She shook her head. "I am an ordinary girl. Very plain. Not very accomplished. My hair is a lifeless brown and my eyes are a muddy gray. I blush when I talk to strangers and I am clumsy when I walk. Nothing like the face, the figure, the woman you see before you."

"But you—then how did you—they *changed* you? Is such a thing possible?"

She nodded. "As you see."

It was clear he was having trouble crediting what he heard. "I don't understand."

She spoke slowly and deliberately. "I assumed a shape that I thought you would like, and I made up a story that I thought would move you," she said. "I came to your house the night of your ball determined to pique your interest. Every word I said, every gesture I made, was calculated to make you want me. If you had not followed me to the inn the next morning, I would have found some reason to stay. But you tumbled so quickly that you made everything easy for me." She caught her breath. "So easy. You did not resist at all."

He was sitting straighter on the sofa now, but obediently he stayed in place. "How did you know me?" he asked now. "Where had you encountered me, that you would want to come to Grey Moraine and ensnare me?"

The word *ensnare* made her flinch, but she answered calmly. "I have lived near this town all my life. Your uncle might have passed me in the street dozens of times, and never noticed me. Indeed, when you first came to take possession of Grey Moraine, you stopped at one of the taverns for a drink. You bumped into me as I was walking past, and you excused yourself very politely. I liked you for that. I asked somebody who you were. And from that day forward I became obsessed with meeting you again. In a different guise. In a shape you would not be able to overlook."

"I did not mean to overlook you at that very first meeting," he said.

She smiled again. "Anyone would have. Everyone did."

"I told you once that I would have found you no matter where you lived and what your appearance," he said. "And I believe, had you given me more time, I would have. What was so awful about your life that you felt you had to take such drastic measures to catch my attention?"

Once more she glanced in my direction. "Nettie might have guessed this, too," she said.

I nodded, my throat so choked that at first I could not speak. "Only because you seemed to despise Sarah Horton so deeply, and for no other reason that makes any sense."

"Sarah Horton? What's she to you?" the master asked, bewildered.

"My father's wife," Lady Charis replied.

There was a moment of stunned silence while he tried to absorb that. I thought it might make more sense to him more quickly if I explained. "Lady Charis is Mr. Horton's illegitimate daughter, or so I have surmised," I said.

"Yes," she replied.

"He has always refused to acknowledge her in any public fashion, mostly because Mrs. Horton will not allow it," I continued. I had to suppose Lady Charis was so grateful to be spared the necessity of making this explanation that she did not care how I had acquired my information. "His daughters do not even know of her existence, though his son and his nephew do." I was fairly certain that a light flirtation—or perhaps a full-fledged affair—with Mr. Horton's bastard child was what had gotten Captain Stephen Horton sent away in disgrace last year, but it didn't seem important to mention it. Charis had so clearly lost interest in the captain as she had gradually grown so much fonder of her husband.

"So you have lived—all this time—within the shadow of your father's grand life and not been invited to partake in any of its luxuries," the master said, slowly putting the pieces together. "And you thought, 'How can I punish him? How can I punish his family?' And you thought, 'If I were the mistress of Grey Moraine, I could practically rule the entire county!'"

"Everyone would bow to me, everyone would be eager to be my friend," she added. "I would be so powerful that my slightest word would see Sarah Horton and her daughters humiliated, and my father confused and embarrassed. Yes. That was one of my goals. But how to fulfill them? Everyone expected Ralph to inherit Grey Moraine, and he had a wife already picked out. 'I will have to move to another city, Lefton, perhaps,' I thought. 'I will have to find a husband elsewhere. I will find a way to persuade him to come to Grey Moraine, and I will do what damage I can during short visits.' Then suddenly Ralph was dead and you were here, and you had no wife in tow, and all at once everything seemed possible."

"How is it that no one recognized your name, if nothing else?" he asked. "If you have lived here all your life—"

"Oh, that was the easiest thing of all to change! I had always been called Cassie, which I hated. Charis was the name I chose for myself when I was a little girl, when I dreamed about the life I wanted. It means *grace*, and I was desperate for some of that." She shrugged. "Sometimes I think I spent my whole life trying to turn myself into the person I am now. And I took the only way I could find—by calling on the demons of the air."

"How did you summon them?" I asked a little fearfully. "What invocations did you use?"

She glanced my way. "I whispered my ambitions into the wind. I said, 'I will do anything you ask of me if you make me the mistress of Grey Moraine.' One day three of them appeared at my door. I didn't know exactly who or what they were—I had paid very little attention to the folk tales whispered in the village, for I was sure I was supposed to be above such foolishness. But suddenly there they were, promising me whatever I desired." She shrugged again. "I did not ask too many questions."

I had never actually spoken to anyone who had had a conversation with the air elementals. "How did they appear?" I asked.

"They looked like men, and yet they did not," she said. "Their hands, when they touched me, felt like dried autumn leaves swept up on a breeze. But when they pulled their hands away, my hair was black and my lips were red and my mirror showed me the most beautiful woman I had ever seen. There was a pile of gold on my mattress, enough to buy my way into my new life. I went to Lefton, after all. Purchased a wardrobe, hired a carriage, and rode back into town. I was here only a day or two before that first ball I attended at Grey Moraine."

She gave the master her full attention now as she continued speaking. "You realize, I was not thinking about *you* as I made my plans. I did not think how *you* might be hurt by any of this. You seemed like a kind enough man, and I liked that, but it wouldn't have mattered to me if you were cruel or ugly or old. I would have followed the same course. I would have made the same bargain. I did not expect that I would love you—or that you would love me. I was not prepared for the calamity I would bring to your life."

"It has been no calamity," he said.

She smiled sadly. "Oh, but it will be."

He leapt to his feet again, no longer able to sit quietly. "Why?" he asked fearfully. "What happens next? Why are you so *afraid* of what happens next?"

She almost laughed. "You mean, if you don't throw me out into the storm?"

He stared. "How could you think that? Why would I do such a thing?"

And now she stared back at him. "Why would you not? I lied to you—I tricked you—I used you. You may decide to show me compassion, but you will find it hard to forgive me."

"I love you," he said. "I forgive everything."

That astonished Lady Charis—and me—so much that there was another moment of profound silence. Finally she said, her voice very low, "Even if that were possible, it hardly matters. You cannot shield me from their anger."

He stepped closer to her. "Perhaps I can. What form will it take? When will it manifest?"

"Very soon, I think," she whispered. Unthinkingly, with her right hand, she rubbed her belly.

"Spirits of the air, spare us all," I whispered, and quickly kissed my fingers and pressed them to my heart. For I knew it was just as bad as it could be.

The master whipped around to glare at me. "What? What's wrong?"

"I'm expecting a child," Lady Charis said calmly, and he spun around to gaze at her again. "That's what's wrong."

His face showed a complex surge of emotions—delight, fear, bewilderment. "But that's—! Charis, that's wonderful! When? How long have you known? Why didn't you tell me?"

She shook her head. "You don't understand. They want my baby. They will take him too—suck the essence right out of his body. Nothing you or I can do will stop them. Nettie, tell him."

"It's true," I said, my voice harsh to my own ears. "She has made a bargain with the wind. And the price is your child's soul. Even now the babe she carries in her womb might not be hers, but theirs—formed like a human, but demonic in his heart."

"I don't believe you," the master said flatly. "Country talk! Ignorant superstitions! You will see—we will have this baby, this beautiful child—and he will be completely ours, body, heart, *and* soul."

He reached for Charis, but she stepped back, quick and decisive. She flung her arms out wide, as if to fend him off, as if to fend off any man or creature who might pull too close, and tilted her face toward the window. Outside, thunder rattled the casements; lightning scrawled indecipherable warnings across the sky.

"You cannot have him!" she cried. "Do you hear me? *You cannot have him!* I renege upon my bargain! I deny the pact! I love him, and I will not bring him harm. I will not give you my husband, I will not give you my child, and I will not give you Grey Moraine!"

And then it was as if every storm that had ever blown across the county suddenly swirled down on top of Grey Moraine. Lightning flashed so brilliantly and so incessantly that the room was graphically illuminated and all our movements looked jerky and incomplete. Thunder bellowed through the canyon; the wind shrieked in hysterical fury.

One window shattered. I screamed, though you could not hear the sound over the roaring of the wind. A second window broke violently inward, then a third. Rain sluiced in past the jagged glass. Lady Charis was twirling about in a mad approximation of a dance, spun into a desperate pirouette by the buffeting of the storm. The master darted along beside her, trying to grab hold of her flailing arms, trying to pull her into a hard embrace, but first one gust and then another knocked her out of his reach. "Charis!" I heard him shout over the rushing, screeching gale. *"Charis!"*

"Duncan!" she answered, and she tried to catch hold of his hand, but something pummeled her so hard that she was pushed all the way across the room. She was so close to the windows now that another shove would send her over the fractured sill. "Duncan, I love you!"

"Let her stay with me!" he cried. "I accept the bargain on her behalf! Let her live!"

But the spirits of the air did not hear him, did not believe him, or were too angry to care. There was another great boom of thunder and the horizon lit up so vividly that the whole sky might have been one monstrous bonfire. I swear I saw two forms take shape from the swirling wind, one on either side of Lady Charis. They lifted her off the floor, guided her almost gently through one splintered pane of glass, and dropped her into the yawning black chasm that awaited outside Grey Moraine.

Five

They never recovered a body. But then, no corpse had ever been retrieved from that unforgiving canyon. Search parties were sent at dawn, of course, at least as far down the slope as it was humanly possible to descend. But nothing was found of the ensorcelled mistress of Grey Moraine.

You can imagine the kind of talk that engulfed the village in the days and weeks to come. Well, perhaps you have heard some of it for yourself—it is the story every visitor is told upon first arriving in our little town. "How were the roads on your way in?" you might have been asked. "Do you find the Red Owl comfortable? Did you hear about the mistress of Grey Moraine? Killed herself one night, she did. Flung herself out of the window in the middle of a storm. Not a soul could tell you why."

I cared very little about such talk, even when it bordered on being true, even when the speaker whispered codas about the elementals and their power over men. All that mattered to me, in those following weeks, was making sure the master did not follow his wife over the windowsill and down the rocky cliffside.

Those first few days he moved through the house in an utter stupor, too dazed to eat or speak or sleep. Ermintrude and I conspired to put food before him, though he refused to sit down for a meal. Harlan would literally lead him upstairs at night and into his room, or otherwise he might never have sought his bed. He refused all visitors. He engaged in no activity. He did nothing, all day, any day, except grieve.

It was clear he had very little interest in living.

I began to spy on him, as I had spied on Lady Charis, surreptitiously checking on him any time I thought he had been alone too long. If he sat in his library for more than an hour, I found an excuse to come bustling in. If he paced around the gardens, his hands clasped behind his back and his head bent low, I crept along behind him. If he headed to the observatory, I picked up my sewing kit and followed him into the room, sitting down across from him as bold as you please. The windows had been repaired the very first day, but I was no fool. Glass is easy to break. A determined man could push himself through them with no effort at all.

During this time, half the neighborhood came to call, as was to be expected. Sarah Horton and the vicar's wife were particularly assiduous in their attentions, but the master never once agreed to see either of them. Men who could more properly be considered his friends also dropped by, and while the master sometimes spoke with them for a few moments in the library, none were encouraged to remain for long. In that first week or two, the only person Lord Duncan spent more than ten minutes with was his estate agent, who rode up one morning and remained until well past dinnertime, closeted with the master in his study. It was bitter to think the agent had cause to be redrawing the terms of the property.

Perhaps three weeks after Lady Charis's death, we had one of the most beautiful spring days that I could ever recall. The sun was warm, the air was sweet, and even gloomy Grey Moraine seemed to lighten with intimations of hope and promise. After the noon meal, I was glad to see the master step outside to enjoy the gardens, which were arrayed with a promiscuous tumble of flowers. I did not begin to grow concerned until I realized he had been outside for more than two hours, unaccompanied and unobserved. Quietly, with the stealth I had honed so finely in the past eight months, I tiptoed out through the kitchen door to begin an unobtrusive search for him.

I was making my way silently around the hedges that outlined the garden pathway when I first caught the sound of someone talking. Surprise froze me where I stood, and I tilted my head to listen more closely. That was the master's voice, no doubt about it, as energetic and laced with laughter as it had always been, and I smiled to hear it. He was speaking very rapidly, and in tones of great excitement, but I was not quite close enough to make out the words. It was not important to me that I know the topic of his conversation. I was just deeply pleased that *some* friend or relative had broken through his hard shell of mourning and induced him to talk at all.

But who was the visitor?

The master did not give his guest much chance to speak, for the words spilled out of him in a passionate torrent, but now and then I caught a syllable, an exclamation, a laugh. I felt my brows pull together. A woman's voice? Which of our neighbor ladies could exercise such a beneficial effect on the heartbroken master of Grey Moraine? Or had Callum and his wife come calling while I was upstairs cleaning out closets? Was that Letitia charming Lord Duncan out of his grief?

No help for it; I must get closer. Moving with even more caution, I stole along until I was nearly opposite the bench where the master was sitting. A small break in the hedge allowed me to peer through, but I couldn't see much, for Lord Duncan and his guest had their backs to me. All I could tell was that she was plainly dressed and had unremarkable brown hair caught up in a severe bun. And that, from the part of her profile I could make out, she was smiling.

The master appeared to be telling her some story from his soldiering days. "I didn't want to travel all that way with a hole in my boots, but there was no time to be fitted for a new pair," he said. "So I found a farmer's son bringing produce to the market and I told him I'd give him five gold coins if he'd sell me his own brogues. Well, he bent down that very minute and stripped off the toughest, muddiest, ugliest pair of shoes you ever saw in your life. Fit me perfectly. Best pair of shoes I've ever owned, to tell you the truth. I think he must have made them himself."

She murmured an answer and he launched into another story, but I didn't pay attention to the words. I was still staring through the greenery, trying to identify his visitor. Who *was* she? A turn of her head briefly showed me her full face, which was teasingly familiar, if not particularly memorable. To my astonishment, I saw that she had laid one of her hands most familiarly on the master's knee.

Some consort of his from his army days? Not a proper person for him to be entertaining at Grey Moraine, perhaps, but for the moment I didn't care. Let him find his way back to the living first; then we would worry about ideal companions.

A cloud drifted over the sun and momentarily shadowed the

whole garden. The young woman gave a start and came hurriedly to her feet.

"I must be gone," she said. "I have sat here too long already."

He was on his feet as well. "No—not so soon. Stay a while."

She shook her head. She was facing me now and I could not have been more amazed. Was this Emmeline Horton? Was *she* the woman with the power to make the master so happy? No—just someone who looked so much like Emmeline that she might have been a—

Even in my own mind, I could not complete the thought. I heard her say, "I must go. I will come back if I can."

And she pressed her hand against his heart, smiled one last time, and vanished.

The master sank down to the bench and rested his face in his hands.

As for myself, I dropped to the ground and stared sightlessly before me. The visitor had looked so much like Emmeline Horton that she might have been a sister. A poor, badly dressed, shy, and disregarded sister.

It seemed that Grey Moraine was once again home to a ghost.

∽

In the days that followed, the master grew visibly happier. He walked through the house with a jauntier step, sometimes whistling as he went. He ate every scrap of the fine meals Ermintrude prepared; he commended Martin on his new mustache. Now and then, he agreed to see callers. Twice he went into town.

But most of the time he kept assignations with the spirit of his dead wife, till it was hard to say which of them haunted certain rooms of the house more. She did not come every day, but the hope of her arrival brought color back to the master's face and eagerness to his stricken eyes. It was no surprise that they spent a great deal of time in the observatory, or that I spent a corresponding number of hours outside that door, catching what I could of their conversation. They could be found a little less often in the parlor, in the library, or in the garden. I followed them to all their trysts.

For ghosts are tricky, even the ones that seem benevolent. They are creatures of the air, after all, though not under the strict control of the elementals. They do what they please, and they often mean no harm, but many of them have forgotten what will hurt a human, and they are careless. It would be through no laxity on my part that the wraith of Charis Baler brought harm to the master.

The rest of the household reacted with various degrees of uneasiness to her presence among us. Ermintrude was constantly kissing her fingers and whispering prayers, and I suspect she warded her kitchen with some kind of dried herbal mixture designed to hold the supernatural at bay. Martin and the underhousemaids claimed they often saw her walking the halls in the very early hours of the morning. Harlan told me privately that he had glimpsed her clearly only three or four times, but he had felt her presence often enough, and every time it made him shiver. Dawson, the head groom, confessed that he had not seen her at all, but that whenever the horses grew fractious, he could tell she was nearby.

Somehow, the news made its way through the neighborhood; everybody knew of the new ghost at Grey Moraine. I heard whispers whenever I went to town, and young girls were always talking to each other behind their hands when I glanced in their direction. More and more often, I was aware that townspeople caught sight of me and then blessed themselves, kissing their fingers and pressing the tips against their hearts. Harlan and Ermintrude reported the same behavior.

Then the stories started to circulate. *Don't ride past Grey Moraine at night. The spirits of the dead will rise up and snatch you from your saddle. . . . I heard of a man who was thrown from his horse and disappeared! The horse came back to the stable, panting and covered with sweat, but the man was never seen again. . . . They say if you kneel at the edge of the property and weep, a woman's hand will appear under your chin and catch your tears. . . . If you stand too close to the canyon on the night the moon is full, you can hear a woman's voice crying, "Save me, save me, I'm falling!" . . .*

Country talk. Credulous fools. And yet Grey Moraine *did* harbor a ghost, and the master became stranger by the day, and all of us realized our household had become very odd indeed.

Ermintrude couldn't take it very long. She quit by the end of summer, and both of the housemaids with her. There was so little cooking to do that I assumed this chore myself, while Martin helped me with the heavier lifting. I found myself unsurprised, however, the day Martin came to me, hangdog and apologetic, to tell me he'd taken a new position with a household in Kingston.

"That's where a bright young lad like you belongs," I told him firmly. "Stay in touch, but go with a light heart."

Most of the other servants followed. For the better part of a year, Harlan, Dawson, and I were the only staff left at Grey Moraine. The master didn't even seem to notice. He continued to fulfill his obligations as a landowner, meeting with tenants and seeing to estate business, but it was clear his heart did not belong in the world of the living. He was pleasant, he was thoughtful, at times he was moved to great acts of generosity, but he had very little attention to spare for anyone outside the spectral realm. Every day he withdrew a little more. He was not sad—in fact, for the most part he was quite cheerful—but he was no longer really present. He grew thin and a little absent-minded. It was possible to think that he was deliberately paring himself down to very little more than a restless soul encased in the slimmest sheath of skin.

It was hardly a surprise when he caught the fever that swept through town with the first of the winter storms. Three elderly women and one infant succumbed to the ailment and died, though anyone with a modicum of physical strength was able to fend it off handily enough. But the master, of course, was far from robust. Three days after he contracted the illness, he was dead.

Harlan wrote the estate agent, and within the week, Callum and Letitia were back at our door. Time for a new master to be installed at Grey Moraine.

∽

I stayed with the house, of course. I always stay with Grey Moraine. I am the guardian of this place, an elemental creature of the earth itself, and my place is here.

Naturally, I could not retain my familiar shape. I waited until Callum and Letitia arrived—bringing, as was customary, their own grooms and butler and a few upper servants. Dawson and Harlan were handsomely pensioned off, and the new mistress began hiring to fill other key positions. I drew Letitia aside and sang the praises of my granddaughter, trained from birth in the intricacies of running a manor home.

"She sounds perfect. Do send her to see me!" Letitia exclaimed. And so Nettie vanished and Norah appeared, and Grey Moraine was still under my watchful eye.

Letitia was glad to have me, and we became quite close within a short period of time. She was so warmhearted and open that it didn't occur to her that a servant girl might not be a proper confidante. She told me everything: of the rare arguments she had with Callum, and of their passionate apologies as well; of her social ambitions, which were no grander than not to be afraid of Sarah Horton; of her hopes and fears and silly dreams. She was an excellent mother, rarely turning the young heir of Grey Moraine over to his nanny, and moving through the days with easy grace when she became pregnant with her second child. Every servant loved her, both the ones she had brought with her and the ones she hired, and not a soul in the neighborhood could say a harsh word against her, not even the vicar's wife.

That didn't mean that everyone managed to be kind. She had not been mistress of Grey Moraine for a day before she heard tales of how its last mistress had died—and how she continued to haunt the property. Callum laughed off the stories, and Letitia was strong-minded enough not to let herself be frightened by whispers and stories. But she paid attention, I could tell. She lifted her head when the wind moaned by, and if a curtain fluttered when there was no breeze, she watched it with a narrowed gaze.

It was almost the end of winter, and she had been in the house for five months, before she said anything to me on the subject. The day had been sunny, though very cool, and she had chased the young master all through the gardens for the better part of the afternoon. When the nanny came out to fetch him, Letitia dropped to the stone bench with a sigh and rubbed her rounded belly.

"Soon I won't be able to run after him quite so quickly, and he'll get into all kinds of trouble," she said. "Norah, sit with me a minute! Have you come to tell me about some new domestic crisis? Surely it can wait for five minutes while we both enjoy the sunset."

I dropped beside her on the bench, which was quite cold even through my heavy dress, and smiled. "No crisis. I was just going to ask if you wanted anything from town tomorrow. One of the footmen will be taking the gig in."

"I can't think of anything at the moment," she said. She pointed, to make sure I did not miss the impressive sight of sunlight streaming down in great differentiated rays and lying across the grass like so many bands of hazy gold. "People say that the most impressive view at Grey Moraine is the chasm, but I love the gentler scenery of the garden and the lawns," she said. "Don't you? The prospect is so pretty."

I wasn't sure how to phrase this. "Some people don't like to look down the canyon because of the way Lady Charis died," I said. "Does it frighten you?"

She shook her head. "No. I am clever enough to stay back from that particular ledge. In any case, I have everything I want. All I would ask of any spirit would be happiness for Callum and health for my babies, and the wind demons aren't likely to grant those favors, anyway."

I just looked at her a moment, surprised into silence. "Milady believes in those country tales?" I said at last.

She nodded serenely. "Oh yes! I was brought up on them. I know all about the elementals, which ones you can trust, and which ones to stay clear of. I suppose Lady Charis didn't learn those lessons in time."

"I suppose she didn't," was all I could think to say.

Letitia stirred restlessly on the bench, and finally spoke in an impulsive voice. "Don't think I'm a silly girl, but I sometimes think—I know how it sounds, but—I believe she's still here. Lady Charis," she said. "I've never seen her, but I've felt her from time to time. Callum says that's ridiculous," she added.

"Most of the townspeople will tell you Grey Moraine is haunted—but most of them have never seen a ghost on this property and never will," I said.

She turned to me. "Have *you*? Why does a ghost choose to show itself to some and not to others?"

I hesitated for a long time, and then finally answered with the truth. "Yes, I've seen her," I said. "Some people are afraid of ghosts, but I've always believed that the ones who see them are the ones who loved them when they were alive. At any rate, my grandmother told me that Lord Duncan would sit in this garden for hours and talk to the spirit of Lady Charis. He was never so happy as when that ghost was sitting by his side."

She raised her pretty blond eyebrows. "Maybe his spirit is still here as well."

I nodded. "Oh, I'm sure of it. I'm sure he walks these very lawns." Now I was the one to point to the sloping landscape before us. The sunlight had all but faded, and most of the view was covered in shadow. It was too cold to be sitting out here this long, and yet I could tell the new mistress did not want to go inside yet; neither did I.

"Why is it that some spirits linger long after their bodies are gone, while other people die peacefully and are never seen again?" Letitia asked.

"My grandmother always said that spirits were anchored to a spot because that was where they had experienced some profound emotion," I replied. "Most people believe that fear or anger or hatred are the great emotions that tie a ghost to a place. But my grandmother said love was stronger than any of those. Lady Charis loved Lord Duncan and she could not bear to leave him behind. She stayed—and because she was still here, his spirit stayed as well, after his body passed on."

Letitia hugged herself as if to try to stay warm. "So love lasts after death."

"Long enough to be visible to the world. Yes, so I believe."

"I would like to see them," she said wistfully. "I would like to let them know that they are not forgotten. I would like to let them know how much Callum and I value Grey Moraine, and how well we will look after it."

"I don't think they care very much about such things any more," I said. "Land and property and the affairs of men. When her spirit first came around, she was almost as substantial as a real woman, but these days there's practically nothing left of her, and he was already a shell of a man before he died. Soon they will wear away completely, I believe, as all spirits do, and then there will be no more ghosts at Grey Moraine."

"I hope I see them at least once before that happens," she said.

"Sunset is a good time for them," I said in a low, dreamy voice. "And this is a good place, because they like the gardens. You have to sit very still and look very closely. We should be quiet now. They won't come as long as we're speaking."

I fell silent, and Letitia sat beside me, soundless as well. Behind us, the sun dropped even farther past the horizon; my skin was as cold as the marble bench beneath me. The wind had died down, and no bird, no animal, no living creature made a noise at all.

And then, I saw them. I pointed again, but Letitia nodded,

her eyes on exactly the right spot. Two figures had emerged from the shadows cast by the tall oak tree and were strolling together across the grass. Their clothes were so faded it was impossible to tell color; their transparent skin held only the faintest phosphor glow. They walked together hand in hand, their heads bent together as if they were whispering. I thought I caught the echo of a woman's laugh. They paused long enough to exchange a single kiss, and then they disappeared.

EARTH

Birthright

JEAN JOHNSON

Author's Note: *Please notice that for all Flame Sea words, "j" on its own is pronounced with a distinct "y" sound, which forms its own consonant-vowel pairing, such as "yih" or "yuh"; "dj" is pronounced like a normal English "j." Endjoj—er, I mean, enjoy!*

One

Arasa scowled at the map the trader had spread on the table between them. The crude markings the barbarians of Kumron had used to draw their landscapes were confusing her. She could read and speak in Kumronite-lon, but it had only been a month ago that she'd heard of a "Womb of Tarden," some holy-place deep within the southern lands beyond the mountain peaks of the Frost Wall. Not nearly enough time to brush up on their map-symbols.

Frustrated, she turned the map sideways, then upside down, hoping that it would make more sense that way. The trader gave her a look that said *she* was the barbarian, and deliberately turned the map back around.

"Here is the Third Tree Pass, which is the one southeast of us, if you follow that road into the mountains," he explained with exaggerated patience in his native tongue. That, and he was having to speak over the drunken laughter coming from two tables over. "And this is the Spotted Deer Path, the main road through this section of Kumron. If you stay on it until you reach the king-state of Copper High, then turn east and follow this road, which is called the Dog's Leg, you will eventually come to the king-state of Flying Fangs. Inside the walled city of Flying Fang Tribe is where you will find the Womb of Tarden. Now, just to view the map is two Moons. To *buy* the map, and take it with you, is two Suns . . . and that, only because I am somewhat familiar with these roads."

Since she was trying to budget her expenses, Arasa grimaced. "How much to just let me copy it?"

"Eight Moons," the leather-clad trader allowed, dipping his head thoughtfully. "Six, if you can copy it tonight, before I retire for the night. And if you must hold it overnight, I'll need collateral to ensure I'll get it back. But good luck finding a scribe in this place."

Since they were seated in the tavern portion of a walled cross between a trading post and a small hunting village, she didn't doubt his skepticism. Scribes didn't exactly flock to such a remote location. "I can copy it myself. So long as this map will take me to the Womb of Tarden and back, I'll be happy."

"It will take you there," the man agreed, holding out his hand. "Two Moons for the viewing, which you will pay now."

One of the other patrons in the tavern, wending his way back from the kegs in the corner, peered over the trader's shoulder as she dug the silver coins out of the pouch slung on her sword-belt. He had odd pale skin flecked with tiny brown spots, and vigorously curly, coppery colored hair. Even his brows and lashes were copper-colored, accenting the green of his eyes. He looked rather exotic, really.

"What's *that* supposed to be?" he asked, lifting his mug to his lips.

"A map of Kumron, just south of here," Arasa replied, sorting out six coins.

The redhead snorted. "And you're *paying* for that?"

The trader craned his head, glaring at the other man. "Do you *mind*? We're in the middle of a business transaction! Business which is none of *yours*."

"You should Truth Stone him," the stranger stated, "to make sure he's not cheating you."

"I would, if I *had* a Truth Stone," Arasa pointed out dryly. "But I don't."

The freckled man flashed her a smile. "Then you're in luck. I happen to have one."

"*You?*" the trader scoffed.

"I'm a mage. I make them. Tell you what," the redhead added to Arasa, nodding at the map. "If he's telling the truth about that being accurate, I'll only charge you a single Star for the use of my Stone. If he's lying, you pay me one of those Moons."

Arasa weighed the cost against the accuracy she needed, and nodded. Her quest was too vital to risk being tricked. Slipping the rest of the coins back into her pouch, she kept one silver Moon and fished out a copper Star. "You have a deal. Bring out the Stone."

"I will not sit here and have my honor questioned like this!" the trader protested, rising from his seat in indignation.

The redhead planted his palm on the trader's shoulder, forcing him back down with a *thump*. "You'll sit here and answer the *sajé's* questions, or be judged a liar and suffer accordingly."

Given that she was still clad in Flame Sea–style clothing— loosely gathered layers of beige trousers, tunic, and poncho, with her hair wrapped up under a turban and a second sash wrapped under her sword-belt—Arasa couldn't object to being pegged for an Imperial. The trader eyed both of them, but subsided without protest. The redhead removed his hand, reaching for the flap of the red-dyed leather bag slung crosswise over his chest. Arasa lifted her gaze from the trader, curious to know what was in the mage's bag beside a Truth Stone.

Snatching at the map, the trader bolted out of his seat, flinging himself between the half-empty tables. Disappointment flooded her. Just when she thought she'd finally gotten a decent lead on where to go, the Goddess of Luck insisted on giggling in her face. She opened her mouth to ask the redhead how he knew the map wasn't accurate, but was interrupted by a roar from one of the other patrons. The trader, dodging through the room on his way to the door, had tripped and stumbled into a large, muscular fellow in a fur-trimmed vest. A large, muscular, drunken fellow, who did not take kindly to having his mug knocked out of his hand and his drink spilled across the table.

With a curse that made her ears burn, the big fellow rose, grabbed the trader by his leather tunic, and flung him into another table . . . which was occupied by more inebriated patrons. Naturally, they took immediate exception to being interrupted so rudely. Blinking, Arasa shoved the two coins back into her purse, yanked the strings shut, and escaped her chair. She would have to circle around the edge of the room if she wanted to get to the door.

A hand caught her wrist as she turned to do so, tugging her toward the back of the tavern. "*This* way," the redhead offered, jerking his head at the door to the kitchen. "There's a door out back."

Arasa winced and ducked reflexively as someone threw a mug past her shoulder. It missed her by a good body-length, but it smacked into the table behind her. Being made of waxed leather, it didn't crack and break, but it did slop its contents all over the place. It wasn't the only mug being thrown, nor the only object. Quickly following her erstwhile guide, Arasa shook her hand free so that she could dodge a chair skittering across the floor, flung by the tavern owner as he bellowed for his customers to behave and settle back down.

The door into the kitchen lay directly across from the door into the backyard of the tavern; it took a matter of moments to make their way outside. While the yelling continued out in the common room, they nodded politely to the harried-looking woman peeling vegetables at the wash-basin. From the look of the place, Arasa was glad she hadn't risked eating any of the food; those counters needed a serious scrubbing.

The night air was cool compared to the heat inside the tavern, but not unpleasantly so. It was early autumn, not exactly the most propitious time of the year to be planning a trip over the Frost Wall and back. Arasa didn't have much choice, however. Her instructions were quite clear: make a barefoot pilgrimage from the Womb to the Heart if she wanted to clear up the dilemma of who should have been born first, herself or her twin Kalasa. If the matter hadn't been so important, she wouldn't have contemplated leaving the Empire of the Flame Sea. The silhouetted shapes of the bushy evergreens ringing the wooden palisade enclosing the trading village were a far cry from the spiky, fan-leafed date palms she was used to seeing.

"I think it'll be safe to go back inside in about half an hour, possibly less," the mage at her side offered. He held out his hand. "I think you'll agree that you owe me a Moon. He wouldn't have run if he hadn't been telling a lie."

"I agree." Fishing out one of the silver coins again, she dropped it into his hand. "Thanks. How did you know it was a lie?"

The mage dug into his satchel, pulling something out. "The Womb of Tarden is located in the king-state of Melting Vipers, which is farther east than that map showed. And Dog's Leg Path lies along the coast of the Hamijn Ocean, not in the midhills region."

Unfurling his fingers, he displayed the white marble disc in his grip, shifting his arm to the side so that the light from the open kitchen door played over his hand. Flipping the disc over, he showed her the backside, where it had pressed against his palm. Pure white, proving he hadn't lied to her.

"As you can see, you just got your money's worth." Gripping the stone again, he added, "My name is Malika." Uncurling his hand, he displayed the blackened outline of his fingers. The marks faded from the polished surface of the stone after a few moments, proving the stone was indeed enchanted to prove or disprove the truth.

"You know your geography. And your Truth Stone spell," she praised as lightly as she could. Disappointment still leaked into her voice. All she knew now was that she had to go much farther east in her quest, adding days of travel to what was already a disheartening distance to contemplate riding across, never mind traveling barefoot, of all foolish things.

"And you sound very disappointed that the map was false. I'm surprised," he stated, leaning back against the wall by the kitchen door. "It's not often that an Imperial is so eager to climb the Frost Wall, given how winter comes sooner, the higher you climb. It's a few months away, still, but it's a very long way to the Womb of Tarden from here."

"I don't exactly have a choice. I don't suppose *you* have an accurate map of how to get from here to this . . . Melting Vipers king-state?" Arasa asked, trying not to hope too much.

"Not really. I know the names of the major roads to take," he said. "But I couldn't draw you a map. I've never been there. Nor would I want to, given Tarden's reputation."

That made her frown softly. "What do you mean, Tarden's reputation?"

"He's one of the less friendly Gods of Kumron. His worshippers venerate the vipers of their tribe," the mage clarified. "Including the poisoning of their enemies. Considering that whole eastern region isn't too happy with the Flame Sea at the moment, what with the Empire pushing them back up over the eastern passes this last spring . . ." He shrugged eloquently.

"Well, as I said, I don't have much choice." The noise inside the tavern was finally dying down. Arasa figured she could go back inside in another handful of minutes. Even if the counters in the kitchen weren't spotlessly clean, it was too early to retire to the stables, where she would be sleeping in one of the stalls claimed by her steed and her two remounts.

Sleeping on the floor, the benches, or the tabletops of the common room didn't appeal to her, but this place wasn't an inn, just a lowly tavern; all they had were benches, tables, and spots on the floor, no real beds anywhere. Not to mention that, traveling on her own, she was safer sleeping with her horses anyway. They, at least, would guard her while she slept.

The curly-haired mage tilted his head, studying her. He stuck out his hand. "Elrik of Snow Leaper."

Since he had helped her, she politely clasped it. His flesh was warm, his grip comfortably firm. She returned the pressure evenly, giving him her name. "Arasa."

"Just Arasa?" Most of his face was in shadow, since the lamps from the kitchen didn't stretch around the edge of the door, but she could hear the skepticism in his voice. "You are UnShijn?"

Clanless? She suppressed a snort at the mere thought. *If only my life were that simplified.* "You know a bit about the Flame Sea, for a Kumronite."

He switched languages, speaking in nearly flawless Adanjé-lon, albeit with a Falijn-lon accent. "I may have been born to the Snow Leaper Tribe, but my grandmother was a mage. She taught at the Academy in Aben-hul out on the west coast, so I went to live with her for several years when my powers manifested at the age of ten. Being fluent in both languages, I ply my trade along the borderlands of the Frost Wall. Not many can bridge that particular gap."

"A profitable niche," Arasa agreed. He was still holding her hand. She freed her fingers with a little wriggle, and he dropped his arm back to his side. Her skin itched a little, almost as if it missed touching him.

"It can be, when the southerners aren't trying to make war across the border, and the Imperials aren't trying to push them back over the peaks." He shrugged, tucking his hands between his back and the wooden wall he leaned against. "At least you Imperials stop yourselves at the mountain passes. I can't say the same for my father's kin. I've always wondered why, though. I mean, you have better technology, better mages, better soldiers. . . . Why hasn't the Flame Sea invaded and taken over the southlands?"

That question, she could answer. "Because of the covenant between the Am'n Adanjé and Djin-Taje-ul, Mother Goddess of All. The Ruling Family may claim all of the land from Wall to Wall and Sea to Sea, but not one inch more. So we can only go up to the peaks of the mountains to the north and the south, and stretch ourselves out from the western to the eastern shore. To go over the Cloth and Frost Walls would be to go beyond them, so we can claim only up to the tops of the peaks and passes."

"A covenant, eh? Do you also follow this covenant of your leaders?" Elrik asked her, curiosity lacing his baritone voice. "Because if you do, it's an odd thing, wanting to travel so desperately to the Womb of a foreign God. I'd think you would be smart and stick to your own Wombs."

Our own . . . what? Blinking, Arasa stared at him. "What did you say?"

"What do you mean, what did I say?" he repeated, pushing away from the wall so that he could stand upright. "I'm just asking why you feel like you have to go visit the temple of a God whose followers would hate you on sight."

"A Womb . . . is a *temple*?" Arasa asked him carefully, needing that point clarified. Her heart pounded in her chest at the possibility.

"Of course. We are born of the Gods—even in the Flame Sea, I know they occasionally say it that way," he pointed out. "So it's only natural to think of a temple as a sort of spiritual womb. At least, it's natural to think that way in the lands of Kumron. I'll admit I haven't heard anyone actually calling a temple a Womb in the Empire, but then I'm a mage, not a priest."

"A Womb is a temple," she repeated, though more to herself than to him. "The Womb is *the* Temple! *Now* it makes sense. Why should I have to go all the way beyond the boundaries of the Flame Sea to some foreign 'womb,' when all I had to do was go to Ijesh?! Mother Goddess, I've wasted *months* on a fool's quest—I could *kiss* you for your help, Elrik. *Thank* you!"

He shifted his weight, moving just enough into the light spilling from the open kitchen door for her to see part of his face. She

watched him blink a little at her words as he did so, looking
a bit stunned. "Well . . . you're welcome. And, ah . . . if you actually wanted to, I don't think I would be inclined to object."

She stared at him for a moment, until his meaning sank in:
he *wanted* her to kiss him. Grinning, Arasa reached up, cupped
his cheeks, and pulled his mouth down to hers. It had been quite
a while since she'd last had the time to spare for such things, but
she hadn't forgotten how to kiss a man. He certainly didn't have
any problems returning it, either, wrapping his arms around her
within moments and nibbling on her lower lip.

Unsure if it was just desire for the mage that flared through
her veins or a combination of relief and desire, she pulled back
after a moment. He let her go with a touch of reluctance, but
didn't try to cling. Well, not exactly; he left his hands resting
on her waist. Licking her lips, Arasa hoped the light from the
kitchen wasn't bright enough to point out the flushing of her
cheeks. "As I said . . . thank you."

"May I at least know the problem I solved for you?"

Arasa cocked her head. "Are you trustworthy? Because otherwise, I'm not going to reveal any of my secrets. They're my
own business, after all."

Releasing her so he could dig into his satchel, he fished out
the Truth Stone again. "I am not inclined to give away secrets
for gossip or money. Which means I'm mostly trustworthy. Provided the secret isn't something that would threaten to harm me,
of course." A display of the stone showed that his words were
true; conditional, but true. Elrik slipped the piece of marble
back into his bag. "So, are you going to tell me?"

She did owe him for helping her solve the riddle. "I have a
problem. I have to figure out who was born first, my twin sister

or me, so that we can settle a family dispute. Our father said we had to come back with proof, otherwise he couldn't assign our inheritance to the right daughter. She went off in one direction, and I went in another."

"How so?" Elrik asked, leaning back against the wall again.

Arasa shrugged. "Her research led her into the laws of the Empire, mine into its customs and legends. I don't know what she found, if anything, but I found a reference to a situation wherein the inheritor acquired the legacy by making a pilgrimage from 'the Womb to the Heart,' to quote the old text. I guessed 'the Heart' meant the Heart of the Empire, the capital city of Adanjé-nal, but the term *Womb* isn't used in the Flame Sea to describe anything anymore. It might've been used back at the beginning, but the definition had been lost somewhere along the way. So I started traveling, hoping that I'd find a reference in records kept elsewhere . . . and that's when I heard about a 'Womb of Tarden,' while I was traveling through the Kumré region, here, albeit in a town lower down the slopes of the Frost Wall than this . . . place."

"The edge of civilization?" the mage quipped, humor in his tone. "Yes, it would make sense for the Womb in question to be found in Ijesh, chief temple-city of the Empire, if it deals with a matter of Imperial custom and law. I've never been there, but I understand it's a long way from here."

"About three hundred sixty *selijm* from here, yes. That's over a month's journey on foot, though it's only three or so weeks on horseback. I'm *very* glad I won't have to walk all the way from the temple of Tarden, which would be even farther away," she admitted candidly, relief in her voice. "As it is, Ijesh is a day's walk from Adanjé-nal. Even to make that much of a pilgrimage is going to be a literal pain in the foot. I honestly didn't know how I'd be able to walk across the whole length of the Inner Desert, but I knew I had to try."

"You don't look sedentary," Elrik observed dryly. "How do you get around, if you don't walk?"

"To make a pilgrimage," Arasa enlightened him, "one must walk barefoot and weaponless. That much of the instructions were clear. For all the Heart of the Empire is in hard-desert, there are still patches of softer soil . . . and that means sand-demons."

"*Weaponless?* In sand-demon territory?" he scoffed. "Who came up with that stupid rule? Barefoot is idiotic enough!"

"According to the legends, Djin-Taje-ul, Herself. Mother of Creation. Since it's the only way I've found to resolve the issue, I'll just have to figure a way around that part . . . so long as I do it barefoot and weaponlessly, of course," she muttered.

"What about magic? If someone were to craft you a protective spell for your feet?" Elrik offered.

She considered it. "I don't know. I'd have to double-check the legend, but given that I found the information for the pilgrimage in the record halls of Ijesh, it's not out of my way to go and check, since I now have to go all the way back to the 'Womb' of the Empire for my starting point."

"How did you end up in this question of who came first, anyway?" he asked her next. "I thought twins came out one at a time, the same as any other birthing."

"Our mother died in childbirth," Arasa told him quietly. "Midbirth. We weren't cooperating and coming out quietly, and the Healers discovered she had torn and was bleeding on the inside. But they didn't know that until after it was too late. They had to cut her open to extract us before it was too late for us, and lifted us out together, since our umbilical cords were tangled up together. Once they got us separated out, Father had us named one at a time . . . but there is some doubt as to whether a naming is what makes someone first born, or if it was being drawn out of our mother's body and how to define that, or if it was the position of the one closest to coming out the correct way, had our mother survived."

"It seems like a rather large fuss to go through, just to settle an inheritance. Can't you just come to an agreement over who gets what, or flip a coin?" Elrik inquired.

She shook her head. "There's magic tied up in the inheritance. It has to be the firstborn child. The legend I found said that that the firstborn must 'walk from the Womb to the Heart in pilgrimage,' and they would be known as the inheritor by the proof of their success. That means I have to return to the center of the Inner Sea, find my sister, and persuade her to take a barefooted walk with me, to see which one of us is worthy.

"I mean, if it were up to *me,* I'd have flipped a coin ages ago and saved us all the trouble," she admitted with a rough sigh and a touch of her chest. "I could accept the inheritance as firstborn and try to do my best with it, or step back and let my twin handle the matter and be content to just advise her from time to time on how to manage it, should she seek any recommendations from me. I could be just as content finding a lesser niche for myself in the, ah, family business. A manager of some aspect of it."

"Is that family, as in kin? Or Family, as in Am'n?" Elrik asked her shrewdly. "Not many Shijn-Clans have holdings large enough to need submanagers."

"Not many, but some do," Arasa returned calmly, hedging

around the question without answering it definitively. She glanced at the doorway; only the sounds from the kitchen could be heard. "I think it's safe for us to go back in again."

"Tell me . . . if this inheritance is that important, and if you can get away with using magic to protect yourself . . . would you be interested in hiring me to do the job?"

Elrik's question surprised her. She blinked at him. "Why? I'm headed back to the Heart of the Empire, which is a very long distance from your profitable niche, here."

"There's an Academy at Ijesh," he said, his tone somewhat diffident and reserved. "It's said to be the best of all the Mage Academies. I've never had a reason good enough to travel that far from the Frost Wall—as you say, my niche is profitable so far—but I would like to go there some day, to further my craft. It would be like a hire-sword wanting to go to the Imperial Salle in Adanjé-nal. I don't even know if I'd be good enough for the teachers at Ijesh to bother with, but I'd like to try. And as your people say, when Djindji-Taje, Goddess of Luck, offers you Her Right Hand, only a fool wouldn't grasp it."

He had a point. Without his help, Arasa not only would have been a few coins poorer for that false map, but also would have found herself deep in barbarian lands without any clue of where to go. Lady Luck had touched her with that Right Hand, with this man's timely presence; it was best if she returned the favor, or risk a whap from the Left. Smiling, she offered her hand. "Why not? Traveling alone gets rather boring, anyway."

Elrik didn't take the offered palm. Instead, he cleared his throat. "Well, then . . . we need to discuss my fee. I have some funds set aside for traveling, but a little income to supplement the journey would be nice. Say, a retainer fee in advance for my services? Nothing much, in case there turns out to be a prohibition against magic . . . but if nothing else, I suppose I could walk beside you, and stab any sand-demons that burrowed too close to you. I'm not the one who has to make a barefoot, weaponless pilgrimage, after all. There'd be a small charge for that once we get there, if you don't mind me being mercenary about it, but lessened by the cost of the retainer fee."

His audacity made her laugh. "No, I don't mind. You have a right to make a living. And I didn't read anything against there being any companions on the pilgrimage, though I should double-check that as well. Would a Moon a day on the journey there be sufficient to retain your services? Plus a bonus for any services rendered at the end of the journey, proportioned to the deed in question."

Wrinkling his freckled nose, Elrik considered the offer. "I suppose that'll do. It's a field-laborer's wage, and not befitting the complex, costly services of a mage . . . but it would get me to the Academy. And to the fabled city of Adanjé-nal. If you've been to Ijesh, did you also visit the capital? I've heard stories about its wonders. Buildings as tall as cliffs, waterfalls cascading everywhere, the Great Dome of the Imperial Hall . . ."

"I've been there. You'll have a chance to see it for yourself, since that's where my kin live. In fact, if you can help me resolve my family's dilemma, one way or another, I'm sure they'd be happy to host you while you were in the area, as a thank-you for your assistance." She flashed him a mischievous smile. "That'll help save on the cost of an inn, which can be rather expensive in the capital. Deal?"

"Deal." Now he clasped hands with her, accepting the bargain. "Shall we go inside and risk a meal together? I'm afraid all I have otherwise is journey bread."

"So long as it's been cooked thoroughly, I think we could

risk it," she agreed, smiling. "You can tell me about your adventures in Aben-hul while we eat. I've never gone there personally, but my twin has."

Returning to the tavern, they commandeered a table in a corner and started talking. It was the dirty looks and grumbles from the sleepy patrons who were staying in the common room overnight, wrapped up in their cloaks wherever they could stretch out, that finally broke off their conversation some time later. Arasa found herself reluctant to stop talking with Elrik; he was both intelligent and widely educated, yet not full of his own self-importance. Barbarian or Imperial, that was a rare quality in a man. His politeness was also appreciated, for when she reluctantly rose, he gestured at the table they had been using.

"Why don't you sleep up here? I can take one of the benches nearby."

She smiled at the offer. "Actually, I'm sleeping out in the stables, tonight."

His coppery brows rose at that. "Now, why didn't I think of that? Do you think they'd rent me room in the hayloft, too?"

"I'm sleeping with my horses, not in the hayloft. But I'll meet you back here for whatever passes for breakfast."

"Ah. Then I'll walk you to the stables," he offered, rising to join her. One of the nearby travelers grumbled a little louder before resettling on his own table. Holding a finger to his lips, Elrik escorted her outside without further protest. The stableyard was in some ways larger than the tavern, since it was designed for modest-sized caravans of goods being transported over the passes. Like most of the local buildings, the barn was built of wood, not brick or stone. It made Arasa nervous about the possibility of fire, but the two lanterns providing a soft light were carefully enclosed within panes of glass.

It was easy to pick out even in low light which horses were hers; none of the others' backs topped the sides of the stalls, but hers did. Their pale palomino backs stood out against the darker browns of the boards, too. Elrik stared at them, green eyes wide, then stared at her as she opened one of the stall doors, slipping inside to join her chief mount, who had been placed in the one loose-box in the barn. There was plenty of hay heaped in the corner for her to sleep upon, and tall enough that, even accidentally, her steed wouldn't be likely to step on her.

"Those mountains are yours? How do you even get up onto one?"

"With lots of practice," she chuckled, rubbing the mare's flank. "This one is Thunder; that one is Cloud, and the one on the other side is Lake."

"They all look alike to me," Elrik muttered. "You're rather brave, sharing a stall with one of them. Aren't you afraid of being stepped on?"

"They're very well trained. And sleeping with them on hand to protect me is good self defense for a woman traveling on her own. Even if I do get tired of the smell of hay and horse at night," she quipped dryly. Thunder nudged her with a long golden nose, whuffling horse-breath down her chest. Arasa scratched around her crest.

"Ah," Elrik pointed at a dark brown mare off to one side. "My horse—singular—is in that stall over there. Juniper. She's half mountain pony, so her legs are short, but she's sturdy and friendly. So long as we don't go too fast, she should be able to keep up with your ladies." Elrik wanted to linger, but knew he shouldn't impose too much. "I'll, ah, bid you good night, and see you at breakfast, then."

"Good night," Arasa agreed. She watched him leave, then

settled down into the hay. Disappointment at seeing him go was tempered by the thought of seeing him again in the morning . . . and for the next month or so, on the journey back to Ijesh. That thought pleased her. Not only was he intelligent, funny, and good at both speaking and listening, she found his pale, freckled skin and coppery-red curls exotic.

Most everyone in the Flame Sea was a heavily tanned blond, their hair and skin matching the color of their homeland. There were darker-haired people, which was somewhat exotic, but not terribly uncommon. Usually, they were foreigners, or descendants of foreigners. Redheads, though, were rare, and freckled redheads even more unusual. Such skin tended to burn easily, or so she had heard.

She hoped he had some spell or ointment to protect his pale skin from the desert sun. It might be early autumn and thus not the worst time of the year to be crossing the expanse of sun-broiled sand known as the Inner Sea—so-named for its slowly shifting dunes and shimmering heat waves—but it wasn't the best time, either. Summer anywhere in the Empire, other than the cooler climate of the hills of Kumré, the region bordering the Frost Wall, was not the best time to travel. At least not during the daytime. There was a very sound reason for calling her homeland the Flame Sea.

Two

Three weeks. Elrik had been traveling with Arasa for three weeks now, enduring the thankfully lessening heat of midday as autumn progressed, though it meant the nights were correspondingly colder. The air around them was warm enough to cause heat shimmers and trickles of sweat, but whenever he thought about the chance of being with her intimately, shivers of anticipation, fear, and desire prickled down his spine. Three weeks was enough time to become fascinated with the woman, even infatuated. Ever respectful, since she hadn't behaved with anything above a warm sort of friendship so far, but he was drawn to her all the same.

He hadn't noticed her eyes at first, since they had initially met in a lamp-lit tavern. They were taupe, a light grayish-beige, bland, yet undeniably unusual. He'd heard that some Imperials had odd, desert-hued eyes, but this was the first time he had actually seen such a thing. Her hair was pale even for a desert-dweller, platinum-blond and almost white. Most of the time she wore it wrapped up in her turban, but she unbound it each night and morning so she could unbraid and brush out her rib-length locks, then replait them again to keep them tidy while riding or sleeping.

Her soft waves were very different from his own vigorous, crinkly, coppery curls, though the lengths were about the same. If one didn't stretch out one of his locks, that was. Stretched out, his hair would fall below his backside. She had touched his hair a couple of times and blushed, muttering something about just being curious, but it gave him hope that she was interested in him. But he didn't press beyond a few touches, a hug, and an occasional, brief kiss.

Elrik wanted more, much more, but for one, she seemed the reserved type. For another, they were now firmly in the desert. The hot, dusty, gritty desert. Except for at night, when it became the cold, dusty, gritty desert.

Even if there weren't a threat of sand grains getting every-where, should they engage in further intimacies, there were sand-demons to worry about, which meant taking turns rest-ing and guarding against the beasts. The scaly creatures literally swam through the sand and their sting was quite toxic, inducing paralysis. Regular steel wouldn't kill them, either; it would hurt them, but their wounds healed unbelievably fast.

Rumor had it they were the remnants of a terrible, ancient magical war, and thus had been enchanted to be difficult to slay. Only silver could leave lasting harm, and only a silvered blade could dispatch the tough little beasts. Most everyone in the Flame Sea carried a silvered knife at the very least for that rea-son, while others carried silvered swords, or silver-tipped spears that could double as walking staffs.

He didn't carry a sword, but he did have a mage-staff with

a recessed silvered steel spike that could be spring-triggered at one end. But neither swords nor staves were easy to use when engaged in amorous activities. And when they did pass through a city on their journey north, she continued to sleep in the stables with her horses. He didn't want to offend her by pressing the matter too much, but it was rather frustrating not to be able to find either time or opportunity to coax her into a decent bed.

Watching her as she checked her Wall-Finder, the compass used to successfully navigate the great expanses of desert wilderness that composed much of the Empire, he wished she'd broken her pattern of avoidance back in the city of Ido-esh. It was their last civilized stop before reaching the religious city of Ijesh, according to his hostess and guide. She had made use of a bathhouse attached to the inn selected for their stay, but had retired to the stables to sleep, leaving him in sole possession of a small but private room.

At least he'd been able to relieve his needs within its privacy. Self-ministration wasn't nearly as satisfying as a romp with a beautiful woman, of course, but at least it was some source of relief. Grimacing, Elrik adjusted his broad-brimmed, conical sun-hat, which gave him more shade than a mere turban, and nudged his mare into following her down the slope of the next dune.

Arasa glanced back at him. He was keeping up with her, though his mare was slowing her down a little. The shorter horse had neither the longer legs nor the exceptionally broad hooves of her own steeds, hooves that supported them on the shifting sands better than narrower surfaces would. She was surprised the half-pony mare had kept up so well. And despite the odd-looking Kumronite hat, he wasn't suffering too badly in the autumn midday heat.

She was also aware of a growing masculine frustration in her traveling companion. She felt a similar, feminine version of frustration, since it had been about two years since her last romp in the blankets. Increasing duties and obligations to her family had supplanted most opportunities, and her quest over the last year to settle which twin was the firstborn had chased away the rest. But he was exotically handsome, engagingly amusing, delightfully well educated, and very, very charming.

It was tempting to rent a room for herself, rather than sleeping with her horses, very tempting, but the more she got to know Elrik of Snow Leaper Tribe, the more she found she didn't want to just have a temporary fling with him. She valued his company . . . to the point of imagining what it would be like if he ever wanted to stay with her beyond the scope of this little quest. And therein lay the problem.

Having avoided most questions about her lineage and parentage, speaking only in broad, vague terms regarding her kin and her "family business," it was going to be awkward, telling him the full truth. On the one hand, she wouldn't mind making love with him while they were just Elrik and Arasa. To be wanted just for *herself*, not for what she had been born, was too novel and delightful to give up. It was why she had kept silent about her kin. The full truth would only have gotten in the way.

Well, at first, she hadn't told him the truth because she was too far from home, and all on her own. That kind of knowledge could lead to trouble, being the kind of secret that could tempt a man to morally stray, even from a Truth Stone confession that he wasn't usually interested in spilling such things to others. However, the more they journeyed together, the more she thought he was trustworthy and might accept her confession without being too upset at her previous silence.

But on the other hand, she had been lying to him by omission. If they made love, and *then* he found out who and what she was . . . well, it would be awkward at best, and deceitful-seeming at worst. Which meant that every *selijm* closer to Ijesh they traveled, the more nervous she was about revealing the truth. She couldn't ride into the Womb of the Empire—what an appropriate name for a city carved out of old caves, now that she knew—without someone recognizing her and spilling the secret. Because it wasn't a secret in Ijesh. And from the top of that dune, she had seen the first signs of the hard desert that contained the canyons hosting Ijesh and Adanjé-nal.

Cloud, whom she was riding today, slowed at the subconscious signals of her reluctant rider. Elrik's shorter mare caught up with her, drawing even as they started up the slope of a modest-sized dune. He adjusted the palm-woven hat covering him from shoulder to shoulder again as a warm, dusty breeze gusted around them. "Is something wrong?"

It's now or never, and you like him too much for the consequences of "never," Arasa reminded herself. Bracing herself, she nodded. "Yes, there is. I, um, haven't been fully forthcoming with you. If you haven't noticed. Regarding my kin."

"I noticed. Are they secretly horrible people, under the surface?" Elrik asked. "You made them sound rather nice."

That was far enough off the mark, it made her chuckle. "No, they're not horrible. They're just . . . socially prominent."

"Ah. So you're *not* UnShijn, after all." He paused a moment, then asked, "If they're socially prominent . . . are they a Family, rather than a mere Clan?"

"You could say that," she couldn't help hedging, staring at the hardpan ground in the distance. They still had several *selijm* to travel before reaching the first of the ravines that would slope down into the valleys and crevasses hiding the capital. She reminded herself again that it was better to tell him now, while he still had time to adjust to the full truth.

"Well, either they are an Am'n, or they aren't. Which one is it?"

"Am'n Adanjé." She glanced sideways to gauge his reaction. His green eyes had narrowed in skepticism.

"Am'n *Adanjé? The* Ruling Family of the Empire?" Elrik could hardly believe her. It had to be a joke. Even a cousin of the Royal Blood wouldn't be allowed to travel across the Empire without an escort, yet here was Arasa, traveling with just three overgrown . . . palomino . . . Imperial Mares, he realized suddenly, wincing internally for having been so oblivious to the truth.

Arasa saw that wince, and cleared her throat. "Well . . . yes. I didn't mention it earlier because it isn't always wise to announce such a fact when one visits the Frost Wall. Or in the northeast corner of the Cloth Wall, up by the Ebrinnish Border. Even if you turned out be trustworthy enough—and you have," she quickly reassured him, "—there are always others who might have overheard, and tried to take advantage of that fact."

Facts gathered and collided in Elrik's head. She was a member of the Royal Family; she was one of a set of twins; and she was trying to determine who was firstborn, on a quest so serious she'd been willing to travel into Kumron of all places. The capital was a long way from the mountains comprising the southern border of the Empire, but even he had heard rumors of the royal heirs being twins. He just hadn't paid any attention to their names.

He was riding alongside, talking with—and lusting after—a royal princess. His wince came back, turning into a grimace as he looked away. *No wonder she didn't want to be "alone" with me. I'm nothing more than a quarter-breed, with most of me a barbarian Kumronite. Educated and traveled, but still a common foreigner.*

"I didn't tell you at first, because it was safer that way. But once you refrain from mentioning something, it's just easier to keep from mentioning it, so long as it remains unimportant to the needs of the moment," Arasa explained. "But I'm going to be recognized when we get to Ijesh. And if I didn't tell you before then, when it would be revealed by others, you'd think . . . well, who knows what. I didn't know you at the start of our journey," Arasa admitted, "but now that I do . . . I wanted you to know."

Elrik nodded. She was letting him down easy, saving him from the embarrassment of trying anything further with her. Ordinary men like him didn't get to have relationships with princesses, however nice and normal that princess might seem. "I understand."

"I'm glad. I know I've pushed to get back to Ijesh, barely even stopping for a bath, but the sooner this question of the succession is settled, the happier I'll be," she sighed. "That, and Ijesh is a lot safer for me. Everyone knows who I am, so I don't have to be on the lookout for trouble. And, to be truthful, if I had let myself be distracted by you, I would've been *too* distracted.

"Normally, some of the Imperial Bodyguard would have accompanied me, but Father didn't want it widely known that the question of who exactly is firstborn is so important. Going all over the place with an entourage wouldn't exactly be quiet . . . and this is something that has to be proven on my own. Or my sister's own. One of us has what it takes to rule the Empire, but it's supposed to be found within us, put there by the Gods," she explained. "The First Emperor didn't conquer by the might of an army; he ruled by a special covenant between him and the Mother Goddess."

A thought crossed Elrik's unsettled mind. "If you're of the Royal Blood, then you could command any of the mages at the Academy in Ijesh to do your bidding. Why did you accept my offer to accompany you?"

"Three reasons. One, I don't like traveling alone, and you were proving to be a good conversationalist, even that early in the evening. Two, you gave me a tap from Djindji-Taje's Right Hand, saving me an utterly unnecessary and potentially quite dangerous trip into Kumron. I owed you for that. If you wanted to go to Ijesh, I'd help you get there. And three . . ." Shrugging diffidently, she told him the truth. "I was attracted to you, and wanted to get to know you, in case it had the potential to go somewhere. I may be 'of the Royal Blood,' as you put it, but I'm still quite normal."

Elrik glanced sharply at her. That sounded like . . . He adjusted his conical hat again, which was being tugged at by the wind now that they were off the up-and-down swells of the dunes. "What do you mean by that?"

She eyed him askance, wondering why he hadn't picked up on her meaning. Somewhere along the way, they had crossed paths in a misunderstanding. Arasa addressed him bluntly to compensate. "I *mean,* I'm still very interested in you. Being a perfectly normal female, and having traveled in the company of an intelligent, amusing, handsome man for the last three weeks' ride, I would very much like to know if you'd mind my jumping all over you, once we get to Ijesh. . . . *After* we bathe, of course. I have grit in places only a sand-demon would enjoy."

That was *too* blunt. It shocked a laugh out of Elrik, not expecting royalty to be quite so forthright. She joined him, chuckling. Shaking his head—carefully holding his palm-woven hat—he asked, "How did you manage to be so . . . *normal*, growing up as a princess?"

"With great care on my father's part. He didn't always have time for us, but he made sure my sister and I visited with our mother's kin, who were given instructions to treat us as just another pair of kids. No spoiling, no laxing of discipline, and no holding back of love. And he made sure that we knew he loved us, just for being ourselves. Our tutors were also instructed to teach us how to see through flattery and obsequious fawning, and to know when someone was being honest and trustworthy . . . though I'll admit that Truth Stones make a nice shortcut." She smiled at him to show she was teasing.

"It's good to know I'll always have employment," he dared to joke back. Her earlier words finished sinking in, making him flush despite the heat of midafternoon. "So . . . you want to know if I'm interested in you?"

"Yes, if you don't mind speaking plainly about it," Arasa said. She reminded herself silently that holding her breath was undignified. "And provided my little revelation hasn't tipped the balance either way, in your original intent."

Elrik could understand that. Freeing one hand from the reins, he dug into the satchel slung at his side, and pulled out the Truth Stone. "I may be a little intimidated—all right, a *lot* intimidated by your station—but I'm still interested in you. Arasa-the-woman. Very interested. More than I probably should be, given your station."

The stone was unblemished when he unfurled his fingers. Arasa blushed. "Well. Now it remains to be seen if you can handle being in the midst of the madness that surrounds my 'station.' At least the bed will be big and soft."

"Assuming your father doesn't have me thrown out, or worse," he muttered. At her sharp look, he gestured at his freckled face. "For being a foreign commoner, and daring to want to touch his child."

"Considering he arranged for my sister and me to have formal instruction in the erotic arts as soon as we reached adult status, plus the necessary contraceptive amulets, and gave us a message to 'play responsibly,' I don't think it's as big a concern as you're fearing," Arasa revealed dryly. "Kalasa certainly took advantage of his tacit permission for such things, but then I've always been more bookish than her. You don't run across that many males who are both interested and young enough in the Royal Archives. They're more apt to be found hanging around the Imperial Salle, which was where she spent most of her own time. She's cultivated a certain . . . oh, I don't know, an allure, I guess, a confidence and charm that makes it difficult for some men to resist her."

From the way she didn't look his way, Elrik guessed she had seen some men who had been interested in her turning to her twin instead, in the past. "Kalasa, that's your sister's name, right?" Elrik asked. She nodded, checking her Wall-Finder again. "Kalasa means 'sunlight' in the Imperial tongue . . . and Arasa means 'moonlight.'" He smiled, looking at the slowly approaching canyons in the distance. "I've always been more partial to moonlight, myself."

Glancing at him, Arasa caught sight of that smirk, and felt warmed by it. "Given how pale your skin is, it's probably a good thing. Time to stop and rest the horses, I think."

Complying, he dismounted with her. While she tended to her Imperial Mares, stripping the saddle off the one she was riding, he removed the saddle from his own petite steed, allowing both of them to air-dry. When he set out the drinking pan for Juniper, filling it with water from one of the skins strapped to the saddle, his horse guzzled it eagerly, all but inhaling the liquid. A brief grooming with her curry brush was all she needed to smooth down the hairs of her brown hide, and when the water was gone, he added a double handful of grain and dried fruit to the shallow wooden bowl, allowing her to lip up the grains.

Elrik moved to help Arasa water and feed her own horses, as he had during the length of their journey. Imperial Mares were known for their ability to fight as fiercely as any Flame Sea warrior, with an almost doglike loyalty to their riders. Yet after he was introduced to each of them by her guiding his hand to their nostrils for a whiff of his scent, they had seemed as tame as plow-horses.

Given their normally fierce reputation, he thought it was little wonder he hadn't made the connection. And it was true that they had stomped on the occasional snake or sand-demon, crushing them flat, but even a normal horse would do that. Even after he knew what they were, he couldn't see a reason to be afraid of them.

It did make him wonder how the courtiers of the Empire would view his presence, and *that* made him nervous. Firming his courage, he asked, "Are you *sure* you want to take me to your chambers, once we get to Ijesh? I don't want to cause trouble with your father's Court. The other Am'n might look down on you."

Arasa quirked one of her blond brows as she stroked her own currying brush down Lake's golden limbs. "Elrik, you're a *mage*. That automatically gives you a high status in the Empire. You don't need to be born to a Noble Family to command a certain respect—if anyone gives you any trouble, just threaten to turn their nose into a sausage, or something."

The absurdity of the suggestion made him chuckle ruefully. "In the southern lands, the suggestion would be to 'turn you into a toad,'" he mock-cackled, curling his fingers and wrinkling his nose. Relaxing, he shook his head. "But I wouldn't turn anyone into a toad in the desert. That's just too cruel."

"Then you're a kindhearted man," she observed, glancing at him. "How do you survive on such a volatile border?"

"Oh, make no mistake," Elrik corrected her, pausing in the middle of brushing Thunder's hindquarters. Unclipping the metal-wrapped staff slung at his side like a sword, he watched an approaching lump wriggling its way toward them, forming a rill of disturbed sand in its wake. "I can and will defend myself. I *have* defended myself, in the past. I just prefer to be politely civilized rather than barbarically belligerent."

A stab of his arm and a jab of his thumb thrust the spring-loaded spike into the middle of the squirming bump. Something squealed, the sand shivered and twitched, and he planted his boot on the mound, extracting the spike without revealing the beige-scaled beast. He'd seen them before; there was no need to see them again. A couple jabs of the silvered spike in the sand helped scrape off the bluish-white ichor; a tap against his boot-heel shook the grit free, allowing him to retract the tip. It would need cleaning later, when they had the water to spare, but then it had needed cleaning after their last pause for rest. Thankfully, once they reached the hardpan desert, where the soil was too solid to burrow through, the sand-demons would be left behind.

The oversized palomino twisted her head around, snorted softly, and flicked him in the small of his back with her tail, telling him silently but eloquently to get back to scratching all her travel-borne itches with that lovely currying brush still in his other hand. No fool—especially now that he knew what the mare was, and what the rumors said she was capable of doing—Elrik clipped the staff back onto his belt and complied. Glancing at Arasa, he smiled wryly. "As you've seen, I can take care of myself, and those around me."

"Sand-demons can be dangerous, but some men can be even more so," Arasa reminded him. "Swatting at mountain-flies for a week as we left Kumré, and then stabbing at sand-demons for two more weeks of crossing the Inner Desert, isn't the same as one moment of heart-stopping battle."

"Sometimes sand-demons swim under the surface with six legs, and sometimes they stride across the land on two. The wise traveler is always prepared against either kind—let us concede each other's point," Elrik added, heading off further argument. "And focus on more important matters. Such as the danger I will be in from Thunder, here, if I do not finish currying her."

✦

Ijesh was a strange but wondrous place. Legend said the place had been inhabited ever since the most primitive of times . . . but legend also said that water had not flowed reliably through these canyons until the First Emperor had come to this place. Now, however, there was an abundance of water, though at first one didn't see signs of it.

The first impression was of sloping, rough rock walls gradually growing taller as a traveler descended deeper into the canyon, then of caravans coming and going, some in the main ravine, others in side-gullies angling off to either side. Gradually, one noticed the holes cut in the faces of the cliffs. The first ones were raw-edged, just holes that had been rough-hewn. A few had troughs cut and filled with dirt and plants, though not many. Then the road turned to the left, rounding the edge of a window-riddled cliff; as the valley floor widened into a stall-lined market, the view broadened into great carved entryways, balconies, columns, and statues.

Almost all of the buildings were cut from the hard white-and-gold granite that formed the stone of the valley walls. Curtains hung in windows; banners fluttered from balustrades and jutting posts. A few structures stood on their own, mortared in blocks of stone; the remainder were temporary shelters of wooden posts and canvas awnings, lending brightly dyed colors to the views. And everywhere, water trickled in aqueducts that followed the rugged curves of the canyon walls, splashing down carved channels in gurgling rills that allowed greenery to grow in vast, stone-rimmed beds.

For all that the wind was quieter down here in the twists and turns of the hidden valleys, the air at least was cooler, moister. Easier to breathe, if perfumed with a hundred or more scents: dromids and horses, goats and chickens, spices resting in market bins, flowers growing on the terraces overhead. It didn't *seem* like a large city, since there was never much of it in view at any one time, but it went on and on, from the market sector, where travelers could find a room at a wall-cut inn, to residential areas, where the bleating of market animals herded to the butchering pens gave way to the chattering of young children chasing each other through the streets. And there were side-canyons that they didn't explore, passing alleys carved by both natural and artificial means.

Elrik would have been lost within minutes, had he not been following Arasa. He certainly would have been separated from her in the crush, if the sight of her three Imperial Mares, two of them on lead-ropes trailing after the one in the lead, hadn't cleared a path ahead of them. It was almost eerie, the way the crowd's awareness of the overgrown horses spread, turning heads and quieting conversations as the inhabitants and visitors shifted out of their way. It made him feel something of a tag-along, an afterthought, riding as he was on mere Juniper, the short, brown, stocky half-pony.

They reached a broad stone barricade, stretching from wall to wall on one side of their winding path and patrolled across its arched top by guards with halberds. Here, Arasa turned her cur-rent steed, Lake, toward the broad, wrought-iron gates flank-ing the archway. Guards appeared, spoke quiet words with the princess through the grille, then swung the gates wide enough for horses and humans to enter. Within short order, Elrik found himself urged to dismount as stable-hands came forward to take Juniper's reins.

Fingers slipped around his, startling him. He had only a moment to glance at their taupe-eyed owner before she was tug-ging him away from the servants handling their steeds. Arasa pulled him deeper into what he realized was one of the most ornately carved canyons seen so far.

Bas-relief panels depicted the history of the Empire, while carved pillars represented the Gods of the Empire. Fountains splashed water, cooling the air even further and moistening both his skin and his lungs. Tugged into the cliff-carved palace, he found himself mounting intricately carved stairs flanked on one side by a gurgling cascade that poured down its own set of channel-carved steps. Vaulted ceilings boasted painted surfaces between their ornately pointed ribs. Decades must have been spent shaping the stone around them, but his hostess barely gave him time to see any of it. Before he could absorb more than a quarter of his surroundings, she pulled him through a pierced stone—*stone*—door into a room three times the size of the tavern where they had first met.

The columns in here were more fluid and the frescoes on the ceiling more abstract, but the walls had been polished to a glossy shine rather than carved with depictions of ancient history. The furnishings were crafted from inlaid wood, bleached leather, and pastel cushions. Gossamer curtains hung across what appeared to be a balcony off to the left, fluttering softly in the slight breeze that stirred the warm air; flanking them were heavier curtains that he realized could be pulled across the opening to protect against the chill of the desert night. Greenery bloomed in planters on the terrace, while more grew in pots on some of the tables, and cut flowers spilled out of ornately glazed vases.

Overall, the sitting room gave the impression of comfortable wealth; not pretentious, but comfortable with itself. Much like Arasa herself, Elrik decided. He turned to her, but found the questions forming in his mind derailed by movement off to the right.

Two women in identical blue outfits moved into the room from an archway opposite the balcony; they stopped and bowed at a respectful distance. Servants. Arasa glanced back at Elrik, smiled at him in reassurance, and addressed them. "This is Mage Elrik, my guest. He and I will be taking a bath as soon as the pools can be filled. Please find something for him to wear while our garments are being washed, and set out fresh clothes for myself as well."

"As you wish, Taje-tan Arasa," one of the ladies agreed, addressing her by the Flame Sea equivalent for "princess," though the title actually only meant "noble heir." The maidservant offered, "Taje-tan Kalasa left just this morning; the bathing chamber has not yet drained itself from her visit, if you wish to soak immediately."

Ambivalence speared through Arasa. She was glad on the one hand that her sister wouldn't be around to interrupt her privacy with Elrik, but on the other hand, she had intended to find and chat with her sister. To miss her by a matter of hours was a definite disappointment. "Where did she say she was going?"

"Back to the Imperial Hall. Something about finding a solution, but needing confirmation." The maidservant flicked her gaze to the freckled mage and back. "More than that, Taje-tan, I could not say at the moment."

"You may speak freely in front of both of us," Arasa reassured her. "Mage Elrik has been assisting me in my own efforts to find a solution to the succession problem. He is my honored guest, for his aid in that matter."

"Of course," the maid agreed, bowing slightly. "The Taje-tan said she needed to check some legal records one more time in the Hall Archives, something about researching a childhood illness. She also said she wished to be informed as soon as anyone had word of your current whereabouts."

Arasa didn't know what a childhood illness had to do with the succession, but she was happy to know her sister was still close by. "Good. Send a runner to let her know I am here, and that I wish to see her return. Tell her that I will meet her here, in Ijesh. I have news of my own, regarding a solution to our problem, and that solution literally starts here." She glanced at Elrik and smiled, adding, "In the Womb of Djin-Taje-ul, or so I suspect. I will be searching the Temple Archives again in the morning with the help of my guest; please let the priesthood know to expect us both."

A bow, and the maid who had spoken departed. The other one shifted back out of the way as Arasa took Elrik's hand again, tugging him toward the archway. Once past the daylight filtering

through the terrace curtains, the passageways were lit by glow-
ing spheres—magelights. Elrik knew how they were made, of
course; it had been a part of his magical education. They were
expensive, though. Even more than the intricately inlaid wood-
work, the number of magelights told him how wealthy the Am'n
Adanjé was, and for one reason alone: not a single oil lamp or
candle could be seen.

Elrik had seen a few fine pieces of furniture here and there,
some artistic carvings, a number of brocaded tapestries, even
paintings and other artworks in his time in Aben-hul, but never
had he met anyone who could afford to use magelights as their
sole source of illumination. This was the level of wealth that
had driven his father's people to invade time and again, seeking it for themselves. It made him feel a little awkward to be
three-quarters Kumronite and a guest inside, if not *the* royal
palace—that was the Imperial Hall in the capital—then at least
a royal palace.

Passing through a chamber lined with benches and shelving,
they entered a bathing hall. The chamber, slightly larger than
the front room had been, took his breath away. It didn't hold a
mere bathing tub, as his own people knew and most inns used.
It wasn't even a bathing pool. It was a series of pools, one cascading into the next, four of them. The one in the far corner of
the terraced room was small, and steamed with visible heat. The
middle two curved around that corner, each larger than the previous one, each spilling into the next.

The bottom one was big enough for swimming, and had
been sculpted to look something like a natural pool, though the
water was clear of both flora and fauna. Clerestory windows
carved high in the walls spilled light, as did sconces of crys-
talline magelights at regular intervals along the walls. Stone

planters grew right next to the edges of the tiled pools, soothing desert-weary eyes with a profusion of greenery and adding to the overall effect.

The smoothed granite floor of the chamber was slightly sloped so that any excess water would flow into drains set here and there, but it wasn't tiled; the pools, however, were. The largest basin was tiled in a pale blue glaze, the next one up in sky blue, and the third in royal blue; he couldn't see into the highest pool, but guessed it was tiled in dark blue, if it followed the theme. Overhead, the faux-vaulted ceiling had been gilded between its granite-white ribs, but the paint had begun to age and flake, no doubt because of all the moisture in the air. Somehow, the sight of that flaw reassured him that this room was real, that he really was in such otherwise magnificent surroundings.

He didn't even notice Arasa removing her clothes until he finally turned to look for her and saw her stooping over next to a bench, removing her trousers and underdrawers together. Her other garments and her boots had already been discarded at her feet. Though her naturally tanned skin was darker in places where the desert dust had infiltrated her clothes, the grime did nothing to disguise the feminine shape of her legs, the slenderness of her waist, the palm-sized curves of her breasts.

Heat prickled across his skin, adding to the lingering warmth of late afternoon. Tugging at his clothes, Elrik remembered after a moment to untie the chin-straps holding his sun-hat in place. With it removed, he could pull his poncho and tunic over his head. By the time he stooped to unlace his boots, she was already sinking into the water of the largest, lowest pool, a pale-haired, golden-skinned, mortal goddess.

"Will you and your guest need assistance with your bath, Taje-tan?"

Three

Elrik jumped, startled by the intrusion of the other maidservant. People in the Flame Sea often bathed together in public bathhouses without thinking twice about it, but they didn't couple in front of an audience; exhibitionism just wasn't done. Wanting very much to be left alone with her, he looked over at Arasa, giving her a tight little shake of his head.

She smiled. "We'll be fine. Give us some privacy for a while, and leave the toweling cloths and some clean clothes in the changing hall."

The blue-clad woman bowed and removed herself from the chamber. Relieved, Elrik finished undressing. Semihard already, he padded somewhat self-consciously toward the steps, outlined along their curved edges in a darker shade of blue that defined their location under the rippling surface.

Arasa watched him ease into the cool liquid, floating half-way across the pool from him. She smiled at his palpable relief. "Feels good, doesn't it?"

"Very," he agreed, wading forward until the water was up to his chest and he was just an arm's length away from her. "Thank you for the privacy. I, um, want to do more than just bathe with you."

"So do I." She wrinkled her nose with a rueful smile. "First times with another person are always so embarrassing and awkward, aren't they?" Lifting a hand from the water, Arasa gestured at a cabinet half-tucked into the greenery. "There's a collection of softsoaps and such over there. I suggest we bathe each other thoroughly, get our hands all over each other's bodies, and then we shouldn't be quite so awkward anymore. What do you think?"

Despite the coolness of the water swirling gently around his body, Elrik felt himself stiffen with interest. "I think that's a brilliant idea."

Grinning with relief, Arasa waded with him over to the cabinet. Half of it opened on the pool side, next to a set of steps, the other half to a path through the greenery lining the chamber, so that it could be stocked. Sea sponges, scrubbing brushes, washrags, and combs occupied one shelf, while jars and bottles lined two more. Selecting a rough-textured sponge, she poured a bit of softsoap from one of the jars onto the sponge. "This one is scented with musk and spices. Do you like?"

He sniffed the sponge and nodded. "I like it. Is that for you?"

"For you," she corrected, working the sponge into a lather. "I didn't think you'd want anything flowery."

"I like some flower scents. Roses, carnations, lily-of-the-valley." He fell silent as she pressed the sponge to his chest, scrubbing him gently.

"Roses are cultivated in the Flame Sea, but not the other

two. Essence of lily-of-the-valley is expensive to import, since it prefers a much cooler climate. And until I had visited the Kumré region, I don't think I'd smelled a carnation, before," Arasa confessed. "Here, get your face wet, so I can scrub that, too."

Complying, Elrik ducked under the water, then obeyed her directions to sit on the topmost step, water lapping at his ankles, while she scrubbed him from head to toe. When she had him stand thigh-deep in the water so that she could scrub around his pelvis, he had to catch her hands to make her go slow. The feel of her fingers guiding the scratchy sponge over his skin, cleaning between his nether-cheeks and beneath his masculinity, was too intimate, too pleasurable, threatening to bring him to an abrupt, premature ending.

It had been a while since his last encounter, too long for his body to withstand a lot of teasing. Heeding his silent warning, she worked carefully, clinically, though shifting back his foreskin to clean around the head of his shaft was almost too much to bear. As soon as she released him, he dove into the water, swimming away from her for several lengths until he had to come up again for air. The rush of cool water against his flesh and the release of energy, if not the sexual kind, helped him regain some control. Reminding himself to be respectful, to go slow, to avoid giving in to the primitive instincts her touch aroused within him, Elrik waded back. He watched her pour more softsoap into the palm of her hand from the red glass jar, and guessed it was for his hair.

"Don't scrub all over, when you wash my hair," he warned her, turning to present his back, then sinking to his knees in the water so that she didn't have to reach quite so high, "or it will tangle hopelessly. Just smooth it on, then gently rub it in with your palms in small circles at most."

Stroking her palms over his dripping wet curls, Arasa did her best to comply. The crinkly texture of his damp locks reminded her of the coarse sponge she had just used. "I don't think I've ever met anyone with hair quite like yours. Not someone I've been close enough to touch. It's rather exotic, and handsome."

"It's a pain to wash, unless I have smoothing crèmes to apply afterward, something to calm the tangles. Here, let me show you." Lifting his arms, he slid his hands over to hers, showing the little circles he used on his scalp with his fingertips. The feel of her fingers bumping against his, learning how to scrub his scalp, seemed even more intimate than if she'd touched his nipples. He enjoyed the sensual torment for as long as he could stand, then broke away and dunked himself under the water again, swishing his hair to rinse it.

When he emerged, she had a handful of something creamy and fruity. He helped her work it into his curls, then left it there while he found the sponge she had used, lathering it with more of the softsoap she had used. It was more gender-neutral than feminine, but he liked the thought of covering her in the same scent as him. He took his time in scrubbing her, too; it had been a while, but Elrik remembered how much women liked a longer, slower buildup to their pleasure than men.

Avoiding breasts and loins until the last moment, he played the sponge over her other curves, watching her beige eyes unfocus with increasing pleasure. The sight of the contraceptive amulet strapped to her ankle reassured him when he reached her feet; for all that he had considered one day becoming a father, today wasn't that day. When he finally circled one breast with the sponge, spiraling in toward her nipple, she dropped her head back, arms braced on the rim of the pool to either side, hips barely on the edge of one of the steps. It was such a wanton pose, he wanted to throw the sponge into the bushes and take her, just take her. Hand trembling, he circled her other breast, and watched her shiver in a minor temblor of desire.

It was all he could do to remain polite and civilized when she stood and guided his hand between her thighs. Not in the sense of being a barbarian Kumronite by birth, but in the sense of being a male on the brink of losing control of his passion. When his fingers encountered slick moisture, shifting the sponge over her flesh, it took a few moments longer for his brain to figure out what that was. His loins knew instantly, stiffening to the point where not even the soothing temperature of the water could calm him. Locking his jaw, Elrik forced himself to finish cleaning her, then gestured abruptly for her to move away from him and rinse her flesh.

Unsure what to make of the stern look on his face, Arasa ducked below the surface and ran her hands over her skin to help remove the lather he had applied. Opening her eyes, she ignored the sting of the water and the slight clouding from the softsoap. The jutting length of him—told its own story. He was on the edge of his control.

The realization aroused her even further. Arasa had been given instruction in the art of sexual pleasure, just as she had been taught how to ride, how to tally, how to wield a pen or a sword, and a hundred other lessons. She had taken well to her sensual lessons, and enjoyed the variety of them. Sometimes she wanted gentle, sweet lovemaking. Other times, she enjoyed a good, hard ride. Though his touch while scrubbing her had been deliciously attentive and gentle, Elrik looked like a stallion exposed to several in-heat Imperial Mares, taut-muscled and wild-eyed, the latter visible even through the rippling surface.

If she let him, he'd probably give her a good, hard ride, and that thought definitely appealed to her.

Rising from the water, she slicked the moisture away from her face, pushing her blond locks back behind her ears. He stared at her, only his eyes moving in his freckled face. Plucking the sponge from his fingers, Arasa tossed it in the direction of the cabinet, uncaring if it fell short or landed in the bushes. All this self-control was good; it spoke well of his character that he hadn't pounced on her despite the desire burning in those gorgeous, exotic green eyes. She just didn't think it was needed at the moment.

"Elrik," she murmured, holding his gaze. "I appreciate your self-restraint; I find it admirable, and civilized. Gentlemanly, even. But I don't *need* a gentleman; at least, not every single hour of the day. Sometimes . . . sometimes I want a barbarian." The passion in his eyes intensified, even as he arched a brow at her. She drifted closer, adding candidly, "And sometimes I want to *be* a barbarian." Her fingers found and encircled his flesh, palpably hot despite the coolness surrounding them. "Do you have a problem with that?"

"Gods, *no,*" Elrik rasped, glad she had penetrated his brain with such tacit permission. Pushing her hand away, he grabbed her hips, lifting her in the waist-high water. Muscles flexing, he sighed with relief as she helped him by parting and wrapping her legs around his waist. A prod, an adjustment or two, and he was in the right place. Hips bucking up into her, he pulled her down onto him at the same time, thrusting deep.

Arasa gasped, startled. She was ready for him, and it did feel good—very good—but it had also been a couple of years since her last joining. Everything was tight, to the point of stretchy-painful. A shudder passed through him, then a grimace; in the next moment, she felt his flesh pulsing within her, dragging a groan out of his throat.

Before any disappointment could sink in, he shifted his grip, wrapping his arms around her shoulders and hips. Squeezing her tight, he thrust into her again, burrowing deeper, pulling her down to meet each of his strokes. Contrary to expectations, he remained hard. Now that the initial sting of his girth versus her tightness had faded, the only thing remaining was the pursuit of a pleasure that literally made waves around them. Clinging to him, burying her mouth against his shoulder, Arasa shuddered with pleasure, then in a second, stronger quake of desire.

Feeling her squeezing around him, Elrik lost a little more of his control. Tangling his hand in her damp locks, he pulled her head back, ordering tersely, "Lean back."

Reluctantly, wanting only to cling and enjoy, she complied. It helped that he shifted away from the stairs, farther into the water, until she was supported by it. The position drove him deeper with each stroke. It also, she discovered with a startled breath, allowed him to bend over and lick one of her breasts. He slowed his hips as he switched to suckling, dragging a moan from her with each circular rub and grind.

Burrowing her fingers into his curls, soft and slick from the crème, Arasa gave herself up to him, trusting in his masculine power. Almost a month of conversations had allowed her to learn the thoughts and opinions of her traveling companion, but only now was she getting to know the man. Unfathomable, intimate, tender yet demanding, he rolled his pelvis against hers until she cried out in a climax larger than the ones before—large enough to curl her toes, spasm her back, and claw her fingernails through his damp locks, arching and tightening against him—and then he gripped her firmly and resumed his previous hard pounding, taking his own pleasure a second time now that she had found hers.

It was exactly what she wanted. Clutching at his shoulders, pulling herself upright in his arms, she shuddered and groaned, enjoying the moment all the way through his stiffening, slowing, and final, deep, twitching-hot stroke. Despite the water helping to relieve some of her weight, her limbs trembled from the effort of keeping herself in his embrace, arms and legs wrapped tightly around his back. She didn't want to let go. Didn't want it to end. Not just for the breathless passion of their lovemaking, but because this moment, this clinging afterglow, was perfect.

Arasa could feel him trembling, too. She relaxed in his arms a little, but he clutched her closer, burying his face in the side of her throat. Freeing a hand, she stroked his damp, woolly-feeling curls. "It's all right, you can let me down; I won't go far."

"If I let you go," Elrik panted quietly, struggling to quiet the racing beat of his heart, "I'll drown. Or I'll die."

"*Or* you'll die?" she found the strength to quip. "If you drowned, wouldn't that be, '*and* you'll die'?"

"If I just let go, physically, I'll collapse and melt into the water," he clarified quietly. "But if I let go of *you* . . . No spell could have more power over me than you do."

Craning her head, she looked into his eyes, his freckled nose almost touching her own. The sincerity and emotion in those green depths shook her. Resting his forehead against hers, Elrik continued, his words piercing straight through her.

"Please, do not take this the wrong way . . . but I don't want you to be firstborn. A mere Taje-tan is at the very edge of my grasp, perhaps even beyond what I deserve . . . but the next Empress of the Flame Sea would be as far beyond my reach as the stars themselves."

Arasa sought to put her own feelings into words. He was wrong, very wrong to doubt himself like this, but she couldn't say it in so many words and have him believe. Searching for the right thing to say, she held his gaze. "Elrik . . . *reach* for me. Take me and accept me as I am now. Whatever happens, I will always be *me*, and the woman that I am wants to reach for and hold onto the man that is *you*. If you want me . . . don't let go. Don't ever let go."

"Never," he promised, burying his face once more in the curve of her throat. This time, his muscles trembled from relief, not release. She stroked him from scalp to spine, soothing his fears. Soothing, and re-arousing him. A rough laugh escaped him a few moments later. "Though I'll have to let go, to finish washing your hair. And to find a bed, so that we won't drown next time. But I won't go far . . . not unless you tire of me, and tell me to go."

"Never," she promised in turn. Not ever, when he made her feel whole.

⚬

"**Here** it is," Arasa murmured. "This is the one."

Elrik abandoned the text he had been studying, joining her as she laid out a scroll. She kept her voice quiet because that was the feeling imposed by the massive, carved depths of the Temple Archives of the Mother Goddess; this deep into the canyon cliffs, the air was comfortably cool and dry, perfect for preserving texts. The spells the ancient mages had used on these scrolls didn't hurt, either. It permitted her to open a six-century-old scroll without fear of the parchment cracking from brittleness.

Unrolling the staves a little further, she perused the inked characters, faded somewhat with age despite the runes along the top and bottom edges helping to preserve the parchment, but still legible.

"... *Then the Mother Goddess spoke unto him, saying, 'Stand you now in the Womb of the World, but a womb is the place of a child, not that of a man; from here, you cannot rule. Go you to the place that you would make the Heart, make of it a pilgrimage of Our Holy Covenant, and the Land will know you as a man, the firstborn and eldest of all. Be humble, for the power you would hold is not to be held with pride; if you wish to rule the Land, you must walk barefoot upon it, with nothing between your flesh and the sand but your skin so that the Land may know and embrace you. Be faithful, for the trust you would find in those you would rule is a trust you must offer as well; if you wish to protect your people, make your pilgrimage weaponless, so that the Land will know its duty is to protect you from all that would bring harm to you.*

"... *Let this be the sealing of Our Holy Covenant, and when you reach the Heart, let the blood of your heart fall, anointing the Land, feeding it so that it may in turn sustain you. Let it know you for Firstborn in the blood you shed, and it shall know all of the firstborn of your Blood, and of their firstborn, and of theirs; let your Family be bound to the powers and responsibilities I give unto you, from now until the Land itself is no more, so long as a single drop of your Blood shall survive, so long as a single drop of your Blood shall be spilled, wherever else you and your Blood may go upon the Land."*

"... *When the Mother finished speaking unto him, and holding himself in the faith of their Covenant, the First Emperor removed his sword and cast off his shoes, and walked in trusting penitence from the Womb to the place that was to be the Heart, from the sheltered life of a child to the responsibility of a man. The Land did indeed know him, and the Land did protect him, and the Land bound itself with him and to him when he spilled his blood upon the sand, rising up and sheltering him at his command . . ."*

Arasa stopped reading at that point, since the rest of it pertained to the establishment of the capital. That one segment contained everything she needed to know about the journey to be made. Except for where the Womb was located, of course. Now that she knew a Womb was another name for a Temple, it made sense. Especially with that reference to *"a womb is the place of a child,"* and *"from here, you cannot rule."* Temples were meant to be places of worship, not leadership.

Elrik wasn't familiar with the archaic script—the runes along the edges were far more readable to him—but he had puzzled out enough of the words to know she had translated it more or less as it was written. "I see what you mean. It doesn't say where this Womb was located, nor how long a journey he made, just that he had to make it, barefoot and weaponless. And it specifically mentions sand . . . so sand-demons are a worry."

"But it says that *'the Land did protect him,'*" she returned, shifting her hand to point at the passage. The scroll, rolled up for centuries, immediately curled up on itself, making her laugh and smooth it back. A rueful sigh, and she shook her head. "Of course, like the explanation for 'womb,' the scroll doesn't say *how* the Land protected him. But I know that there were mentions of sand-demons in even earlier texts, and that this is the best clue I have for figuring out who is firstborn, between the two of us. If Kalasa and I make a pilgrimage from the Mother Temple—and where else would a "womb" be found, but in the home of a mother—and we do so barefoot and weaponless . . . the Land will know which one of us is firstborn."

"Yes, but the implication is that the other twin will *not* be protected," Elrik observed dryly. "So that twin will risk having a sand-demon sting her. In fact . . . it looks like the only way to tell one from another is to *let* a sand-demon sting one of your feet. I strongly suggest you bring enough people along with you—with boots and weapons to protect themselves, though not you—so that they can lift and carry whoever must succumb. I don't *like* it, but letting one of you fall unconscious from the venom looks to be the only way to tell for sure."

"I agree," Arasa concurred. "Whoever does fall should not be left on the ground for the sand-demon to colonize." She shuddered at the thought. "That is a *very* nasty way to die."

Elrik touched her arm, reassuring her. "I won't let that happen to you. With my boots and my staff, I can protect myself, and I'm strong enough to carry you." He wrinkled his nose and added wryly, "Unlike you, I don't have the slightest chance of being firstborn, and no chance at all of the 'Land' protecting me. However it may do so."

Nodding, she rolled up the scroll. "There's nothing more to be done until my sister returns from the capital, except put this back where I found it." She paused, bundled parchment in hand, then set it down and looked up at him. "You said you were interested in the Imperial Academy. Would you like to go and have a tour today?"

The offer was appealing. Elrik almost said yes, but then she licked her lips. It was just a reflexive act, moistening them without thought, but it reminded him of the way she tasted, and the way she felt.

She noticed his interest. "What would you like to do with the rest of the day?"

His mouth curled up on one side. "As you say, 'whatever I

like' . . . and I would *like* to spend time in your company. Private time. Not necessarily coupling—though that is on my list of things to do today—but just spending time with you."

She smiled and stepped into his arms, wrapping her own around his waist. Being half a foot shorter, she was the right height to rest her cheek on his shoulder. It was a comfortable place to be, and even more so when he returned her embrace.

Elrik hugged her close, enjoying the musky-spicy scent of the softsoap he had used on her now braided hair. They weren't traveling through the desert at the moment, so she had left her turban behind this morning. Just as he had left his woven hat, though he had been careful to stay out of the sun as much as possible on their way to the Mother Temple.

Of course, he hadn't *seen* his hat since the bathing hall last night; their clothing had disappeared at some point after they had left, stopping in the antechamber for the towels and fanciful garments left in their place. Brocaded fabrics in rich colors, rather than the simple linens and cottons of desert travel. Shoes made of ankle-high soft leathers, rather than the stiffer, knee-high material of riding boots. She looked beautiful in shades of golds and creams accented with red, while someone had been smart enough to give him garments in hues of green and blue accented with silver. His best clothes, while brocaded, were made from cotton bought from the modest weavers of the Frost Wall, not silk that was grown, spun, and woven by the much more renowned weavers of the Cloth Wall, but they were in flattering blues and greens.

However, like everything else washable, they had disappeared. Even his worn leather belt had been replaced with a much newer, metal-studded version, though at least the servants had clipped his staff and slung his coin-pouch in the proper places

on it. On the one hand, the new garments helped him blend in
better with his surroundings. On the other hand, they weren't
his clothes; he knew it was meant as hospitality, not charity, but
it was something he would have to get used to accepting, if they
kept their relationship.

If she wasn't firstborn, he would support himself as much as
possible as a mage, to prove to her family that he would be an
equal in their marriage, not a burden. If she was firstborn . . . he
would have duties as her Consort. If she still wanted him in
her life. Those duties would include public appearances, which
would require suitable clothing befitting such a high station, but
he wouldn't be sponging off her. Even he knew a consort's job
helped a kingdom run more smoothly, and that it took a lot of
work to be one. It was that way in the king-states of the south-
lands, and it would be that way here, as well.

Either way, he realized he would have to be a source of
strength for her. It wouldn't be easy, stepping back and letting
her do the greater work, but he would do it if she turned out
to be the firstborn heir. Certainly he could at least try to give
her what a more likely prospective consort wouldn't be able to,
and that was a sense of normalcy in her life. Elrik wasn't noble-
born, wasn't politically ambitious, wasn't motivated by greed
for all the wealth a position at her side would provide, either as
the Consort to the Empress or the husband of a mere princess.

He was just a man, one who had fallen for just a woman.
Just a wonderful, intelligent, delightful, funny, down-to-earth
woman. A woman who shifted in his arms after he sighed in
contentment, glancing up at him.

"What are you thinking?"

"That I've fallen in love with you."

The unadorned, quiet truth held in his words made Arasa

blush. She cleared her throat. "Well. It seems we've been thinking the same thing. That I've fallen in love with you, too. I was just standing here, in your arms, thinking how I never knew I was missing something in my life, until you came along and helped me out. I'm thinking how much I care about you, now that you're in my life. And how much I'm afraid of the future, in case things go wrong, or turn out to be overwhelming . . . because I'm afraid you might leave me, and make me face that future alone."

A wry chuckle escaped him. Elrik kissed her braided head. "And here I was thinking I'd have to learn how to be a source of strength for you, so that you'd never feel you had to do it all on your own, from now on."

"Well, if you're planning on sticking around and helping me," she dared to tease, snuggling closer, "then I should think of some way to reward you."

"I think we should go back to your quarters before you give me this reward, so that we don't end up accused of blasphemy for 'unbecoming conduct' in Djin-Taje-ul's Temple."

Chuckling, she left the scroll-filled room with him.

∽

Head on her palm, elbow propping her sideways on the bed, Arasa studied the freckled, masculine face of the man sleeping next to her. Early-morning light seeped through a gap in the velvet curtains drawn over the windows, shutting out the cold of the night. The glow illuminated the room in soft gray-white. In direct sunlight, his curls gleamed with almost metallic highlights, but right now they just looked reddish-gold. Even his lashes were reddish-gold. In a land filled with pale blonds, golden blonds, ash blonds, dark blonds, the lesser-seen shades that were light browns, chestnut browns, medium browns, and a few with hair even darker than that, red was very rarely seen.

Certainly freckles were even more of an oddity. She wanted to touch them, to try to feel any tangible difference to his skin where it was spotted in brown, but knew there wasn't. Elrik didn't seem to think he was special, and maybe he wasn't; maybe there were plenty of freckled men and women down in the south-lands beyond the Frost Wall, but she had seen the appreciative looks her fellow countrywomen had given him. Coupled with refined masculine features, a nice, lean amount of muscle, and those green eyes when he was awake, he made her body ache, he was so extraordinary, so handsome.

But it was his personality that made her heart race. Arasa had been raised to be a strong person; she needed an equal in her life, someone who could keep up with her intellectually, work beside her in whatever she needed to do, and not be jealous of her socially. Of course, if she didn't turn out to be the firstborn, then it would be a case of her working beside *him*. There was no doubt in her mind that she could be the wife of a mage; she'd still have certain familial tasks and duties to perform, obliga-tions to the bloodline and to the nation, but she could support him in his career. If she did turn out to be firstborn, she knew it would be far easier to accept the responsibilities of being the heir with his support.

Djindji-Taje, I owe you a pouring of Suns and Moons into both your Right and Left Hands, for bringing this man into my life . . .

If it weren't for his timely aid, she would have been deep into the southern lands by now, lost, alone, and quite possibly in dan-ger, all on a misunderstanding. Walking from Ijesh to Adanjé-nal was considerably shorter than from somewhere south of the

Frost Wall. By caravan route, it was a distance of ten *selijm*, the distance a man could walk on foot in ten hours. But for those who knew the route through the mazelike crevasses connecting the two cities, there was a path that would take only seven hours, whether on foot or on horseback; its only drawback was that the way was too narrow for the bulky loads of most caravans to pass.

Both routes passed through patches of sand where the sand-demons could burrow. Only a few things could discourage the creatures from tunneling wherever they willed: hardpan desert, where the earth was baked so hard that it was difficult to dig even a few inches down; the tough, deep-rooted grass that grew at the verges of the typical desert oasis; arm's-length tiles of stone and pottery pounded into the ground with no more than a thumb's-length of space between them; and sowing the soil with powdered silver. The lattermost option was too expensive for most to implement. Cities, towns, villages, and even the lowliest farmer's holding were walled, with broad stone thresholds at their entrances, too broad for sand-demons to feel safe about crossing. They were often carved with repelling runes, too, and well worth the expense, since a carved rune could easily last for generations.

But where she and her twin had to go, barefoot and weaponless, there were no grasses, no tiles, no runes, and certainly no powdered silver.

Voices pricked at her ears. There shouldn't have been anyone making noise at this early an hour; the servants generally went about their early-morning chores quietly when they knew one of the Am'n Adanjé was in residence. Arasa heard a laugh and widened her eyes in recognition: that was her twin's voice! Giving Elrik one last glance, she eased out of the bed, pulled on a burgundy silk lounging robe, and padded out of her bedchamber in search of her sister.

"I'm sure she's still asleep," she heard Kalasa say, with that lilt to her voice that said she was flirting with someone. "And if she's here, then the baths are still filled. So if you would like to join me for a bit of fun in the water . . .?"

"If she is here, and asleep, now might be the time to approach her," a vaguely familiar male voice said. They were in the front room up ahead.

Arasa stopped in confusion. *That was an odd thing to say . . . approach me while I'm asleep?*

"I don't want to talk about that." The teasing had left her sister's voice, leaving her tone flat and unhappy. "Perhaps we should just order a meal, and retire. I am tired from traveling all night."

The reminder that her sister had traveled to see her at her request spurred Arasa into moving again. Crossing the last few body-lengths, she entered the front room in time to see her sister unwinding her turban from her head. She couldn't stop the smile that spread her lips, and didn't want to; she hadn't seen her twin in more than a year. "Kalasa!"

"Arasa—it's been too long." Abandoning the length of linen on a table, Kalasa met her twin halfway, embracing her tightly for a long moment. When she stepped back, there was an odd, almost melancholic edge to her smile. She looked very much like her twin, too, having the same height, the same build, the same pale hair color. Only her eyes were different, with hints of orange flecks warming the beige. Kalasa released her twin, turning to introduce the dark blond man in the room. "You've met Hallakan, the Taje of Am'n Paikan, haven't you?"

"*Taje?*" Arasa repeated, surprised. She hadn't realized his father had passed on, leaving the leadership of his Family to him. If the law of primogeniture didn't apply to the Noble Families as well as the Royal Bloodline, she would've voted for someone else to have taken his place. She hadn't had a lot of contact with Hallakan in recent years, but Arasa did remember he had been rather arrogant about his status as a noble-born, and a little too interested in political power for her tastes. Not that it was her place to disapprove of her twin's choice in companions . . . but she did.

Of course, to be fair, most of the noble-born sons around the Empire were a bit arrogant about their birthright, and a little too interested in political power, but then most of the Families tended to jockey for a position on the Imperial Council.

Hallakan answered her implied question. "Yes; my father died of an adder bite eight months ago. It was very tragic, and unexpected," he added. "I've had the runes to our Family estate revised to include a repelling of poisonous snakes."

If Arasa remembered right, the Am'n Paikan had holdings not far from the border with Ebrin. That was where adders lived, in the northeasternmost corner of the Empire, and it could have been possible for a snake to have wandered a little farther than normal from its usual territory.

Hallakan glanced over at Kalasa, and smiled. "I wouldn't want anything to happen to our possible future Empress, after all."

At her twin's puzzled look, Kalasa blushed and held out her hand to Hallakan. She faced her sister as he clasped it. "Arasa . . . I have accepted Hallakan's offer of marriage. We'll be wed by this time next month."

Shock held her still for a moment, then Arasa moved forward, embracing her twin. "I'm . . . happy for you! Shocked, but happy—I never thought you'd settle on just one man," she teased her sister, pulling back with a grin. "He must be something special, to have captured your heart."

Kalasa smirked. "Well, let's just say I finally succumbed to his charm."

"I feel like the luckiest man in the world," Hallakan added, smiling at Kalasa and making her blush. "To be wed to the most beautiful woman in the whole world is a rare honor; she lights up my life like no one else. She is the Sunlight of her name, and all other men pale with envy that she is to be mine."

"Not every man," a voice behind Arasa stated. Elrik, clad in a deep blue lounging robe, padded into the front room. The partially open robe showed off a long strip of his chest, including the sparse scattering of his copper-red hairs and spice-brown freckles. "I prefer moonlight, myself."

One of Kalasa's brows arched up as she glanced at her twin for an explanation. Hallakan eyed the foreigner, his lip curling up slightly on one side. "A foreigner."

"Elrik, I present my sister, Taje-tan Kalasa Am'n Adanjé, and Taje Hallakan Am'n Paikan, overlord of the city of Paikan," Arasa introduced. "Kalasa, Taje, I present Mage Elrik of the Snow Leaper Tribe of Kumron, and a graduate of the Academy at Aben-hul."

"*Sajé,*" Hallakan murmured, using the commoner-honorific, and not bothering to nod his head in greeting. He was still arrogant about his social status, Arasa noted. At least her sister nodded politely.

Elrik nodded at the other man, then dipped a little lower in a half-bow to Kalasa. "Taje, Taje-tan."

"Well," Arasa said, covering up the awkward tension. "You've probably had a long journey and are tired. Why don't you go and sleep for a while, then perhaps you can come with me to the Mother Temple later this afternoon? I have something important to show you, Kalasa, something I think will clarify the succession question between us once and for all."

Kalasa and Hallakan exchanged a look, and the other woman nodded. "That would be good. I would like to hear your solution."

"I heard you had a possible one yourself," Arasa observed. "I'd like to hear it, too, after you've rested."

This time, Hallakan looked at Kalasa, but she looked away from him. "Let's discuss that later," Kalasa stated. "And I'd like to hear your solution, first. You've been gone longer than I have, after all. But it'll be after we've rested."

"Of course." Stepping aside, Arasa watched her twin leave the room, Hallakan at her heels. She caught Elrik's puzzled look and shrugged. "I can only hope her solution turns out to be a lot easier than mine. Shall we go back to bed?"

He nodded, then paused. "Arasa . . . *after* this is over, if you aren't firstborn . . . I'd like to discuss the, ah, possibility of my asking for your hand in marriage. If that's all right with you."

She flushed with pleasure, then narrowed her eyes in dismay. "And if I *am* firstborn? Are you going to run away?"

Rubbing at the back of his neck, Elrik shrugged. "No . . . but I thought that I'd leave the asking up to you, at that point. If you aren't, I'll ask. If you are, *you* ask."

It was a silly division of responsibility, one that made her want to chuckle, but she could see the logic in it. Only a man with very little political ambition would put it that way, reassuring her that he wasn't trying to marry her for her station. "Tell you what. I'll remove all doubt, and ask you, here and now: Elrik, will you give me your hand in marriage, and promise before the Gods to become my husband at some point within the near future?"

"Yes." He flushed and smiled, closing the distance between them. A light brush of his mouth against hers sealed his acceptance.

Four

Kalasa's relief slumped her shoulders and turned her voice into a sigh. "Oh, yes . . . this is *much* better than the solution I had found. We'll do this one."

Hallakan leaned over his betrothed's shoulder, frowning at the text. "*Walking* from Ijesh to the capitol? That's all you do? And 'the Land will know' which one of you is firstborn?"

"Yes," Arasa confirmed, looking up at him from the other side of the table, her hands holding the scroll open so they could read. "If it worked for the First Emperor—and it does say the Land will recognize all of his firstborn heirs—then it should work for us."

"This isn't even one of the official history-scrolls!" the dark blond man scoffed. "You said you found it in a collection of tales intended for *children* to read."

"Yet it is undeniably a part of the history-scrolls that the First Emperor *did* travel 'from the Mother Temple to the place where he made his capital,'" Arasa stated. "And that the walls of the Imperial Hall did rise up around him in proof of the Cov-

enant between him and Djin-Tajeul. Both tales are accurate in
that much detail, so why shouldn't this one be?"

"*Walking,*" Hallakan sneered. "Barefoot and weaponless,
putting your trust in a child's tale of a promise given to an ancestor, but *not* given to you! Our way is much surer—"

"We will *not* use that option," Kalasa stated sharply, cutting
him off. "I have made up my mind on that matter. It will *not* be
discussed."

"What option?" Elrik asked.

"It doesn't matter. This is the better solution. I will put my
faith in the Blood of my Family," Kalasa returned tersely.

"You would put your faith in a fool's quest," Hallakan muttered, his tone slowly sharpening with disdain. "It has been
more than six hundred years since the Covenant was first pro-
claimed, and the Flame Sea first conquered at its heart—and
it was *conquered.* The Empire has been expanded and made
strong because of the might of its warriors and the careful planning of its people. Not by putting *blind faith* in the Gods—do
not the teachings of Djindji-Taje say that the Gods will help
those that help themselves?"

"There are things about the Royal Blood that you do *not*
understand," Kalasa retorted. "Hold your tongue on the matter, or depart, so you will not be tempted to use it!"

Trouble in their oasis? Arasa wondered, glancing silently
at Elrik. He raised his brows briefly, but didn't say anything,
either. Hallakan glowered for a moment, then drew in a deep
breath and let it out, composing himself.

"I apologize. I am concerned for your safety. If you are barefoot and weaponless, anything could happen, whether it's an
attack from a sand-demon or stepping on a sharp stone. And
what if one of you *is* stung?" Hallakan asked Kalasa pointedly.

"That's why I'm going with Arasa, shod and with weapons of my own," Elrik stated. "I will not interfere, unless and until she is stung. If she is, I will catch her and carry her, until we are safe on hard rock, or until she revives. And if it is her sister who is stung, I will also—"

"—I will carry her," Hallakan interrupted. "She is *my* betrothed. My place is at her side. I presume that we'll be taking the shortcut through the canyons, the one not used by the caravans? That would cut three *selijm* off the way."

"Of course," Arasa agreed. "The important thing is to make the pilgrimage from the Womb to the Heart, to renew the Covenant by walking the Land; the exact path and its duration are not as important. Besides, even barefoot, it won't take us more than eight or nine hours to make a normally seven-hour journey, but taking the caravan road would make it more than a reasonable day's march. And I want this settled."

"Then it will be settled," Kalasa agreed, looking at the other two. "Tomorrow, we'll gather our provisions for the trip, purify ourselves with prayer and a daylight fast, then eat well as soon as night falls, sleep deeply, and begin our trek from the Mother Temple to the Imperial Hall at first light, two days from now."

From the subtle rolling of Hallakan's eyes at the part about prayer and fasting, Arasa got the feeling he was definitely not a religious man. She rolled up the scroll and returned it to its place in the latticework holding the ancient texts. "I think we should send word to Father about what our solution is, so that he can be ready to welcome us upon our arrival. And we should mark down this solution in the more commonly referenced texts, in case this problem ever comes up again."

"*After* we know it works," Kalasa cautioned her, glancing briefly at her betrothed. "I sincerely hope it does."

⌘

Riding on a horse, Elrik decided, lifted one a couple of feet off the desert floor. Which lifted the traveler just high enough to dissipate some of the heat reflecting off that floor. Unfortunately, he wasn't riding on a horse anymore. Mopping his face with a scrap of fabric drawn from his satchel, he grimaced against the glare coming from the sandy ground. For all this was midautumn, the sun was still high overhead, and the heat was becoming fierce.

Replacing the kerchief with his waterskin, he drank a couple of swallows to replace the sweat he had just shed, and envied the twin princesses. Hallakan was sweating the same amount as he, but the two women didn't seem affected by the heat—in fact, they had chosen to forgo turbans and ponchos as well as footwear, leaving them clad in sleeveless cotton shirts and sashed trousers gathered and tied at midcalf. Their gaze was focused almost entirely on the ground, watching where they placed their tanned feet. This might be a sandy stretch, which carried the potential for a sand-demon or two, but it also had crumbled bits of rock, swept about by the strong storm-winds that sometimes wracked the desert.

Hallakan, striding to the right and a little bit behind his betrothed, was watching the rugged stone walls ahead of them. This was one of the open stretches where their path crossed the winding caravan route. There weren't any burdened pack-animals, merchants, or guards in sight, but there were plenty of churned hoofprints in view. Sand-demons could be killed by crushing with a very heavy weight, like a horse's hoof or a dromid's tough-skinned foot. Unfortunately, most humans weren't strong enough for the task, since sand-demons rarely left their soft soil home;

sand-dunes just weren't solid enough to effectively stomp against. But then, the nasty beasts wouldn't stick around when a large caravan came by. The potential to be crushed was far greater than the chance to sting a victim.

Lifting his gaze away from the pale sand, Erik studied the next crevasse they had to enter. It was narrow, just big enough for someone to ride an Imperial Mare, but no bigger. If he tipped his head just right, his conical hat shaded his eyes from the glaring blue-white of the slightly hazy sky while still allowing him a view of the tops of the cliffs. The granite at this section was redder than it was back at Ijesh, and the darker color was easier on his eyes than the glare of the yellow-cream sand.

For a moment, he thought he saw something moving up there, and glanced at Hallakan to see if the other man had seen it, too. Hallakan shook his head, though. It was a slight movement, one that took a few moments to register. Not that it had happened, but that the man hadn't been looking at Elrik at the time. Hadn't known—*couldn't* have known—that Elrik was curious whether he had seen that movement as well.

Something wasn't right. Elrik knew he was being influenced by his impression of the other man: arrogant, condescending, proud, disdainful . . . suave, very charming, there was no denying that, but there was something more. That first morning, when Hallakan had argued about the strength of the Empire, he had backed off when Taje-tan Kalasa asserted herself, and then . . . he had ingratiated himself back into her good graces. Charmed her, soothed her ruffled feathers. Placated her.

Made sure she still considered him valuable enough to keep at her side.

Elrik didn't know where that thought came from, but he knew

he didn't quite trust the man. Hallakan seemed ambitious, and very interested in settling the succession, even if he didn't believe in religious texts or ancient agreements between mortals and gods. Elrik had to concede that he himself wasn't overly religious either, but his was more a matter of agnosticism; he was merely a mortal man, relatively unimportant in the grand scheme, and unlikely to be visited by the Gods of either his father's or his grandmother's peoples. But he did believe they existed, with or without any fervent worship from him personally.

Hallakan murmured something, moving to get ahead of the women as they entered the crevasse. Elrik held himself back, taking up the rear position; there was just enough room to walk in pairs, but not comfortably. Surrounded by rock, the heat felt closer, yet cooler, mostly because the cliffs were close enough to cast a bit of shade despite the height of the sun. Lifting his waterskin again, Elrik drank. When he lowered it, he saw Hallakan looking up and shaking his head slightly a second time.

Odd. Surreptitiously, using the brim of his sun-hat to shield the direction of his gaze, Elrik searched the cliffs again. Now that they were crossing hard rock that was dusted with sand too shallowly for sand-demons to feel comfortable swimming through, he didn't have to worry about one of the two women being stung.

It wasn't until several minutes later that he thought he saw movement again. Someone was following them, up along the top of the ravine. Movement to the other side, a turbaned head clad in desert shades, told him more than one person was up there. Elrik wasn't a fool. Two people, following and flanking their position, and one of their own party members shaking his head, suggested the staving-off of an ambush.

But why? Only a fool of a bandit would think their plainly

dressed party had any money, since even Hallakan had for-gone colorful silks for plain, sturdy linen. Bandits wouldn't stay their hand, but rather dump a small avalanche upon them to dig through the rubble and search all their bodies afterward. He'd seen the aftermath of similar tactics up in the Frost Wall passes.

But an avalanche would put Hallakan at risk, and he was still traveling close to his chosen princess.

A cold shiver raced up Elrik's spine, widening his eyes. There *was* another way to guarantee which woman was firstborn. He wasn't completely sure, since there was this Covenant thing and its Goddess-based magics entangled in the matter . . . but if one of the two women died, with no offspring to follow after her and cloud the issue . . . the survivor *automatically became first-born*. At least, that was the commonly held law of the king-states down in Kumron.

The thought, stark and horrible, hurried his steps. Crowding behind Arasa, he made her close the small gap that had started to grow between her and her sister. So long as they were too close together to risk an avalanche, Hallakan would be forced to continue to shake his head in negation. Unsure of just how closely he himself was being watched, Elrik didn't unclip his mage-staff from his belt, but he did grip it with his hand, focus-ing his inner energies into the crystal-studded shaft. A warding-sphere would prevent them from being attacked by falling rocks, flying daggers, or soaring arrows. It would also keep out charg-ing swordsmen, if he could gather enough energy beforehand.

Nothing happened for several more minutes, just the four of them wending their way through the narrow defile, but he didn't relax. It looked like the ravine widened up ahead into a small valley. Once they were free of a possible rock-fall, there would be other ways of being attacked. Unhooking his staff, Elrik held it close by his hip while he whispered under his breath, concentrating his magic. The Land might know and protect one of the women just ahead of him, but he didn't know which one, and he couldn't take the risk that it would protect only the firstborn of the two from its own dangers. Emperors and Empresses had been killed by the efforts of mere mortals in the past, though it was a rare thing.

With half his attention on Hallakan and half on the cliffs, he saw the moment when the turbaned lord nodded, ever so slightly. They were away from the rock walls, away from tumbled boulders that might have served as defensive shelter. Elrik snapped up his staff, releasing a rippling, spherical wave of air outward with the release of the prepared spell. It fluttered the folds of his garments, washed over the bodies of Arasa and Kalasa, tugged at Hallakan's clothes, and stopped with a *thwack-thwack* as it encountered two small arrows, off to one side. Crossbow bolts, rather.

From the angle of them, he figured they had been meant for both Arasa and himself. With the mage in their midst as dead as the princess, there would be no witnesses, and the attack could be called the work of bandits without being contradicted. Arasa glanced between Elrik and the thickened air, confusion in her eyes. Her twin blinked and frowned at the rippling air, while Hallakan glared at the spell-stuck bolts.

Eyes narrowing, Hallakan spun to face Elrik. "*You!*"

"More like *you*," Elrik retorted. "I saw you signaling to them. Who are they, your guards? Hired trash? Someone you can claim were just bandits, killing the two of us so there would be no contention for the throne, and no witnesses?"

Arasa's gaze snapped to her sister's flushed face. "*That's* what this is about. With one of us dead, the other is automatically the heir!"

"I didn't want to do it!" Kalasa protested, backing away from her twin. "But I couldn't find any other way! Not until you showed me that scroll—"

"—Oh, stop putting your faith in a bunch of tales told by the priests to keep us all 'morally responsible'!" Hallakan snapped at her. "The Gods—if there *are* any—only support Their promises on a random whim at best."

"When a firstborn dies without any heirs, the next child becomes the firstborn. That's what you were looking at, wasn't it?" Arasa asked her twin, advancing one step at a time. "I remember, now; the eldest of one of our Empresses died of a childhood disease and her brother became the firstborn heir . . . and thus the next ruler of the Flame Sea. Only in our case, it doesn't matter who is really the firstborn, because whoever survives will automatically become that firstborn. But you didn't even have the courage to make it a fair fight—a challenge, a duel!"

"I didn't *want* to kill you. I don't!" Kalasa argued, backing up. "Hallakan may not put his faith in the Covenant, but I do!"

Elrik was aware of movement along the periphery of the warding-sphere. Flicking his gaze away from the other three, he counted four, five . . . seven men surrounding them. So long as he held the barrier against them, they could not interfere, and no one could—

Steel rasped, recapturing his attention. It was Hallakan, drawing his sword. Someone *could* hurt them, someone who was within Elrik's warding-sphere. The nobleman was armed against sand-demons, as was Elrik, but Elrik needed to keep focusing his magic through his staff; he honestly didn't know if he could divide his attention well enough to keep out seven determined would-be assassins *and* fight off a man who probably knew how to use that narrow, curved blade very well. A blade that was too close to Arasa.

Elrik lunged forward anyway to try to block the blow with his metal-bound staff, but he was too far away. The blade slashed through the air—and missed. Arasa had swayed, twisting away from the blow. Almost all of the blow; the tip of the blade scored her upper arm. But to both his and Hallakan's shock, she didn't move back. Instead, she stepped in closer, ignoring the scrape and the danger.

Angered by this betrayal, Arasa snapped her hand up, grabbing the sword as Hallakan brought it back for a second strike. She stopped it before it could gain momentum with a full swing, and the sharpened edge bit in her palm as a result, but she stopped it. Stopped it, and squeezed it deeper into her hand, ignoring the aching, bone-deep pain.

"Traitor," she growled, staring into the nobleman's startled brown eyes. Blood trickled from the cut, racing down the underside of her forearm. "Traitor to the woman you would have wed, for *ambition's* sake. Traitor to her sister, to myself, who would have been *your* kin, too."

The line of crimson thickened and lengthened, more flowing down her skin as she squeezed his blade tighter, preventing him from tugging it out of her grasp.

"Traitor to our father, your undoubted Emperor! Traitor to the *Empire*, for threatening its *heirs*!" she snarled. Dark red swelled at the point of her elbow and dripped onto the hard desert ground beneath her bare feet. It impacted with a sound that all of them *felt* with their bones, as well as their ears. "*Traitor to the Blood!*"

Dirt exploded around them in a cloud of dust and grit, heralding a scraping, screeching, grating cacophony. Spires of reddish granite thrust up around them, unfurling and striking like some sea-creature's tentacles. Wincing from the bursts, squinting against the debris, Elrik heard the men on the far side of his shield yelling in fear, and saw their bodies thrashing against the solid bonds that had captured them, holding them at wrists and ankles. Inside the sphere, which was half-smothering them as it contained some of that choking grit, tendrils of stone had grabbed Hallakan by his arms and his legs . . . and they had grabbed Kalasa as well.

The sword, torn from its owner's hand, dropped from Arasa's now very bloodied grip. Her breath hissed through her teeth at the pain, and she cradled her wounded limb against her chest, trying not to cry. It hurt; her hand hurt very badly, but the greater pain was the stab-wound of her sister's betrayal. She couldn't tell whether Kalasa was telling the truth about not wanting to kill her, nor whether her sister would have suggested an honorable death-challenge, rather than this assassination attempt of Hallakan's . . . but her twin *had* considered it as an option. That hurt more than if she'd had her whole hand severed, rather than just gouged all the way to the bone.

Elrik ended the warding-sphere; it was only keeping the dust trapped inside with them, preventing any breeze from clearing the air. With their ambushers trapped by a display of magic far greater than his own, he didn't need to shield against them. Clipping his staff back onto his belt, he crossed the sand to his shuddering betrothed, digging into his satchel. He had some bandages he could wrap around the injury, embroidered with runes to cleanse and seal the wound and keep out infection while it healed.

Neither of them said a word while he gently wrapped her palm. The others cursed, coughed, and struggled against their bonds while the air slowly cleared, but none of them moved. With a hand-length's worth of solid granite wrapped firmly around their limbs, none of them were going to be able to free themselves soon, if at all. They could be dealt with later; Arasa's injury concerned the two of them right now.

When her hand was wrapped, Elrik held Arasa for a few moments. She buried her face against his chest, letting him shelter her while she tried to come to grips with what she'd done, and what must happen. Imperial law was very clear regarding the fate of undoubted traitors. But to make sure they were undoubted, they would have to be questioned. And she couldn't pass on the responsibility to another.

At some point in the future, her father would either die or step down from being Emperor, and then all the tough decisions of running the Flame Sea would be hers. Sending soldiers to fight bandits and repel border invasions would be no less difficult than deciding the fate of a person who had tried to kill her. More so, in some ways, for soldiers were loyal and obeyed their orders, trusting that their leaders would not risk their lives casually or carelessly.

Composing herself, she pulled free of his embrace and stepped back, squaring her shoulders. "Do you still have that Truth Stone on you?"

Nodding, Elrik fished it out of his bag, passing it to her. Padding barefoot across the now quiescent ground, Arasa moved to the farthest of the seven men caught and held in her stone-wrought bonds. The granite tentacles hadn't been a deliberate choice on her part, just an overwhelming need to *stop* everyone from harming her and Elrik. The Land had responded to her need, as it had responded to the need of her ancestor six centuries ago. Stepping up to the scared-looking man, she pressed the disc against his brow.

"Did you agree to help kill me and my companion? Yes, or no."

"No!"

Lifting the stone from his skin, she checked the far side. An imprint of his forehead and part of his nose blackened the white marble. He could see it, too, and struggled fruitlessly against his bonds. Moving away from him, she crossed the sandy ground to the next captive, and repeated the question as soon as the disc touched his cheek. He stayed silent, refusing to answer.

"If you do not answer, I will have to believe your answer is yes, you deliberately chose to assist in assassinating me, and with it, committed treason. I ask you again, did you agree to help kill me and my companion?"

The man stared over her head, refusing to meet her gaze, let alone respond. Arasa sighed. "Then you are as culpable as he is."

She worked her way around the ragged circle. Two of the others stated a bold, almost proud "yes," one stayed silent, and one spat at her for his answer. The last tried to plead that he had been threatened with death if he didn't comply, that he didn't know until the end that he'd been hired to assassinate a Taje-tan. When she examined the Truth Stone, Arasa found it to be almost entirely white, with only a hint of gray. Probably whatever money he had been paid for the job had enticed him just enough into ignoring the fact that he was being bought to commit a murder.

Crossing to the fallen sword, she picked it up in her uninjured right hand, carrying it by the hilt. Sand had crusted to the blade, glued there by her drying blood. She didn't bother to clean it, just held it at the man's throat and *willed* the Land to release him. The rock holding him rumbled, creaked, then shuddered and retracted rapidly under the thin layer of sand coating the valley floor. It was hardpan desert, with only an inch or two of semisoft soil on top; there were no sand-demons here. But to get out of here, he would have to cross soft, loose sand at least a foot deep, and that was where the beasts preferentially lurked.

With the would-be assassin held at the point of the blade, she ordered, "Drop your weapons and strip off your boots. Do not think to attack me. I have renewed the Covenant of Am'n Adanjé, and the Land *will* take offense, if you do."

He blinked, hesitated, then lowered his hands slowly to his belt. Unbuckling it, he dropped it and the sheaths bearing his sword and two knives at his feet. Then, lifting one leg at a time while balancing awkwardly on the other, he unlaced and removed his boots. It was a wise choice; stooping might have made her think he was reaching for a weapon. Once he stood on feet as bared as her own, she flicked the sword in her hand away from his throat.

"Leave. That way," she added, tipping her head off to the right. "Go that way, and you'll reach the caravan path within a quarter *selijm*. If you make it back to Ijesh without drawing the attack of a sand-demon, then the Gods will have forgiven you for what you tried to do . . . but do not cross my path again. Do not come back here, either. Nor seek to give these others the mercy of a swift death, or you will share their fate," Arasa added, catching him glancing at his companions, "rather than *generously* escape it."

Stumbling over his belongings, he edged around her, backed up several feet, then turned and ran in the direction she had indicated, limping a little whenever a bared sole landed on something sharp or hard.

That left her with only two more prisoners to interrogate. Moving up to the imprisoned Hallakan, she touched the Truth Stone to his face, pressing it in place as he tried to turn aside. She didn't ask him the same question as his accomplices, however. "Now that you have seen the power of the Covenant, and how the Land itself has responded to my need, declaring me the undoubted firstborn of the Royal Blood . . . will you still try to kill me, to secure my sister as the firstborn with my death?"

He didn't answer her.

Elrik moved up beside her. He had a question of his own. Now that he knew the so-called nobleman was capable of killing to gain political power, he had to know. "Did you deliberately arrange for that adder to kill your own father, securing the leadership of your Family?"

Hallakan's jaw worked for a moment, then he spat at the mage. It splattered on his victim's chest. Wrinkling his nose, Elrik wiped the spittle from the front of his poncho. A glance at Arasa showed her own jaw tightening, but not to spit; rather, she was holding back her contempt. Leaving the dark blond man, she approached her twin last of all. Kalasa seemed to be holding her breath, until the cool white disk touched the bare skin of her shoulder. She let out the air in her lungs in a rush, then spoke without prompting.

"Yes, the death of one was the only way I'd found over the last year to ensure that the survivor was the firstborn. No, I wasn't happy about that sort of solution, and yes, I prayed to Djin-Taje-ul that you'd found some other solution . . . and yes, I told Hallakan of my findings. He wanted me to challenge you as soon as I could, but I wanted to find another way, had *hoped* you had found another way."

The stone was white, unblemished when the firstborn twin

pulled it back. Arasa stared at it for a moment, then pressed it against her sister's arm again. "And if there had been no other way, what would you have done? Challenged me to a duel? Or stabbed me in the back?"

"I would have *talked* about it with you, first. I wanted to avoid fighting with you, because I knew I was the better swordswoman, and you wouldn't likely have won. Hallakan was the one pressing for me to fight you right away!"

Turning over the disc, Arasa saw a tinge of gray on the marble. It faded, and she pressed it against her twin one more time. "But you would have fought me. Tell me something. Knowing that the Covenant and its powers are just as real as all the tales we were told as little girls, that as the firstborn, I clearly have the power to command the very soil of the Flame Sea to do my bidding . . . do you still want to be firstborn?"

Kalasa didn't answer for a long moment. Only when Arasa shifted to take away the disc did she speak, and speak quickly. "Not at the expense of your life!"

The Truth Stone, when examined, was an unblemished white. Clenching her fingers around it, to the point where it dug into her flesh with a bruising pain somewhat like the throbbing of her wounded palm, Arasa made up her mind. Rock groaned, flexed, and dropped, releasing her twin. Kalasa collapsed to her hands and her knees, choking a little on the dust stirred by the retracted tendrils.

Returning to Elrik, she handed him back the marble disc, then raised her voice, addressing the remaining prisoners. "By your own actions, you have been accused of treason against the Empire. By your own words, or your deliberate lack thereof, you have testified. By Truth Stone, you have been judged, and found guilty of attempted murder of an innocent life, and attempted assassination of one of the Royal Blood, which is treason beyond all shadow of a doubt.

"Though the soil is too hard, its softness too shallow to host sand-demons for the full punishment of your crime, the law is clear: you are to be staked out spread-eagle, and left just above the desert floor, so that if you strain, you will not touch the ground. Normally, someone would be sent around to check on you, to kill any sand-demons *after* they have colonized you, so that it cannot continue to render you peacefully unconscious during its offsprings' hatchings and depredations. Though you may not be colonized by a sand-demon in this particular place . . . there are still vultures and fire-ants, scorpions and insects who will undoubtedly take their place."

A sweep of her arm, a thrust of her intent into the soil listening under her feet, and the granite pillars groaned, spreading out. They didn't shrink down, but instead lifted legs and arms until the struggling ambushers and their leader were splayed out nearly a body-length from the ground. Arasa heard her sister sob, saw Elrik shudder, but kept her will firm.

"Let these pillars stand throughout the ages, once your bodies have rotted and your bones have vanished, as a warning against any further such treachery. Don't bother crying for help; the nearest curve in the caravan path is beyond the reach of your lungs."

Without further word, Arasa strode out of the ragged circle, Elrik quickly joining her. Kalasa remained where she was for a long moment, still on her hands and knees, then came to her senses and scrambled to follow them. "Arasa, wait!"

Arasa slowed, but only by a fraction, forcing her twin to hurry and catch up with her. "What do you want?"

"What . . . what are you going to do with me?" Kalasa asked, her tone hesitant.

"Right now, I am very angry at you, that you would even *consider* killing your own twin—!" Biting back her anger, or trying to, she continued. "I do not think it would be wise for you to stand on the very soil I can command with a thought, while I am so angry with you," Arasa added tightly. "But I don't want to kill you. We may be twins, but I am very different from you, in *that*."

Kalasa flinched back from her vehemence, falling behind. Elrik passed her without a word, smart enough to know it wasn't his place to intercede. If Arasa's anger got the better of her, he might have to try, but wisely Kalasa reminded behind them, following silently in their tracks. They still had two or three more *selijm* to go before reaching the Heart of the Empire.

I began this pilgrimage with the intent of finding out which one of us is the true firstborn, Arasa thought, struggling to calm herself. *I may as well finish it, and finish renewing the Covenant of my Family, so that no one else will doubt it any further.*

A shadow crossed her vision; it belonged to Elrik, who had moved to walk beside her, since the valley floor was still wide and unhindered. They were headed for another narrow crack in the cliffs forming ragged walls around them; he would have to walk behind her then, since he didn't know the way . . . but she was grateful he was walking at her side right now. Except he was walking on her left, which was her injured side.

Glancing at the sword in her right hand, she cast it aside, letting it bounce and skitter under a tough, leafless desert bush. She didn't really need it, though it had made a tangible threat against that one would-be bandit. Crossing behind him, she offered Elrik her uninjured hand once they were even again. He didn't hesitate to clasp it, giving her his silent support. She needed his strength, for the stone-trapped men behind them started yelling again, this time for help.

Reminding herself that they had deliberately been trying to kill both her and Elrik, she kept herself moving, walking away.

⌗

Two and a half hours of walking brought them to the outskirts of the capital. Like Ijesh, it was first a view of caravans coming and going, then of rough-hewn openings in the canyon walls, then of water in aqueducts and greenery in planters, of carvings and banners and people all over. There was more in the way of stone buildings, since the valleys around the Imperial Hall were broader than those around the Mother Temple. Unlike Ijesh, the people here seemed to be expecting them, for the pedestrians and riders immediately moved out of their way, clearing a path. That path soon became a corridor as citizens young and old began to line either side of the way to the palace.

Two and a half hours of walking had also brought some equanimity into Arasa's mind about what she had done. If she hadn't carried it through, her father would have been forced to do it; the law was the law, and no one was above it, not even the Emperor himself. If he had done that for her, she would have had to rely on others to carry out such orders in the future. No, better for her to shoulder the responsibility herself; if she didn't, it would be perceived as a weakness, a bad thing to see in a ruler of such a huge nation.

The law could be changed . . . but those men would have just tried again, had she left them to live. The Truth Stone results were the proof of that. Hopefully their deaths, though gruesome, would serve to discourage others from trying again. She really didn't want anyone trying to attack her again.

Some of the people had flowers in their hands. Arasa came out of her thoughts with a blink of surprise when she saw someone tossing some of the blossoms onto the path a few yards in front of her. They weren't the only ones; more flowers had been cast down on the road ahead. She slowed in surprise, and more were added. There was only one reason for this display: someone from the palace must have spread the word that one of the twins would be selected as the true heir by the time they reached the palace. She knew it had been a source of concern for the Empire, but this much a concern, that they would seek to line her entrance as the heir with a carpet of flowers?

A cushion of cut flowers. Cut, and thus dying or dead. Not still living, not still growing. Not still part of the land. Something about that stopped her just before she reached the point where she would have to walk more on the flowers than on the age-worn paving stones under her feet. It didn't feel right, separating her skin from the Land before she had completed her pilgrimage.

Elrik glanced down at her, curious to know why she had stopped. Shaking herself mentally, Arasa gave the Land an order. The flowers and leaves rippled, parting in front of her. Not by much, just a strip wide enough for her bare feet to touch the undecorated ground. The display startled the gathered people into silence for a long moment; then the noise picked back up again, quickly growing louder than before. With the way cleared for the soles of her feet, she moved forward, Elrik at her side and her twin at her back. They could tread on the flowers; she needed to complete her pilgrimage on the Land.

The Great Dome of the Imperial Hall appeared before her. Unnaturally large, the structure soared hundreds of feet in the air, arcing above the high walls of the canyons sheltering the capital. It spanned an equally broad distance, ribbed with ornate stonework that, if legends were true, had been grown, not carved.

Having seen for herself what she could do with a thought and a bare foot on the ground, Arasa realized the legends were all true. This was the Heart, as the Mother Temple was the Womb. This was where her ancestor had ended his journey, spilled his blood upon the sand, and declared it his home.

The crowd lined the broad, shallow steps leading up to the vast Hall. Here, as below, the Land shifted a narrow path through the flowers, just enough for her to walk unhindered, but without making it seem as if she were rejecting the blooms being offered in homage. Indeed, the petals had piled high enough to tickle her ankles as she mounted the steps. Inside the great doors, nobles and servants lined the way. She padded through the corridor they had made, across the broad flagstones of the Hall floor to the shallow steps of the dais.

The top of that dais was unusual, for though its throne was carved—or perhaps shaped—from the same reddish-golden granite as the rest of the hall, the surface of the dais itself was a broad, shallow depression filled with desert sand. Now, she knew why. She could *feel* why; it was Land itself that surrounded the throne. Not quarried stone, but sand taken from the desert beyond the canyon walls. It tied the throne, and the one who sat upon it, to the whole of the Flame Sea . . . though she suspected that, without the pilgrimage in recent centuries to tie ruler and Land tightly together, it was only a long-standing tradition that had kept the top of the dais filled with the golden-cream grains.

Now she knew what awaited her.

Elrik freed his hand from hers when they reached the bottom of the steps. It wasn't his place to mount those stairs just yet, though her twin did follow in Arasa's wake; he was tactful enough to acknowledge it. Soon he would follow her up those steps, when they were married and he was her Consort, but not just yet. Kalasa showed equal tact, stopping two steps below her sister, as Arasa halted one step from the sand at the top.

Their father awaited both of them on that sand, his pale hair subtly streaked with silver, his gold-and-white robes blending into his chest-length locks. Taje-ul Melekor Am'n Adanjé looked as strong as the weathered but still graceful carvings that graced the canyon city, and just as imposing. Yet to Arasa, he was the man who had cuddled her and her sister as children whenever he could spare time from his duties. An expectant silence filled the hall as every eye watched the tableau.

"Well?" her father inquired, the single word warm with anticipation as he glanced between her and her sister.

Arasa wondered briefly how the first Emperor had managed to cut his hand, after making the same journey weaponless and barefoot. All she had was a wounded hand that had scabbed over during the last few hours of their journey. A moment later, a hand touched her elbow. It was her sister, offering her a small knife. From the shape of the hilt, it was of Kumronite manufacture, though the blade itself looked like it was silvered. Once more, Elrik had come to her aid, passing the blade up to her through her twin. Pricking the skin at the edge of the cut, Arasa held her breath and reopened the wound. Just enough to bleed in a scarlet trickle to the edge of her palm, where the liquid gathered.

"In accordance with the ancient Covenant between Djin-Taje-ul, Mother of All, and the Family Flame, the Am'n Adanjé, I spill my blood as Firstborn of the Empire, in renewal of that Covenant."

She had given some thought as to how she would prove, beyond all doubt, that she was truly the firstborn during their two-plus-hour walk. While the ability to reshape the earth itself had been considered a family legend for a long time, other abilities were not. Many members of her family could, in times of great need, whistle up a strong wind, even a whirlwind, or more commonly, calm an approaching sandstorm. They tolerated greater extremes of heat and cold, and could grab the burning end of a torch without flinching or blistering. Fire was as comfortable as ice to them.

They could also use drops of their own blood to draw forth water. All that someone born to the bloodline of Am'n Adanjé had to do was spill a drop of that blood on the ground, and they could summon up a small trickle of liquid, just enough to quench the thirst of a modest group of travelers in a place where no water had risen before; they didn't have to be firstborn. The Emperor or Empress could do more, though, supporting whole cities from the willful drops they shed. Fully one third of the cities in the Inner Desert had been founded by the spilling of royal blood.

Now, as a single drop collected, then fell to the stone under her feet, she pushed her will into it, and from it, into the Land.

With a rumble more musical than the ragged ones of before, a small bud of stone rose up through the stone at her feet. It swelled to the size of her head, then split open, unfurling into basin-shaped petals. A moment later, water gurgled up through a small hole in the center of the stone rose, spilling over and trickling down from petal to petal until it fed back into itself through a set of drain holes in the lowest petal-tiers. It was a very small piece of Covenant magic, but she didn't need to erect a whole new Hall to prove her birthright.

Rebinding her hand, she looked up at her father. "Taje-ul . . . Father . . . do you accept my claim, and my proof as your first-born heir?"

"I do." Holding out his hands to her, the Emperor guided her up to stand at his side. "Imperials of the Flame Sea, I give you Taje-tan Arasa Am'n Adanjé, my undoubted heir!"

They cheered, pleased that the succession had been settled, and a little stunned at the miracle of the miniature fountain as well. Under the cover of their chattering voices, her father murmured in her ear.

"You will have to tell me what happened in greater detail, later. Now, why does your sister look like she thinks she's in trouble?"

Most of her anger had faded, but Arasa knew not all of it had. It would take a little time for the events of midday to fade from her memory. "I think my sister would like to be sent to the Ebrinnish Court as an ambassador for a little while. To help clear her head, and ease any lingering discomfort of not being proven firstborn."

"And what of her betrothed, Taje Am'n Hallakan? I do not see him here."

"He has been judged and sentenced under Truth Stone as a traitor to the Empire, along with six others who tried to ambush me." Catching Elrik's eye, she gestured for him to mount the steps. After a moment of hesitation, the freckled mage did so, pausing to bow at the next-to-last step. "Father, this is Elrik of Snow Leaper Tribe, a mage of some skill . . . and the man who helped me solve the riddle of how to prove which one of us is firstborn. He also helped protect me against Taje Hallakan's treachery earlier today . . . and he is the man I'm going to marry, with your blessing. Elrik, this is my father, Melekor Am'n Adanjé, Emperor of the Flame Sea."

"Taje-ul," Elrik bowed respectfully, though his freckled cheeks were a little red from the proximity to royalty. He had

met with the rulers of Kumronite king-states in the course of
his work up and down the Frost Wall, but they were little more
than overly arrogant noblemen, as Hallakan had been, rulers of
cities and farms spanning mere tens of *selijm*, if with more exaggerated titles. But this was a man who commanded hundreds of
selijm and thousands of warriors. A man whose veins flowed
with the same Goddess-blessed blood as Arasa's. Even his eyes
were the same taupe shade. It was awkward, being singled out
like this . . . but at least she hadn't cast him aside.

"You saved my daughter?" the Emperor asked him, arching
a sandy blond brow. "A southlander? Why?"

For a moment, his mind was blank. Not because he didn't
know the answer, but because to the mage, it was so blatant, even
an emperor should have seen it. "Because I love her . . . and . . .
and because I would wed her even if she fed the chickens. I think
I'd *prefer* it, if she were a chicken-feeder . . . but I love her all
the same."

For a moment, Elrik feared he had gone too far. Then the
Emperor's mouth split in a grin, and a remarkably hearty chuckle
escaped his lungs. Arasa caught his hand in hers and kissed him
on the cheek, making the crowd cheer and making Elrik's face
redden until his freckles threatened to disappear. Holding her
hand, looking into her exotic eyes, Elrik didn't know what
impulse had made him glance down at that map a month ago.
But she *was* worth the fuss of an emperor and the embarrassment of a watchful nation.

Smiling, he kissed her back, and blushed again as the crowd
in the Hall roared its approval.

Unmasking

CAROL BERG

1

Water reveals truth. So Ezzarian mentors teach us on the first day of our schooling. Toss your conjured rose into a stream, and if it be but a glamored thistle or a clothed vapor, the water will unmask it. If the velvet petals float away from the thorny stem and yet fill the air with sweetness, you have worked true sorcery and not paltry illusion.

Water has caused the downfall of many a slacker among those of us training for our part in the demon war; mentors do not hesitate to throw a student and his or her creation into the nearest pool or stream to test enchantments. Not that we have so many slackers. When the gods have given your race the sublime gift of true sorcery and charged you to stand between the unwary world and the invasive evils of the rai-kirah, even the youngest students take their preparation seriously. Some of us just fail.

Of course, no heady matters of truth or illusion had sent Kenehyr and me to the pool in the Wardens' Grove that night. Spring in Ezzaria brings incessant rain and cool mists to our forests, and the completion of our day's training exercise—a difficult Search scenario that had led us through a conjured city the size of Zhagad itself—had kept us late, leaving all the temple purification to my partner and me. By the time we had cleansed ourselves, the vessels and cups, and the mosaic floor of the open-sided temple, and we had stood in the rain to complete our chants at each of the temple's five porticos, we just wanted to get warm.

"Aelis will have our heads for this," I said, already having second thoughts as I followed Kenehyr downhill through the dripping woodland toward the encarda. We named the pools "fire spouts" because the water rose from the depths of the earth so hot that all but the most foolhardy bathers used enchantments to protect their skin.

"Who's to tell her?" my partner called over his shoulder. "All the Wardens are sent off south to work with some swordmaster, and no one else dares come to their pool. My mind is set. *Hot. Bath.*"

"After my wretched performance today, she already believes me hopeless. If she hears I've trespassed a restricted grove for a bathing party . . ." *Joelle,* she would say, *are you* determined *to fail?* "She'll not allow me beyond the border until I'm thirty."

Before Searchers could begin their work to seek out those souls possessed by demons, they were required to serve an apprenticeship in the outside world. Those few months ensured that our long years of training in investigation, languages, customs, geography, and sorcery could be brought to bear not only in conjured scenarios, but in real cities and villages . . . amid strangers who knew nothing of the dangers that threatened them . . . amid filth and corruption . . . in places where Ezzarians were known as naught but odd barbarians from the forests beyond the southern mountains. But before we were allowed to cross the Ezzarian border we had to pass five rigorous days of testing.

I was already two-and-twenty, the age at which most of the power-born had taken up their duties in the war, and I held superior proficiency in every Searcher's discipline, even the physical skills that often posed difficulties for women. Yet every time I attempted a full testing scenario, my carefully constructed enchantments collapsed. Had we been on real missions instead of training exercises, Kenehyr could have died for my errors and the victim remained in thrall to the rai-kirah. I should be studying, practicing, working to rid myself of flaws. My mentor would rightly reprimand me for this frivolity.

"How are we to do this?" I said, hopping over a fallen branch to catch up with Kenehyr. "Polluting an encarda with clothes would compound—"

"We'll shuck them. We can take turns, if you insist, or I'll close my eyes while you get in. For certain, *I've* little to hide." Pale light gleamed from my partner's hand as he left the path, slipping and sliding down a steep embankment. His laughter rippled through the night like a swarm of glowflies.

I sighed. There would be no dissuading him. Kenehyr could work exquisite spells. With his Comforter's enchantments, he could create mind links over vast distances, binding a possessed victim to those who could rid the ravaged soul of its demon. He could also sing like a lark, could craft riddles and puzzles with the finest minds in Ezzaria, and would stand fast at a friend's shoulder until the end of time. But he could only hold one thought in his head in any instance. Once he had set his focus, holy Verdonne herself could not budge or distract him. He was going to the encarda. Unless I was willing to give him up to Aelis or lie to her, I might as well follow.

"At least slow down and stay quiet," I said, yanking at my sodden skirt as it snagged in the gooseberry thicket. "A quiet trespass seems somehow less heinous than a noisy one. Perhaps it will make me feel better."

"Not as much better as the pool will leave you. You take life much too seriously, Searcher." He paused to wait for me, his dark eyes merry in his round face. Slight, soft, and smooth-skinned, he might have been a boy of twelve. But indeed he had lowered his voice and dimmed his handlight.

Kenehyr refused to proceed with his own testing until I could be ready, which left my failures more of a guilty burden. Whatever victims of the rai-kirah he might succor—the Suzaini merchant who would one day come home from his shop in an inexplicable rage and murder his wife, or the kindly Manganar woman who dreamt of burning her fields and her children, or the Derzhi lord who could feel the urge at any moment to flay his slaves—must hold out against their creeping madness because Kenehyr was not yet available to bring them help. Because his partner was as thickheaded as a talentless tenyddar.

"Tomorrow I'm going to persuade Aelis to pair you with someone else," I said abruptly. "I swear it."

"Silly girl, what pairing would suit better?" He held a dripping fir branch so it would not slap me in the face. "Kenehyr, who cannot see, if he happens to be eating, nor hear, if he happens to be working magic; and Joelle, who can juggle complex sorcery, maps, cities, languages, weapons, demon signs, signal messaging, and a victim's contentious family members, while yet taking time to glory in the fine weather. We are *meant* to be together just now, partner fair." Then he smiled in that way he had, as if he knew some magical secret that even our mentors had not guessed.

The night seemed deeper as we descended into the grove, where the boles of the oaks grew thicker than five men could circle with their arms, and the scent of sulfur tainted the damp. As we slipped through creeping wood sorrel and the knee-high larkstongue that would bloom in brilliant blue spikes come summer, I found myself spreading small enchantments to mute the sounds of our passing, as if we were engaged in yet another training exercise that required a stealthy approach.

As we neared the heart of the grove, I laid my hand on Kenehyr's shoulder to slow him and on his lips to quiet him. With a quick gesture, I summoned finer senses, stretching my hearing through the trees. Hurried, muffled footsteps approached the pool from the far side. Someone besides two cold, wayward students intruded here. Yet the Wardens were in the south, and their training grounds were forbidden to all others . . .

We Ezzarians kept well hidden in our forests, safely tucked away behind the craggy barrier of the mountains so that we could prepare for our difficult work unhindered by the common wars and politics of those we protected. We remained ever on the alert for intruders, especially in this particular settlement, so near the mountains. Strangers could bring corruption—paths for unseen demons to insinuate themselves into our ranks.

Pressing Kenehyr to wait behind an ash, I slipped forward, loosening the dagger sheathed at my waist and readying my supply of defensive enchantments. A Comforter's safety was his Searcher partner's responsibility.

I settled onto the spongy litter of the forest floor and crept to the boundaries of the clearing at the grove's heart. A man stood bent over beside the steaming pool, heaving deep breaths and resting his hands on his knees as if he'd been running. A lantern, hung from a branch, suffused the rising steams and mist with a golden glow, as if this were divine Valdis himself come to the Wardens' Grove.

He straightened, unknotted his belt, and pulled off his common brown tunic and shirt, easing my concerns. The straight black hair cropped about his face and neck, the copper hue of the skin he was rapidly baring, and the slight angle to his dark eyes named him wholly Ezzarian. Long arms and shoulders knotted with muscle, his lean face intelligent and intense, he was the very image of a Warden—a warrior destined to step into the living landscape of a possessed soul and do battle with demons.

Odd that I didn't recognize him, though. A scar marred one high cheekbone. His black brows angled downward more than most. And surely I would remember that long, clean jawline. As one of the power-born of Ezzaria, I had been schooled with most of the student Wardens, certainly those near my own age as this man was, and certainly all who trained here in the northern forests. Who was he?

He stripped off his boots, breeches, and leggings, though not without a glance about the grove, as if to make sure none witnessed his brazen immodesty. My own cheeks heated. Yet, indeed, my eyes refused to look away. A man's body was so . . . different.

This had seemed such a harmless adventure when Kenehyr had proposed it, and I'd been so tired and cold and discouraged. Now here I was, shamelessly intruding on a man's privacy.

He dropped to one knee, calmed his breathing, and bent his head. Spreading his arms wide, he murmured words I could not distinguish. Prayers. Fire's daughter! What if he was no student, but a true Warden, purifying himself after a demon battle?

Dismay, embarrassment, and self-reproach scorched my heart.

To intrude on a man when he was trying to put his world back in balance, to reconnect himself to sanity and light and the gods, was inexcusable.

When he rose and stepped into the pool, I jumped up, intending the splash and his immersion to cover my retreat. But he had scarcely dropped beneath the steaming surface when he lunged right back out again with a choked cry. Coughing and gasping, he crawled away and huddled in a quivering, dripping knot, his curved spine rigid with pain.

Abandoning caution, I sped across the clearing and dropped to the flat rocks beside him. "Master Warden, do you need help? Could I fetch someone?"

Before my concern was half spoken, he bounded to his feet, snatched up his clothes, and backed away, knocking the lantern with his head. His face could have fired my father's kiln. "Goddess mother!"

"Forgive my intrusion," I said, bowing my head so as not to embarrass him further. The yellow light danced wildly on the wet rocks. "When I saw—I thought you must be injured."

"Why have you come here?" he said, his voice harsh.

"No excuse but curiosity, Master Warden," I said, my cheeks aflame, my stomach curdling in humiliation. I stood and folded my hands properly at my back, keeping my eyes averted. Gods, I felt like a chit scarce out of reading school. But lying was useless—Kenehyr couldn't lie if his life depended on it—and more complete truth would only compound my offense. "I've never seen a man's body . . . entire."

The choking noise that followed this confession sounded distressingly close to laughter. "What is your name?"

Humiliation slid toward despair. He'd never ask so personal a question unless he planned to report my violation.

"Joelle, sir. My mentor is Aelis of the Searchers."

"Power-born!" His shock erased my last hope. What might be excused for one of lesser responsibility would not be ignored in my case. "Well then . . . go on. Get out of here."

"Of course." I spun in place and marched away, attempting to retain some dignity. Spying on a Warden . . . sweet Verdonne . . . I'd be forty before I got into the war. Forty! What a damnable, rotten, horrid day.

Kenehyr met me at the verge of the trees. "Stay out of sight, fool," I mouthed through clenched teeth.

"He's not going to see me," said my partner at a volume that had me cringing. "He's gone."

I whirled about. Naught remained but steam and mist and the swaying lantern.

Every hour of the following morning, as I reviewed Kuvai dialects for our next exercise, I expected to be summoned before a mentors' tribunal or at least before Aelis herself. I spent the afternoon sparring with another aspiring Searcher, and when we broke for water and rest, Kenehyr waited in the doorway of the practice arena. My heart faltered.

"Shall we try again for our hot bath?" he said, all innocence. "We could rendezvous at midnight."

"Absolutely not," I said, pushing past him so I could sit on the bench outside in the welcome sunlight. "There are reasons for the rules. Everyone deserves privacy for their prayers and cleansing, Wardens most of all. We trespassed for naught but childish amusement."

Kenehyr joined me on the bench, instantly sober. "We may be students, Joelle, but we are not children. Enjoyment is no betrayal of our purpose. Besides"—his more usual mischief sparked his eyes—"the fellow wasn't exactly following the rules either. His hands were filthy. Some of us who are not constructed so ... advantageously ... as Wardens, *do* manage to keep ourselves clean at the least. Or perhaps you didn't notice his *hands*."

"Begone with you, troublemaker," I said, shoving him stumbling off the bench, resenting the laughter he raised in me. "Aelis is bringing some retired Warden to assess my knife work next hour. The last thing I need is a fool's distraction."

As it happened, I *hadn't* noticed the Warden's hands—a matter that disturbed me almost as much as hearing they were dirty. A Searcher must stay alert for even the smallest details. What kind of Warden would bring dirty hands—the very emblem of corruption—to a sanctified pool? And I had felt sorry for the man!

⟡

My mentor, Aelis, relished hammers. Whenever she was not teaching in the temple or the practice arena, one could find her engaged in some building project about our settlement, whacking away at a loose joist or asserting her mastery over shingles or beams. Her father was a carpenter, one of the eiliddar or skillborn—those judged to have too little talent for sorcery to stand in the forefront of the rai-kirah war as Searchers, Comforters, Wardens, or the like. My own parents were eiliddar too, my father a potter, my mother a spelltasker whose small enchantments kept my home settlement free of vermin.

All Ezzarian children were tested at age five to determine their natural level of melydda or talent for sorcery. Though all attended reading school together, valyddar—the power-born, like me—were immediately assigned mentors and guidance to determine our true calling. The skill-born apprenticed in crafts or teaching or spellmaking, whatever fit their particular skills and interests. Those few of us born without melydda—the tenyddar or service-born—left school at ten and were assigned to work the fields, care for beasts, hunt game, or the like.

Early on the hazy morning two days after the ill-fated venture to the Wardens' Grove, I found Aelis repairing a fence around her brother-in-law's horse pasture. Using a hefty sledge, she slammed an iron wedge into the end of a log as I crossed the field to join her. No man could deliver blows with more authority. The crack split the rail near halfway down its length.

"You should be writing your review of your last exercise," she said by way of greeting. "Your investigation was flawless. Not one in twenty Searchers would have discovered that the child had slain her father. And the wards you wove to keep Kenehyr and the child hidden from her mother and her clansmen were inventive and perfect. But you must explain why they failed in the end. I cannot take you further until you understand it."

I blotted my face with my damp sleeve. "I've not come about the exercise, mistress, or about me at all . . . or at least not with regard to my studies . . . or failures. It's about someone else. Of course, it was my own fault for being there, and I'll accept the consequences, but I cannot let it go . . . because of the risk. It's about a Warden . . ." Aelis rested her arms on the fence as I told her of the encounter.

I had wrestled with the dilemma through two long nights. The Warden had not reported me. He had been hurt . . . and grieving, I thought, as his cry echoed in my memory. Yet of all Ezzarians, Wardens must avoid the least taint of corruption, lest the demons they fight gain a foothold in their own souls. And though failure to report a petty trespass was a small matter—and polluting clean water with dirty hands only slightly worse—we were taught that small corruptions could signal larger ones. Even if it meant restriction or dismissal, I could not ignore his violations to hide my own. The threats we lived with were very real.

"I don't know of any Wardens who've come to our temple to work of late," Aelis said when I finished my tale. "We've not so many in all of Ezzaria that his identity should be a mystery."

"He's none I've met, mistress." At least her concern bolstered my wavering conviction. The tale had sounded so silly.

"I'll discuss the matter of the Warden with Galadon." Swiping at the mixed gray and black strands of hair the damp had stuck to her knotted brow, she reached for her sledge. "Were you a child, Joelle, I would restrict you to your quarters outside your training time. As it is, I need to give deeper thought to the consequences of your actions. For now, resume your studies."

✧

Though I returned straightaway to the house where I'd been fostered since coming to train with Aelis, I made very little progress on my assignment. In a dismal fret, I mulled what I might do with myself should Aelis recommend termination of my training.

At midmorning, a pounding on the door announced a runner. "A Searcher is returned from Azhakstan and is resting at the Weaver's," said the slim girl who proudly wore the woven belt of the Weaver's official messenger. "He'll share news in the schoolhouse at noontide."

My skin prickled with excitement. The visit of a countryman newly returned from the outside world was not to be missed. Fresh news, new books, tales of adventure . . . Everyone in the settlement would be there. "Thank you, Cadi," I called after the child, as she ran off to the next house. "Wish your mother a fruitful day for me."

But I had scarce donned my cloak when my conscience got the better of me. Kicking the door shut, I sat down to work again, forbidding myself diversion until I understood why I kept failing at the thing I desired most in the world.

Throughout the long afternoon, I sketched diagrams, wrote explanations, explored alternatives, seeking some imperfection that could have caused the test to collapse. The whole scenario had been fraught with risk. Such dire evils. So many people involved. Every decision I had made in the ill-starred exercise had been designed to protect Kenehyr and to secure the young Derzhi victim and her family. The child's mother could not be allowed to know that her young daughter had actually done the murder, lest she slay the child and free the demon. The members of her clan who lived close by must be kept out of the way, especially the girl's brother and the clan warriors; children and those who lived in violence were especially vulnerable to a displaced demon. With ruthless precision I had constructed barriers of enchantment to warn of intruders, to disguise our activity, to deflect physical and spiritual attacks. I had turned myself inside out to be certain of every detail. But at the end, as Kenehyr laid hands on the child to trigger his linking magic, the girl had cried out in fear for her dog, of all things. My impregnable circle had collapsed, the clan warriors had seen us, and the rai-kirah had taken warning. I thanked holy Verdonne yet again that the disaster had been but a grand illusion. A roused demon could have ravaged both the child's soul and Kenehyr's.

I tapped my pen on the smooth oak table, then threw the implement across the tidy room. Perhaps I should resign myself to cooking or repairing clothing or digging vegetables like an unschooled tenyddar. What use having "extraordinary melydda" if you caused more harm than you healed?

Another knock on the door roused me from my uneasy meditation. "The Weaver summons you to meet with her and Aelis, Joelle," said the solemn Cadi, her cheeks flushed. "Just after lamp-lighting, if you please. And you are not to speak of this summons to anyone."

Why were they making the meeting secret? And what did the Weaver have to do with anything? A village Weaver did not involve herself in matters of mentoring or discipline. My heart sagged into my stomach as Cadi vanished into the stand of white-trunked birches. They would not dismiss me for trespassing. They could not.

2

As the evening mists began to rise, I hurried out of the wood and cut across a soggy pasture toward the whitewashed reading school, the records house, and the Weaver's cottage. Stragglers called greetings to me as they strolled down the main track from the gathering at the schoolhouse back to their homes or work.

Ezzarians built their homes and temples deep in the forest, clustered together where the abundant life fed our power for sorcery, and each of these unnamed settlements chose a Weaver as its guardian. Though always a woman power-born, she did not stand in the war or fight demons directly. Rather she wove protective enchantments into the trees—wards that would rouse us when intruders, especially unseen demons, entered the wood. Only the Weaver slept outside these protected boundaries, lighting her lamp each eventide to assure all that her wards held secure.

Though I returned their waves, I did not join my friends and neighbors to share news, as I would on any other day. A glimpse of Kenehyr engaged in conversation at the schoolhouse door sped my steps across the road. Kenehyr could sniff out a secret from a doorpost.

Unfortunately my partner caught sight of me and met me as I swung my legs over a sheep fence. His black tunic was sweaty and his chin-length hair disheveled. An angry scratch reddened his cheek.

"Is your conscience sufficiently eased, partner fair? Gruffyn says I'll spend the next sevenday sparring as reward for our midnight trespass." Kenehyr hated combat training, and his mentor knew it.

"I didn't mention your name," I mumbled. "I just needed—"

"Spare me your reasons!" he said. "I can reconstruct them for myself. So what is to be *your* penance? Let me hear it, so I can take some satisfaction as Gruffyn chases me about the arena with sharp objects."

"I'm left to stew," I said. "I would far rather be fighting. After an entire afternoon working at it, I've come up with exactly no way I could have prepared for the dog. I thought perhaps I would find Aelis here and talk to her again."

He shrugged tiredly. "She's gone into the Weaver's house with the Searcher."

"Oh . . . well then . . ." I stammered, relieved that I'd not need to lie to him. "I suppose I'll go there to find her."

"Shall I accompany you, lest she have her favorite hammer to hand?" A smile twitched the corner of his mouth as he nudged my shoulder with his. "You know I'm not *so* angry."

"No! I mean . . . I need to face up to this myself. If they're going to dismiss me, then I must come to terms with it on my own."

"It won't come to that, partner fair. You just haven't found your way yet. But I've faith that you will. Only for you would I put up with another year of Gruffyn."

I kissed him for that. Right in the middle of his damp, grimy cheek. Right in front of every passerby who would be scandalized at such unseemly behavior between two not married. But no woman had ever had such a partner . . . such a friend. And, truly, it cheered me inordinately to walk on to the Weaver's house, leaving Kenehyr with his mouth open and naught coming out of it.

I worried sometimes that Kenehyr might feel some . . . fervor . . . for me that I had not experienced for him as yet. For me, the disciplines of training—the need to stay clearheaded—precluded such personal indulgence. Yet, if we chose to marry, as happened with many pairings who worked out in the world, I took comfort that holy Verdonne herself could offer me no better man.

∽

The Weaver's lamp hung from the eaves of her stone cottage, alongside drying fleeces dyed blue and red. Its new-lit fire washed the oaken door with gold, as Dai herself answered my knock. Her cheeks crinkled in pleasure, deepening the fine lines about her coal-dark eyes. "Welcome, Joelle. Come in. Come in. Too long has it been since you've come to weave with me."

All power-born Ezzarian girls learned to weave. The rhythm and intricacy of it teaches much of spellmaking. Anyone could understand that. But I found it a tedious craft and could never guess what colors and patterns might appeal to anyone.

"Blessings of evening and springtime, Dai. I'm sorry to have neglected to visit, but my head is jammed full of work just now. Soon, perhaps, I'll have more time for other pursuits." Too soon, if Aelis had given up on me. A friend had told me that Dai had once trained to be a Searcher. Perhaps she had failed, too.

Gold glints in the Weaver's eyes seemed to pop against my skin like sparks from a bonfire. "When the day comes you feel the need, I will delight in welcoming you back to the loom."

Dai drew me into a warm room smelling of tea and splashed with color. Rugs of scarlet and goldenrod softened the stone floor. Cushions of emerald and indigo graced the wooden chairs and benches. And all the colors of Ezzaria—the amber of our barley fields, the myriad greens of our woodlands, the pure white of our stone temples, and the variegated hues of our magics—lived in the vibrant threads of the weavings that covered the gray walls.

Aelis glanced around when I walked in. Her scuffed leather breeches and muddy boots hinted she'd come directly from her fence-mending. Beside her stood a square-jawed Ezzarian of middle years—the visiting Searcher, I guessed. Gray had touched his dark spiky hair, yet his shoulders and chest were broad, and his belly tight and flat like that of a younger man. His sun- and wind-scoured face spoke of long sojourn in Azhakstan, the desert land of the Derzhi horse warriors. He was no one I knew.

"This is the student who encountered the unidentified man," said Aelis, returning her attention to someone seated behind her. "She is quite capable of all we require. But I still believe someone more experienced—"

"We need young people clearly in their prime," said their hidden companion, a woman. "Encountering them in a homely setting will lure him into the trap, make him confident. We must give our quarry no reason to doubt his conclusions. Too old and he will suspect deception. Too young and he will blame immaturity. And we've no time to recall a person with the proper skills, the proper age, and more experience."

Dai nudged me gently toward the others. Their conversation had already confused me, but when I recognized their seated companion as the queen of Ezzaria, I was completely confounded.

"Blessings of evening, Lady," I said, when I recovered my wits enough to stop gaping. "I'd no idea you were come to our vale."

"Blessings of evening and springtime, student."

Queen Tarya, her black braids twisted tight about her head, welcomed me with a frankly examining eye and an outstretched hand. Though her short, thick fingers were stained with blue dye, as if she had been working alongside the Weaver, their solid, confident warmth spoke the language of pent power. In every way, our queen lived as any one of us, yet the conduct of the demon war—the safety of the world—rested in those woad-stained hands. Power, intelligence, and determination, not birth or family, brought an Ezzarian queen to her office.

"I understand you did not attend Evrei's gathering this afternoon," she said. "I should think an aspiring Searcher would be eager to hear his tales."

"Of course I wished to attend, Lady," I said. "But I felt obligated to work on my studies. To abandon work for sheer enjoyment seemed—" I broke off, my cheeks heating when I realized how foolish I sounded. How could I name hearing news of the world frivolous, when my greatest desire was to serve humanity's cause by living in that same world?

My mentor's bony face hardened in disappointment. "I told you of her flawed judgment, Lady."

"Overzealous studying is not an *insurmountable* flaw, Aelis." The queen's wry smile discounted every report I'd heard of her inflexible sobriety and earned my dearest gratitude.

Politeness bade me speak to the Searcher, who had raised his wiry brows and pursed his lips in amusement. I placed my fist on my heart and closed my eyes. "*Lys na* Joelle, Master Searcher," I said, offering him my name in trust.

"I am honored, Joelle," he said, bowing politely and placing his fist over his own heart. "*Lys na* Evrei." Though Tarya had already spoken his name aloud, his gift gave me permission to address him by it. Names held immense power, giving entry to the soul. Rai-kirah used them to enthrall the unwary.

"My apologies, Master Evrei," I said. "I *did* wish to hear your reports, but I've reached an unhappy impasse in my work and chose to hammer away at the problem while the events were fresh in mind. Naught but foolish pride, I think."

"I understand," he said, gravely. "Mistress Aelis, if you think I might be of some assistance with Joelle's training while I remain in country, please let me know. Such talents as I've heard described should not be left idle."

Aelis nodded, her lips thin as willow whips. *Talent,* she would say, *is no measure of success.*

Tarya waved us impatiently to the benches drawn up near her. "Searcher Evrei has brought disturbing reports from Azhak-stan, Joelle," said the queen, once we were settled among the bright-woven cushions. "We need your help to counter a threat to our borders. Are you willing to interrupt your training to aid in such work?"

"Of course," I said. "If you and Mistress Aelis agree . . . if you think . . . if I could possibly be useful." *My* help?

Tarya accepted a cup of tea from the Weaver. "Evrei, if you please . . ."

The Searcher leaned forward, forearms braced on his knees, his big, well-scrubbed hands clasped loosely between. "In summary, the sleeping giant to our north is stirring. Half a year ago, the Derzhi Emperor commanded his son Ivan to subjugate the kingdom of Hollen, as he had tired of tithing to the factors who control grain shipments through Holleni seaports. Hollen fell in less than a month. Rumors have long hinted that Prince Ivan has a yearning for glory and an iron hand. Reports out of Hollen confirm it. When Kozur joins his fathers, Ivan will be a different kind of emperor. Restless. Dangerous. He casts his eyes beyond the Empire's borders, while gathering loyalties from their most powerful clans and most influential factions . . . such as the Derzhi Magicians' Guild."

Now I felt the shiver of true danger. Few people in the world besides Ezzarians bore any trace of melydda . . . a seer or hedge-witch here or there, a woman who worked healing potions, a man who predicted the weather . . . But among the horse clans of the Derzhi had grown up this clique who named themselves magicians. Most of their work was sleight of hand and common trickery, but a few possessed talent enough to generate impressive illusions.

Such insignificant power was no threat to our work. But their jealousy . . . Reports said the Guild ruthlessly hunted down rumors of sorcery within the Empire and eliminated the practitioners, lest their own prestige be diminished among the horse clans. Searchers and Comforters who worked inside the Empire were extremely careful never to leak hints of their talents and never to cross paths with the Guild.

"And so to our current problem," said Queen Tarya. "The problem Evrei did *not* report to today's gathering."

"On my journey home, I rested one night at a hostelry in Karesh," he continued, speaking mostly to me. "So near our border I pay close attention to the other guests. When I noted two men wearing the yellow badge of the Guild on their vests, I paid *especial* attention. The two were awaiting a third companion who had been assigned to 'cross the mountains and assess the nature of barbarian sorcery.' They marveled at their companion's talent at 'impersonation,' such comments leading me to believe that he can craft an appearance very like to ours."

A kiss of mountain winter stung my skin. "The man I saw in the Wardens' Grove! Verdonne's child, do you think he was a Derzhi spy?"

"We must not ignore the possibility," said Tarya. "You saw this Warden come out of the water, did you not? Was he changed . . . unmasked . . . by the pool?"

I closed my eyes and recalled the stern face that had glared at me through the mist and lamplight. The copper skin and black hair. The dark, wide-set eyes. His body's speech expressing pain and embarrassment, not arrogance or apprehension. "When he came out of the water, his back was to me, and he looked up only when I spoke. Yet I would swear on my mother's head no change had occurred. He appeared true Ezzarian, Lady."

"And what were the nature of his enchantments?"

I blinked, and my stomach knotted. "I don't think—I mean, I didn't sense any enchantments. I was—I can't say."

A Searcher's senses must remain ever alert to spellworking without one thinking constantly about it. On any stroll through the village, the common wards and spells brushed my skin like a cat's fur tickling my ankles. Had the man truly used no enchantment to enter the pool, or had I, distracted by the sight of him, merely failed to perceive it?

Aelis sighed and kneaded her brow with two fingers. "Try to remember, Joelle. If he can maintain his appearance through immersion or with undetectable enchantment, we have an entirely more serious matter than unmasking an illusionist."

The human face was highly resistant to change. To mask it with illusion was difficult. To alter it with true sorcery—a transformation of the features—was one of the most difficult of all workings, a level of sorcery we did not believe existed outside a very few of our own practitioners.

"I'm sorry," I said, chagrined. "My memory tells me he was Ezzarian and used no enchantments at the pool. But I cannot swear to it." I rose, expecting that my usefulness was ended.

"Sit down, girl," said the queen. "Your lapse of attention means only that you've no choice but to engage in this venture. You *would* recognize the face you saw?"

"Indeed yes, Lady." Straight-backed, I sat again, trying to cool my flaming cheeks.

"Your mysterious Warden may or may not be the Derzhi spy." The queen pinned me to my seat with her black gaze. "But in either case, we face a dilemma. To seek out this spy and slay him for naught but possibility is blatant murder, a corruption of our values and purposes that I cannot allow. Yet to permit a member of the Magician's Guild to wander Ezzaria and gain any idea of our true capabilities risks our safety from this day forward in increasingly dangerous times . . ."

". . . and so we must deceive him and send him back misinformed." My conclusions took voice as if Tarya had dug them out of my head and dropped them in my lap.

The queen looked satisfied and turned to the others. "Dai,

the Weavers must account for the possibility that the spy is already among us, as well as the possibility that he is on his way through the mountains—a much more difficult task than we thought."

The Weaver stood, arms folded, behind Aelis. "Weavers' wards throughout Ezzaria can be tuned to direct the spy wherever you wish. He will believe he chooses his own path."

"And you say you've chosen a reliable subject to bait our trap?"

"The young man I've recommended is eager to help and quite intelligent."

"It is more important that he be obedient," said the queen.

"That is unquestioned. It is his life he offers." Dai's response was uncharacteristically curt. Again the gold sparks from the Weaver's eyes pricked my arms like spiders' feet, though we no longer stood near her great lamp.

"Just so. We will be very grateful." The queen accepted Dai's implied rebuke in astonishingly equable fashion. Tarya might dye her own wool and clean her own kitchen, but her decisions were our law. I'd never imagined village Weavers holding much place in her councils.

"Aelis, you will prepare Joelle," said Tarya. "Evrei, you will instruct the tenyddar in his duty. Here is our plan . . ." As I listened in increasing dismay, my sovereign queen laid one Ezzarian man's life and our land's security in my incapable hands.

3

"**Dai** vouches strongly for this man," said Aelis as we halted at the edge of the trees. We overlooked a soft fold of the green foothills, where a thatch-roofed hut squatted beside a tidy field of vegetables—straight rows of cabbage, feathery carrots, onions, and numerous other plants I could not identify so early in the season. The vale smelled of mud and spring greenery and the deep, clear stream that watered its length. "Evrei reports that he seems steady, understands his duty, and will yield to your direction. But he *is* tenyddar—ever a risk for corruption. You must be vigilant. Tell him no more than necessary."

Having no melydda of their own, the service-born could shape no internal barriers against demon infestation or nefarious enchantment. It was no fault of theirs, only unfortunate truth.

"Was he told that I am . . . untested?" It seemed only fair to inform a man standing on the verge of a cliff that the person holding his rope had a habit of losing her grip. My stomach had not stopped gnawing itself for the entire revolution of night and day since Queen Tarya had given me my mission.

"Evrei told him you were Searcher-trained and would arrive by sunset. No more." My mentor grabbed my shoulders and swung me around to face her. I thought her fingers might leave holes in my bones. "I did not favor your selection for this task, Joelle, yet you possess every skill necessary to succeed. Your failures are not bound up in your talent, but in your fears. You arrive at the point of commitment and withhold."

"But I—"

"The queen believes that the reality of responsibility will push you to the final step. I pray her insights are keener than mine. Now go. The Weavers' web may already be drawing our quarry to this place. Search your heart and mind. Practice and be ready. And if your test comes, hold back nothing."

"I'll do my best, mistress. I swear it."

"I know you will." She laid her bony hands on my cheeks,

kissed my forehead, and smiled kindly. Yet the ridges of worry on her brow did not soften, for the same reason my stomach ached as she disappeared into the forest. When had I ever done less than my best?

Thunder rumbled from the mountains. The granite ramparts that shielded Ezzaria from the violent world seemed to have moved closer in our few hours' walk from the settlement. The gray masses covered half the northern sky, mists coiling upward from green notches and rifts that seamed the lower slopes. I shifted the pack on my shoulders to ease the bite of the straps, and hoped the rain would hold off until I reached shelter.

Did not favor your selection . . . your fears . . . you withhold . . . Aelis's judgment dogged my steps as I tramped through thick wet leaves of burdock and milkweed that left my boots and leggings soggy. Halfway down the steep hillside, a rock rolled out from under my foot, and I stumbled and hopped to keep my balance, twisting my ankle. The next rock I encountered, I kicked out of the way. And the next.

Aelis was wrong. Of course I was afraid—of demons, of violence, of death. What shame in that? We were taught not to throw our lives away. But I had never shaped a plan around my own safety. Everything I wanted in the world was to serve in the demon war . . . to crush the rai-kirah who distorted human lives so dreadfully . . . to prevent the horrors they wreaked.

The mist settled into a light rain. The hut was situated slightly above the field, atop a modest knoll beyond the stream. Crossing the field instead of going around clotted my boots with muck. And then my slimed boots skidded on the bridge of twin logs, near toppling me into the deep-flowing water. By the time I reached the top of the knoll and faced the thatch-roofed hut, its neat wood stacks, and the open shed that covered piled crates and casks, a worktable, barrows, and tools, frustration had me near bursting.

I reminded myself that another human being awaited me—a man powerless and barely schooled, who must depend upon my talents and judgment for his life. I marched up the well-trod path and rapped on his door, straightening my back. The least I could do for the fellow was demonstrate a bit of confidence. "Greetings of evening!"

The soft rain whispered in the thatch. Down below a fish plopped in the stream. A shiver raced up my back. Sweet Verdonne, what if the spy had arrived early?

With the proper techniques, those of us power-born could choose to extend the range of our senses, even without the interplay of sorcery. But even heightened hearing could detect neither a scritch nor a breath from within. Summoning a blasting spell to one hand and a light to the other, I pressed down on the iron latch with my wrist and nudged open the door. "Greetings of evening . . ."

My handlight thrust back the shuttered gloom to reveal a single cramped room, unoccupied. The meager furnishings—a straw pallet rolled up in one corner, a square table and stool, a wooden chest, and a few shelves holding a variety of dishes and boxes—seemed undisturbed. Casks had been shoved into the corners, and copper pots and a pile of wood sat beside the blackened fire pit dug right into the center of the stone floor. The place smelled of straw, damp, and smoke—unsurprising, as a hole in the thatch served as the only chimney. A bleak, barren room.

What had I expected? Tenyddar left school at ten. They lived wherever they were needed, did what they were told. So why wasn't the fellow here to meet me? All the previous evening, and all this day, Aelis had reviewed the techniques I would need to carry off this deception, but they were worthless if the man could not interpret my instructions.

Wind gusts rattled the shutters, heralding another squall rolling off the peaks. Deafening thunder followed hard upon the lightning. Rain and hail soon battered the hut.

I pulled the door shut, shoved aside the scraps of wood that littered the table, and set down my pack, allowing my handlight to die. Melydda should never be wasted on mundane tasks. A heavy winter cloak hung from a hook beside the door. I appropriated a second hook for my own dripping cape, then searched for a lamp to stave off the early dusk.

Net bags filled with onions, aged turnips, and yams dangled from the rafters. Tools and implements adorned the support posts. I shifted an ax, a straw broom, and several other tools out of the corner where they stood beside an ale cask. The next corner yielded naught but a barrel of flour and a small wooden box of salt. Pegs in the wall above the wooden chest supported an unstrung bow and a well-stocked quiver. No lamp anywhere.

As the rain moderated, I reopened the door to admit the murky daylight. A fire was laid in the pit, and so I shifted my search to flint and steel.

The shelves yielded wooden bowls, spoons, small crocks of butter and honey, and a few packets of herbs, but no flint. Exasperated, I knelt beside the wooden chest and raised the lid.

"What do you think you're doing?" The words were softly spoken, but very precise. His body filled the doorway, only its dark shape visible against the rectangle of cloudy twilight.

I dropped the heavy lid, jumped up, and mustered my composure. "The Searcher told you to expect me this afternoon."

"He said you'd come at sunset. He didn't say you would walk into my house uninvited or slop my floor"—he brushed his foot on the stone floor, where even the gray-blue light from behind him showed my muddy footprints and the spreading puddle from my cloak—"or pry into my possessions."

My cheeks heated. "It was raining, and I was hunting a lamp."

"I don't keep lamps in my clothes chest," he said, slinging something from his shoulder into one of the copper pots by the hearth. The odor of fish wafted about the room. "Do you?"

He stomped his muddy feet on the threshold, sat down on a bench just inside to the left of the doorway, and proceeded to remove his boots.

"You'll find what you want above the door," he said, shoving his boots under the bench.

Indeed a lantern-shaped blotch sat in a shadowed niche above the lintel—a perfectly sensible location. He must think me an idiot.

"When I knocked and you didn't answer, I thought perhaps the sp—I thought you might have come to harm."

"Then I suppose I must thank you for the intrusion."

He lifted the lamp from its nook and crouched beside the dark firepit. In moments a steady orange glow appeared among the ashes. A taper flared and transferred the spark to his lantern. A simple enchantment. But then I remembered that he had no power for sorcery. "How did you—?"

As the lamplight flared yellow and revealed his face—lean, intelligent, brows that angled more than most, scar on his right cheekbone—my words caught in my throat, and I pressed my back against the wall, splaying my left hand where the blasting spell yet twined my fingers. My feet demanded to run, my hand to release destruction.

But necessity and duty strangled my fear with caution. I

folded my fingers inward and held them tight. Let the spy reveal himself.

"Banked coals," he said. "No sorcery required. There exist useful skills beyond magic, you—" When our eyes met, guilt wrote itself plainly on his every feature. "Ah, powers of night, it would have to be you."

I picked carefully among the comments that came to mind, trying to sort out how much he knew. If he *was* the Derzhi spy, and Evrei had revealed the queen's plan, then he had already learned a great deal about Ezzarian sorcery—too much and I must prevent him leaving this valley. My soul chilled at the imagining.

Yet, he could simply be the man Dai knew—a tenyddar who had been trespassing in the Wardens' Grove. "You're not a Warden," I said.

"No." Abandoning the lamp, he returned to the open doorway. He ran his fingers through his wet hair, cropped short about his face and neck. "This business you need me for . . . Dai said it was of great importance and that time was critical. I can still do what's needed. That night in the grove—I never meant—I did nothing but enter the pool with prayer and respect."

"Your hands were unclean," I said.

"Ah." He extended his hands in front of him, and examined the wide palms and long graceful fingers as if they belonged to someone else. Even from across the room I could see the calluses and grime. "Soak them in lye, if you will, and perhaps that will clean them to your satisfaction, for neither soap nor prayer nor anything else I know will do it. Work the land for a few years—" He closed his eyes and inhaled deeply. "Forgive me, mistress. If my violation leaves me suspect, then report me as you must and find someone else to do whatever it is you need. I would not risk your corruption or your failure in a critical task."

His quiet anger resonated with sincerity. It was tempting to believe him. Yet in a matter of such importance, I dared not relax my vigilance. A spy who could hold an illusory mask so long—keeping his face so distinctly Ezzarian and so exactly as I remembered it—might have wandered through our settlements for days and learned many things. He could have wit enough to take up Evrei's mention of Dai's name and speak smoothly of cleanliness and corruption. What tenyddar would be so well spoken?

"So tell me why you went to the pool," I ventured. "Perhaps if you explained, I might overlook your trespass."

"No." He did not raise his voice, but neither did he hesitate.

"But—"

"My reasons are my own, like the contents of my chest. If I am formally charged with corruption and must prove myself, I might consider exposing my soul to the first student Searcher who barges through my door and demands it. Report me or not as your conscience requires. Just make up your mind what you want to do. These fish will spoil if I don't cook them soon."

We glared at each other across the fire pit, and I took no satisfaction when he turned away first, spitting a breath of exasperation. I would discover nothing if I didn't push. "How do you know Dai?"

Resting his back on the doorpost, he closed his eyes and folded his arms across his body. "She is my mother's cousin. What does that have to do with my trespass?"

Hoping for a better view of his face, I strolled across the room and perched on his stool, as if I'd no concerns worse than a tenyddar who had violated a sanctified pool. "You agreed to assist me, did you not? To do what I say?"

"Yes." His answer cracked like a dry stick. "Dai said a tenyddar was needed for some unusual kind of mission to secure the border. The Searcher said you would explain what I needed to know."

So far, so good. I toyed idly with the straps of my pack. "I've no desire to walk half a day to consult with Dai. But I can neither judge your possible corruption nor conjure illusions to protect you if I don't know something about you."

He blinked and stared at me, clearly puzzled. "Isn't that what Searchers do? Expose corruption? Ah"—his face cleared in understanding—"so your methods are not entirely sorcery then. You learn to interview your suspects and weigh their answers, listening for telltales of wickedness. Examine their faces as they speak. Watch their reactions. Pry. Spirits of night . . ."

His indignation seemed genuine. But I had worked hard to avoid reliance on instinct. Facts and evidence were an investigator's best tools. I pushed on. "So tell me something that does not violate your privacy. Mere stated kinship is useless, but I've studied weaving with Dai . . . know her a little. She's never mentioned you until now."

Even across the room I felt his resistance. But he answered. "Dai traveled to our settlement when I was five to confirm my testing. My parents were . . . disbelieving."

As would be the parents of any child judged tenyddar, I would imagine. Clearly the man knew something of Ezzarian customs. Yet his frank, unemotional reference to the disaster that had shaped his life unsettled me. The service-born stayed apart, even in reading school. I had never actually spoken with one of them about what it was like to live powerless among a people whose sorcery defined their every moment, every activity, every choice. But how could any man comprehend the true meaning of being tenyddar and not rage at the gods every hour at the gift they had withheld?

"Go on," I said.

"She would have had no reason to mention me. She visited our house from time to time when I was a boy, and looked in on me occasionally after I finished reading school and was sent south to work. More often since I was sent here, so close to her own settlement. I think, perhaps, she arranged my assignment here." He stiffened and his face took on a sudden distress. "Gods, you won't report her for that? Dai doesn't know about the pool . . . what I've done. You must believe that. All she's done is offer me her friendship all these years."

"Of course, Dai would never countenance a violation," I blurted. "She's recommended you highly."

Sentimental idiot, your task is not to reassure him. "Come." I stood and waved him out the door, where pink and white lightning flickered in the boiling sky, giving me an idea of how to finish this. "Before it rains again. Show me what you do here in the vale."

"What I do? You want to see the field? So late?" Agitated as he was, my request seemed to confuse him thoroughly, which was exactly what I wanted.

"The twilight will linger for a while yet. I must judge whether my plan will work here."

Shaking his head, he returned to the bench and shoved his feet in his boots. "I do hope you'll tell me about this mission," he said, yanking the laces tight. "Dai told me she would withdraw the wards about the valley. I'll say, it's unnerving not knowing what's like to fall on my head at any moment."

"Of course I'll tell you." What I could. What was necessary. If he was who he claimed to be.

"I don't know what you want to hear," he said, as we walked out his door and headed down the path toward the stream, the log bridge, and the field beyond. "This is my fourth season in this valley. Dai's told me your settlement's grown by half again since they brought student Wardens there to train, so you need a larger food supply. It's the first time I've opened up a new field on my own . . ."

Why had I assumed a tenyddar would be tongue-tied and sullen? As he spoke of using the natural vegetation to decide what to grow here, of breaking virgin ground with only the settlement's mule to help, of expanding his plot by half again each season, of his second season's bounty and his third season's disaster when rain pushed planting late and wild pigs and early frost combined to ruin his harvest, his discourse was articulate and unreserved. I learned more of Ezzaria's land and seasons in that hour than in all my two-and-twenty years.

". . . and so this winter past I began the logging for the fence, hauling birches from that forested notch on the mountain behind the house. Now planting's done, I can get back to it, start the building, cut more timber. Notched rails are easy to tear down if I'm sent somewhere else. I'm not permitted to leave behind anything I build." Indeed, our law forbade those without melydda to shape anything of permanence, whether a spoon or a buckle, a fence or a child's mind, lest they leave their creations flawed and thus at risk for demon corruption.

He halted by the log bridge. "Forgive my prattling. Having three visitors in a sevenday has unbridled my tongue."

A wind gust snapped my hair into my eyes. The sky rumbled and flickered.

"You enjoy this work—farming." I stepped onto the wet log, and when I wobbled, he gave me his hand—rough, warm, steady.

As I set my footing, I felt his hesitation. Then he gave a small shrug. "I am happy to do what I'm given to do. And there are undeniable satisfactions. But . . . no."

Had not the approaching storm chosen this moment to abet my design, this frank—and wistful—avowal might have precluded its execution. But in that very instant, jagged forks of pink and orange split the sky overhead, illuminating the soggy landscape with summer's brilliance. Using its cover, I released my own thunderous bolt from my left hand straight into the man's chest, toppling him into the swift-flowing water. As he yet held a firm grip on my other hand, I crashed right on top of him . . . and made sure he was fully submerged.

When I splashed backward and relieved his legs of my weight, he burst above the surface, spluttering and coughing and pressing one hand to his heart. He would likely have scorch marks on his shirt and a bruise the size of my fist just above his breastbone. "Mistress!" he croaked, gasping for breath. "Were you struck?"

Water cascaded from his dark hair and over his fine cheekbones and long jaw—all entirely unchanged from the moment before my blast. I felt no hint of enchantment. If he was a Derzhi illusionist, I was a sprig of knotweed.

We sat facing each other in the chilly water, and I felt like crowing in relief. My jellied knees and fluttery stomach told me I'd been more frightened than I'd guessed. "I'm quite well now," I said, grinning even as he wheezed and grimaced. "As are you."

"What do you—?" Even in the failing light, I saw his expression freeze. He surged out of the water and climbed the steep bank in giant steps. "I hope you're satisfied, Mistress Searcher," he said, bowing stiffly, his shoulders still hunched from the impact. "Unless you have further tests for me, I'll be inside where it's warmer and drier."

As I scrabbled my way up the sodden, weed-choked bank, I mumbled and groused that he had no reason to be offended. I hadn't actually injured him, which I'd come awfully close to doing when I recognized him—which was his own fault for bathing where he didn't belong.

By the time I had slogged halfway up the muddy knoll, I had gotten over my annoyance and was searching for words to explain why I'd had to be sure of him. It must be a constant frustration to a tenyddar, to be forever suspect, to be kept forever ignorant, to know that anything you built must eventually be destroyed. I'd never considered how difficult such a life must be.

But by the time I reached the hut, I had set aside my apologies. Whatever offense the man might have taken at my testing was wrongheaded. I had to be sure of him. Ezzaria was in danger, and personal sympathies must not confuse our priorities. We needed to prepare. Somewhere lurked a true Derzhi spy.

4

"**Everything**—the fish, the cheese, the kale—excellent," I said, scraping the last bits of the savory fish from my bowl. "Who taught you to cook?"

"No one." He held out his hand for my bowl and spoon.

My host maintained the close-mouthed sobriety he had assumed since my strike on the log bridge. Perfectly polite, strictly correct in his preparations—from providing a separate basin and towel for handwashing to his careful cleaning of the fish and greens and disposal of the waste—he demonstrated no emotions of any sort. I would have been more comfortable if he had thrown something or yelled at me. But I would not apologize for doing what was necessary.

My dishes—implements I had brought with me to avoid using anything he had made—soon joined the other clean bowls on his shelf, and he carried the washing water outdoors and dumped it where it would not sully the stream. I did not need to follow him to believe all was done properly.

"Beginning tomorrow I will take on the cooking and cleaning duties," I said, as he sat down on his bench to remove his boots.

He looked up, genuine surprise breaking through his restraint. "Why? Dai herself could not be more careful. I *do* understand the risks of what I am."

"It is naught to do with your practices, which are impeccable." No matter how obedient he might be, his role would require his active participation. I could not shield him from the truth. "We believe a spy has broached our border for the specific purpose of investigating the nature of Ezzarian enchantments. Our purpose is to demonstrate our incapacity for true sorcery and send him back where he came from. Derzhi see all females as subservient. He'll never believe a serving girl would have power for sorcery."

"Derzhi! The 'someone' you thought might have done me harm . . . a Derzhi warrior." His deep-set eyes widened with the surge of understanding. "And the Weaver has removed the wards around this valley. So he is allowed to come here apurpose, *because* I am tenyddar."

He slumped heavily against the wall and stared at me in utter desolation. "I am to be served up to the Derzhi to prove that Ezzarians have no war skills. Dai warned this venture could cost my life, but she never said—sweet Verdonne, the Derzhi take slaves . . . chain them . . . cut off their feet . . ."

"You are not to be *served up* and dragged off to the Empire," I said quickly. I'd not realized he knew so much of the outside world. Fear wasn't going to help us weave a convincing deception. "The spy is not a warrior, but a magician. We yet believe the mountains sufficient to keep the Empire out of Ezzaria. Trees, rocks, and a few patches of arable land are not worth their trouble. But if the Derzhi Magicians' Guild comes to believe that barbarian Ezzarians possess true sorcery, they might convince the Emperor that we are a threat. So we need to send this fellow back with a different view."

"How are you going to convince him of that—bind me to a post and let him have his way with me until he is convinced I can't conjure a drop of spit?" His eyes nearly drilled a hole in my forehead. "Gods and spirits . . ."

"I'll not let it come to that." Aelis and I had discussed innumerable tactics. Unfortunately none ensured that this man would remain undamaged. All I could do was help him understand the need.

"You'll but play a part," I said, jumping up from the table and warming my chilly hands at the fire. "Rumors of Ezzarian sorcery have persisted for decades, too long for us to convince anyone we've no power at all. So the queen believes we'll do better by making the Guild believe that we can do no more than they—that a male Ezzarian in his prime can work simple illusions and naught else. We'll show him some tricks and send him home laughing at us. My Searcher's training has taught me to work enchantments through another person's body—make it appear as if that person is working magic. You'll be able to see fire shooting from your fingers."

"At age seven, I might have appreciated that." His short laugh was fraught with despair. "Don't mistake me, mistress. I'm willing to do whatever's needed. Of course, I am. Grateful for the chance to serve—pitiful as that sounds. But I can't see why you would jeopardize your outcome with so complicated a plan. Certainly we can't risk one of the power-born, but surely one of the skill-born could do this more convincingly than I . . ."

He paused for a long while, leaning his elbows on his knees and pressing his forehead into his fists. Better if he worked it out for himself.

And so he did. Eventually he raised his head enough that his chin rested on his fists. ". . . But if your deception fails, and the spy . . . presses . . . hard enough, one who can work even a bit of true sorcery might cast some spell to save himself. Whereas if the subject has naught to yield, our secret is safe. And a Derzhi would not think twice if the serving girl were to vanish into the wood. It is clever. I'll give you that."

"We're not going to fail. My mentor reviewed my plan. I've only to develop the details and execute it."

Another abortive laugh. "Could you at least use a different word?"

From the bench beside him, he picked up the bits of wood he'd rescued from his table—thin, odd-shaped little pieces of varying lengths that I had assumed were kindling scraps. But he arranged the pieces carefully on the table as he straddled the stool I had vacated. Some he turned crossways to each other and fitted together, so that they formed a latticework no bigger than his two fingers together.

"So how do we manage this?" he said, his eyes fixed on his odd little business.

"We must settle a few things here at the beginning. Be attentive; I'll keep things as simple as possible."

"I'll do my best to keep up." I heard a trace of irony—amused?

More likely resentful. The man was so difficult to read. He seemed
intelligent, as Dai had indicated, and sincere in his intent. I wish
I'd known he was Dai's kin. I'd have asked her more about him.

I tore my eyes from his long, sure fingers and gathered my
thoughts that seemed to be scattered from the Wardens' Grove
to his carrot patch to an odd, hollow ache beneath my breastbone to the delicate oddments in his hand. I had no time to tip-
toe about his pride.

"Names and stories, first. You are Bran. You call me *girl*.
My actual name will be Teleri, and I came with the land and
the hut when they were granted you by our chieftain. You must
treat me—"

"Our chieftain?"

No mistaking the amusement this time. Better to hear than
despair or bitterness. It reminded me of Kenehyr, and for the
thousandth time I regretted that I'd been forbidden to tell my
partner of this mission. Surely he could have advised me how to
teach an inexperienced vegetable farmer to stay alive.

"Derzhi believe us to be barbarians. We'll not show him
differently. You must treat me with contempt, as he surely will,
while portraying yourself as bold and skilled in magic . . ." I
recited the other bits and pieces of the history I had devised so
that we could present a coherent and unenlightening story as to
"Bran's" position in life. Then I moved on to the more important
matters.

"The spy may approach aggressively—attacking or trying to
take us captive right away. We'll deal with that if it comes. I've
been trained to fight and, with your help, should be able to take
care of one magician. But that will be our last resort."

I held back a number of things, such as the prearranged signals that could bring aid within the matter of an hour. Such

signals required spellworking, and the less he could reveal to a determined questioner, the better.

"We've evidence that he may try more subtle means," I said, "perhaps even trying to pass as Ezzarian. So I'll warn you—"

"—to keep conversation general, and not back him into any corners with detailed questions. Our purpose is not to expose him. I do have a smattering of common sense." He glanced up. "Would you like to sit here at the table . . . Teleri? I could move back to the bench."

I had been circling the small open space beside his chest and rolled pallet. "No. I think better when moving. That was good to call me Teleri. We should use only our false names from now on."

He pressed another splinter, the size of a small nail, into his little construct. "You've not asked my true name."

"That's not necessary." I folded my arms across my breast. "I've come up with three illusions for you to use—"

"Somehow it would be a comfort if the enchantress holding my life in her hands knew my name," he said, glancing up from his scraps.

He behaved like the yarn in Dai's loom—apparently pliable, but coming up knots even here at the beginning. "It is for your protection," I said. "What I do not possess, I cannot yield. Now, we should—"

"Would it not induce me to even more caution, lest my talentless weakness jeopardize your safety?" With a knife pulled from his belt he began to notch the edge of a thin strip of pine the length of his middle finger. "I know *your* name. You gave it at the encarda. I would never presume to use an ill-gotten prize, but I'd like to give you some assurance. Unless—" He looked up sharply. "Do you prefer *not* to know it?"

"That makes no sense. It makes no difference if I know your

name." His reference to the incident at the encarda threatened to fluster me entirely. "Come, we really must practice. We'll master one of the sequences of false magic tonight and the others in the morning. We've no idea when the spy will arrive."

He laid down his knife and his oddments, and held out his hands, fingers stiffly spread. "Teach me, mistress."

"No, no, you mustn't hold them out so oddly. Or look at them so intently." This was going to be more difficult than I'd thought. "Go back to what you were doing. Let me consider how best to go about the teaching."

He returned to work with his knife and slips of wood, but he continually glanced my way. "What now?" he said.

"Keep on with it." I waved him off, watching until his glances became less frequent. The moment I felt his focus actually shift away from me and onto his work, I carefully, delicately claimed his right hand. Commanding a person to yield control of his body could end up a nauseating wrestling exercise. It was far easier to accomplish it by subterfuge.

He sneaked another glance at me, but without focus. He did not yet feel what I'd done.

"Pretend that an unwelcome visitor has cast her eyes to your clothes chest," I said softly. "You wish to prevent her from prying. So move your right hand as if to protect the chest."

Brow knotted, he pushed his stool away from the table.

"No!" I snapped. "Stay where you are."

"But how—?"

"Do as I said. Move your hand."

He settled on the stool again and waved his right hand. Straightening his three long fingers, I induced a sharper, quicker motion than he'd begun and shot a stream of orange flame from his appendages to encircle the wooden chest.

"Spirits and demons!" His stool crashed to the floor as he jumped to his feet. His flailing left arm sent his knife and his wood slivers flying, while he stretched his right arm until his shaking hand was as far from his body as he could put it.

"To end it, curl your fingers."

"I cannot," he said harshly.

"Begin the motion! Do it!" When he managed a jerk, I finished it, sweeping up the enchantment in his tight-closed fist. The tether of fire vanished.

The flames from his fire pit paled beside the scarlet of his face. His chest rose and fell rapidly. His mouth and jaw might have been forged steel.

"Again!" I said sharply, before anger or fear spilled out of him. "Right hand . . . move it."

I could not have said whether it was terror or compliance that made his hand twitch, but I grasped the motion and repeated the sequence. No matter how strong the link between us, I could not induce movement from absolute stillness. Fortunately, few people had self-command sufficient to maintain perfect stillness.

"Again. This time, the ale cask. Do *not* look at me." The rope of flame encircled the barrel in the corner.

"Now the fire pit itself. Use a grander gesture . . ." And the small efficient fire left from his cooking burgeoned near as high as the thatch, before we tamed it again. No scorch marks marred his walls or floor, nor was his thatch at risk. Illusory flames did not truly burn.

"The movements must be as seamless as a dance," I said, moving around behind him, "and your eyes must never rest on me." We repeated each variation twenty times over before I called it enough.

He stared at the hand lying in his lap as if it were some creature crawled out of nightmare. I had prepared words to soothe
his fear and to answer questions. But the intensity of his quiet
stilled my tongue. When he moved at last, he was out the door
so fast he didn't even stop to put on his boots.

I debated whether to follow. He couldn't mean to go far without boots. But I should have made it clear that he was required to
remain with me at all times. Goddess save us if he blundered into
the spy.

Yet forcing my presence on him as he considered what I'd told
him . . . what he had guessed . . . what I had just done . . . would
surely be cruel. He was so fiercely protective of his privacy.
I'd used these skills frequently in training—and often without
forewarning—but the subjects had ever been the humanlike
conjurings who populated our temple exercises, or my mentors
or fellow students, people who understood the limits of what I
did. I had never practiced on a living human person who had
not been taught the secret workings of sorcery. Whatever he
felt from it—fear, confusion, humiliation, excitement—must be
near overwhelming.

I picked up his spilled wood bits and laid them on the table,
noting how precisely they had been cut and smoothed, notched
and fitted. Though I could not imagine what they were, every
piece was purposeful: some thin, flat strips, some the splinter-
like sticks, some grooved, some delicately carved with repeated
shapes of whorls and spirals. I took my hands away quickly,
feeling as if I were spying on him naked again.

After some interminable time—likely not more than an
hour—I had fidgeted myself out of sympathy. It was irrespon-
sible of him to vanish for so long without even a word. Chafing
for occupation, I laced up my own boots—still sodden from my

dunking—grabbed the lamp, and went out to assess my prospects for the night. A serving girl who did not share her master's bed would sleep in the shed, not inside the house.

The sky had cleared. Stars pricked the night's dark canvas, and the air smelled sharply clean as it does only after a storm. Searchers and Comforters who had lived outside Ezzaria claimed that the stench of cities assaulted the senses, worse even than their noise. Our mentors could not waste their conjuring skills on such details in our test scenarios, so I had ever tried to imagine what it might be like. Stink and clamor seemed such a small price to pay for the variety of marketplaces and temples; the throngs of people so different from our kind; the great houses, shops, and artwork one would find in landscapes so different from green forest and hills. From my first days in reading school I had longed to see such wonders, resenting the simplicity of Ezzarian life where the only marvels were those we conjured for the demon war. Yet how much more confining must our life seem for those who had no magic? Tenyddar were forbidden to cross the borders or even to interact with non-Ezzarians.

Blast the man! Was that the truest risk of his kind—not so much that they were a channel for demon infestation, but that they created such a distraction when one got involved with them? A responsibility akin to children . . . only they were not at all childlike.

I rounded the corner of the house and poked through the clutter of his shed. Even so mundane a venue as the work shed bore his stamp. Neat stacks of slender birch trunks, some of them already cut to length and notched for his fence, took up half the broad shelter. From the rafters hung the hooks and ropes he used when he hauled the logs down from the mountainside. No wonder he was muscled like a Warden . . .

Shocked at the unseemly imaginings that crept into my head, I set to work. First I cleared out a small space snug to the house wall and a stack of crates, then grabbed an armful of leafy branches from a heap of trimmings and piled them in my corner. Empty flour sacks and seed bags pulled from a cask made a softer layer atop the branches. As I worked I sorted through phrases about duty and necessity, composing a reminder that his obligations must keep him at my side.

His bare feet made little noise on the path up from the bridge. Rather, it was his hard breathing that first warned me of his return. It sounded as if he'd been running.

"I am capable of making my own bed," he said from the verge of the shed.

"Teleri's proper place is out here." I arranged the last of his seed bags on the pile. My carefully contrived reprimand stuck in my throat. Now he stood ten paces behind me, and all I could add was, "Are you all right?"

He didn't respond.

I turned to read the answer for myself, but he had vanished. *Confounded man.* Had I insulted him again? He needed to *tell* me what he was thinking.

I'd scarce got to my feet before he'd come back again, his arms laden. He set my pack beside my bed and pushed a woolen bundle into my arms. "You'll need these. Nights are cool here all year. If you require more, you can use my winter cloak. Tomorrow I'll build a partition to give you a bit more privacy."

"That's not what you need to be—"

"*After* we finish my practicing, of course. For the other illusions."

Sweat dripped from his face and hair. His feet and worn leggings were splashed with mud halfway to his knees. Yet such solemn dignity enveloped him in that moment that my entire being ached for the beauty of him. I had no name for the yearning that waked in me.

"Thank you . . . Master Bran," I said, attempting to hide my confusions as I dipped my knee. All I could do was play my part. *"Nevaro wydd."*

"Nevaro wydd, girl," he said, and the beginnings of a smile illumined his face. But he took the lamp and padded quietly away before I could glimpse its fullness.

Nevaro wydd . . . sleep in peace. I feared that might be impossible.

5

The night in the shed was *not* the most uncomfortable night I'd ever spent. Searchers in training spent plenty of time living rough, from the arid northern slopes of the mountains to the sticky, insect-plagued fen country that bordered the jungles of Thrid to the south. I felt snug and safe in my little corner of the tenyddar's shed. But truly I did not sleep overmuch. The birch limbs cracked and poked every time I shifted position, as I fretted about the mistakes I'd made with the tenyddar and the many lessons I yet needed to teach him. My doubts and frustrations— and my misconceptions about him—had led me into prideful, overbearing behavior that had no place in the person I was striving to become.

As the outlines of barrows and crates slowly emerged in the gray light, I was ready to get up and strive to do better. If only the morning weren't quite so cool . . .

I tucked the soft wool blankets under my chin, rolled over

to ease my aching back . . . and then sat bolt upright. A hands-breadth separated my nose from the tenyddar's knees.

"I wasn't sure whether to wake you," he said, retreating immediately toward the stacked timbers. "But it seemed my serving girl ought to have my breakfast out by now. I've thinned three rows of beans and set a span of fence already."

"But it's only just—" Far later than I'd imagined. Golden sunlight shimmered beyond the shady boundaries of the shed. "Just so. Give me a moment and I'll be along, Master Bran."

"Good." He rummaged through the birch rails.

I threw off the blankets, noticing for the first time how beautiful they were. Despite wear that had left the edges frayed, the colors held true—deep vibrant reds intricately patterned with rich hues of pine and healthy earth.

"Where did you come by these?" I asked, but he had already set off down the knoll, a notched trunk across his shoulders. I would wager this was not his mother's weaving, but Dai's. My finger traced a deep green thread. Warmth and comfort settled into me—an enchantment so faint as to be unnoticeable to one who was not looking for it, a gift from a friendly kinswoman to a lonely child.

Over my shift and leggings, I donned a shapeless tunic suitable for a despised serving girl. By the time I struggled into my damp boots yet again and gave up on taming the hair that had escaped my braid in the night, the tenyddar had returned to retrieve another slender trunk. From the shelter of the stack of crates, I watched him work, strong and sure and entirely self-contained.

He called to me over his shoulder as he retraced his route down the hill. "My cold-store is in the stream bank just down from the back of the shed. I've eggs need to be used." No mistaking the cheerful underpinning to his direction. He was enjoying this part.

The bank he spoke of did not border the stream that traversed the valley floor through the middle of his field, but a rill that trickled down from a great green cleft in the mountains. It joined the wider flow downstream from the log bridge. After splashing my face with the breathtakingly cold water, I located his eggs, along with a wheel of cheese, a side of smoked bacon, and a basket full of sorry-looking apples, in the stone-lined larder tucked into the steep bank. I stuffed four of the apples in my pockets and, though I'd truly have preferred a slab of the bacon, took three of the eggs.

As I rolled the thin flat stone back across the mouth of the cold-store, a sensation like the flutter of moth wings tickled my ears. I spun and gazed up the steep, forested cleft, stretching my sight and hearing to the barren heights beyond the wood. I could not pinpoint the disturbance that had roused me at such a distance, but I caught sun glints just above the dark line of the trees. Metal. Moving downward. The spy was on his way.

I scrambled up the bank and to the empty house. Cursing the tenyddar's diligence, cursing my choice not to push him the previous night, I deposited the eggs and pelted down the path. He was working at a near corner of the field where his rail fence had begun to take shape.

As I sped across the bridge, he straightened up and leaned on a bow saw, mopping his brow with his sleeve and eyeing my shabby attire. "This isn't news of breakfast, I'd guess."

"He's descending the cleft behind your house, just entering the wood. It's too steep for a horse, which means we've— How long?"

"Half a day," he said. "Likely no more than that for a determined Derzhi, though it's a rough go down the notch. He'll not see sky till midafternoon, when he comes out of the wood."

"We *must* prepare a few more illusions or we'll never convince him. Last evening . . . perhaps I should have explained more."

"Don't trouble over last evening," he said softly.

But he'd had every reason to be angry and afraid. "I am a student, it's true, but it's only my final testing that I've not accomplished as yet—and those exercises are much more complex than this. I excel at every Searcher's discipline. The queen would not have sent me did she not believe I could keep you safe."

"Dai told me you would match her skill some day. I've rarely known her seeings to be wrong." He waved toward his half-raised rail. "Should I keep working as you begin?"

"No," I said, puzzled at his reference to *seeings* and Dai's equating of a Searcher's skills with those of a Weaver. But then, who knew exactly what Weavers did?

He nodded. "Then I'll cover these, lest a rain come."

He laid his saw and hammers on a length of canvas beside his ax and iron wedges, tossed a few iron spikes into a canvas bag hung from his belt, and dropped the bag next to the tools. After folding in the ends, he rolled the canvas, tools and all, into a long bundle.

When he stood up again, he dropped his hands to his sides, flaring them slightly as if giving me a gift. "Do as you will with me."

Such responsibility laid so gracefully in my hand. Neither my first combat training, nor my first day in the temple, nor even my first sight of a demon-possessed victim brought into Ezzaria for healing had humbled and terrified me so much as that gesture.

Necessity forced me stumbling ahead. "You must— To do

this requires— I must be able to take control of your hands over these next days to work our illusions. I can do so when you are preoccupied, as I did last night, but that can be slow and unreliable. Which means you must learn to *yield* control. That can be difficult, and I understand if it makes you angry, but we've no time for you to grow comfortable with the idea."

"So that's why you're treating me as if I've glass bones. Blessed spirits, I thought I'd been too forward or too thick skulled." He riffled his hair, relief and apology softening his serious demeanor. "I wasn't angry last night. Certainly not. Truly it was a wonder— to see fire magic happening as if I'd done it myself. Something so marvelous, so *immense*. Something I'd imagined so often, yet believed that in all of time I would never see. A bit frightening, too, I'll confess, though I've had this belief—well, no mind to that. When I get so wrought up in thinking about how things are in the world and with me, I just need to *go*. Just to *do* something lest I burst, which would be a most unpleasant sight, I think. So I run. It clears my head. Settles my mind." He held out his hands. "Take them. Do as must be done. I've naught else to give."

"I'll do my best for you," I said. "I swear it." And though I meant what I said, I wanted to kick myself for speaking it aloud, and to kick *him* for forcing such an oath out of me.

Never, *never*, befriend a player in a combat scenario. I had etched that rule on my soul long years before, when girlish sympathies and sentimental misjudgments had caused my earliest failures. Were the subjects Derzhi torturers or Ezzarian farmers, I gave everything I could.

Yet indeed, this man was possessed of a profound grace. I scarce touched his grimed and calloused hands, and they were mine.

༄

"**So** when your signal spell wriggles my right thumb, and I yield control of my hands, you'll make the fire rope. Wriggling my left thumb signals the apparition—whatever object you think fits the occasion. And the scents . . . you'll signal with a finger to my nose, along with your promise not to poke my eye."

"That happened only once, and you jumped," I said, grimacing at his sidewise grin. "And we'll only do scents inside the house." I wished I could feel some hint of good humor. My plan that had felt so solid when I discussed it with Aelis seemed, of a sudden, flimsy as moth wings.

We sat on the log bridge, basking in the late-morning sun, as if our test were not bearing down on us from the north. We were eating the soft old apples I'd pulled from my pocket, or rather I was eating, as he'd finished his three in three bites each, half the seeds and core as well, and tossed the tiny remainders into the grassy distance.

"I've a thought about the scents," he said, hesitantly.

I didn't really want to hear. Better to stop thinking for a little while, to rest and recover here in the sun, so we could be fresh when the challenge came—so my stomach might stop devouring itself. We had reviewed every scenario I could devise, and practiced the illusions until they seemed to engrave themselves in the air. The tenyddar had heeded my direction without complaint, repeating his stories and practicing his movements without reservation. Indeed, his performance had astonished me. He had incorporated my enchantments smoothly into his body's own language, and when I triggered one of my signal spells, he opened himself so completely to my will that I felt as if I could walk into his skin and share it with him. He deserved to be heard.

"Go on," I said.

"This Bran would have no reason to make the girl's cooking smell better. Come the end of a work day, I can eat sour cabbage and old beets. But scent attracts beasts. It would be useful to a hunter to lay down a scent to attract prey—apple, acorns, clover, honey."

"Yes, that makes a lot of sense." Assuming this spy did not try to capture us right away, we could make something of it. We talked for a while of possible scenarios, then fell quiet again.

Useful . . . that was an important distinction. In the way of jugglers or acrobats, members of the Derzhi Magicians' Guild created entertainments. But Derzhi warriors lived for their pride, and would no more use a magician's illusion to bait a beast than they would use an acrobat to fight a battle for them. A barbarian farmer would have no such luxury. His enchantments would be useful—devised to improve his life. Or to defend his family or his property.

I had designed the fire rope and the scent illusions as lures—minor evidence that Bran could work sorcery. The heart of my plan lay in the illusion of solid objects—magic that could be clearly unmasked in front of the spy. I intended to use a jeweled pendant, or some similar valuable that would appeal to the intruder. Drop such an apparition into a pot of water, and it would reveal itself as no more than a length of yarn and a stone—and Ezzarian sorcery as petty illusion. I stared through the deep, clear stream to the moss-covered stones beneath its silken flow, and like a night-blooming lily, heavy with scent, a new plan blossomed in my head. Far more dangerous . . . but far more convincing.

"We need to work on one other illusion," I said, jumping up. An anxious survey of the mountains and its dark rift revealed no telltale of the spy. He would be well hidden under the canopy of the wood. We'd not see him—and he'd not see us—until he emerged from the trees and walked into the valley.

"A fourth illusion! Because I've learned my lessons well?" My companion's quiet smile instilled such a burden of dread in my breast, I could scarce breathe. Duty demanded dreadful deeds. Mortal deeds. Dai had warned him.

No. We would *not* fail. I would not allow it. I closed my eyes for a moment and stripped away the weakness and sentiment that could cloud my resolve. Only then could I inhale, and answer, and begin the lesson. "You've done very well. I'll signal this one by clenching your fists, and instead of your hands, I'll need you to yield me everything . . ."

Once I had built the trigger spell—the link from my fists to his that would tell him that the time had come—I taught him to grant me his entire body as a canvas for my spellmaking. Only then did I create the new illusion. A few tweaks of the enchantment itself to create a truly fearsome result and the soft-spoken farmer stood in his vegetable field clad in armor of fire. His breastplate blazed as a whorl of scarlet, his chausses and greaves gleamed orange, and his helm scalded the eye with the yellow of the sun at midmorn.

"We're out of time," I said, dismissing the illusion with a twist of my will. The sun had begun its slide downward from the zenith. "I'd like to practice more, but we dare not let him see. If we come to this, you will engage the spy wherever he might be and fight him with whatever skill you can muster."

The tenyddar's smiles and wonder had long vanished. He did not question. Did not ask why I had created so warlike an illusion. Did not ask how an untrained farmer might "engage" a Derzhi of any ilk, or why I had not told him how or when we would use this, as I'd done with each of the other illusions. Did

not remind me that I'd said I would defend him against physical harm. He must have guessed I wasn't going to answer. Silent
and expressionless, he nodded, hefted his bundled tools, and
struck out for the hut.

I fenced my heart in steel and spoke no comfort to him. Not
just his safety, but Ezzaria's, depended on my talents, wit, and
will, and on his continued obedience . . . and good heart. Surprise and fear and righteous anger would enable him to use the
armor and make the spy believe. Until then, we could afford no
comfort and no distraction.

∽

The spy arrived with the sunset, skittering and sliding down
the last steep drop out of the trees. He waved and hallooed in
a friendly manner when he caught sight of us beside the shed,
where the tenyddar had set out more birch trunks for notching.

As we watched the slender figure climb the knoll, I broke
out of our roles for one last time. "Give thought to every word,
every action, for the sake of those souls we protect."

"I'll do as I've sworn, mistress, and I will obey your commands and yield to your wisdom on every matter save one—I'll
not be used as if I'm no more than a post or a rail to be put
in a fence." The tenyddar set aside his ax, closed his eyes, and
clenched his fist over his heart. "*Lys na* Gareth. It's only right
you know my name."

6

"**I'm** called Haine." The slight, dark-haired man drained the
wooden mug and smiled blissfully as he wiped his mouth with

a ragged sleeve. "Never tasted such fine ale. Water may be the root of life . . . but it's no compare to the best of the barley after such a journey as mine. I should have guessed my kin would do right by me."

The red-gold light enhanced the coppery hue of his skin—so like to Ezzarian skin. His eyes, dark brown, not black, and with only the slightest angle to them, *hinted* at Ezzarian roots, rather than claiming them. But then, the newcomer did not claim full blood.

"You say your mother was Ezzarian," said the tenyddar—Gareth—standing cool and wary a few paces in front of his door. "It's rare for any Ezzarian to intermarry, even one wayward enough to venture the filthy world. Especially a woman. Our gods frown on it."

I, the serving girl, stood humbly to one side, trying to cool my fury. *Inexplicable* fury, for I could not even begin to explain why Gareth's revelation rankled me so sorely.

"I guessed as much," said the spy, tossing me his mug and flashing a most charming grin as I snatched it from the air to prevent it from dropping in the dirt.

His teeth gleamed evenly white in his rich-hued skin. And his movements were quick and sharp, like the expressions that danced across his angular features.

"Mam didn't have so much as one Ezzarian friend. She didn't tell me much, as she died when I was a brat. But I remember her saying her people didn't like their ways talked about, and I should only ever come here if I was desperate. An Ezzarian man came to my shop once, and I tried asking him about Ezzaria and if he knew my mam, but he closed up tighter than a miser's fist. Not one of you I've ever encountered wished me so much as a good morrow, so I've long called a pox on the lot of you."

He held up his hands defensively. "I'm just being honest, Good-man Bran; you know your own people well enough. But since the Guild took up their mission, I've learnt the true meaning of *desperate*."

My every sense stretched to its limit. I tasted the air around the newcomer, listened to it, smelled it. No enchantments masked his face or tainted his actions. I was as sure of that as I was of my own name.

"We care for no man's opinion of our ways," said Gareth. "What is this Guild you speak of?"

Truly the tenyddar was better at this than I'd any reason to hope. He could almost have fooled *me* with this staunch and guileless manner. He held out his own empty mug without so much as a glance at me. I took it, then scurried over to the cis-tern and ladled water into the mugs, rinsing and emptying them while Haine talked.

"The Derzhi Magicians' Guild," he said. "Sorcerers—the fin-est in the Empire. They serve the Emperor and the Twenty Fam-ilies, raking in gold by the cartload for their magics. But they aim to keep it all to themselves. On one hand, a man can't get into the Guild lest he's got Derzhi clan connections—and my da was a Fryth sweeper who didn't stay around even long enough to see me birthed. And on the other hand, if the fellow prac-tices a bit of sorcery outside the Guild, he's marked and warned off. If he's *good* at what he does"—he snapped his fingers and a shower of rose petals swirled about him like a whirlwind, drifted to the ground, and vanished—"he's marked for dead. I've been on the run for most of a year. You can see what I've come to."

In cheerful chagrin, he spread his arms. His ill-fitting breeches had lost their knee-buckles long ago, and his shabby layers of shirt and tunic, stained and threadbare, hung loose on his slight frame. The metal I'd glimpsed in the morning sun was likely the battered hilt of a sword that dangled from a greasy rucksack. The dagger sheathed unobtrusively at his waist appeared better kept.

Gareth clasped his hands at his back and strolled around Haine. "Our life here is not so easy."

"I feel a shameful beggar," said Haine, seeming wholly unembarrassed by the scrutiny. "To have spoke so ill of Ezzarians while I prospered with my bead shop, and now that I'm in penury to ask those same folk for sanctuary. But I'm healthy and willing to work, and have skills to offer, so I asked myself who would appreciate them more than kinsmen and fellow sorcerers?"

Only forewarned would I have recognized this subtle gambit. With his frank and engaging speech, plausible story, and unprepossessing body—on size alone, Gareth could snap him like one of his wood splinters—it would have been so easy to take Haine at his word. Surely our goddess and her son must have been watching out for us when Evrei caught wind of this plan.

"You seem a right fellow, Haine," said Gareth, reclaiming his position between the stranger and his front door. "And I've no grudge against words spoke in ignorance. But no matter your skills or blood claim, I cannot give you leave to make free of our land. Only my chieftain can do that, and if you've brought Derzhi on your heels, he'll have your skin off your bones before you can whistle."

"I've left the pursuit in the wastes, I'll swear it," said Haine, waving northward. "So I'd be grateful if you could point me to your town where I might parley with this chieftain. Even better were you to guide me there yourself . . ."

Gareth snorted. "Leave my fields just when the beasts get a hunger for tender plants? Not for my own mam would I do that. And it's worth my life to let you wander Ezzaria on your own."

"What of the girl then? She could take me." Haine's sharp gaze crawled up my leggings and across my breasts to my face. I averted my eyes and felt the urge to wash.

"Girl's bound to the land," said Gareth, with a huff of derision. "Not allowed to go elsewhere. Besides, she's got the wit of a tree stump and is as like to lead you off a cliff as to anywhere you'd want. No, we'll wait right here for Ogul's son. He's to bring a mule and help me break a new field come the new moon. He'll decide if his da wants to see you or not. 'Til then, you stay where I can see you."

Three days until the new moon. We'd see how eager Haine was to meet other Ezzarians.

"Fair enough," said the spy, cheerfully. "I'll work for my keep. Teach you some magics, if you like."

"You'll get no thanks for it," I mumbled, just loud enough to be heard—my own opening play. "Bran don't know the word."

"Quiet your sour tongue, girl, and move your lazy bones," snapped Gareth. "Our guest and I need supper—bacon, cheese, and new bread. Put his things in the house, and make him a bed. He's to sleep inside." He motioned Haine to drop his rucksack by the door and follow him. "Keep your magics. I doubt a half-blood Fryth would have much to teach an Ezzarian in the way of sorcery. Come and I'll show you what work needs done . . ."

I dipped my knee and jogged off to the larder for bacon and cheese, scarce able to suppress my satisfaction—Gareth could not have played it better. As I cooked bacon and bread, the men strolled about the field. Though I fretted at not hearing their every word, my role precluded my being with him at every moment. Three days, I'd wager, and we'd have this done.

∞

The first rounds of bread came off the hearthstones at deep twilight, a perfect time for our first test. Gareth and Haine lingered beside the new span of fence. My blood pulsed hot in my veins as I sped down the path toward them. Rousing will and magic, I brought forth a shadowy beast far across the vale.

". . . by end of summer, I should have the new field harrowed. I can fence it over winter. I've no shortage of trees, but I could use help with the felling—"

"Supper's on, master," I blurted as I joined the men. And even as my conjured sow wandered down the distant hillside and toward the field, I wriggled my left thumb . . . and Gareth's.

To his credit, he jumped only a little and recovered nicely. "Interrupt me again, thimblewit, and you'll go to bed hungry."

He waved me aside and turned back to Haine and the field, squinting into the dimness. I had prepared him for what he'd see. "Ah, Valdis's hammer, a blighting pig!" With a grand gesture appropriate to the size of the task, he swept his hand outward, yielding me control . . .

. . . and my sinuous, golden rope of flame looped about the field. As it settled into a knee-high, burning barrier, the shadowy sow squealed in fright and lumbered away.

"Oh, well done!" said Haine, approaching the fiery boundary sprung up ten paces from his feet. He crouched and held his hand near the fire . . . then plunged it in, laughing as the flames danced around and through his fluttering fingers. "Wouldn't do for baking your girl's bread, though."

"The appearance is enough," said Gareth. Though his voice

remained cool, excitement brightened his eyes and curved his lips once Haine's back was turned. The spark died quickly when his gaze flicked to me. "This will do until I get the fence built. Let's to supper."

I trudged up the hill behind them, feeling hollow and guilty. That's why I resented Gareth telling me his name. As if he wanted me to know him. As if I dared consider his wishes or his needs or anything but what I must do with him.

꘡

My mediocre cooking provided ample demonstration of Master Bran's scorn for his serving girl. Haine's attention never wavered from our sparring. I'd vow he could have recited every word we spoke on any matter. Once the men had finished their meal, and I sat in the corner eating bacon rinds and burnt corners of the bread, the visitor probed Gareth about Ezzarian life, expressing hopes and eager curiosity about his chosen "sanctuary." Did we trade? Work metal? Herd beasts? How were chieftains named . . . the strongest in magic, perhaps? His investigation was well done. Subtly done.

Bluff and hearty, Gareth incorporated the misguiding tales I'd taught him into his own words, gaining confidence with every exchange. When Haine's questions ventured beyond our preparations, the tenyddar blithely invoked Ezzarian custom to explain his reticence.

The spy asked Gareth why he had no wife. To my amusement Gareth responded solemnly that as soon as he had earned enough to buy himself a goat, his chieftain would reward his diligence with a bride. "What of your own family, Haine? What came of your wife and children when this Guild chased you from Vayapol?"

The goat story was Gareth's own invention. Perhaps it had sprung from his private imaginings, for in truth, his kind rarely married. It was not a matter of law. No evidence claimed that children of tenyddar would inevitably inherit the parent's impoverishment. But who would ever risk such a grief?

"I never could choose one woman to settle with," said Haine, picking his teeth with a splinter from the woodpile. "They're like beads—so much variety, all desirable. Being a beadmaker as I was, I always had my pick of the ladies." He waved his hand as if scooping a hole in the air, but when he held out his hollowed palm, beads of stone and glass and delicately engraved metal filled it. Every size. Every color.

Sensing an invitation, I crept forward and knelt by his stool. "Oh, so pretty," I said, gasping. "Such like the goddess herself must wear as she walks the holy wood."

When I glanced up, he winked and flashed his teeth, deepening the attractive creases alongside his mouth. "Go ahead. Touch them. I'll guess Master Bran doesn't gift you such pretties."

"Nawp. He never would," I said and fingered the beads. Their texture was excellent—metal, glass, and stone entirely distinct, though the relief of the engravings felt muddy. The metal beads felt warmer, the stone and glass cold. I dropped my voice low as if Gareth weren't sitting on the bench five steps away. "Master Bran only wants to take. Not give. But I won't, and the law forbids him forcing me."

Gareth's stillness near paralyzed the room. This was not part of our planned story. I wanted him unsettled. Haine would notice it.

Haine picked out a few of the beads and tossed them to Gareth. Caught by surprise, Gareth snared only two. The remainder bounced onto the floor at his feet.

"Watch closely!" Haine said, laughing. He poked thumb and forefinger into the handful of beads and slowly drew them out again. Clasped between was the end of a string. He pulled out an entire length of string threaded with every bead I had touched. After knotting the ends, he dropped the necklace over my head.

"Oh, good sir," I gasped as I fondled the beads. "I feel like a chieftain's consort!"

"Perhaps you were chased out of town because your beads were false," said a scowling Gareth. He snatched the loose beads from the floor, but Haine vanished them right out of his hand before he could inspect them closer.

The spy shrugged and laughed. "The beads in my shop were true for the most. I've a hand with tools and fire, as well as magic. Come, show me something finer, Bran. If you can."

A brazen challenge. I retreated to the corner by the ale cask, fingering the necklace, relishing the opportunity. I twitched my right thumb.

Gareth did not jump when his own thumb responded, but rubbed his mouth thoughtfully. Without even a glance at me, he held his palms a handspan apart, then closed his eyes and brought his hands together sharply, just as we had practiced. When he opened them again, an emerald the size of a walnut lay in his calloused palm. I'd seen only one emerald in my life, so I was not so sure of it. But imperfection was a part of our game.

Haine applauded and reached for the emerald. He ran his fingers over the facets, pursing his lips as he exposed it to the firelight. He nodded in approval. "Nice work. Edges not quite sharp, but clean, nonetheless. And a good, deep color. Alas"—he scraped a dirty fingernail across one edge—"hardness is difficult to get right."

"My cousin once sold one of my gems to a woman in Karesh," boasted Gareth.

"If one could rely on a ready supply of ignorant buyers, we would all be rich. I'll advise you not to test your luck in a real marketplace, unless you relish farming with one hand." Haine tossed the emerald into the air. His catch was awkward, especially for a man with such clever fingers. Thus I judged it no accident when the fumbled gem fell into my basin of washing water. "Ah, pardon . . ." He pulled out a dripping gray pebble, grinned, and flipped it back to Gareth. So he knew of water's unmasking.

Clutching my false beads, I buried my satisfaction and drew two mugs of ale.

It must have been near midnight as I waited for Gareth in the thick scrub that surrounded his latrine. Once he had served necessity, I stepped out to meet him. He started like a sparrow, his dagger in hand swifter than Haine could juggle his beads. I'd filled his ale mug neither so deep nor so often as the spy's.

"Verdonne's child," he sighed, when I raised just enough pale light he could recognize me. "I'm not made for this." His hand trembled as he sheathed the knife.

"You did well today," I said allowing my light to fade, lest Haine's raucous snores be false. "Exceptionally well. Just two things. Tomorrow we go boar hunting, as we planned. And Bran must continue to demonstrate his disdain for Teleri . . . but also clear jealousy of Haine's attentions."

"Jealousy? You're not thinking of—"

"Just follow my lead." Ezzarian modesty had no place here. "Remember all we've practiced. Remember obedience."

Gareth's hand touched my elbow as I turned to go. Even through my sleeve I could feel his blood racing. "He's good, isn't he? With the magic?"

"Very good. But it's all illusion."

"You'll take care with him, watch yourself with whatever this is you're planning to do? I think . . ." Uncertainty slowed his tongue. "I think he suspects you're not what you pretend. And he walks like a Warden."

A good thing the darkness hid my own worries. "Don't think overmuch. Just play your part as you've done. I'll take care of the rest."

He laughed a little as we set out across the hillside toward the hut. "I should have known I'd get no enlightenment. I just don't see— You've the skill to make me seem something I'm not. You've the wit to put all these stories and tricks together. And you've the courage to put yourself in the way of danger and corruption to protect Ezzaria—naught can cleanse the way Haine looks at you. How is it you're yet a student?"

"Searchers' testing is much more complicated than this." Though I was well practiced at humiliating confessions, I saw no benefit in undermining his confidence with my history. "I can do what's needed."

"I'll not renege on what I've sworn. I just . . ." His voice took on a note of urgency. "I feel the need to know you. When you appeared at the encarda, so kind and lovely, offering your help, I thought that holy Verdonne herself—"

"And then you learned I was but another trespasser." My cheeks could have cooked our breakfast.

"But you didn't run away. You revealed yourself—jeopardized your own future—to aid me." He halted just below the crest of the knoll. "I've never played a part in fateful events and likely never will again, no matter how this ends. But to understand the other players—to understand what drives this brave, determined Searcher who commands me—might help me understand my own part."

Had his request stemmed from simple curiosity or fear, I might have bristled and refused. But his desire to find order in a terrifying world struck some respondent chord in me, as a harper's fingers pluck a stretched wire and bring music, where another's elicit only noise. Against all intent, I sat on the grass in the midnight dark and told him of my training, my hopes, my doubts, and my failures . . . even to the illusory Derzhi child who had murdered her illusory father, and the collapsed enchantment that had condemned her to madness. ". . . but we've only one spy to deal with here and no rai-kirah. We're not going to fail."

"What was her name . . . the child?"

"Sonya . . . Sachka . . . something like. My partner knows their names. I did my best for her."

He sat on his haunches beside me, little more than an outline against the starry sky. "Perhaps you didn't fail. Perhaps she couldn't be saved."

"I won't believe that."

"Dai once told me something—a seeing she had. Doesn't matter what, but it got me thinking. I'd heard that jumping into an encarda without use of magic was the first trial in a Warden's training—a test of strength and faith and possibility. Since Dai's seeing, I've trespassed a Warden's encarda twice a year. Twice a year I jump in, thinking this time it won't scald me, this time I'll manage to stay in the water more than a heartbeat, this time I'll discover . . . something. Twice a year I fail. It's a fierce hurt, to be sure, and likely naught will ever come of it. But I've come to 'eve it's the trying that's important. The caring." He stood.

"I trust you. And I thank you for your caring . . . and for trusting me. Good night, mistress."

He strode off toward the house and in moments the door closed behind him. I stared after him for a long while . . . telling myself that a tenyddar farmer could not possibly have explained a puzzle I had been trying to unravel for so many years. Never in all my training, in all my thrashing, studying, and analyzing, had I ever considered that some of my tests had been designed to fail.

7

"**You** *will* come, girl," snapped Master Bran in our tenth argument of the morning. "You don't eat if you don't work. And women's work is what men say." He grabbed the bead necklace and with one great wrench snapped the string, sending beads flying all over the trampled ground in front of the hut. "What their *masters* say."

I grumbled wordlessly and rubbed my stinging neck. Haine watched us as he buckled on his swordbelt.

We were going pig hunting, and Teleri was commanded to go along to haul back the meat. It had not been difficult to act out my disgust for the task—death, blood and entrails, the sheer difficulty of maintaining the cleanliness our people prized. Thank the goddess and her son, my conjured sow would prove elusive, and we had no intention of bleeding our true quarry.

I snatched up the frame harness Gareth had dropped in the dirt in front of me and jammed my arms through the worn leather straps. As he struck out for the wood beyond his field, I spat on the ground behind him. We had both taken on our roles with extra vigor on this day.

Haine shrugged and grimaced in friendly sympathy. With a twist of his hand he vanished the scattered beads. "I'll replace them tonight," he whispered, his smile gleaming. Then he bowed to me, shouldered the boar spear we had given him, and followed Gareth down valley.

Mist coiled out of the hollows like smoky fingers of dawn, dampening skin, cloth, and leather alike, yet my throat felt as parched as the deserts of Azhakstan. I saw no evidence that Haine judged me anything but a besotted maidservant, but Gareth had been right about one thing. Though the spy behaved like a cocky magician—part juggler, part sorcerer, part scoundrel—he carried himself with the confidence and reserved strength of a warrior. No matter his small frame and dark coloring, I'd wager his father was no Fryth servant, but purest Derzhi. There was no measuring the danger in a physical confrontation with one of the warrior race. I swallowed bile, hefted the frame, and hurried after the men. We would need all the strength, faith, and benevolent possibility we could manage.

The day sped by. Haine seemed impressed by Bran's laying the scent of acorns to attract the sow and then quickly surrounding the rooting beast with a rill of flame. But when clumsy Teleri dropped the pack frame and rattled the butchery knives, thus sending the illusory beast charging straight at our blind, it was Haine who raised our protective fire to the height of a man and endowed it with a searing heat that convinced the mind it truly burned.

The sow, of course, turned tail and barreled into the wood. We gave chase, but came up with naught but one broken spear and a brace of rabbits. I was grateful for the overcast sky. Large, complex illusions could appear transparent in full daylight—especially at such close quarters.

Gareth shoved me stumbling up the path as we slogged back

to the hut in the steamy afternoon. "Fool of a girl. I should bind you to Ogul's mule when it's brought—to show there is no difference between you."

"Do it!" I spat. "I would sooner bed the mule than you."

Haine stayed out of our bickering. He had been quite companionable all day, allowing Gareth to lead the futile hunt, helping me gather dill and garlic shoots along the way, and expressing naught but whimsical humor when Gareth insisted he skin and gut the rabbits fifty paces from the stream. "I've known no gods so enamored of inconvenience," he'd said. "I always thought Mam had it wrong that we must be mindful of every puddle."

Once we arrived at the hut, Gareth retired to the shed to repair his broken boar spear, while I built up the fire and put water on to boil. Haine borrowed oil and sharpening stone and sat next the fire to hone his sword and dagger. "Your master is a strange one," he said after a while.

I dropped the disjointed rabbits into the pot. "He's a prideful devil," I said. "His head is rock. And he's a wicked liar."

"Ahhh . . . I think you favor him, Teleri. Is it you who refuse his desires, or he that refuses you?"

"I hate him! My da worked this land, but drank himself to death before he had it half broke, and he never paid the chieftain a fee for it. Ogul decreed I had to stay with the land till I was wed and my husband could pay the fee. Then he gives the place to Bran Prickhead, who'll have none of me within the law, as he's lusting for Ogul's daughter. What man'll ever look my way, thinking Bran takes his pleasure with me?" I whacked the roots off three leeks and dropped them into the pot. Casting an anxious glance at the doorway, I lowered my voice. "You oughtn't trust him. Nor Ogul, neither."

As I chopped garlic, enchantment teased my skin. Two quick footsteps and a solid weight draped round my neck. I looked down to see a necklace of bloodred glass beads laid on my breast.

"Oh, noble sir . . ." I touched the gleaming strand of purest illusion.

"I told you I would replace the others," he said, running his hands along my shoulders. "I was right that red would look fine with your dark hair and dark eyes. You are quite a pretty girl, you know."

"Bran won't let me keep them. He'll—" I snapped my mouth shut and tucked the necklace inside my tunic. Catching Haine's hand, I tugged him downward, until he crouched beside me. "He's no friend of yours, great sir. No friend of any stranger comes to Ezzaria."

"I'm not afraid of him." Haine pulled back, eyes glittering in the firelight. His smile chilled me deeper than flames could touch. "I've skills beyond beadwork."

"You *ought* to fear him," I said, my shivering no playacting. "He's got such magics—" I broke off and stirred my soup until the splash near doused the fire.

Gareth's boots thumped outside the door.

Haine's breath teased at my ear. "What magics?"

And so was my fish hooked. Scarce containing a ferocious joy, I planted a quick kiss on Haine's stubbled cheek. "Come to the bridge tonight when he sleeps."

⌀

At supper, Gareth eyed Haine and me, one and then the other, as if he knew something had changed. "I must mark the new field tomorrow," he said, spearing a chunk of meat with his knife and pointing it at Haine. "But first I'll show you the birch grove up valley. Fell enough trees, and you can eat another day. I'm done filling your belly for no return."

Haine rose from the bench, passing me his empty bowl. "I'll not dispute that, kinsman. You've treated me better than I'd any right to expect. But for tonight, I'm swagged, so I'll bid you fair dreaming—and you, too, Teleri."

"You're not to wish the mule anything, Fryth. She's naught to you." Gareth's ferocity heated the room as if he'd raised Haine's fiery wall.

"As you say, goodman."

While I knelt at the fire pit, cleaning pots and evaluating the possibilities of the next few hours, Haine retired to the corner by the flour cask and rolled up in Gareth's winter cloak. Head propped on his rucksack, sword and dagger within reach, he was soon snoring.

Gareth drank the last of the rabbit broth from his bowl and offered the dish to me with a shrug and an apologetic smile. Wound tight as I was, I could not return his smile. I jerked my head in the direction of his own pallet and mimed that he should stay awake.

He understood. After wiping his knife on a rag, he rose and stretched. "Finish your chores and get you to bed, girl," he said. "We've a full day tomorrow, even for lazy sluts the likes of you." His insult bore a harshness entirely at odds with the hand that so gently settled on my hair. Such comfort flooded from his touch, such care and apology and . . . forgiveness . . . that I almost dragged him from that hut and sent him running for safety.

"May devil spirits carry you to everlasting fire this night, Bran Prickhead," I muttered.

I finished my cleaning, banked the coals, and did not so

much as glance the tenyddar's way as he retreated to his own corner of the hut.

c/p

Haine's footsteps squelched on the muddy path long before I made out his trim shape moving through the dark. I waited on the verge of the sloping stream bank, one of Dai's wool blankets spread on the grass beneath me, the laces of my shift undone. Magic thrummed in my fingertips, in my head, in my spleen. Every mezzit of the vale was laid out in my mind, along with its scents and tastes and the slightest variation of its air—a map to guide my feet and my senses, so vivid that I marveled the spy could not see it waiting with me in the dark, right alongside the monstrous presence of my fear.

The deep water burbled and slopped underneath the bridge . . . and he was there, kneeling on the blanket, just behind me. The muffled clank of metal on rock and the aroma of grimed leather spoke of swordbelts and rucksacks. *Good.* That suggested he saw an end to his mission.

"Are you wearing your beads, pretty girl?" His silken voice touched me just before his hands.

"Aye, sir." I neither flinched nor shuddered as his fingers glided down my neck and located the necklace. The crimson glass began to glow. "Oh, blessed Lady, they are so beautiful."

He stretched out beside me on the blanket, leaning on one elbow, and idly traced the line of my cheek and my bare arm with his clever fingers. After a brush of my hip and thigh, he stroked the length of my leg through my woolen leggings. "Such a sweet thing you are to warn me of your heartless master. I've brought you another gift."

He withdrew his hand, and a loop of brilliant green appeared in the night, casting its glow on his sharp face. Faceted beads, like tiny emeralds—ten strands of them bound together—dangled from his finger. "They're for your ankle. Though"—he yanked them back from my grasping fingers—"it would be a shame not to see them against your smooth skin."

"Oh, sir!" Eager—loathing—I giggled and shucked my leggings. "They're so lovely."

I reached again for the beads. Again he dangled them out of reach. "First tell me of your master's fearsome magics—and of this chieftain, Ogul."

Sighing, I bent forward as if the stream or the bridge might overhear. "Ogul has been chieftain of this north country near forty summers. He fears all who live beyond the mountains. He forbids us to cross, and he gives his sons and favorites these border lands, teaching them his most fearsome powers to make war. Tomorrow Master Bran will lead you to the birch grove, making sure you get confused as to the way. Then he'll don his magical armor—"

"Armor?"

"Aye, armor of fire and sorcery. Naught can harm him when he wears it. He'll bind you in the birch grove, and only when you are half mad and half starved and swear on your mortal life to carry the tale of our monsters and haunted mountains back to the Empire will he let you go."

"He has done this before with . . . strangers?"

"Aye." I shifted position and nestled close to him, where I could not avoid his unwashed stink. "You must leave here tonight, get safely through the mountains before he wakes. You could take me with you. I could show you the easiest paths."

"Run away?" He cocked his head to one side, as he stroked my bare leg with the emerald beads, charging my body with revulsion. "I don't think so. Not yet. I've questions must be answered."

"Can I have the beads now, sir? They shine so." I stuck out my bare foot, scarce able to breathe as I waited.

"Soon, pretty girl." Smooth as a hunting cat, he sat up, pressing close enough to cup my chin and rub his thumb across my lips. "Tell me: what kind of magics do Ezzarian women wield?"

I crushed a glimmer of panic. He was but probing in the dark. He'd see no evidence lest I gave it to him.

"None but what the *men* teach us." I shoved his hand aside and flounced away from him in a pout, turning my back and kneeling up as if ready to bolt. "Always *men* must do as they please. My da said he'd teach me magic when I was gone twelve, but he drank himself dead before that. Bran would rather yell that I'm stupid and lazy than teach me to make fire to keep wildcats away. Sure you're as bad as the lot of them . . . teasing me to get what you want."

Quick as a weasel his body enfolded me from behind, legs and arms like straps of steel confining my limbs. His hand gripped my hair and yanked my head back onto his shoulder. "I don't believe you," he whispered in my ear.

I spat on his cheek, twisting and writhing to get loose. Yet when I wrenched one leg out from under me, I did not slam my heel into his groin. Neither did I conjure snakes to crawl up his shirt nor spark true fire from my hand to set his hair aflame. Rather I scratched his arms and bashed my head into his chin, whimpering like a powerless serving girl. "Devil spirit!"

Haine chortled and with effortless strength wrestled me onto my back, straddling me so that I felt the vile heat of him through my thin shift. But what froze my gut was how he pinned my hands to the earth beside my head, his palms pressed flat with mine, our fingers interlaced. I could not make a fist.

He throttled my rising wail with a grinding kiss, then held his face nose to nose with mine. "Something is very odd about you, Teleri. I've seen it since the beginning. Tell me what magics lie within these clean fingers, or I shall snap them off one by one."

"Naught, Master Haine. Naught..." And I babbled and moaned to please him.

Praying I could initiate the armor spell with power alone, I stretched my melydda to the hut where my rescuer waited, his heart galloping, sweat dampening his back. Pressing my will against his natural resistance, I reached for control...

...and like a worn bowstring, my magical tether snapped, blinding me for a moment with its recoil. He was too tight. Too focused.

Haine gripped harder and thrust a knee between my legs. "I'll wager I can persuade you to tell me what I want to know."

Seven times over, I cursed myself for linking the signal to my hands. Without the signal, Gareth did not know to yield me his body. But I had neither time to wait for opportunity nor weapons to break through his barriers. I was no Comforter like Kenehyr, who could bridge vast distances to speak in a listener's mind.

Despairing, I averted my face from Haine's hard lips and scratchy chin. But as I swallowed my disgust, thoughts of a Comforter's enchantments reminded me of the weapon that had been given me in trust. Using his gift to force submission would violate that trust, yet he had told me to take what I needed of him. And so again I stretched out my melydda to the hut, and this time I bound my enchantment with all the power of Name: *Gareth*.

When he came roaring down the path in his fiery armor, he

might have been a blazing meteor shooting through the night sky, or divine Verdonne's son Valdis, waging war on the Nameless God.

In one furious motion, he dragged Haine off me. Overbalanced, the two men slipped and slid down the bank, grappling in a blazing knot. No matter his strength and size, a tenyddar was unlikely to best a trained warrior, even if I had cloaked him in true fire rather than illusion. Yet in those first few moments as I scuttered away and drew Dai's blanket about my quivering shoulders, I thought he might actually prevail.

Gareth took the spy to the ground, but Haine twisted out of the bigger man's grasp and scrambled up the bank toward his sword. With a ferocious growl Gareth pounced, but snared only Haine's legs. The wiry Derzhi twisted loose again, and this time booted Gareth in the face. By the time Gareth recovered and sprang to his feet, Haine had drawn his dagger.

They crouched low. Haine danced here and there, never still. His blade glanced off the gleaming mail at Gareth's neck. Gareth caught the wrist of Haine's knife hand and grabbed for his throat. But they lost footing on the muddy bank, stumbling and sliding downward.

A thudding blow and a bitten cry told me when Haine's blade struck home. As with the emerald, the solidity of the illusion was ephemeral and could not long resist steel. Indeed, I had planned it so.

Another strike landed true, stalling Gareth as if he'd collided with a tree. Growling, he shook it off and engaged Haine yet again, obedient, as he had promised. The brilliance of his flaming coat seemed to dazzle the spy. Haine repeatedly swiped his eyes with his sleeve or hand, and numerous strikes missed their mark entirely. The illusory heat seared my skin, even at a distance.

I clenched my jaw and held my magic tight bound. *Think, you cursed fool of a Derzhi! End this.* The damnable, snarling warrior just didn't seem to recall how close he was to the water and the very answer he'd come here to learn. If Bran could work true sorcery, this armor would surely be its manifestation.

"Stop! Please stop!" I shrieked. "Master meant only to fright you." I grabbed a handful of stones and pelted the struggling pair . . . and made sure some flew off course and into the water. The largest one made a great loud *thunk* and splash. And then I bolted. Haine's interest must not revert to me. A roundabout course took me into the stream on the far side of the bridge, where I could peer under the logs without being seen.

Haine had disengaged and backed up the bank a few steps.

Gareth, breathing hard, one arm clamped to his middle, advanced warily. Haine feinted, appearing to overbalance. But when Gareth rushed in to take advantage, Haine slammed the pommel of his dagger into Gareth's head. Gareth wavered, stunned. Planting his foot on Gareth's chest, Haine threw his weight forward and toppled the bleeding man backward into the stream.

Water reveals truth. The blazing illusion was snuffed out.

Gareth emerged with a great gasp, shoulders hunched, arms flailing. Slipping and staggering, he lunged forward, but stumbled hard to his knees before reaching the bank.

As Gareth heaved and coughed and struggled to rise, the Derzhi darted up the bank and retrieved his sword. Winded himself, he stepped and slid downward, sword raised, the tip circling as he approached the kneeling man.

"Come, surely you can do better than this, Ezzarian. Sorcerer. Farmer." With every word, his scorn swelled. "Will you allow your drudge to buy your life, Goodman Bran? Will you die for your pitiful secrets?" He touched his edge to Gareth's neck.

Gareth did not move, save in the struggle of his breathing.

Ah, holy ones . . . I could not aid him. As a Weaver defends her settlement, I must maintain the barriers that kept Ezzaria inviolate. Humankind needed our gifts lest the innocent suffer from demon madness . . . and the life of one tenyddar, no matter how faithful, could not even shift the scale.

In a move that stopped my heart, Haine whipped his sword in a sidewise blow. Gareth crumpled without a cry.

Haine climbed out of the water. When he reached the top of the bank, he spun in place, calling out, "Teleri! Here's your pay, pretty girl!"

I did not answer, did not move, did not breathe.

A loop of sparkling emerald flew through the air and fell to earth halfway down the bank. Then Haine snatched up his rucksack and strode northward toward the mountains.

As the spy's footsteps and merry whistle faded, the night fell dead. The flowing water nudged the still form toward the bridge. Even so, I dared not move, but near shredded my ears with listening. Only when my senses detected no lingering trace of the Derzhi did I fly from my hiding place.

When I lifted Gareth's head and shoulders from the frigid water, blood leaked from the side of his skull. "Get up. Come on. I'll help, but goddess save me, I can't carry you."

He weighed like lead and remained limp as a rotted fig as I hauled him onto the muddy bank. "Wake up!" I mumbled. "You swore to obey me, so wake up. Breathe."

I rolled him onto his back, tapped his cold cheeks, and blew into his mouth again and again. And at last, in a blessed explosion of coughing and choking, he spewed water and gasped for air.

I risked a faint handlight, using my body to shield it from Haine's likely route up the mountainside. Goddess . . . Gareth was bleeding everywhere. Besides his head, three . . . four . . . separate gashes on his arms, another in his shoulder, another in his thigh. A bone-deep slice across one palm. Nothing mortal as long as I could get him warm and stanch the blood.

His eyes dragged open, cloudy and confused. He coughed and shuddered.

"That's better," I said, smiling in relief. "Keep at it." I reached under his arms to drag him farther up the bank. That's when I noticed the dark fluid welling from his side. *Goddess mother . . .*

I clamped his pale face in my hands until he focused on me. "Have you medicines at the house?" I said. "Teravine? Yarrow? Shavegrass?" Sorcery alone could not heal such a wound or put blood back where it belonged, but my enchantments could enhance the effects of medicines.

"Tin box. In the chest," he croaked, squeezing his eyelids shut as if the words were blows.

I shook his chin hard enough to jar them open again. "Have I your permission to open the chest?"

The weak smile brought his face back to life. "Whatever you need of me."

I tied one of my abandoned leggings around his lacerated hand. Then I balled up the tail of his shirt in his other fist, positioned it over the hole in his side, and tied the second legging about his middle to hold it in place.

"Press as hard as you can bear. I'll be back before you can blink." I tucked Dai's damp wool blanket around him and let my light die.

As I stood to go, his bandaged hand touched my ankle. "We did well? He believed?"

"Marvelously well. He saw your greatest illusion unmasked. Now stay awake until I get back."

My bare feet pounded the path. Gareth's side and his dreadful hand were going to need sewing. Once I slowed the bleeding, I'd need to get him up to the hut. But in no way could I do this all myself. Wrapping enchantment about my will, I sent out the call to Aelis. An hour, and help would be here. So why did my mind refuse to declare victory?

Stretching my senses into the house, then past its walls and up the notched mountainside, I listened, felt, tasted—nothing. The spy was gone, and Gareth would live if I stopped dawdling. Surely it was only Gareth's wounds that left this soured taste upon the air, and the memory of Haine's heated touch that roiled my belly.

I hurried into the shed and grabbed my rucksack and the second of Dai's blankets. The enchantments of her weaving might bring Gareth some healing benefit. Inside the house I lit the lantern and grabbed a tin basin, a flask of clean water drawn from the cistern, and the winter cloak Haine had left crumpled in the corner. Then I dropped to my knees in front of the wooden chest.

Ah, Verdonne's child . . . It was a man's soul I found carefully tucked away amid folded shirts, winter leggings, and worn linen towels. At least twenty well-used books filled the corners, their titles an incredible range—histories, fables, works on astronomy, on tools, on the sea and the weather, on the uses of herbs and the structure of the human body. Stacked with them were journals—the thin booklets of bound parchment we used in reading school—pages and pages written in a careful hand. And in a box lay the answer to the mystery of the wood slivers—a wooden sailing ship the size of my two fists, lovingly detailed, lacking only rigging to complement its three masts. I felt as if Haine's knife had pierced my own breast.

I grabbed the linen and a painted tin box containing a few

vials and packets, bundling them with the basin, flask, and blanket. Making sure not to damage his work as I closed the chest, I snatched up the lantern and ran.

Gareth had vomited while I was gone, and now sat up, his head resting on his knees. His skin was cold and damp, the beat in his wrist racing. I threw the second blanket over him and set the lamp close.

He groaned and buried his eyes in his unbound arm. "Head," he whispered. "Goddess mother . . . like hot irons."

"He must have whacked you with the flat of his blade." Ever grateful for the goddess's gift of magic, I set water to boiling for steeping his dried yarrow.

"Why?" he mumbled. "Why didn't he finish me?"

"He likely—"

My hands fell slack. Of a sudden, the night pressed in upon our little circle of light, all my uneasiness taking shape in that simple question. The bead anklet lay gleaming faintly in the trampled sedge. I snatched it up and used it to focus on the Derzhi, scouring the vale for some sign of him.

I neither smelled nor heard nor saw nor tasted him. Had this been two days previous, I would have declared our venture finished. But somehow, with my spirit so full of Gareth, I detected the weight of malevolence directed his way. Every instinct, every pin's weight of logic in my bones, told me that our enemy approached. Haine. Creeping our way ever so quietly to see what we would do with Gareth's wounds. Healing enchantments wrought fundamental changes in the body—always sorcery, never illusion.

The knife in my breast twisted. The spy must be given to believe that Bran could not heal himself, and that Teleri either could or would not heal him. A devoted Teleri would not abandon Bran before he was dead, and it was too late to pretend indifference. Yet I dared not be here—dared not risk Haine questioning me—for all the reasons Gareth had guessed. No matter that I would give my hands or eyes to protect this man, we had to play one more scene.

"You damnable, cursed, stubborn pig!" I screamed and flung the basin across the stream.

Gareth raised his head, wincing at the movement, the noise, and the light. "What?"

"Did you not think I'd notice that Iola gave you this?" I waved the painted tin box, scattering the precious vials and packets across the mud and water. "Bran Prickhead. Bran Cheatheart. Bran Devil. Chasing Ogul's daughter while I slave at your hearth."

I had vowed to use my knowledge and talents to save lives, to save minds and souls, which were life's essence. To lose the subject of your scenario meant failure to a Searcher, and in fear of failure—and the pain it must bring—I had ever sought an impossible perfection in my work, withholding my heart while pursuing my own flaws. But Gareth had been right. Some tests were fated to fail. Some victims could not be saved. You had to embrace them and care for them and keep trying.

"Ah," he said, softly, glancing here and there into the night. Then he forced his voice into a loud, quavering croak. "Teleri, I can explain!" Brows raised in good humor, his dark eyes flicked from my face to his bandaged hand, where he wagged his thumb. Offering. Yielding. "You're bound to me, girl!"

Tears coursing down my cheeks, I claimed his hand, dribbling weak fire from his fingers, and at the same time kicked him flat. Then I rolled him back into the water, turned my back, and walked away.

༄

From my hidden vantage across the valley, I could not decipher all that ensued. I saw the dark, slight shape return to the stream. I heard splashing. I heard Gareth's screams. I heard Haine rage in frustration. For every moment of an interminable hour, I prayed. But I did not stop it. Just because I knew a man's name and that he built ships and read books and tested his faith in steaming pools could not change what had to happen. I stayed and I watched and I cared.

When the dark shape vanished into the north beyond the range of all my senses, I ran. And when I found the stubborn farmer yet breathing, I sat in the water and held him as it washed us clean, wrapping him in all I could of warmth and care. "Bravely done, son of Ezzaria. Bravely done."

8

"**Ready** for final testing . . . Joelle, are you sure?" Aelis's hammer rested against the fence in rare idleness.

"Absolutely sure. Our venture did not conclude perfectly. Haine might yet carry some suspicion about Ezzarian women. But he believed he saw the best magic our men can do—illusion—unmasked. Gareth's ordeal proved an Ezzarian man could not save himself with sorcery. And thanks to Gareth and Queen Tarya and you, when the test came, I did not withhold."

My mentor nodded.

Now for the more difficult part of this meeting. "Mistress, I know I've spent years of your time, years of everyone's indulgence. But once my testing's done . . . instead of moving into the field right away, I'd like to spend some time with Dai. She sees things others don't, and she protects far more than village boundaries. I feel the need to sit at the loom and learn from her. I can't explain . . ."

Aelis sagged against the fence. "Well, Verdonne's child be praised. You've pulled your head out of the bog at last."

I had no idea what she meant, until later that afternoon when I announced my plan to Kenehyr. ". . . and I know this means delaying your own field work or starting over with a new partner."

He grinned, leaned his mouth next my ear, and whispered. "Don't let on I've told you, but I've been working with Kirsa for six months now, since Aelis told me you had the makings of a Weaver, if you ever got your head out of your . . . bog . . . and saw it. Sorry as I am to lose the fairest of partners, Ezzaria—and the world—will be the richer."

He must have seen my bewilderment.

"You *do* know they reserve our strongest to defend Ezzaria?" He chortled and crowed and then kissed me straight on the lips. "Now go to him. You've been twitching since you heard they'd brought him here."

Still trying to take in what all this meant, I hurried through the birch grove, bright with new green and dappled sunlight. The house of healing was quiet and spare—a few tidy beds rowed on an expanse of polished wood, great windows that flooded the room with light. He was the only patient on this day. The attendant smiled and left us alone.

I watched him sleep for a while, and a fevered warmth raced through me when his first groggy glimpse of my face suffused his own with pleasure.

"Never thought you'd come here, mistress."

"They say you'll be abed another fortnight, so I didn't want you to feel dull." I slipped Kenehyr's book of sailing ships under his pillows, then scowled in mock severity. "Besides, we've a few things to settle."

The cloud that shadowed his poor bruised face forbade me prolong my teasing.

"First, to remedy a dreadful rudeness." I laid my clenched fist on my heart. "*Lys na* Joelle."

Embarrassed, pleased, he stumbled through the response. "I am honored . . . by your trust . . . Joelle."

"And second, you've left me with a pestiferous curiosity. You never told me what Dai saw."

He burst out laughing, only to gasp and clutch a pillow fiercely to his bandaged middle. I raised a hand to summon the attendant, but he shook his head. "No, please, I oughtn't laugh anyway. It's just . . . Dai is so wise, but in this instance, her sight is surely flawed. A fellow who ends up twice drowned and his gut holed like a sieve is not what she saw."

I arranged his pillows to support him better. "Let me judge. As I'm to be Dai's student, I need to weigh her insights."

"You're to work with Dai?" An inordinately cheery smile replaced his grimace. "Then, who am I to argue?"

He dropped his gaze as he turned his mind to his story. "When I turned ten and walked out of reading school, knowing I could never return, I was near inconsolable. Dai was waiting for me. She told me she had seen something in her weaving, and that I must hold to it through every day." He glanced up, wincing as if sure I would laugh. "She said my life would be the key to the war's end."

A flutter of moth wings brushed my skin. I did not laugh. "That is a wonder. What else did she say?"

"Nothing." His brow drew tight. "So often I've wished she'd not spoken. I study the books she gives me. I keep strong and live with what honor I may, so as to be ready. But what vegetable farmer ever ended a war? So twice a year . . ."

". . . you jump into an encarda, believing the pool might wake some dormant melydda inside you."

A trace of scarlet livened his pale cheeks, and he smiled ruefully. "Many years have gone since I believed that. No, I've just felt that if I kept at it, as with my running and my reading, then the goddess would have ample opportunity to tell me whatever she wished—even if it was only that I would ever be tenyddar and must spend my days with turnips."

I smoothed his rough hand that had found its way to mine. "Sometimes the Lady's course is very hard."

He raised our joined fingers to my lips. "Ah, mistress, speak no ill of holy Verdonne. I'm thinking she *did* reveal a path on that night in the Wardens' Grove. I'd like to follow, if you're willing. As to where it might take us . . . what comes, comes."

What we'd done these past days would not end the rai-kirah war. At most it would stave off the dangers of the world for a few more years. But Gareth's faith had changed whatever part I was to play in the war—and in all my days of living. Perhaps a vegetable farmer could not end a thousand-year war by himself, but who said he had to attempt it alone?

I bent close then and made it clear that I was more than willing to explore the goddess's path. When we caught our breath, we talked long of books and ships and magic, and I sat with him as he drifted back to sleep, leaving my hand in his, lest he dream himself alone. Then I hied off to the Weaver's to begin my work anew.

Huntress Moon

REBECCA YORK

One

The ancient ones have always understood the wolf. Their totems often show the animal with eyes that are calm, focused, benevolent. Yet other totems depict the wolf with red eyes and fangs bared, his visage—for want of a better word—tormented.

"**W**hich do you choose? Disgrace or slavery?"

Zarah sat very still, her hands clasped in her lap to keep them from trembling.

"What if I choose disgrace?" she asked.

"The tumor in your mother's breast is growing. You will watch her die a slow, painful death."

Zarah struggled to keep her features even. Since the moment she had entered Scanlon's massive stone and timber mansion, she had known from his expression that he was holding the trump card in a game of power and politics.

Now she sat in his comfortable reception room with an untouched glass of red wine resting on the wooden table in front of her.

"How can you let a helpless woman suffer?" she asked.

Scanlon smoothed a hammy hand down the edge of his embroidered tunic, his fingers like sausage links. With his broad shoulders and long legs, he might have been athletic in his school days. Now his body had gone to fat. And his long hair hung limply around his ears. He had been the head of the council for more than seven years. A long time in the political life of White Flint, where alliances constantly shifted. And a particularly long time for a man with only minimal psychic talents.

"Fenda's plight is not my fault. Your father should have thought about his wife and daughter when he embezzled money from the treasury."

"He was an honest man. He would never have broken our laws."

Scanlon gave her a knowing look. "Not even to import spices from the south?"

She blanched. She knew that her father had dealt with smugglers who avoided the city-state's import taxes. All the nobles did it. It was a small sin compared to stealing money from the treasury.

"He was caught, convicted, and executed," Scanlon said, his voice low but firm.

She wanted to scream that it was a lie. One of his enemies on the council must have arranged for him to be caught with White Flint money bags in his strong room. But there was no use protesting his innocence. After the presumed crime, the trial and the execution had been carried out with lightning speed.

Her father was gone. Her coward of a brother had stolen the emergency money hidden in the house and fled into the badlands. And she was left to deal with the consequences of the whole mess.

Scanlon looked like a jackal that had cornered a rabbit and was anticipating a tasty meal. "I don't expect you to stay a slave forever. Once you find out what Griffin is hiding, you're free to come back to White Flint."

"And how would I get home? Sun Acres is miles from here."

"I'll send a crack team to kidnap you from the city and bring you back, once you've gotten the information I need."

Was that possible? Or was Scanlon offering her hope when she had none?

"If I agree, you'll have an expert psychic treat my mother's illness while I'm gone?"

"Of course."

"How will I know you're fulfilling your part of the bargain?"

"You have to trust me," he said, his voice smooth.

Impossible. But her choices were limited.

She licked her lips. "What do I have to do?"

"You agree?"

"Tell me the whole thing."

Scanlon took a sip from his wineglass, then leaned back in his comfortable leather chair and looked her up and down, his gaze lingering on her blond hair, her well-shaped lips, and her high breasts.

"As you know, Sun Acres had been a threat to us for years. After one of their leaders, Falcone, disappeared, a man named Griffin stepped into the power vacuum."

She had heard her father talking about Griffin. He'd admired the man's progressive policies. Apparently, in this world of shifting alliances and private armies, Scanlon disagreed.

"For several months, Griffin has been acting secretive. He's hiding something and we want to know what it is. We have discovered that he is looking for a slave girl to share his bed. I'll make sure it's you. And that will put you in the perfect position to spy on him. Then you can send information back to me—using your skill with the flame."

She stared at him—stunned. "His bed?" she whispered. She'd been raised as the daughter of nobles. And she'd expected to marry one of the powerful men of the city—a man seeking an alliance with her family. Now that would be impossible.

Scanlon gave her a knowing grin. "He's reputed to be a skilled lover. You won't be disappointed."

"But I . . . haven't . . ."

"My dear, your virginity is part of your charm."

She was still absorbing that when a flicker of movement made her head whip around. A short, spindly man wearing a blue tunic stood in the doorway.

"Are we ready to start?" he asked.

She gaped at him. "Alroy?"

He gave her a quick half bow. She'd known him since she was a little girl—when she'd been taken away from her family and sent to the school where psychic talents were nurtured. He'd been one of her teachers. A harsh man who was quick to use a switch on children who were slow to learn.

He knew all her skills. And all her weaknesses. And when she'd graduated two years ago, she'd thanked the Great Mother that she was never going to see him again.

"What are you doing here?" she asked.

"We're going to establish a communications link."

Her chest was so tight that she could barely breathe.

"We?"

"You're adept with the flame. So am I."

"I . . . was never that . . . good . . ." she stammered.

"You didn't have to be an expert at anything, because your

father had other plans for you. Now you're going to reach your full potential."

And if I can't, will you whip me? She kept the question locked in her throat, because she knew that voicing it would only make things worse.

"Come with me."

She looked at Scanlon. "You assume I've agreed?"

"Have you?"

"Yes," she whispered.

"Then go on. The sooner you pass the tests, the better."

Feeling like she was going to her execution, she followed Alroy down the hall to a small room with a wooden table and two chairs. When he ordered her to sit, she sat, as though she were back in his classroom.

He pulled two small oil lamps from the bag he was carrying. "Let's get started."

She answered with a tight nod. She had come to the end of life as she had known it. And the sooner she finished her assignment, the better.

He pushed one of the lamps toward her. "Use your thoughts to light the flame."

She gulped and tried to focus on the wick. But she was too tense to make anything happen.

"Do it!" he said in a steely voice.

She tried to clear her mind and obey him.

᙮

Griffin paced the length of his bedroom, then stopped at the window and stared out into the walled garden where the shapes of trees and bushes blurred in the moonlight. He had always liked night better than the day.

But no more.

He squeezed one large hand into a fist and slammed it against the other flattened palm, welcoming the pain of knuckles striking flesh.

He was a tall man with dark hair, a powerful intellect, lips that women had called sensual, and deep-set dark eyes that could make an opponent in the council chamber stop talking in midsentence.

He knew the world had once been very different. With governments of countries, not cities. But he had to work within the system that existed now. Lucky for him he had been born into one of the city's noble families. But he had never taken the privileges of birth for granted. Not in a place like Sun Acres where you had to rely on talent and cunning to get power and keep it.

He had worked hard to become one of the top men on the council. And he wasn't going to make the same mistakes as his former associate, Falcone.

The man and some of his private army had apparently paid with their lives for his miscalculations, although no one seemed willing to claim credit for ridding the city of the menace.

That was six months ago, and while nobles were jockeying with each other, Griffin had quietly consolidated his position. It helped that he didn't want the glory. He was content to work behind the scenes.

Life in his little corner of the world might not be as safe and comfortable as in the old days before the psychic change, but he could make things better—at least for some of the residents of Sun Acres.

He had been content with his life. He had thought about forging an alliance through marriage. And then disaster had struck.

His own private disaster.

"Carfolian hell," he muttered under his breath.

He had a problem—a sickness—that threatened to destroy him. Yet he could trust no one to help him. Because the moment he whispered his secret to another living soul, he was finished.

So he had started doing his own research, plowing through the library of the school where children with psychic potential were trained. Every city-state had a similar facility, and he had spent ten years of his life being trained and indoctrinated. He hadn't been one of the most talented students. But he was an adept, nonetheless.

He had watched and listened and learned everything he could, and he was sure that some book in the restricted library would hold the key to his salvation.

He wanted to go to the school now. But under the present circumstances, that would be taking too much of a risk.

So he paced back to the low chest along the wall and picked up the bottle of spirits that sat there.

After pouring several inches of the amber liquid into a glass tumbler, he held it up to the light, swirling it in the vessel.

The glass was ancient and rare. From the old times before the change. When household goods had been manufactured in smooth-running factories. He took a swallow of the fiery liquid, then another, feeling the heat hit his belly.

With luck, it would settle him down so that he could sleep.

Two

Zarah had suffered through a week of agony and humiliation. She had survived this long. She could survive the rest of it because she had to.

She and the fourteen other slaves had been chained hand to hand as they walked toward Sun Acres. But now her hands were free, with the chains still dangling. To control her movements, her right foot was secured to a post pounded into the ground.

Maybe a strong man could have worked it loose. But she was too exhausted to even try.

Her feet were sore. Her muscles ached. And her stomach clenched with hunger. Never had she put out so much effort with so little to eat.

She and the others in the group had walked all day—away from the only home she had ever known, and into the badlands, the lawless void between cities. Were they ten miles from White Flint? Twelve? She couldn't be sure. But she knew they were heading northeast, unless Scanlon had lied about that.

Two of the guards rode horses. But most walked alongside the men and women secured in a line like animals going to slaughter.

The guards held their spears and whips at the ready, partly to keep the slaves in line and partly to protect their owner's property. Zarah and the other captives were a valuable commodity that would fetch a good price in Sun Acres.

Her blond hair was matted. Her knee was scraped where she had fallen. As she lay with the thin blanket folded around her, the ground was hard under her slender frame. But she was exhausted enough to sleep.

A rough hand on her shoulder woke her. She would have screamed, but another hand clamped over her mouth.

In the light from the fire, she saw a man hovering over her.

Was this a raid? Thieves bent on stealing the slaves?

But no one else moved, and she realized with a sudden jolt of fear that the attack was only on her.

She felt something cold against her neck.

"Scream, and I'll slit your throat," the man hissed, his breath sour in her nostrils. He must be one of the guards.

She clenched her teeth, trying to evaluate her options. Was he fool enough to destroy valuable property? She didn't know.

From the smell of his breath, she thought he had been drinking. Maybe liquor had shattered his judgment.

One of his hands pulled the blanket aside and groped at her breasts through the bodice of her shapeless dress. The other hand reached for the hem, pulling it up above her thighs.

So rape was going to be the final humiliation of the day. Or was death better than this life that had been thrust upon her?

Remembering the chain that still dangled from her right hand, she raised her arm in an arc, slamming the metal links down on the back of the man's head.

He screamed, and she pushed against him, trying to roll him off her body.

Roused from sleep, the woman next to her reared up, reaching for the assailant's hair, pulling as she called out in a loud voice, "No! Stop! Get off her."

"Bitch."

He lashed out a hand, slamming it across the other woman's face.

More slaves had awakened. Wide-eyed, they stared at Zarah and the other captive struggling with the guard.

Then strong hands lifted the man away and flung him to the ground.

"You fool! She's being sold as a virgin. You can't bring down the price we'll get for her."

The whole camp was awake now.

The rapist gasped as something solid connected with his midsection. Then he screamed.

She didn't see what happened to him. She only knew that one of the guards dragged him off into the bushes and left him there.

She turned her face away as the man in charge crouched beside her, then grabbed her chin and brought her face back to his. "Did he penetrate you?"

Zarah swallowed hard. "No."

As she tried to shrink away, he reached between her legs, poking at her, then lifted his hand and examined his fingers in the firelight.

"No blood. Good."

Sick and humiliated, she fumbled for her blanket, pulling it over herself again. Tears stung her eyes, and she fought to hold them back.

When a hand reached toward her, she jumped.

But it was only the woman who had come to her aid.

"Thank you. I should have thanked you," Zarah whispered.

"That's okay."

"You could have gotten hurt—or punished."

The other woman shrugged. "I was pretty sure some-one would stop him. It was a matter of holding him off," she whispered.

The woman rolled toward Zarah, clasping a hand across her shoulder, silently stroking her back and hair. "It's all right to cry."

"No."

She didn't want to cry. She wanted to show these bastards that she was strong. But she couldn't stop the tears from leaking from her eyes and sliding down her cheeks.

The woman rocked her, soothed her. After a few moments, she said, "It's going to be all right."

"How could it?" Zarah managed.

"I don't know. But I think I feel it. You were strong. You fought him. Few slaves would do that. He was counting on your being weak and afraid."

Zarah nodded, then whispered, "Can you read the future?"

The woman hesitated. "Sometimes."

"Do you know my fate?"

"No. They've given me a drug that dampens my powers."

Zarah nodded. She had been given drugs for the journey, too, because the men who were taking her from White Flint to Sun Acres had no idea of her clandestine assignment. But the dampers would wear off—she hoped.

"My name is Quinn," the woman said.

Up until now, Zarah had tried to keep to herself in this terrible time of humiliation. The other slaves were a sorry, beaten-down lot. But this woman seemed different. Quietly, she whispered her own name. "Zarah."

"You haven't been a slave for long," Quinn murmured.

Around them, people stirred, probably trying to get back to sleep—or maybe listening. What if one of them was a spy? What if this woman was?

Zarah lowered her voice. "How do you know?"

Quinn laughed softly. "You're not worn out. And you have a way about you. The way of a free woman who has lost her position."

"Yes," Zarah admitted, then asked, "Were you born a slave?"

"No. I was free until I was ten. Then my city—The Preserve at Eden Brook—was raided by soldiers from Hammond Town. We lived near the outer wall. They took my family captive. And they discovered I had talents. So I went to the school for psychics in Hammond Town."

"What can you do besides read the future?"

"I . . . run equipment. I can light an oven and keep it hot. Or I can make a water pump work."

"Ah . . ."

So, as an adept and then a skilled worker, Quinn had been treated relatively well.

"A few months ago, Hammond Town was raided by White Flint. That's how I ended up here."

"But why are they selling you? You have valuable skills."

She spoke in a barely audible whisper. "The woman who ran the kitchen where I was sent had fewer talents than I do. She's the love child of a noble, so she had enough influence to get me out of there."

"I'm sorry," Zarah answered.

"Quiet!" one of the guards shouted, slapping a whip on the ground close to Zarah's cheek. Instantly she closed her mouth and rolled to her back.

She had a long day of walking ahead of her. And another after that. And perhaps another. She already felt like she might die of fatigue. That part of the ordeal would be over when she reached Sun Acres. The next part might be worse.

Alroy had made her practice with the flame—over and over. He'd set up tests where they had to communicate from different rooms of the mansion. Then from across the city. After five days, he had told Scanlon that she was ready for the assignment.

She hadn't felt ready. What if she couldn't do it from so far away?

She thought of her mother, living in a small room in the servants' quarters in Scanlon's great house. Her mother had been a beautiful woman who was proud of her thick golden hair and her smooth skin. Now she looked old and sick. She'd tried to hide her pain and fear, but Zarah had seen it all too well.

Scanlon had given them a few minutes alone to say good-bye. Probably because he knew that would stiffen Zarah's resolve to carry out her assignment. He'd been right. She'd promised fiercely that she would save the two of them. In the next few days, she had to make good on that promise.

Three

As a noble's daughter, Zarah had loved the market where her father and the other men bought and sold purebred horses. She'd sit in the visitors' gallery watching the magnificent animals and listening to the discussions about their good points and their bad.

But she had never been to a slave market. Never known that it was the same for people. Only the slave-animals could listen to the discussions going on around them.

The Sun Acres slave auction was in a large stone building in the commercial quarter of the city, with open display areas and many small rooms where the consignments were housed.

The guards brought the captives from White Flint to a dining hall where they were given a decent meal for the first time in days. Bread and cheese and even some fresh fruit and vegetables.

She and Quinn looked at each other across the table. Zarah

longed to ask what would happen next. But they had been warned not to talk. So she only ate and drank—and worried.

Then the men and women were separated. First they were given a medical exam. Since Zarah was being sold as a virgin, she had to lie down on a narrow table and spread her legs so that a wrinkled old woman could probe her private parts to confirm her condition.

"There was an incident on the trail," the tall heavy man who seemed to be in charge of the auction said. "Is she still untouched?"

"She's a virgin."

The man, whose name was Teledor, stroked his chin. "I'm almost disappointed. I'd like to fuck her myself before I sell her off."

Zarah sucked in a sharp breath, but they ignored her.

"She's pretty. And refined. She'll fetch a good price."

"I know a couple of nobles who will be interested in her."

"Griffin and Lloyd?"

Griffin. That was the man she'd been sent here to spy on. She wanted to hear more about him, but she didn't dare ask.

They kept talking, but not about Griffin.

"The last woman Lloyd bought died."

"He said it was an accident."

"He gets his pleasure from hurting his partners." The old woman glanced at Zarah and saw that the blood had drained from her face.

She touched the slave master's arm. "Come into the hall."

He glanced at Zarah, then nodded.

In the hallway, they continued talking in low voices. Then the woman returned. "You can rest in your cell for a few hours. Then we'll take you to the baths."

❦

Griffin turned the message in his hand. It was on heavy paper, a rare commodity in Sun Acres.

"Private slave viewing at 8 P.M. The woman will interest you. She will be for sale at the morning auction. Reply to Teledor."

He knew the procedure. The woman would be taken to one of the bathing rooms. And she would think she was alone. But men would be watching in darkened cubicles behind the grille-work that covered what looked like decorative panels.

He'd been there before. They'd never shown him a woman he wanted for a bedmate. Nevertheless, the experience had turned him on.

Tonight he hesitated. There was danger for him going out after dark. But he knew he would be in a private room. If anything went wrong, he could leave without being seen.

So he sent back his acceptance, then wondered if he was making a mistake.

❦

Slave women led Zarah to a large bathroom with a tile floor and walls and a large candelabra hanging from the ceiling. As she watched, they filled a large wooden tub with hot, scented water.

"Why are they letting me bathe?" she asked.

"So you'll look nice and smell nice tomorrow."

"The auction's tomorrow?"

"Yes. There's good soap. And lotion for your face and body. You should take advantage of them."

After the dry dusty walk across the badlands, the idea of soap and hot water was heavenly.

"Thank you."

"Take off your clothes. We'll bring you a clean gown. Better fabric."

She looked at the women, then pulled the rough dress over her head. The other slaves studied her body with interest. When one of them glanced toward the grillework halfway up on the wall, she followed the woman's gaze. "What's up there?"

"Nothing."

"Enjoy your bath," the other woman said quickly.

Zarah suddenly wanted to cover her breasts with her arm. And shield her thatch with the other hand.

Instead she climbed quickly into the tub. Staying as far down in the water as she could, she began to wash.

They had made her think she would be alone here. But now she had the horrible feeling that she was being watched—by men.

Closing her eyes, she enjoyed the hot water and the soap. Finally, the two women came back and ordered her to get out. The towel they gave her was too small to wrap around her body, so she dried as quickly as she could. When she started to pull on her dress, one of them stopped her.

"Dry your hair first."

"Why?"

"So your dress won't get wet."

She did as she was told, wondering who was enjoying the view of her naked body as she stood with her arms raised above her head, rubbing the strands of her hair with the towel, making her breasts jiggle as she worked, trying to pretend she was alone.

❧

The next morning, as she waited in the holding room, ready to go on the auction block, she couldn't see what was happening in the arena, but she could hear nobles bidding for another woman.

She glanced at Quinn, who was among her group.

"It will be over soon," the other woman whispered.

If only that were true.

Her heart was pounding when the man named Teledor pointed to her. "Let's have this one now."

Two guards pulled her to her feet and marched her out the door, to the side of a room with a waist-high barrier separating the center ring from what must be a viewing area—like at the horse auction. Bright lights shone on the center of the room, and she cringed away as she saw a large wooden cross on a small raised platform. The audience was in shadow, but she sensed a crowd of men beyond the barrier, and her stomach tied itself into a knot.

"We have a very exciting offering. A woman from a noble family. Refined and certified as a virgin. Well educated and modest in her demeanor. Her name is Zarah."

Before she could gasp, one of the guards pulled the gown over her head, leaving her naked.

Then he and the other man each took one of her arms and marched her to the center of the room and up onto the raised platform. Each of them fixed one of her wrists to manacles on the horizontal beam of the cross. Then they spread her legs several inches apart and chained her ankles to rings on the floor.

She was naked and exposed, and one of the men wound a crank, turning the platform on which she stood, giving a view of her naked figure to all sides of the room. From beyond the lights, she could hear men commenting on her body.

Teledor walked to her and lifted one of her breasts, then squeezed her nipple.

When she winced, he said, "She's very sensitive to touch. And ripe for the picking."

He ran his hand down her body, stroking his fingers through her pubic hair, and she heard herself make a whimpering sound.

When he let her go, she stood rigidly, staring toward the top of the wall, wishing she could simply die.

"We'll start the bidding at one hundred new dollars," Teledor said.

"One hundred."

"One hundred and fifty."

"Two hundred."

"Two fifty."

At first there were many voices from beyond the lights. Then only two.

The bidding went up and up. And she knew that these two men must want her badly.

She fought not to take her lip between her teeth while they decided her fate.

Was one of them Griffin? And one Lloyd? She had no way of knowing for sure. But she used every ounce of mental power she possessed to reach out to the one named Griffin.

"Damn you," one of the voices growled. "She's not worth that much, and you know it."

Footsteps stomped out of the room, and she held her breath.

"Sold."

Great Mother, who had bought her?

Four

"**Y**ou can fuck her here, Griffin. In one of the private rooms," a man in the audience called out.

Others laughed.

She cringed away from the voice and the laughter. Yet at the same time, she let out a sigh. It was Griffin. The man who had bought her was Griffin. Had someone mentally guided his desires? Was that why he was willing to pay so much for her?

"Put her gown on and take her to the side door. I have another purchase to make."

The guards released her hands and feet. One of them threw her dress at her and she quickly pulled it over her head. They took her out a different door, then led her to a small room with wooden benches along the wall.

She waited for almost half an hour. When the door opened, she expected to see the man who had bought her. But it was Quinn who stepped into the room.

"What are you doing here?" Zarah asked.

"The same person bought me."

"Thank the Great Mother," Zarah breathed, then felt her breath hitch.

Quinn crossed the room and gave her a hug. "Was it bad?" she whispered.

"They stripped me—and chained me to a cross."

Quinn winced. "They didn't do that to me. I guess because I'm only going to run kitchen equipment." She looked quickly away.

"And I'm going to the master's bed," Zarah whispered.

The other woman glanced around, then drew Zarah into the corner of the room. "Maybe that's not so bad. I heard them talking about him. He's a fair man."

Zarah licked her dry lips. Before she lost her nerve, she asked, "Quinn, have you been with a man? In bed?"

"Yes."

"Was it good—or bad?"

"I was with the boy I loved, and it was very good."

"But with Griffin, it could be bad."

"With the other one—Lloyd—it would have been worse than you can imagine."

Zarah sucked in a sharp breath. "How do you know?"

"They had you isolated from the other women. But where I was, I could hear some of the slaves talking. About Lloyd. And Griffin. Lloyd . . . likes to hurt women. That gives him sexual pleasure."

Zarah made a strangled sound.

"Griffin isn't like that. I think he'll want to please you."

"Why do you think so?"

"I saw him. He looks like a decent man."

"He can do anything he wants with me."

Quinn laid a hand on her arm. "It's better if you don't assume the worst."

"I'm scared," Zarah whispered, surprised that she'd been able to admit that much—to a slave girl. But now she was a slave girl, too. And Quinn was the only friend she had.

The other woman raised her head and gave Zarah a direct look. "Did you ever . . . touch yourself? Give yourself pleasure . . . between your legs?"

Zarah flushed scarlet, and her voice thinned. "How can you ask me that?"

"Because I'm trying to help you. When sex is good with a partner, that's what it's like—only better."

"Really?" she whispered, her face still hot.

Quinn kept her voice even. "Did you play with your breasts?"

"No!"

"Why not?"

"I . . . never thought of it."

"But you thought of the other."

She struggled to stand there facing Quinn. She could never have imagined this conversation. Not in a thousand years. And she had as good as admitted something shameful. Something she never should have done.

Quinn must have followed her thoughts. "It's good that you did. Because you know what arousal feels like. And sexual climax."

"Is that what it's called? The part at the end?"

"Yes. Or coming."

The need for information overcame her embarrassment. "With a man . . . he . . . puts . . . his penis inside you?"

"Yes. Don't you know anything?"

She answered with a nervous laugh. "Not much—apparently. Most of what my mother told me was about keeping anyone from doing that—until I was married."

Quinn snorted.

"Doesn't it hurt?" Zarah asked quickly. "When he does it? I mean—how can it feel *good*?"

"It hurts the first time." She was silent for a moment. "Not after that."

"Why did you hesitate?"

"Because it depends . . . on if he wants to please you. And if you want to respond to him."

"You're making it complicated."

"It's not. The most important thing for you to remember is that it should be . . . pleasurable. And if you let him arouse you, it *will* be. So don't try to protect yourself by keeping your mind away from what he's doing. Let yourself get into it."

"How?"

"When he touches you—and kisses you—let it make you hot. Kiss him back. Touch him."

"His penis?" she managed, hardly able to picture touching him there.

"Well, he won't expect a virgin to be that bold. But maybe his nipples. He'll like that."

"His nipples—what should I do to them?"

"The same thing he does to yours."

Zarah took that in. She was getting up her courage to ask another question when the door opened, and she snapped her mouth closed.

Another man stepped in. He was balding and dressed like a servant in a short tunic and leather sandals. Zarah looked him up and down. "You're not Griffin."

"Hardly. I am Philip. I run his household. I'm to take you home."

He pulled manacles and a chain from the leather bag slung over his shoulder.

"You don't need those," Quinn said. "We're not going anywhere."

"I'm sorry. City rules," he muttered as he clamped a cuff on her left wrist, then joined it by a chain to Zarah's right hand.

He led them from the room and into a hallway. A man was waiting there—watching her. A craggy-looking woman was standing beside him, her dark eyes fixed on Zarah.

Suddenly she felt as though the woman could see into her head, and she looked quickly away.

"You lost the bid, Lloyd," Philip said.

"I wanted to have one more look at her."

He stepped forward, and Zarah instinctively cringed away.

Philip moved quickly between her and the other man. "Try to be a good loser," he said.

"You dare to talk to me like that?" the man named Lloyd asked.

"She belongs to Griffin now. You've lost."

"We'll see," Lloyd snapped, then turned away.

Zarah stood there trembling.

Philip turned to her. "You don't have to be afraid of him."

Easy for him to say. Lloyd hadn't looked at Philip with lust and something else. Something she couldn't name.

When Philip led them out of the building and into the street, Zarah felt as if a hundred-pound weight had been lifted off her chest.

Trying to take in her new surroundings, she gazed at the

cobbled streets, the buildings stained with wood smoke, much like a scene in White Flint.

People walked past, some of them stopping to look, and Zarah cringed as they stared at her chains. Then Philip hustled them into a horse-drawn cart with wooden hoops over the top holding up a cloth roof.

Philip climbed in front, leaving the new slaves in back.

"Griffin's rich," Quinn whispered.

"Yes."

Small windows were cut in the side of the cloth, and Quinn and Zarah stood at the side of the conveyance, holding on to wooden posts so they could keep their gazes glued to the opening as the horses pulled them slowly through the streets.

The view was severely restricted, but Zarah got the feeling that Sun Acres was larger than White Flint.

Once she had worn an expensive watch. Now she could only estimate the time that passed. As far as she was concerned, the ride could take forever, but she thought it was probably an hour later that they pulled through large metal gates into a paved courtyard.

The gates clanked closed behind them. The house beyond was bigger than where her parents had lived. Apparently Griffin was rich indeed.

Her mouth was so dry she could barely swallow. She had survived thus far. Now her real job would begin.

⌒⌒

Griffin stood at a window on the second floor, looking down at the wagon. When Philip opened the curtain at the back and the two women stepped out, he felt a jolt of anticipation, his total focus on Zarah.

She was small and delicate, with a heart-shaped face and a slender body, with high, firm breasts.

Pound for pound, he had paid a fortune for her. More than any slave woman was worth. But he had been taken with her as he'd watched her bathe the night before. Then, this morning, the idea of Lloyd getting his hands on her had made him sick, so he'd kept bidding. And now he had her.

He pressed his palms against the sides of his tunic. He was standing at a distance from her again—watching.

At the bath and in the auction, he'd had no choice. Now she was his property, and he could do whatever he wanted with her.

He wanted to get his hands on her. But he didn't want to screw up their relationship.

Their relationship? With a slave?

Well, it was obvious from the way she held herself that she had once been more than that.

Did she know her place now? Was she really what he wanted?

⁓

Zarah was given a small room to herself, a luxury that surprised her. The toilet was down the hall.

A middle-aged woman named Branda, who was in charge of the female slaves, told Zarah to dress for dinner. She would be taking her evening meal with the master.

The clothing in her closet was not so different from what she had worn at home, although none of the dinner dresses were as modest as she would have liked. Of course, Griffin had seen her naked and chained to a cross. Shuddering, she thrust that image from her mind and picked a gown from the closet. The fabric clung to her body and was cut high under her breasts, but the neckline was high. And the green color matched her eyes and brought out the warm tone of her skin.

The room also had two mirrors, a long one on the wall and one at the dressing table—another luxury.

As she studied her reflection, she felt a chill travel over her skin. She was making herself attractive to Griffin so he would take her as his bedmate. But she didn't want to sleep with him. And she didn't want to spy on him, either.

Then she thought of her mother back in White Flint, and she firmed her resolve. Sitting down at the dressing table, she began to stroke on some lip and cheek color and found she had to rest her elbow on the table to steady her hand.

Branda opened the door without knocking. "Hurry."

Zarah stood, swaying a little on her bare feet. She had been given no shoes and no underwear, so that she felt at a disadvantage.

The other woman swept her with a studied appraisal. "You look lovely. He should be pleased."

Zarah swallowed and said nothing as Branda led her down the hall toward an isolated wing of the house. Two guards stood on either side of a wide doorway. One of them gave her a knowing look as he opened the door.

Her heart was pounding as she stepped through, and he closed the door behind her.

She went very still, looking around. She was in a small reception room. Beyond was a garden courtyard with plants and a bubbling fountain. A man stood with his back to her. He was dressed in an evening tunic of rich burgundy and he wore leather sandals on his feet. His hair was dark, his shoulders were wide, and his legs were muscular.

She had been told this man was evil. An enemy of White Flint. And here she was—at his mercy.

When he turned, his gaze went straight to her, and she felt as though he could look right through the gown.

Maybe he could. Maybe that was one of his talents.

"Come in," he said in a deep, masculine voice.

She came toward him, trying not to look like she was studying him.

A slave didn't study her master, but she couldn't stop herself from taking in details. He wore just the sandals and tunic. No jewelry. Dark hair showed above the deep vee at his neckline. Raising her eyes, she saw that the hair on his head was dark and thick and cut short. His brows were wide above chocolate brown eyes.

She knew a few basic facts about him that Scanlon had told her. Griffin had been to the school for adepts. His father had been a minor council member who had died five years ago. His mother had been one of the young beauties of the city. In some ways his early life had been like hers. But when he'd grown up, he had chosen to become a power in Sun Acres.

Now, here she was with the man himself. And in the next second, he could order her to go to his bed and take off her gown.

When he spoke, his words came to her over the buzzing of her own blood in her ears.

"How are you settling in?" he asked politely as though she were a guest in his house, not a slave.

"Well," she answered, wishing she could match his tone. But she heard the slight tremble in her own voice.

"I've had dinner sent over from the kitchen." He gestured toward a table set in one corner of the courtyard. It had a white cloth, gleaming cutlery and fine china plates that must have been manufactured long ago. A cart with covered dishes sat next to the table.

Griffin lifted a lid, and the delicious aroma of roast chicken wafted toward her. To her embarrassment, she heard her stomach growl.

"You're hungry," he murmured.

"I . . . yes."

"Sit down."

She sat and he served her some of the chicken, then what looked like mashed potatoes—only more yellow.

He also poured her a glass of white wine. She had never drunk much. But because she was nervous, she took a swallow, then another.

He served himself, then sat down opposite her, as though they were equals.

She studied him from under lowered lashes and decided she liked his looks, even if she wished he were a little less formidable.

They both ate some of the chicken, which was tender and delicious, and she silently ordered herself not to gulp down the meal.

The man and the wine were making her light-headed. Was the drink drugged? Was that part of his plan for her? He'd drunk some, too. But not as much as she.

He had the power to do anything he wanted, yet he seemed nervous.

"You're well educated?" he asked.

"I went to the school for adepts."

"Ah. So you have hidden powers."

"My talents are small."

"And they are?"

"I can . . . soothe away minor pains in others."

"A convenient skill."

"And I can calm animals."

A look she couldn't read crossed his face. "Interesting. What else?"

She shrugged. She couldn't tell him about her communication power with the flame. She must keep that hidden. "I think they kept me in the school as a courtesy to my family. My father was on the council," she added and wished she hadn't felt it necessary to add that detail.

He touched his temple. "How did you get that scar?"

"When I was a little girl, I fell and hit my head against the edge of a table."

He nodded, still staring at her. "So how did you end up as a slave?"

She almost choked on the bite of chicken she'd just eaten. After swallowing carefully, she said, "My father was convicted of a crime he didn't commit. And executed."

"Oh?"

"They said he raided the city treasury. He would never have done that."

"Then how was he convicted?"

"He had enemies—just as you do," she snapped, then realized that she had stepped over the line with Griffin.

He kept his gaze on her. Instead of responding to her comment, he asked, "What about your mother?"

She recognized the danger in that question, then considered the answer carefully. "She's dying," she finally said.

"Of what?"

"She has . . . cancer."

"I'm sorry. Can't they treat her?"

"Perhaps. But they didn't think the wife of an executed criminal was worth saving."

He answered with a tight nod, and she hoped he was satisfied with the answer.

"What was your father's name?"

"Arturo."

"I haven't heard of him."

"You have spies in White Flint?" she asked, then knew at once that she had made a mistake by bringing up the subject. Intrigue wasn't her strong suit, and already she was getting herself into trouble.

Griffin tipped his head to the side, studying her. "That's not a subject we should be discussing."

Five

"**I'm** sorry. I overstepped," Zarah whispered.

"Try to remember your place," he said, his voice sharper than it had been.

"Yes, sir," she said, hating the subservience in her voice. Clearing her throat, she said, "You're on the council here?"

"Yes."

"What's your most important goal for the city?"

He looked startled, then sat back in his seat. "Keeping us safe. Making sure there are jobs for everyone. Stopping the endless wars."

"How do you do all that?"

"I'd like to form an alliance with one of the nearby cities—so we stop draining our resources in fighting. Along with that, I'd like to set up trade agreements. Each city could produce what it does best—and sell it to the other at a fair price."

She stared at him. "That's very . . . progressive."

He laughed. "Maybe in today's world. But the ideas are quite old. Have you ever read the old books—about what life was like before the psychic change?"

"No. The old books were forbidden in White Flint."

"They're forbidden here—to all but a few men." He shifted in his seat. "You've never heard of the United States of America?"

"No."

"That's what they used to have here. A confederation of states—that all cooperated and ceded many powers to a central government. The seat of that government was Washington—a city not too far from here."

She blinked. "You know a lot."

He shrugged. "I've made it my business to educate myself—to learn more than they taught in school."

She nodded. She'd been told that this man was evil. Instead, she found him intelligent and fascinating.

He ate in silence for several minutes. She'd lost her appetite when they'd talked about her family. Now she took a few more bites of food.

A small bell rang, and she looked up, startled. "Pardon me," he said and got up from the table. Opening the door, he took a folded piece of paper from a messenger and read it. His face turned to a scowl.

"There's trouble at an entertainment venue in the city. I'll need to send soldiers. I'll be back," he said.

He left her alone at the table. After a few minutes, she got up and wandered around the room, examining the plantings and the stone planters. Another door led to a large bedroom. His bedroom. She wanted to stay away from it, but she was drawn to the softly lighted room. She could see a wide bed with four posts at the corners and high shelves crammed with old books.

He would take her to that bed tonight. She shivered. She was attracted to him. But she was sure he wasn't going to give her time to get to know him before he . . .

She cut off the thought and focused on the bookshelves. She longed to take some of the volumes down and examine them.

He read a lot. And he seemed to have the best interests of his city at heart. She sensed he was someone she could like and admire—if the circumstances had been different.

But he had bought her like a thoroughbred horse. He could do what he wanted with her. And she was here to please him—and spy on him.

Suddenly it was difficult to catch her breath. A faint breeze was blowing through one of the open windows, and she walked unsteadily to the grillework, where she stood breathing in the cooler air.

She heard a door open, heard footsteps cross the courtyard. She went rigid as she felt him come up behind her and put his hands on her arms.

"I'm sorry to have left you."

"You don't have to apologize. I know you're a busy man."

"This has to be difficult for you."

"Yes," she whispered.

"How are you feeling?"

"A little shaky," she managed to say.

He turned her slowly toward him, and she ordered herself not to resist when he pulled her body against his.

She trembled as he stroked his hands over her shoulders and down her back.

"Perhaps we can help each other out."

When she didn't answer, he murmured, "Relax."

"That's difficult."

"Because I frighten you?"

"No," she said quickly, probably too quickly. "You're not what I expected at all."

"What did you expect?

"A man who would exercise his . . . rights over me."

His voice was low and steady. "Is this so different than it would have been? Your father would have arranged a marriage for you. Probably to a man you hardly knew. And you would have had no choice about marrying him."

"Marrying . . ." she answered, suddenly remembering what her life had been—and what it was now.

"We'll try not to make this too unpleasant for you."

She stood stiffly as he tipped her head up, then slowly lowered his mouth, lightly stroking his lips against hers.

Her stomach clenched, and she ordered herself to relax. He could do anything he wanted now. But she remembered what Quinn had told her. It could be good with him, if she let herself enjoy it.

She focused on the sensation of his lips moving against hers. She had kissed a few men. And she hadn't thought the experience was anything special. But she liked the way Griffin's lips felt, liked the way he moved them against hers. And when his tongue stroked against the seam of her lips, she let herself open for him.

He made a sound of approval as he played with her mouth, his tongue stroking the sensitive tissue just inside, then playing with her teeth and finally sliding his tongue against hers.

She might have been shocked, but she reminded herself what Quinn had advised. So she focused on the sensations he was creating. What he was doing felt wonderful.

She could do a lot worse. No—she shouldn't think in those terms. This was not her husband. Not a permanent relationship. She had been sent here to spy on this man.

The thought made her stiffen.

He felt her muscles tighten and misinterpreted the reason. "Let yourself enjoy this."

His hands slid up her ribs, then along the sides of her breasts, and she made a shocked sound.

"You've never let anyone do that?" he murmured.

"No."

He worked his fingers inward, skimming over her nipples through the thin fabric of her gown, and she realized that the cold air had made them bud. Or perhaps it was his touch. When he stroked the hardened tips, hot sensations shot through her, and she caught her breath.

The gown had a row of buttons down the front. He slid the top six open, one by one, then reached inside, cupping her breast in his large hand before pushing the fabric aside and lowering his head so that he could stroke her nipple with his tongue, then suck it into his mouth.

"Oh!"

He blew gently on the wet bud, then spoke with his mouth centimeters away. "You like that?"

"Yes," she managed, then remembered what Quinn had said. "Can I touch you there?" she asked in a voice she couldn't quite hold steady.

"Gods, yes."

He quickly unbuttoned the top of his tunic, and she slipped her hand inside, stroking the hair on his chest, then encountering a flat nipple. When she slid her finger back and forth across it, he made a low sound of approval.

While she was still exploring his chest, he reached down and pulled up her gown, raising the hem so that he could slip his hand under and stroke her knee.

She tensed as his fingers glided their way up to her thigh.

"Relax."

She tried, but she was scared now. It was one thing to talk about this. It was quite another to have a man she had just met working his hand up her leg. But those were the rules of the game that she had been ordered to play.

Trying not to think about the role that had been thrust upon her, she focused on physical sensations.

He kissed her neck, his lips and tongue spreading warmth downward through her body. And she found she liked that as much as his lips on hers.

"You're very sensitive. That's good."

As he spoke, his hand traveled higher up her thigh, then glided into the most intimate territory.

She had touched herself there. Given herself pleasure. And what Quinn had told her was true. She had prepared herself for a man's attentions. She closed her eyes as he slid his hand through her sensitive folds, finding the bud where the greatest sensation lay, then stroking downward again. From the way he touched her, she knew that he understood a woman's pleasure very well.

She gasped as he did what she had never done herself, slipped his large finger inside her.

"Does that hurt?" he asked urgently.

"No." She swallowed, then answered honestly. "It feels good."

She felt him smile as he bent to nuzzle his lips against her breasts while his finger stroked in and out of her, then traveled upward again, driving her toward what she knew was the ultimate pleasure.

He kept her poised on the edge of completion, and she tried to increase the friction by pressing against his fingers.

"You need to come."

"Yes," she gasped, hardly able to believe she had made such an admission.

When he moved his hand away, she cried out in frustration. But he only lifted her onto the wide window ledge, pressing her back against the grillework, lifting her skirt to her lap, and opening her legs.

A jolt of alarm lulled her from her sensual haze. "What?"

"Shhh." He went down on his knees, so that his mouth was at the level of her hips.

She didn't understand what he meant to do, and for a moment she froze in embarrassed shock as he knelt on the floor, his face level with her woman's parts.

She tried to struggle away when he leaned toward her, but he held her in place with his large hands on her thighs, then pressed his mouth to her.

"Don't!" she cried out in panic.

"It's all right. Don't fight me," he answered, then began to caress her with his lips and tongue, using them as he had used his fingers. She went rigid at the intimate contact. But she was too aroused not to respond. As he licked and sucked at her and stroked his finger in and out of her, the exquisite attentions brought her up and over the edge, so that she cried out as she reached sexual climax.

While she was still vibrating with the aftershocks, he stood and pulled his tunic aside.

Again, she had no idea of what he intended. He took her by surprise, when her body was still limp with pleasure.

There was a moment of pain when his large penis penetrated her. But the pain was over by the time he began to thrust. She held on to his shoulders, her heart pounding as she listened to his jerky breathing.

Then she felt his body shudder, felt him pour himself into her.

He made a rough sound and gathered her close, holding her as his head sank to her shoulder.

When he withdrew from her, she stared up at him.

"You tricked me," she murmured. "I thought you would take me to bed to do that."

"Was the outcome worth the subterfuge?"

"Yes."

"Good." He lifted her in his arms and carried her through the courtyard and into the bedroom. Setting her on her feet, he pulled the gown over her head and tossed it away.

Before she could react to her nakedness, he put out the lamp on the table, pulled the covers aside, and eased her into the bed.

Then he pulled off his own tunic and sent it to join the gown.

Naked, he climbed into the big bed beside her.

"Are you all right?" he murmured as he stroked her arm.

"More than all right."

"It wasn't so bad?" he asked, his voice teasing, or perhaps he wanted reassurance.

"You know it was . . . good."

"I hoped it would be."

"Why?"

"I want lovemaking to be good between us."

She wanted to ask what he intended for the future. She had sense enough not to demand answers. And what did it matter what he intended? She wouldn't be here long—would she?

He kissed her cheek. "Sleep."

Physically and emotionally exhausted and at the same time relieved that the sexual initiation was over, she closed her eyes. He could have raped her. Instead he had very skillfully seduced her and given her intense pleasure. She was grateful for that. And also sick and shaky. She was supposed to be spying on this man. He was supposed to be her enemy. But Scanlon felt more like the enemy than Griffin.

She liked him. Liked what he had done with her and the way he had done it. He'd gone out of his way to be tender and generous. And she felt emotions she hadn't expected blooming inside.

Which made her predicament all the more difficult.

She lay next to him, unable to sleep. She hated being forced into the role of liar and spy. She ached to throw herself on his mercy—to tell him why she was here and ask for his help.

But she had sense enough to know that the gentleness he had shown her could turn instantly to anger.

So she lay silently next to him.

She had finally drifted off when something woke her, and her eyes snapped open.

In the darkness, she felt Griffin lunge from the bed.

"What?" she asked, hardly able to see him.

He answered with a low curse, already on his way out of the room.

Six

Zarah climbed out of bed and snatched up her gown, folding it around her as she followed him into the courtyard. He plunged through another door, leaving her alone.

Where had he gone in such a hurry? And what should she do?

She was alone, but was he coming back soon? Did she have time enough to communicate with Alroy? And where would she find a lamp? It couldn't be a hurricane lamp. They were too large for her psychic communications powers. She needed one of the small oil lamps that was like a flat little pitcher with a wick.

In some other part of the house, she heard a grandfather clock strike the hour and stopped to listen. One, two, three, four strikes.

Four in the morning.

She could stay here and wait for Griffin to come back. But she'd be missing an opportunity.

She put on her gown and buttoned the front, then picked up

the hurricane lamp from the table. Griffin had put it out, but even if she couldn't use it to communicate, she had the power to ignite the flame with her thoughts.

With the lamp in one hand, she walked to the entrance where she'd first come into the courtyard. When she opened the door, a sleepy-looking guard snapped to attention.

"Where are you going?" he demanded.

"I . . . I need to go back to my room," she improvised.

"Has the master given you permission?"

"Am I expected to stay in his rooms all the time?" she challenged.

"Let's ask him."

"He's sleeping," she answered quickly.

"And you took it upon yourself to sneak away."

She adopted the voice she had been accustomed to using with servants. "Of course not. Where would I go? I need another gown, so I'll look fresh for him in the morning."

He considered her request, then waved her through the door.

When she was out of sight, she breathed out a small sigh. She had made it out of Griffin's rooms. But she still needed a suitable lamp, and a place where she could use it.

She went first to her room and stripped off her gown, then took the time to wash, using the basin in her room. When she washed between her legs, she found blood on the cloth and sucked in a small breath.

She was no longer a virgin. No man of her station would marry her now. She forced her mind away from that topic. She couldn't worry about her own future. She thought of her mother, alone and sick and scared, and her heart contracted. She had to save her mother's life. And get back home so she could take care of her.

After washing, she changed into another gown, one that would be more suitable for the morning. She wanted to rush out and take care of the job she'd been given, but she took the time to brush her hair and make herself look presentable so that her story of preparing herself for Griffin would hold up.

But she wasn't going back to his room. She was going to the servants' hall, off the kitchen. Down there, when she'd first come in, she'd seen some of the small lamps.

And if she was asked, she could say that she hadn't been able to eat much at dinner, and she was hungry.

Of course, no slave would dare to take food without permission. But maybe they'd think she was slipping back into her old role—now that the master of the house had bedded her.

She cringed as she contemplated that excuse, then tried to come up with something else, but her brain felt paralyzed.

She kept walking, into the kitchen wing. Although the guard outside Griffin's door had challenged her, she didn't encounter anyone else, thank the Great Mother.

The lamps were kept on shelves just inside the door of the servants' hall. Zarah grabbed one and shook it gently. It was full.

She'd practiced communicating with Alroy. But only in White Flint. She was far away now, and she had no idea if she could establish the link. But she had to try.

And then what? What would she say? She had learned nothing important. Or had she?

Why had Griffin rushed out of the room? He'd seemed in a terrible hurry to get away from her. Did that have to do with his secret? Was he meeting someone? Or was he feeling sick and didn't want to embarrass himself in front of her?

And what if he came back and found her gone? Would he be

angry? Would he think she was trying to escape? Well, that was hardly logical. Where would she go?

With the lamp in her hand, she hurried through the darkened room, then into a large pantry area. She was about to light the lamp when a hand came down on her shoulder, and she screamed.

∽

"**Stealing** food?"

The voice was harsh and accusing. Zarah turned to find herself confronting Branda.

"I . . . no . . ." Zarah stammered, struggling to speak when her heart was blocking her windpipe.

The supervisor rested her hands on her hips. "Then what?"

"She came to meet me," another voice said.

Zarah looked up to find herself staring at Quinn.

"We came from White Flint together. And we were worried about each other. We promised that we'd try to meet and tell each other that we were all right. She came to me because I couldn't go to her."

"Prowling around the house in the middle of the night is forbidden," Branda said. "You will stay in your assigned area—unless you are told to leave it."

Zarah swallowed. "I'm sorry," she said in a small voice, looking from Branda to Quinn and back again. "I was worried about my friend."

"You should worry about yourself. Did Griffin send you away?"

"No! He left the bedroom . . ." Her voice trailed off.

Branda gave her a sharp look. "Well, go back to your room and wait until he sends for you again."

"Yes, ma'am."

Zarah bent her head and started back the way she'd come, the lamp clutched in her hand. Branda stayed right behind her. And when she'd stepped into her room, the supervisor closed the door firmly behind her.

Zarah leaned against the door, breathing hard, feeling as if her heart might pound its way through her chest. She'd gotten caught sneaking around, and Quinn had come to her rescue.

How had she known that her friend was in trouble? Or had she just been in the right place at the right time?

Whatever the reason, Zarah was profoundly grateful. Now she had the lamp. And she was in her room. But did she really have privacy? She looked at the door. It had no lock on her side. Branda could come bursting in at any time. But would she?

Zarah swallowed. She had to take a chance on communicating now. Because she knew that Alroy would be impatiently waiting to hear from her. And if she didn't do her job, her mother would suffer.

She hurried to the farthest corner of the room and crouched on the floor, hoping she wouldn't be heard. Then she decided that if Branda did come in, it would look strange to find her on the floor. So she moved back to the bed and settled down with her back braced against the wall.

Picking up the small lamp, she focused on the wick, willing the flame to spring to life. Nothing happened, and she felt her chest tighten. Panic leaped inside her, and she ordered herself to relax. She had lit the hurricane lamp. She could light this one. But not if she was too nervous to function.

She took a moment to calm herself, breathing slowly and evenly the way she had been taught in school. Then she focused on the flame again. This time it flickered, and the oil caught.

"Thank you, Mother," she murmured.

Now came the hard part. She knew Alroy was standing by. He'd have his own lamp lit so that he could receive a message from her.

The idea of reaching out toward him made her stomach clench. She hated his cruelty and what she had been ordered to do. She was no huntress, yet she had been forced into that role.

If she had been on her own, she might have severed all ties with White Flint and taken her chances here. But that left her mother in terrible danger.

Take her chances here? Was she making too much of her relationship with Griffin?

He'd fed her dinner. Talked to her. And fucked her—to use the crude word that she had heard several times in the past few days.

But what did that mean to him? He'd left her bed in a hurry. Maybe he was going to meet some other woman.

She thought back over the way he'd acted and concluded that he wasn't meeting a woman—not unless she was a witch who had put a compulsion on him.

With a grimace, she ordered herself to stop obsessing about Griffin. She was stalling, and she needed to establish the link and get on with her assignment.

So she focused on the flame, sending her consciousness drifting into the small fire that she had created, letting her thoughts fly toward that other flame. Toward home. As she'd been taught, she reached out for Alroy—and came flying up against a barrier. It was like flying down a hill on a sled and smacking into a stone wall.

It knocked the breath from her lungs.

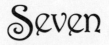Seven

Zarah almost dropped the lamp but managed not to set her gown on fire.

As she struggled to catch her breath, she tried to figure out what had happened.

Did Griffin have a shield around his house that was designed to prevent psychic messages from breaching his enclave?

Did the city have such a shield? Was some person interfering with her? But who would that be? Branda? Or had Quinn somehow stopped her? And why would her friend do that?

Zarah stared at the flame, struggling to calm herself. Maybe this was a warning that she should give up her assignment. At least for tonight.

Every protective instinct urged her to put the lamp out and try to get a few hours of sleep. But she couldn't do that. Not and save her mother.

So she took a deep breath, then began the communications process again. She couldn't have explained to anyone how she did it. Just the way she couldn't explain the theory of using the flame for healing. She had never been asked to do that. But she had used the communications link many times since Alroy had begun training her for this assignment. And she was more comfortable with the flame than at any other time in her life.

The lamp flared up suddenly, and a man's voice filled her head.

Was that you?

She jumped again, only this time her hand was firm on the lamp. It was Alroy. Even if she'd come up against a wall, he'd sensed her presence at the other end of the communications link and reached out to her. Because he was older and more experienced, he'd been able to bridge the gap.

"Yes," she answered, speaking the word aloud, then realizing that it would be safer to keep the conversation silent.

What have you found out?

I just got here yesterday.

Did Griffin bed you?

She winced. She didn't want to discuss her personal life with Alroy.

Did he? the man at the other end of the communications line demanded.

Yes, she answered, her inner voice very faint.

Speak up!

Yes.

Was he as good a lover as they say he is?

Yes, she answered, glad Alroy wasn't in the room with her.

And what have you found out about him?

He's intelligent. He has the welfare of his city at heart.

What about his secret?

I don't know!

You have to do better than that.

She hesitated. She could tell Alroy about Griffin leaving their bed. But what did that prove, really? Instead, she looked toward the door.

There's someone coming, she whispered inside her mind. *I have to go.*

Wait.

I have to go, she said again, then blew out the flame and sat with her head thrown back against the wall, breathing hard. She had lied to Alroy. She had been anxious to cut off the conversation, so she'd manufactured an excuse.

Next time, he would ask her about it. And she had better be prepared with an answer.

✑

The clock struck nine, and Griffin sighed. No more stalling. He had to meet with the man who had been cooling his heels in the reception area for the past two hours. He was a fellow named Preston who spoke for the city's tradesmen. And Griffin had a pretty good idea what he had come to complain about.

He was glad he had an excuse to be late. Everybody in the city knew that he had bought a new slave at the auction the day before. A virgin whom he'd snatched from the clutches of Lloyd. They would know that he'd taken her to bed. And he might be tired from his night's exertions.

He might have made love to her again in the night. Or in the morning. But he'd left their bed rather precipitously. According to Branda, Zarah had gone down to the kitchen area after that. Still in the small hours of the morning.

She'd said she was worried about her friend, Quinn, another

slave who had come from White Flint. But was that really true? Did she have some hidden agenda that he didn't know about?

He clenched his hands into fists.

He'd enjoyed the woman. Enjoyed her intelligence. Enjoyed seducing her—and giving her pleasure.

He'd thought they'd gotten on well together. Until he'd had to run from the room.

"Carfolian hell," he muttered. He'd thought—

Well, what exactly *had* he thought? That making love with her was going to save him?

He snorted.

He'd better watch himself. He could picture getting emotionally involved with Zarah, and that might be a big mistake. He knew nothing about her, beyond what she'd told him. It could all be lies. And he'd better find out. He thought about his spies in White Flint. He had adepts who could send a message to one of them—a man named Dell, who was posing as a wine merchant. That gave him license to pass out drinks freely. And when he loosened the tongues of White Flint residents, he often came away with very interesting information.

He was also a powerful adept who could send and receive messages just through mind power—when he was sober. Which wasn't always the case. But he was loyal. And he would send back credible information—if he could discover anything about Zarah, daughter of Arturo.

Griffin wanted to have Blayden, his man here in Sun Acres, make the contact with Dell. But first he had to deal with Preston. So he took a deep breath, then strode into the reception room as though his ankle weren't aching. He'd covered the wound with a bandage and a pair of boots. But it was an effort not to favor his left leg.

Preston, who had been sitting in one of the straight chairs, jumped to his feet. "Sir."

"Good to see you," Griffin said, sticking out his hand. As they shook stiffly, he saw the tension around the man's eyes. "I take it you came to discuss some problem."

Preston nodded, tightly, and Griffin could see it was something the fellow didn't want to talk about.

"Just tell me," Griffin prompted.

"There was another incident with a werewolf in the city," Preston blurted.

"How do you know it was a werewolf?"

"How would a real wolf get in here?"

"You have a point. What happened?"

"It killed a dog."

"Did the dog go after him?" Griffin asked.

"No. It was tied up. It was an unprovoked attack."

Griffin listened to the man. Was he lying or had he been misinformed?

Griffin knew exactly what had happened with the damn dog.

Because he'd been there—as the wolf.

The dog hadn't been tied up. It had leaped out of a passageway between two houses when the wolf rushed past, grabbing his left hind leg in its teeth. When he'd turned to protect himself, the dog hadn't the sense to run. It had gone in for the kill, but he had gotten to the animal's throat first.

He'd taken the dog out, then run for his life, with residents of the neighborhood shouting behind him.

"Did he injure any people?" Griffin asked.

Preston scuffed his foot against the antique carpet. "A child."

Griffin swore. "Bitten?"

Preston looked uncomfortable. "The child might have been injured earlier, and the family is trying to connect it to the attack. In case the city is planning to provide some compensation."

"We can do that," Griffin said. "How about a hundred dollars to the child's family? And twenty-five for the dog."

"That would be satisfactory," Preston allowed, but he remained where he was standing.

"What else?" Griffin asked.

"We need to do something about the animal."

"You have a suggestion?"

"Set a trap."

"You don't think a werewolf would be smart enough to avoid a trap?"

"There's a special kind of trap that lures a shape-shifter and incapacitates the beast so it can be killed."

"That's not permitted inside the city," Griffin snapped.

"But we may have to use it, if the creature is menacing the community."

"I can't authorize it. An innocent shape-shifter might get hurt."

"The people are frightened. If the wolf attacks again, we'll have to do something."

And the people are lying about what happened, he thought, but kept the observation to himself.

"I'll have the night watch patrol increased."

"That may help. But we want to make sure nobody else gets hurt."

He managed to keep his temper, then ushered the man out. When he was alone, he walked to the table at the side of the room where he had a pot of tea keeping warm under a small blanket. He poured himself a cup of the brew and drank it down. It was an herbal mixture that was designed to calm the nerves. He was pretty sure it wasn't doing him any good. Absently, he rubbed his ankle.

He'd thought . . .

Well, what exactly had he thought? Had he believed that old wives' tale that deflowering a virgin would cure illnesses?

He laughed. Apparently, it wasn't true. And all he'd gotten out of it was a good time. A very good time, he reminded himself. Yet good sex was no reason to rush into a relationship.

He'd been hot to satisfy his lust with his new purchase. Now he had some time to think about his screwed-up life.

He'd been on top of the world until disaster had struck. He'd been a werewolf all his life. He'd found that out when the elders had dragged him off to their school for psychics. A slave girl named Rinna had been the best student in the shape-shifter classes. After they'd graduated, she'd gotten into trouble with Falcone, who'd wanted her to give him a child who was a powerful psychic.

Falcone and Rinna had both disappeared from the city. He could believe the noble had come to a bad end. He hoped Rinna was living happily far away from Sun Acres.

For himself, Griffin was barely hanging on to his life by his fingernails. He'd always had control over the change—until last year. Now, he'd feel the aura coming over him and he'd know it was going to happen. At first it had only been once a month—at the full moon. But lately it was more than once a week. He'd turn into a wolf, and he'd struggle to control the savage impulses that came along with the change.

He hadn't killed anybody yet. But he'd come close. And the savagery he'd felt when he'd torn out that dog's throat made him sick now.

He paced to the window and looked out at a wagon being unloaded. Yesterday he'd received a delivery of women. Today it was vegetables.

And maybe he'd better keep his relationship with one of those women on the level of the vegetables.

He'd bought her for his bed. And his emotional involvement with her had been intense. Which might be dangerous to him.

Let her do some work in the kitchen for the next couple of days, while he figured out whether he wanted to keep her or put her back on the auction block.

So Lloyd could get his hands on her?

No, he told himself firmly. If he gave her up, he'd arrange a private sale. Of course, that didn't mean that Lloyd wasn't going to find out and offer a tempting price for her.

Eight

In the morning, one of the servants came to Zarah's room and handed her a dress that was much less delicate than the gowns she'd been given by Griffin.

Then she was told to report to the kitchen. Her hands were shaking as she changed her dress.

Last night, she'd thought she and Griffin had gotten along very well. Until he'd rushed out of the room.

What had happened to him? And why was he discarding her now? Had Branda said something? But the woman paid no particular attention to her.

After a quick meal of bread, cheese, and weak coffee, she was put to work peeling and cutting apples that were going to be made into jam. She'd never done anything similar before, and she cut herself when the blade slid off the apple skin.

A supervisor came rushing over. "Don't get blood in the apples," she ordered. Come here and wash your hand."

Zarah followed her to the sink, where she washed off the

blood under cold water and wrapped a bandage around her hand.

Quinn was sitting on a stool in the corner of the kitchen, her gaze focused on one of the big ovens, and Zarah knew she was firing the heating element. Quinn glanced up and gave her a smile of encouragement. "Are you okay?" she mouthed.

Zarah nodded and decided that it couldn't have been Quinn who had tried to prevent her link with Alroy last night.

She went back to the apples, working more carefully this time and getting chastised for not cutting them quickly enough.

The other women in the kitchen looked at her as she worked.

"Didn't the master take a fancy to you?" a woman with unkempt yellow hair asked.

"I thought he did," she said in a small voice. She'd expected to be called back to his rooms. Maybe he was waiting until the evening. Maybe he was going to put her to work during the days.

The girl looked to see if the supervisor was nearby. When she saw they weren't going to be overheard, she said, "He's strange."

"Strange? How?"

"He used to be . . . normal. Now you never know what he's going to do."

Zarah nodded. Was that enough to send on to Alroy? Would it satisfy him? Or would he be angry again?

When the supervisor came back, the gossipy woman clamped her mouth shut.

They worked for three hours, and Zarah was feeling exhausted by the time they broke for lunch.

She was quiet as they took their food. This time it was pota- toes with a little fatty meat. Not a dish she would have been served in her father's house. But she was glad to eat the simple dish and wash it down with a mug of water.

She watched the other women and listened to their talk and their laughter. Most of them were uneducated. And she didn't know how to fit in with them.

Quinn sat next to her.

"So it worked out okay last night?" her friend asked.

"Yes."

"Did you hear there was a werewolf in the city last night?" one of the women whispered.

Zarah shivered. She'd known a few children at school who had that trait, and she'd been wary of them.

"Preston—the man who speaks for the tradesmen—came to tell Griffin about it. He wants to kill it."

"Did it hurt anyone?" Quinn asked.

"It hurt a boy."

"Is he all right?"

"He was torn up bad."

Everyone around the table nodded.

"I'm glad I don't have to go out at night," a redheaded girl said.

There were murmurs of agreement around the table.

"He's evil," an older woman with bright red cheeks said. "They should put out traps to catch him. And kill him."

"Maybe the story is exaggerated," Quinn said.

"How?"

"Who really saw what happened?" Quinn argued, then said, "And maybe the werewolf is just sick. Maybe he just needs psychic treatment."

"What do you mean?"

"I've heard of a disease that affects them sometimes. Usually they can decide when they change. But if they have that disease, they can't control it anymore."

"You're acting like you know everything," the woman challenged.

"How do you know so much?" another woman asked.

"I learned it in school," Quinn said

"School for adepts?"

"Yes. In Hammond Town."

"They say the people in Hammond Town practice the black arts."

"Not as far as I know. The people there are like people anywhere," Quinn murmured. "They just want to live their lives in peace."

"So you think you're hot stuff because you went to a school for psychics?" the woman with bright cheeks challenged.

Quinn grinned at her. "Hot stuff. Oh right. Well, I did learn how to run an oven."

The women laughed, and Zarah admired what Quinn had done. The others were ready to brand her as a snob, but she'd turned the comment around immediately.

One of the women glanced at Zarah, and she thought she was going to be singled out. She had also heard about the were-wolf disease in school, but she wasn't going to call attention to herself by mentioning it. And she certainly wasn't going to give away anything by saying that her flame was sometimes used as a cure.

Just then, Branda came over and told them it was time to get back to work. With a mixture of relief and weariness Zarah returned to peeling and cutting fruit.

She worked steadily throughout the day. After an early dinner, she was sent back to her room, where she waited for Griffin to ask for her.

When he didn't, she felt her stomach knot. He had made love to her in a way that made her think that he cared something for her. But maybe he had just been amusing himself with his new slave.

With her lips set in a grim line, she got out the lamp that she'd kept in her room. She had no trouble lighting the flame, but this time when she tried to make contact with Alroy, the wall between them was thicker, and there was no way she could punch her way through.

She kept trying, then gave up in defeat, brushing back tears. Either she was too off balance to use her talent, or someone was preventing her from connecting with her old teacher.

After the failed communication session, she lay down. But she hardly slept. She felt shaky and confused. She should be loyal to her own city. But she felt more for Griffin than for the man who had sent her here. She wanted to be with him. What had gone wrong between them? Had he discovered why she was here?

But how could he? No—she had displeased him.

She hugged her arms around her shoulders, rocking herself to sleep. And in the morning—as if to prove her failure—she was sent to the kitchen again.

✍

Griffin sat back in the chair behind his desk, schooling his features so that he didn't look as if he had any personal stake in the conversation. "You have information from White Flint?" he asked Blayden.

"I had some trouble rousing Dell."

Under the desk, Griffin clenched his fist.

"But I finally got through to him," the adept said.

"Sit down," Griffin invited, then waited for the man to settle himself in one of the desk chairs facing the desk.

"Could he find out anything about the woman, Zarah?"

"The daughter of Arturo?"

"Yes."

"It's common knowledge in the city that her father was convicted of embezzlement and executed."

"Was he guilty?"

"That's difficult to determine. He had enemies in the city. Like all the . . ."

Blayden stopped short, and Griffin gave him an impatient wave of the hand.

"Yes, I know I have enemies. I watch my back."

The adept nodded.

"So the daughter was sold into slavery. And what about the mother?"

"She died a few days ago."

Griffin winced. "I should tell Zarah."

"Is she better off not knowing?" Blayden asked.

"I believe in honesty."

Although the adept nodded, Griffin wasn't sure the man agreed.

They talked for a few more minutes about politics in White Flint and how it might be relevant to Sun Acres.

"See if there's more you can find out about the family—and about the woman," he said. He thought for a moment. "Is there some way we can find out if she's really the daughter of Arturo?"

"Does she have any distinguishing marks?" the man asked, then flushed.

He thought of her perfect face, marred by one small blemish. "She has a scar on her right temple, running into the hairline."

∽

Zarah tried to keep her panic—and sadness—from showing on her face. Apparently Griffin had changed his mind about any personal relationship with her. Too bad he had paid so much for a woman who wasn't very good at kitchen work.

A shiver skittered over her skin. He could sell her to another owner to get some of his money back. And then she'd have no way to carry out her mission.

Alroy would say that was her fault. And he'd certainly take that out on her mother.

She was cutting a chunk of meat into cubes for stew when she heard a stir among the slaves.

Looking up, she saw Griffin striding across the courtyard. When he saw her, he stopped and stared directly at her.

Her breath caught, and she couldn't stop herself from pushing back the lock of hair that had fallen across her forehead. She knew she looked like a mess, and she wished she weren't sitting there with bare legs sticking out below a shapeless dress that was smeared with blood from the meat.

He took a step toward her, then stopped when he saw that everybody in the courtyard and the kitchen was staring at him.

Instead, he changed course, kept walking, and disappeared into the building, leaving her with a terrible tight feeling in her chest.

She went back to cutting meat, working automatically, ordering herself not to cry and trying to keep her thoughts focused on the job and not herself. Or Griffin.

After dinner, she returned to her room and washed the blood

off, then changed into a simple gown. Not that she expected Griffin to send for her. But it made her feel a little better to have the soft fabric next to her skin. If she lay down and closed her eyes, perhaps she could pretend that she was back in her old life.

She lay in bed, listening to the tall clock announce the hours. At two in the morning, her door opened, and she sat bolt upright in bed.

"Zarah, you're awake."

She could only make out the silhouette of a woman in the doorway, but she recognized the voice.

✍

Quinn had kept her thoughts tuned to Zarah and to Griffin, and now she knew she had to act.

Zarah sat up, peering into the darkness. "Quinn? What are you doing here?" she asked, her voice edged with puzzlement.

Quinn dragged in a breath and let it out. "I woke, and I knew he needed you."

"Who?"

"Griffin."

"How do you know?"

There was no way she could explain the knowledge that had brought her here. "I *just do*. You must go to him, and take your lamp."

Zarah tipped her head to one side, staring at her friend.

Quinn crossed to her and took her by the shoulders, trying to convey her own urgency. "Please. You must help him."

"At school—there were people like you. People who . . . *knew* . . ." Her voice trailed off, as though she couldn't articulate exactly what she meant. Her breath hitched. "If he wanted me, he would have sent for me."

"He *needs you*." Quinn snatched up the lamp and handed it to Zarah. "Take this. Light it now."

Zarah stared at her. "You know I have . . . abilities with fire?"

Quinn swallowed. "Yes."

"How?"

"That's not important. What's important is getting to Griffin before it's too late."

Zarah shivered, then bent toward the lamp and shook it. "I've . . . used a lot of the oil."

"Let's hope there's enough left."

Zarah twisted off the burnt end of the wick. Then she stared intently at the braided threads, creating a spark.

The wick flamed up. "Okay."

"I can't go with you."

To Quinn's relief, the other woman answered, "I know."

They both stepped from the room, and Quinn watched Zarah hurry down the hall. When she'd first met Zarah, she'd thought she was a spoiled noble brought low by circumstances. Now it was clear she had guts.

∽

As Zarah hurried toward the master's rooms, she expected Branda to leap out at her. But, thankfully, the woman wasn't around. However, there was still the guard at the door to the courtyard.

Zarah stopped short when he snapped to attention.

"What are you doing here?" he demanded.

"Griffin has sent for me."

"He didn't send a message."

She raised her chin. "Yes he did. A psychic message."

The guard studied her. "How do I know?"

"Do you want to get in trouble for not letting me in?"

"I could get in trouble for letting you pass."

"Call the master and ask him."

"I'm not supposed to disturb him," the man answered, obviously torn. Zarah stood in front of him, holding her breath.

Finally, he stepped aside, and she let the breath trickle out of her lungs. Once inside the reception room, she closed the door behind her, holding up her lamp as she looked around.

The courtyard was dark and silent. But as she strained her eyes and ears, she heard a low, anguished sound coming from a doorway opposite the bedroom.

The hair on the back of her neck prickled, and she wanted to turn and run. But this might be her chance to get the information Alroy had demanded. Or her chance for . . . for what? She wasn't sure, and she didn't dare give voice to her half-formed thoughts.

The sound came again, peppering her arms with goose bumps. Gathering her resolve, she walked toward the door.

Slowly, she reached for the knob. Then, before she could stop herself, she pulled the door open.

Beyond was a sight that froze the breath in her lungs.

Nine

In the corner of the room an animal with fierce yellow eyes pawed the ground, then bared its teeth and snarled at her.

She knew that it must be the werewolf that had terrorized the city two nights before.

It was here. In Griffin's private rooms.

How had the creature gotten into the house? Into the master's private quarters?

The only possible answer hit her with the force of a tornado slamming into the side of a house.

"No," she whispered.

But even as she voiced the denial, she was coming to grips with reality. Scanlon had told her Griffin was hiding a secret. And this was it.

He was the werewolf—backed into a corner, looking like he was going to spring at her. And she remembered what the women had said about the cruelty of the animal. Or had any of that been true?

"Griffin?" she whispered.

He growled deep in his throat, as though he was warning her to get away while she could. She should be terrified. She could have turned and run screaming from the room. Instead, she felt her heart going out to Griffin. He was in a terrible situation, and she understood that very well. The feeling of being helpless. Powerless. The knowledge that you were at the mercy of forces over which you had absolutely no control. That understanding made her stiffen her legs and remain facing the beast that had terrorized the city.

"Griffin," she said again.

The animal reared back.

"It's all right," she whispered, even while she wondered if she could possibly be speaking the truth.

Her grip tightened on the lamp. "Griffin, I know what's wrong with you. Something that people only whisper about because it's so . . . frightening. You have a sickness that sometimes affects shape-shifters. I learned about it in school. You can't control the change. You studied it in school, didn't you?"

Slowly, he nodded his head.

She swallowed hard, wondering how she was going to manage the next part because she had to give him an explanation—even if it wasn't the whole truth.

Speaking quickly, she went on, "When you asked me about my powers, I was afraid to tell you all of them. I studied how to use the flame—to cure illnesses of the mind."

She asked the Great Mother for strength to tell her big lie. "I didn't want to admit it because people in my city stay away from those who can work that kind of cure—because they think the illness can infect us."

When he stayed where he was, she went on. "I think I can help you—if you let me."

Or that was what she hoped. Because she had never used that

skill. But Alroy had forced her to practice with the flame—over and over. And she knew the principle was similar. She must send her mind into the flame. Then direct her power toward Griffin's consciousness.

"Will you let me try?" she whispered, her heart pounding.

He kept his gaze on her, then slowly nodded his head.

"I have to get inside the flame," she murmured, struggling to hold her voice steady.

The flame was already lit. She stared into its flickering depth, trying to center her consciousness.

As she let herself slide into the heat and light, she sensed the wall that had stopped her before.

She would have whispered her protest, but she knew the wolf was watching her. And she had to keep her outward calm—for him.

When she had used the communication method, she had always gone to the flame. Now she tried the opposite. Forcing herself to remain still, she invited the fire toward her, invited the heat and the power into her mind.

This time she broke through the barrier. And she felt the transition as a burning sensation inside her skull. It might have frightened her, but she had no time for fright. Not if she was going to help the wolf standing in front of her.

She took a step toward him, then another. Holding the lamp in one hand, she reached out with her other—trembling as she laid her palm on the wolf's head.

She felt his hair bristle under her fingers, felt his muscles tense. Unsure of what she was doing, she let the fire guide her as she struggled to stay merged with the flickering flame and at the same time reach for the wolf.

It was different from what she had done before. It felt as if her mind were frozen in amber, and she asked the fire to melt the rigid substance that held her fast. To her relief, she felt it start to give way.

The wolf made a sound low in his throat, and she knew that he felt it, too.

She kept pressing forward, and suddenly everything changed. She was one with the wolf. One with the flame. One with forces in the world that she had never understood.

Not the world. The worlds. All at once she knew that there were worlds beside this one. Existing alongside this universe. They were the same, but different, too.

She wanted to escape to one of them. And somehow she knew in that moment that a werewolf had escaped there. A woman named Rinna.

She could join her. She could live in a better place.

No, that was impossible. She didn't know how to get there. And even if she did, she must stay here—with Griffin and the flame. She must cure him—if she could.

She kept one hand on his head and one hand on the lamp, sending healing energy into the wolf. It was working. She could feel it deep inside herself.

Then the flame began to flicker, and her breath caught.

She was running out of oil. Running out of time.

"Griffin, you have to change. Do that for me. Change. Before we lose the fire."

He made a strangled sound, and she knew he was trying to follow her command.

She didn't know whether he could do it in time.

Ten

The flame sputtered, and she was sure it would go out. Then from some source she didn't understand, the fire surged up. She felt the wolf's skin ripple, felt something happening within his body.

She wanted to snatch her hand away, but she kept it where it was. He was transforming, and her breath caught as she watched his muscles contort, his limbs lengthen, the shape of his head change. The gray fur on his body disappeared—replaced by skin.

And from one breath to the next, the wolf was no longer there. Instead, a naked man was on his hands and knees before her. Griffin.

He pushed himself up, staring at her, his face contorted with a wealth of emotions.

"How did you know?" he asked.

Afraid to give Quinn away, she stammered, "I—sensed it."

"Thank the gods!"

"You're not angry with me?"

"How could I be? You saved me."

"You may need the flame again."

He nodded, and she wondered if he had heard that part as he gathered her close. "This must have been the reason I bought you. The gods told me I needed you."

"Then why did you . . . send me to the kitchen?" she managed to ask.

"That was a mistake," he answered, then lowered his mouth to hers for a long, heated kiss.

She wanted to continue the discussion, but he wasn't in a talking mood. His kiss turned frantic as his hands moved over her body, stroking her arms, her shoulders, and traveling to her breasts.

She cried out as he teased her nipples, then took them between his thumbs and fingers, squeezing and twisting, sending heat shooting downward through her body.

"Oh!"

He pulled her gown over her head and tossed it away before folding her into his arms.

She was as naked as he, and the feel of his skin against hers was intoxicating.

His hands slid down her back, over the curve of her bottom, pulling her against his erection.

"I want you," he growled.

"You're grateful that I cured you."

"Yes, but gratitude is only part of what I'm feeling. I was powerfully drawn to you. And that frightened me. That was why I tried to stay away from you."

"I was powerfully drawn to you as well," she whispered, as terrible, conflicting emotions tore at her.

She had forged a strong connection with him very quickly. But she had been sent here as a spy. And she wanted to tell him about that. But she wasn't free to speak of her real slavery—to Scanlon.

She sensed she was headed for disaster, and that made her frenzied to show him her true feelings.

Reaching up, she pulled his head down to hers, kissing him with a passion born of need—and fear for the future.

He must have caught only the passion, because he kissed her with renewed hunger.

Then he raised his head, looking frantically around the darkened room. In one corner was a sofa and chair facing each other across a rug. He swept her up and carried her to the rug, then laid her down and followed her to the padded surface.

"The bed's too far away," he panted as he trailed kisses down her throat, then her collarbone, working his way to her breasts. He turned his head one way and then the other, kissing and licking at her, driving her wild with need.

And when he sucked one tight bud into his mouth and drew on it while using his fingers on the other, she thought she would explode.

Last time he had taken her by surprise. This time she knew exactly where they were headed.

His hand slid down her body, then into the triangle of blond hair at the top of her legs before reaching lower to glide into her folds. She was swollen and slick for him, and he murmured his appreciation as he made the journey from her most sensitive flesh to the opening of her womanhood, where he thrust one finger inside her, then brought it almost out again, circling the opening, making her reach out and grab his shoulder.

"Please."

His eyes were fierce when he turned his face toward her. "What do you want?"

"You know!"

"I don't want you to be shy with me."

"I want you inside me."

"My finger?"

She moaned. "Not your finger."

"Then what?"

"Why are you torturing me?"

"Say it."

"I want your penis in me."

"Gods yes."

He moved over her, angling his body so that his penis slid against her. "Take me in your hand; guide me to your opening."

She was embarrassed and, at the same time, too far gone to deny him anything.

She took his firm, full shaft in her hand and pressed the head to her vagina.

He did the rest.

The first time with him, she had suffered through a few seconds of pain. This time he slipped easily into her, and she absorbed the sensation of fullness.

She hadn't had time to think about it before. Now she marveled at the way her woman's body was made to receive him and marveled at the way she clasped him tightly.

"That's so good," she murmured.

"At this end, too." He grinned down at her, and then his face sobered. "Last time was fast. You probably think I can't last more than a few seconds."

"I don't know much about this."

She kept her hands on his back as he bent to kiss her,

then began to move his hips, drawing almost all the way out of her, then gliding back in, the measured rhythm teasing and inciting her.

"Please . . ." she moaned.

"Reach down and press your hand against your clit," he said again.

"My what?"

"Your sweet spot."

She understood what he meant, and heat flooded her face. "In front of you? Is that . . . all right?"

"Very all right."

Embarrassment warred with need. But she did as he asked, because her body clamored for release.

As she used her hand to push herself toward climax, he picked up the pace, his movements going from slow to rapid in the space of a heartbeat.

She climbed toward the top of a high peak, where the air was almost too thin to breathe. And as she toppled off, she felt him follow her into free fall.

He clasped her to him, calling out her name as his body jerked.

He lay on top of her, breathing hard, then shifted to his side, taking her with him, clasping her sweat-slick body.

"Thank you," he whispered. "And I don't mean just the mind-blowing sex."

She laughed. "Mind-blowing?"

"A nice turn of phrase."

He held her for a few moments, then felt her shiver. "You must be cold."

She swallowed. "Yes."

"Come to bed."

He helped her up and kept his arm around her as he led her back to the courtyard, then into his bedroom. He'd left a lamp burning on the table, and it looked like he'd been in bed when the attack had struck him. When he started to straighten the covers, she helped him.

After they had both climbed in, he reached for her again, and she clung to him. When he cleared his throat, she tensed. "What?" she whispered.

"I have something bad to tell you. Something I learned yesterday. I . . . should have already told you."

She braced herself.

"Your mother is dead."

She pushed away and stared at him. "How . . . how do you know?"

"I have several men in White Flint. One has the psychic ability to communicate over long distances. He sent a message back. I'm sorry, she died of her illness."

Zarah struggled to catch her breath. "My mother . . ." she gasped.

"I'm so sorry."

"She was sick. I thought . . ."

"What?"

"I . . . didn't expect her to die so soon," she managed to say as her mind spun. Scanlon had lied to her. He'd had no intention of treating her mother's illness. Maybe he'd even killed her. Zarah tried to take in the horror of that, praying her mother's death had been quick. Then she thought of something else. Scanlon had sent her here with a mission, and now she had no obligation to complete it. She was free. She could . . .

What? Tell Griffin that she'd come here as a spy? Oh sure. He'd be delighted to hear that.

When she started to shake again, he gathered her close. She buried her face against his shoulder, and he stroked her hair. Tears filled her eyes, and she struggled to hold them back.

"I'm so sorry," he murmured. "The past few weeks must have been horrible for you. The shock of your father. Your being sold into slavery. And now . . ."

He stopped speaking, his hand moving more swiftly across her shoulder. His voice was tight when he said. "I bought you and took you to my bed. Would you stay with me if you were free?"

The tears in her eyes spilled over, and her shoulders began to shake.

"Is the idea of staying with me so terrible?" he asked.

"No!" she managed to get out. If her life had continued in the old way, she would have been sold by her parents—to a noble of their choosing. She might have been married to a partner she hated.

But she knew Griffin was a good man. She'd gotten to know him, and her feelings for him were very strong. Maybe she had fallen in love with him. But she didn't think he'd believe it if she told him. Because it had happened so quickly.

"You can live as a free woman in my house, while we get to know each other better. Unless you hate the idea of living in Sun Acres."

She struggled to contain her emotions. "I would never go back to White Flint—not after what happened. But I'd want to earn my keep here."

"I think you can do that with your healing abilities."

"I . . . haven't done that before."

He pulled back and looked at her. "You healed me—and you hadn't done it before?"

"I studied it at school. And when I saw you, I knew I had to try."

"Yes."

"And you have to remember that you may need more treatments."

"Yes."

He pulled the covers up around her shoulders, then slipped his arm around her. "You're good with the flame. You must have practiced with it."

She gulped, thinking about Alroy's making her practice the communications skills over and over. She had to tell Griffin about Scanlon and Alroy. But when she imagined his reaction, she pressed her lips together. She'd have to find the right way to tell him. But for now, she felt a terrible mix of emotions. The sadness of her mother's death tore at her. And at the same time, it freed her. For what? To face Griffin's wrath.

She slept for a few hours, then woke with a start when she felt the covers slowly slipping down her body.

As her eyes blinked open, she saw Griffin leaning over her, tugging on the blanket.

He smiled as he exposed her breasts, then her ribs, then her navel. When she tried to stop the downward progress, he grabbed her hand and pulled the blanket all the way off.

She felt herself blushing at his blatant stare.

"You're . . . embarrassing me," she whispered.

"Why? Your body is very beautiful," he murmured.

"Is it?" she asked in a shaky voice.

"Oh yes."

Before she could stop herself, she asked, "Were you looking at me that first night I was here in Sun Acres? When I took a bath?"

He looked momentarily like a boy who'd been caught with his hand in a cookie jar, but he recovered quickly. "Yes. But then I could only look."

He began to touch her, watching his fingers make her nipples contract. He slid his hand lower, his gaze following along as he circled her navel, then skimmed into the blond triangle of hair, tangling his fingers in the springy curls.

"Open your legs for me," he asked, his voice husky. "And reach your hands over your head. Grab the edge of the headboard."

She swallowed, but she did as he asked, closing her eyes as he shifted his position so that he could watch his fingers stroke her folds.

"Don't close your eyes."

She opened them again, staring up at him.

"I want total honesty between us. And this is part of it. You totally vulnerable to me—and knowing I want only to give you pleasure."

Total honesty. She gulped, and he thought she was still abashed.

She must tell him her secret. But she couldn't get the words out. Not yet. Not now.

So she gave herself totally to the physical pleasure, knowing he was watching intently as her body responded to his attentions.

"You like that?"

"You know I do."

His finger circled inside her channel, then slid up to her clit and back again. "Let go of the headboard and touch your breasts. Play with your nipples."

Her face flamed. "I . . ."

"I want to see that."

She obeyed with shaky fingers, increasing her arousal as he'd known she would. And when her hips were rising and falling with unendurable need, he finally covered her body with his and plunged into her.

They climaxed together, and he held her for long moments before easing away, smiling down at her in satisfaction.

"You were embarrassed at first, but you liked that."

"Yes."

"Next time, you can be the one in charge and tell me what you want me to do. Unless you don't want to."

"I do—because it's with you," she said quickly.

"Good."

He stood and stretched. "I have meetings this morning. I'll come back in a few hours. And I'll have one of the women bring you breakfast."

"I can eat in the kitchen."

"No more of that!"

She gave a little nod. He was changing her status, and that made her feel strange, since she'd come to this house as a slave. She wanted to tell him to free all the people who worked here. But she knew that was a pipe dream. At least she knew he treated his people well.

He had a luxurious bathroom, and something she knew few houses boasted—a wood-burning stove that also heated water for the tub.

She let herself enjoy the hot water, then dried off and put on Griffin's robe so she could go down the hall and put on one of her gowns.

On the way back, she could hear Griffin's angry voice coming from a reception room.

Wondering if it had something to do with the werewolf, she walked closer.

When she saw who was talking to Griffin, her throat closed. It was Lloyd—the man who had wanted to buy her.

"I brought an adept, Tolara, with me. She said there was something funny about the girl."

"You're making up a story—because you're angry that you didn't get her."

Lloyd laughed. "I'm relieved. She was sent here from White Flint as a spy."

"I don't believe that."

"Have you seen her with a lamp? She uses it to communicate with someone in White Flint."

"How in Carfolian hell would you know that?"

"I suspected she was doing something, so I had Tolara monitor her."

"You violated the privacy of my house?" Griffin asked in a slow, deliberate voice.

"I was doing it to save your hide. My adept, Tolara, caught her trying to send messages. She blocked her twice. But I believe the bitch did get through one time."

Zarah gasped, and the men turned toward the door. Lloyd strode forward with a look of triumph and pulled her into the room, his grip painful on her arm.

"And here she is—spying again," he said as he flung her forward. She lost her footing and stumbled across the floor, catching herself on a chair.

Eleven

Zarah felt Griffin's hot gaze on her. She had felt heat coming off him before. This was quite, quite different.

His eyes and his voice turned glacial, he asked, "Were you sent here as a spy?"

She swallowed, trying to moisten her mouth so that she could speak. "Yes. And I was trying to find the right time to tell you about it."

He made a derisive sound. "You expect me to believe that?"

"No."

"Why did you do it?"

"Because Scanlon was holding my mother captive. He was supposed to have her illness treated, but he lied to me."

"You had an opportunity to tell me about that last night. And again this morning."

"And you would have been angry with me," she answered in a small voice, knowing how pitiful that excuse sounded.

"As opposed to being angry with you now?" he asked.

Lloyd leaped into the conversation, his eyes gleaming in anticipation. "Let me take her off your hands. I can punish her appropriately for you."

Griffin looked from the other man to her and back again, and she was sure he was considering the offer.

Time stretched like a vine reaching to choke the life out of a tree. When Griffin finally spoke, his words came to her above the buzzing in her head.

"I'll take care of my own problem."

"But . . ."

"Thank you for providing me with the information," he said, his voice firm.

Lloyd opened his mouth, then closed it again. He gave her a murderous look, then strode from the room, and she was left alone with Griffin.

The man who had made love to her so tenderly had vanished. This man was angry—and disappointed.

"You made love with me—then betrayed me."

He kept his gaze on her, and she wanted to shrink away, but there was no place to hide from his anger—and her own shame.

"What was your assignment—specifically?" he asked.

"Scanlon said you had a secret. I was supposed to find out what it was."

"You did."

"But I didn't tell him."

"I kept you too busy last night I was so grateful. I was going to free you."

She struggled to keep her tone even. "I was so happy to be with you again. But I was afraid it couldn't last."

He snorted, his gaze raking her.

"And now what are you going to do?" she managed to ask.

"I don't know. But I'm not going to make any snap decisions. The way I did when I bought you."

She felt as if the atmosphere around her had thickened, so that it was almost impossible to draw air into her lungs. She reached out her hand toward him, then let it drop back to her side. "I never gave Scanlon any information," she whispered.

"Because Lloyd's adept kept you from doing it," he answered instantly.

"I talked to Scanlon's man a few days ago. I didn't tell him anything."

"You didn't know anything," he snapped.

"You've never been put in a position like this," she whispered. "Where you have to let your mother die or betray the man you love."

He made a harsh sound. "The man you love! Oh please. You've made love with me three times! Are you trying to make me believe . . . we forged a bond?"

She hadn't meant to speak of love. It had slipped out of her mouth. Her lips trembled, and she looked down, so he wouldn't see the tears glistening in her eyes.

"Who was your contact in White Flint?" he demanded.

"Alroy. My old teacher."

"I'll find out if you're lying."

"Why would I?"

He laughed mirthlessly. "Because it gives you a feeling of power—when you have none?"

"It gave me a sick feeling," she said.

He shot her a penetrating look. "But you managed to do it."

When he turned away from her with a look of disgust and strode toward the door, she took a terrible chance, snatching up a small lamp and slipping it into her pocket. If he found it, he would probably kill her on the spot. But she did it anyway.

He came back with a guard. "Get her out of my sight. Put her in one of the cells."

The man grabbed her arm and led her out of the room and down a flight of stone steps to the basement of the house. Some of the rooms were used for storage. Some were empty, and he shoved her into one and slammed the door.

A bit of light came from a small, barred window. When her eyes adjusted to the dark, she saw that she was in a cell, with a waste bucket in one corner, a pile of straw for a bed, and a scratchy blanket.

It was cold in the basement room, and she crossed the floor and draped the blanket around her shoulders, then sat down on the straw, shivering. Her life had changed abruptly again. And this time it was her fault. She should have told him last night and risked his wrath. Or this morning. She could have told him then—if she had been brave enough.

She drew up her knees and pressed her forehead against them, struggling to hold back her tears. She wanted to die. And maybe she would—soon.

∽

Griffin wanted to break something delicate. An old plate or a wineglass perhaps. But he kept the impulse in check, then called for Blayden.

By the time the adept arrived, Griffin was sitting at his desk looking calm, he hoped.

"I want more information about the woman named Zarah. Or about her family. I need to know if she was really Arturo's daughter or if she was a slave groomed to play that part. Ask about that scar on her forehead."

"I'll contact Dell."

"And find out about a teacher from the psychic school named Alroy. Where is he now?"

"Yes, sir." Blayden hesitated.

"What?" Griffin snapped, then was angry with himself for betraying his roiling emotions.

"Another woman came from White Flint with her. Quinn."

"Yes. That's interesting. Do you think she's involved?"

"Hard to say."

"I'll question her later." *When I'm calmer,* he thought.

✑

Quickly, before she lost her nerve, Zarah pulled out the lamp and held it in her hand, then focused on the wick, kindling the flame.

As the small fire flickered, she said a little prayer to the Great Mother, asking for strength.

Now that Lloyd had reported his news to Griffin, would he still be checking up on her communications? She prayed that he and his adept weren't focused on her now.

With her heart pounding, she stared into the flame, sending her mind into the flickering light.

"Careful," she whispered to herself. "Don't rush it. Work carefully."

After firming the contact between her mind and the lamp, she caught her breath, then reached out toward White Flint.

Alroy had taught her well. And she followed his instructions. Even so, the last time she'd tried, she hadn't been able to get through. This time, to her relief, the communication slid into place almost at once, and she breathed out a small sigh. She had done that much. Could she do the rest? For herself. And for Griffin. It was clear to her now that Scanlon was planning some kind of attack. Could she change that equation?

Alroy?

She was sure she had done everything right. But when he didn't answer, panic leaped inside her. Struggling for calm, she tried again. She couldn't expect him to be sitting beside the lamp every minute. But what if he didn't come back for hours?

She huddled on the straw bed with her heart pounding.

Should she put out the lamp to conserve oil? Then try again later? Or was that only increasing the chance of getting caught?

It felt like centuries before his silent voice filled her head. But really, she didn't know how much time had passed. *Where in Carfolian hell have you been?*

She dragged in a breath and let it out. *I tried to get through to you last night, but something was interfering.*

Did Griffin get wise to you?

She clenched her hand around the lamp, steeling herself to lie. *No.*

Then what?

I found out something important.

What? Alroy demanded.

First, tell me how my mother is doing.

She's fine!

Was that what he'd been told? Or was he lying through his teeth because he needed her cooperation?

Good, she managed to answer. *I wish I could speak to her.*

You can speak to her when you come back to White Flint. What information do you have?

When can I come back?

When you complete your assignment. Tell me your information.

I want to tell Scanlon personally.

He's busy. Tell me.

I'll only tell him.

Impertinent girl! You will do as you are told. Your mother will be hurt if you don't cooperate with me.

Get me Scanlon. This is too important to trust to a servant.

You dare . . .

Get him.

Alroy sent a string of curses down the line, curses unsuitable for her ears. Then he went away, and she sat on the straw, barely breathing, waiting for him to return.

Finally, his voice filled her head again. *Scanlon is here.*

How do I know?

You have to trust me.

Have him put his hand on you. I'll feel him.

She felt Alroy's anger blaze up again. But then she sensed the shadow of another presence beside him. It might be Scanlon. Or it might not. She had no way to figure that out from where she sat in this cold cell in Sun Acres. But she knew he had brought another man.

What's your information? Alroy demanded.

Griffin has developed a weapon of great power. She spoke the words mechanically, holding him at the other end of the communications line while she gathered her thoughts, gathered the energy of the flame. Not just this flame. All the flames that were burning in the great house. She didn't know exactly how she was doing it. She only knew that desperation had made her strong. Desperation and determination. She had come to Griffin's house as a spy, but she could do one important thing for him.

What? Alroy said, and she struggled to focus on his words while she readied herself.

I don't know.

What use is that to us? Alroy demanded.

There's more. Listen to this!

She had gathered as much power as she could. Praying that it was enough, she rolled it into a ball of fire and sent it shooting down the line to Alroy.

She heard him scream. And she heard another man too, and knew it was Scanlon.

That was the last sound that rang in her head before the fire came roaring back toward her, and she fell over on the stone floor, unconscious.

❧

Griffin was sitting at his desk, staring at the flame of the lamp in front of him. A lamp was such an everyday thing. Yet it had brought him salvation. And then sent him to Carfolian hell.

He dragged his mind back to the lamp on his desk. It had flickered and almost gone out a few minutes ago. He'd gotten reports that all of the lights in the house had dimmed. What did that mean?

Was Lloyd somehow attacking this compound? He'd thought he had wards against psychic interference; he should make sure they were working properly. Or had the woman spy somehow worked an evil charm on his household?

He kept himself from rushing downstairs to confront her. Even saying her name was too painful, although eventually he'd have to do something about her. Probably sell her to get her out of his sight. But not to Lloyd. The thought of her with that sadist made his stomach twist.

She had made a fool of him. But he wasn't going to make her suffer in Lloyd's torture chamber.

❧

Quinn gripped the tray in both hands. If she got caught by one of the supervisors, she was in big trouble. But as soon as she'd realized what was happening, she'd had to come up here.

She knocked on the door.

"Who is it?"

"I have your food."

"What food?"

Without answering, she pushed open the door and stepped into Griffin's office, holding the tray as though it were a lifeline.

The master looked at the plate and mug in confusion. "I didn't send for this."

She set down the tray. "I know. I needed a way to get to you."

He leaned across the desk, fixing his angry gaze on her. "You're called Quinn, right?

She blanched but held her ground. "Yes."

"And are you working with . . . Zarah? Did you come to kill me?"

"No."

"Explain why you came here," he said with deceptive calm.

She couldn't tell him everything she knew. "I feel things. Strong emotions."

"Well, then you sense that I want to be alone."

There was no way around it. She had to tell him—and quickly. "Zarah has . . . used the lamp. . . ."

"Lamp!" he roared, jumping to his feet. "What the hell are you talking about? She's not supposed to have a lamp."

"I think she took one. And I think she wanted to free herself from the man who forced her into slavery." Quinn gulped. "She will die unless you save her."

He charged around the desk and grabbed her shoulders. "What kind of trick is this? Are you trying to change my mind about the woman who deceived me?"

"It's not a trick. And yes, I'm trying to change your mind," she said, her voice strong and clear.

"What do you get out of this?" he snarled.

"She's my friend. I know how hard this is for her."

"You didn't come here as a backup spy?"

She swallowed. "No."

He kept his gaze on her, as though he could make her confess.

"I'm not sure exactly what happened," Quinn lied. She'd sneaked down to the cellar to bring Zarah some food and talk to her. And she'd seen what her friend was doing. Breaking Zarah's concentration could have been fatal. As fatal as what ultimately transpired. Now she had to get Griffin down there.

She continued in a rush of words. "I think she sent a . . . a killing blow down the line to White Flint and . . . it came back to her. She did it for you—and for herself. And now she's lying on the floor in her cell. She's not moving."

~

The grim words spurred him to action. The woman might be lying, but what if this was not a trick?

He dashed out of the room, Quinn trailing him as he took the stairs at a fast clip. In the cellars, he charged down the hall, looking in the windows of the doors until he saw Zarah lying pale and still on the stone floor. A lamp lay beside her, flickering in the dim light. She was lucky it hadn't caught the straw on fire.

He threw open the door of the cell and rushed inside, then knelt and gathered her to him. Her skin was chilled, and her chest was barely rising and falling. When he pressed his fingers to the artery in her neck, her pulse was very faint. He tried to hold back his fear, but it ripped through him.

In panic, he looked toward Quinn. "What should I do?"

Her gaze shot from him to Zarah and back again. "It depends on what you want to happen. If you're going to cast her away from you, then you may as well let her die. That would be kinder than bringing her back to life and making her suffer without you."

"She betrayed me!"

"She had no choice. You've never had to make agonizing life-and-death decisions about someone you love. You've never been a slave. You have no idea what she went through when powerful men in White Flint said her mother would die if she didn't do their bidding. On the way here from White Flint, she had to fight off a guard who tried to rape her."

He blanched.

"And how do you think she felt when she was naked in the auction house in front of all those men? You're lucky she didn't go insane. But she was strong enough to bear it."

"You dare to talk to me like that?"

"Someone has to." She kept her gaze on him. "You have a choice now. You can hold to your precious nobleman principles and your pride. Or you can give Zarah what she needs."

"How?"

"Do you love her?"

He felt his expression turn fierce. "Damn all the gods! Yes. How can I save her?"

"In school—did you practice combining your energy? And giving it a focus?"

"Yes," he whispered.

"You have to do that now."

Quinn stepped into the cell and reached for his hands. She placed one over Zarah's heart and the other on her forehead. Then she pressed her hands over Griffin's. "Send her your love and your energy."

Although he hadn't practiced this skill since his school days, he tried to do it. But it was no use. He couldn't find the right focus.

Then he felt energy flooding into him—from Quinn, directing his mind and strengthening the bond between himself and Zarah.

"Tell her," she whispered. "Tell her how you feel. Don't hold back."

He was one of the most powerful men in Sun Acres. But his voice was low and strained as he began to speak. "Zarah, I'm sorry. I was afraid of my feelings. I was afraid of how much I came to need you in such a short time. And when I found out what you had done, I couldn't deal with it. I sent you down here. I wanted to send you away because I was afraid. Don't let my weakness take you from me. Come back to me. Please come back. I'm begging you."

At first nothing happened, and he felt the world closing in on him.

Desperation made his voice hoarse. "Zarah. Please. I need you. You said you loved me. If that's true, come back to me. Come back now."

He felt her stir. Felt warmth returning to her body. But he knew it wasn't enough. Not yet.

He had given her words. Now he opened his heart. Opened his mind. Made himself totally vulnerable to her.

He felt her breathing change. "Griffin?" she whispered.

"Yes, love."

"What are you doing here?"

"Quinn was brave enough to tell me what happened." He leaned down and rubbed his lips against hers.

Her eyes blinked open and she stared at him. "You were angry."

"Not now."

"Scanlon is . . . gone," she whispered.

"Don't try to talk. Just rest," he murmured.

She looked past him and saw Quinn.

"You . . . brought him."

"I knew you were in trouble."

"You . . . risked . . . a beating . . . or worse."

"What's that—compared to your life?" Quinn turned and looked over her shoulder. "I'd better get back."

"Thank you," Zarah whispered.

The other woman nodded.

"We'll talk later," Griffin said. "If the supervisor is angry, tell her I authorized your departure."

"If she believes me."

"Tell her she'll answer to me, if she doesn't."

As the woman disappeared down the hallway, Griffin gathered Zarah closer. "I almost lost you. Don't ever do anything like that again."

She swallowed. "All right."

"I want you with me. As my wife."

"Don't say that. Not yet. We should get to know each other better."

"I was totally open to you a few minutes ago. You know what's in my heart."

"But I betrayed you."

"And you killed the man who sent you to Sun Acres. You almost killed yourself."

She answered with a tight nod. "He was ruthless. He told me he would take care of my mother. And he probably murdered her as soon as I left the city. I hope she didn't suffer," she whispered.

"I hope not."

He stroked her hair. "I'm betting Scanlon learned of your talent from your teacher, then framed your father—to force you to cooperate."

She sucked in a sharp breath. "You think so?"

"Yes. He was probably looking for just the right person." He kept his gaze steady. "Just so there's no misunderstanding between us—I free you now. You can leave if you want."

The breath was frozen in his lungs until he heard her say, "I don't want to leave."

"Thank the gods."

He helped her up, keeping a tight hold on her as she wobbled on her feet.

"I'm going to call in a psychic healer," he said.

"I'll be all right."

"You will be. When I get you out of the cellar and up to my bed."

She stumbled beside him, and he swept her into his arms and carried her up the steps.

A crowd of household workers had gathered in the exterior courtyard. People scurried away when they saw him with Zarah. He knew they were curious, and right now he was too focused on the woman in his arms to complain.

And maybe their seeing him was an advantage. He wasn't going to have to worry about people understanding his relationship with Zarah. By the time the clock struck again, everybody in the household would know.

He carried her through the courtyard, then to his private wing on the other side of the house.

When he'd gotten her into his room, he stripped off the gown she'd worn while she was lying on the straw and helped her into his robe. Then he laid her in the bed and kicked off his sandals. He hesitated for a moment. He'd like to strip off his tunic. But under the circumstances, he thought getting naked was going too far. So he climbed in beside her, still wearing his day clothing.

He held her close, stroking her hair, her shoulder, relieved when she relaxed in his arms.

"They sent me like a huntress—to run you to ground," she whispered. "And I hated it."

"I know that now. I know. But that's all over now. For good." He dragged in a breath and let it out. "I want to do something to make up for being an ass," he said, his voice gritty.

She made a sound that might have been a laugh.

"I'm serious. What privilege can I grant you?" he asked.

Zarah stirred against him, then raised her head and looked into his eyes. "Free your slaves."

He stroked his hand up and down her arm. "I thought you'd ask for that. And you've certainly made me think about slavery differently. In an ideal world, I could do it. I think you know I can't do it here."

When she started to speak, he went on quickly. "It would make my household weak. And I can't afford that—if I need to convince the members of the council that I can keep them safe."

She nodded against his shoulder, understanding, even though she wished life in Sun Acres could be different.

"But I can institute new policies here. Policies that will make their lives easier."

"I think your people are already better off than most," she whispered.

"I've tried to be . . . fair. You've made me see the problem from a different point of view. And I can free Quinn. She saved your life. And saved mine."

"Thank you," she breathed, then sat up. "I need to talk to Quinn. Can you send for her?"

"Now?"

She nodded and ran a nervous hand through her hair.

He climbed out of bed and padded barefoot to the door.

Quinn was there two minutes later, her face pale and strained.

"Will I be punished?" she asked.

"Of course not," Griffin answered. "I'm going to free you."

Quinn stared at him in astonishment.

"You saved the woman I love," he said.

Zarah kept her gaze on her friend. "I need to ask you something."

Immediately, Quinn's expression turned wary again.

"Were you the one at the slave market who influenced Griffin to buy me?"

Quinn hesitated for a moment, then said simply, "Yes."

"Why? How?"

"Scanlon gave me a special treatment to boost my powers so I could influence Griffin—to buy us both. Then he sent me with you, to watch out for you."

Griffin's face contorted, but Zarah laid a calming hand on his arm.

Turning back to Quinn, she said, "Thank you for telling me all that."

"I lied to you before," the other woman murmured.

"But you became my true friend. And you saved my life today. You could have let me flounder here. But you didn't."

"I was happy about his assignment. I wanted to get out of White Flint. I hated it there. I thought anything would be better."

Zarah stood and embraced her friend. After a moment, Quinn hugged her back. "Thank you," Zarah whispered again.

When she stepped away, Quinn glanced nervously at Griffin. "I couldn't tell you the truth," she murmured.

"But I am in your debt." He walked to the table in the corner and took a sheet of paper—a precious commodity—then wrote with a quill pen.

When he handed it to Quinn, she read, "This paper frees the slave known as Quinn, who came to Sun Acres from White Flint." She looked dazed. "Thank you."

"Show it to the kitchen supervisor and have her show it to Philip. Tell him I said to make you comfortable in a guest room, and we'll talk later."

Quinn held the paper tenderly in her hand. "Thank you," she whispered again, then departed.

Griffin helped Zarah back into bed. "How did you know?"

"I figured out Quinn was always there when I needed her."

"So Scanlon launched a conspiracy against me. And it backfired on him."

Zarah nodded, then thought of something they'd said a few minutes earlier. She felt tension gathering inside her, and realized he felt it.

"What else do you need to tell me?" he asked, and she knew he was struggling to keep his voice even.

"You said—in an ideal world we wouldn't have slaves. I think there's more than one world. Maybe not ideal. But different."

His expression was guarded. "Tell me why you think that."

"When I went into the flame, I felt . . . another place. Well, more than one, really. But one that was very much like this."

"Yes. One of the council members, a man named Falcone, took the idea of that other world seriously. My spies told me that one of his adepts opened a portal to a universe much like ours."

"The council members spy on each other?"

"Yes. This is a dog-eat-dog society—in case you haven't noticed. Or dog-eat-wolf."

He'd given her the opening to ask, "What really happened that night—with the dog and the boy?"

"The dog wasn't tied up. It attacked me. The boy was nowhere in sight. That part was a complete lie."

Her fingers closed around his and held on tight. "You must have wanted to shout out the truth. You must have wanted to protest that the wolf didn't want to hurt anyone."

"Yes. But I couldn't." He cleared his throat and shifted the conversation away from himself. "Do you know that this world used to be very different?"

"What was it like?"

"More civilized. And more comfortable. There were machines that did a lot of the work. And ways to travel that were faster than horse-drawn wagons. People came from all over the world to a big fair in 1893—in a place called Chicago. They had all kinds of exhibits there. Agriculture. Machines. Medicine. Science.

Anything people might be interested in. A man named Carfoli came to the fair and set up a tent—where he said he could give people psychic powers. Whatever he did, worked."

Zarah blinked. "I never heard that. Is that why we say . . . 'Carfolian hell'?"

"Yes. He turned this world into a kind of hell. When he created people with psychic powers, it sent society into chaos. Factions were afraid of each other—and fought each other. People gathered together for protection—which is how the city-states were born. But I think that in the world Falcone discovered, things are different. More like in the old days."

She stared at him, fascinated.

"I think one of Falcone's slaves found the portal. A woman named Rinna."

"Yes! I sensed that when I sensed the other world."

"She and Falcone and I were all at school together. She was a werewolf, so we had some classes in common."

She had been listening intently. "You were friends?"

He made a rough sound. "Falcone had alliances—not friends. And I was prejudiced against Rinna, because she was a slave."

Zarah felt her chest tighten. "I acted that way, too," she said in a small voice. "I thought I was better—because of an accident of birth."

"The curse of being a noble." She looked up at him, then away.

"What?" he asked quickly.

"Maybe your new attitude will help you do something for the city."

"I hope so."

She reached for his hand. "I want to help you, if you'll let me."

reward. It was just starting, and she knew it would last so much longer than the terrible time that had come before.

"I've found the perfect man for me," she whispered.

"And the perfect woman," he answered.

And then he claimed her mouth, and the talking was over for the time being.

reward. It was just starting, and she knew it would last so much longer than the terrible time that had come before.

"I've found the perfect man for me," she whispered.

"And the perfect woman," he answered.

And then he claimed her mouth, and the talking was over for the time being.